REALM OF DARKNESS

PAUL DOHERTY

HEADLINE

First published in 2022 by
HEADLINE PUBLISHING GROUP

1

Cataloguing in Publication Data is available from the British Library

ISBN 978 1 4722 8479 2

Typeset in Sabon LT Std by
Palimpsest Book Production Limited, Falkirk, Stirlingshire

Printed and bound in Great Britain by Clays Ltd, Elcograf S.p.A.

MIX
Paper from
responsible sources
FSC
www.fsc.org FSC® C104740

HEADLINE PUBLISHING GROUP
An Hachette UK Company
Carmelite House
50 Victoria Embankment
London EC4Y 0DZ

www.headline.co.uk
www.hachette.co.uk

To my very good friend and supporter
Yollie Calingacion of New York,
in thanksgiving for her constant
support and encouragement.

CHARACTER LIST

The Court of England

Edward I	King of England 1272–1307
Edward II	Son and heir of the above, King of England 1307–1327
Isabella	Daughter of Philip of France, wife of Edward II
Peter Gaveston	Edward II's Gascon favourite, created Earl of Cornwall
Thomas, Earl of Lancaster	Cousin to Edward II and his most inveterate opponent
Warwick, Hereford, Pembroke	Leading earls opposed to Edward II
Lady Beatrice Saveraux	Principal lady-in-waiting to Isabella
Stephen Filliol	Squire, royal courier, mailed clerk and ardent admirer of Lady Beatrice

The Royal Clerks

Sir Hugh Corbett	Keeper of the Secret Seal
Ranulf-atte-Newgate	Principal Clerk in the Chancery of the Green Wax, Corbett's henchman
Chanson	Corbett's henchman, Clerk of the Stables

Faucomburg	Leading clerk in the household of Thomas, Earl of Lancaster

The Court of France

Philip IV	King of France
Monseigneur Amaury de Craon	Philip of France's Keeper of Secrets, head of the Chambre Noire in the Louvre Palace in Paris
Philip Malpas	De Craon's principal henchman
Gaston Foix, Jean-Claude, Augustin, Sebastian, Lavelle, Ambrose of Amboise	The Sacred Six, the household clerks of Monseigneur de Craon

The Abbey of St Michael's in the Woods

Abbot Maurice	
Prior Felix	
Brother Norbert	Principal porter
Brother Mark	Guardian of the Silver Shrine
Brother Henry	Librarian
Brother Aidan	Kitchener
Reboham	The anchorite
Brother Simon	Sacristan

The Mummers

Megotta the moon girl	A mummer but also Corbett's spy
Lord Janus	Leader of the mummers group The Apostles, camped on Bloody Meadow close to St Michael's Abbey
Osbert the owl boy	Lord Janus's messenger

The Swallow	A one-masted cog out of Harwich
Master Barclay	Master of *The Swallow*
Matlock	Barclay's henchman
Delit	Lookout boy

Others

Lady Maeve	Corbett's wife
Edward and Eleanor	Corbett's children
Ap Ythel	Corbett's friend, Captain of Tower Archers
Master Crispin	Mine host at the Wodewose tavern
Sir Miles Kynaston	Admiral of the Seas
Ralph Swinburne	Constable of Wallingford

HISTORICAL NOTE

By late spring 1312, Edward II of England was hurtling towards a bloody confrontation with his leading earls, led by his cousin Thomas, Earl of Lancaster. The great barons fiercely resented Edward's favourite, the humble Gascon, Peter Gaveston, whom Edward had promoted to be Earl of Cornwall, even marrying his cousin to the hated favourite. Lancaster and the others regarded Gaveston as the King's catamite and, in a word, they wanted him dead as swiftly as possible.

Across the Narrow Seas, Philip of France closely watched events in England. He was pleased to see the division and dissent as he knew this would give him a chance to meddle and interfere in England's affairs. Philip also quietly rejoiced that his one and only beloved daughter, Isabella, Edward II's young wife, was now *enceinte* and would in due course give birth to what Philip truly believed would be a male child. Philip was convinced that his vision of Europe was becoming a political reality. He had married his three sons to Europe's richest heiresses and now his daughter would give birth to his grandson, who would wear the Confessor's crown and sit on his throne at Westminster. Philip was determined to meddle even further. He wanted Edward of England at his mercy and the French king even nursed dreams that England would fall fully under his power. However, everything had to be in due order. Philip had destroyed the Templar Order and tried to seize a great treasure once held by the Templars: the Glory of Heaven. Philip wanted this exquisite diamond once owned by Charlemagne, fitting treasure for Philip who viewed himself as Charlemagne's true successor, Emperor and Pope of Europe. In pursuit of his dream, Philip despatches Monseigneur Amaury de Craon to England and, when he does, the darkness begins to gather . . .

The quotations before each part are from *The Life of Edward II*, a contemporary chronicle by the so-called Monk of Malmesbury, covering the period of this novel.

PROLOGUE

LENT, MARCH 1312

'Neither man nor beast, more a statue.'
The Bishop of Pamiers

Philip, king of France allowed himself a faint smile, which played about his full lips but never reached his icy light-blue eyes. He secretly conceded that the Bishop of Pamiers had neatly caught the character, mood and disposition of his King. Philip deeply rejoiced in that. He always wore a mask so as to appear the most inscrutable of monarchs. He prided himself on being able to observe the rest of the world through slits in that mask without betraying any emotion. Philip sat back on his throne, carved out of the costliest oak, polished and embroidered with glistening silver leaf. The French king pulled his blue silk robe, adorned with golden fleur-de-lis, closer about him. One hand stroked the purple-dyed ermine that lined this cloth of state. Philip then stretched out both hands as if to admire the jewelled rings which adorned his long, claw-like fingers. Lost in his own thoughts he twisted his hands. He watched the jewels catch the light from the host of pure beeswax candles fixed in their gleaming spigots and placed down the centre of the long, oval council table. Philip glanced quickly at his Keeper of Secrets, the principal clerk in the Chambre Noire which housed all of Philip's most confidential matters, a place of constant darkness at the very centre of Philip's fortified Palace of the Louvre. The clerk was now busy, deciphering a document using a key known only to him and his royal master. Philip glanced once more at his bejewelled rings.

'Amaury, Amaury! The Glory of Heaven! God's most precious jewel.'

'Your Grace?' The clerk, Monseigneur Amaury de Craon, raised his head as he placed his quill pen neatly back into the chancery tray on the table beside him. 'Master,' he murmured. 'Do not worry. The diamond will soon be ours.'

'If Reboham plays his part.' Philip hissed like an adder ready to strike. 'Why?' he whispered hoarsely. 'Why does he assume such a name?'

'I believe there's good cause, your Grace, but what does it matter as long as he plays his part? Either he does, or Thomas Didymus will never see the light of day. Rest assured, your Grace, Reboham has been bought, both body and soul.'

'And The Apostles?'

'Reboham has these all organised. They will strike at the appropriate time. Once the pawns have been removed, the bishops, knights and castles, not to forget the queen, will be taken.' De Craon pointed across at the gleaming, ivory chess set laid out on its specially designed table. 'All is ready, your Grace. Perhaps we could indulge ourselves with one more game? The day is not yet done and we have time before your evening prayers?' De Craon gazed round the dark, tapestried chamber. 'Though it would be good to rest from here. Perhaps we could play our game in some other room?'

'No, no, Amaury, we still have so much to do. Now, is all set for fair sail to England?'

'Your brothers Charles and Louis are ready, as are their retinues. The gifts and documents for your son-in-law, the esteemed Edward, are safely stored aboard *The Temeraire,* our most powerful and majestic war cog. Your Grace, I repeat, you should not worry.'

'I do not worry.' Philip snapped back so sharply, de Craon winced and quietly cursed his mistake. Philip of France openly proclaimed he had no fear of anyone. Indeed, he had spent most of his life proving that to the rest of the world. Only recently, Philip had seized and held captive that tub of lard, Pope Boniface VIII, at Anagni, whilst Philip's assault on the Templars had been most successful. He had destroyed that fighting order with a farrago of lies as well as the threat of the gibbet, the rack, the gallows and the stake. Philip believed that no one could resist him or his dreams. The House of Capet was the most sacred in Europe, its blood was pure, its destiny laid out by God himself. Philip was simply God's representative on earth. The French king abruptly sprang to his feet. De Craon meant to follow, but Philip gripped his henchman firmly by the shoulder, so tight that de Craon winced at the pain.

'Sit and listen, my friend, whilst I express a thought which I have shared with you before.' Philip released his grip and began to pace up and down the chamber, its floor tiled with gorgeous stone proclaiming the royal arms of the King and those of his ancestors, the Capets. Philip's velvet-slippered feet made no sound as he walked up and down. This was his sanctum locum, his holy place, where he could sit and share his most secret thoughts. The chamber slightly frightened de Craon, its dancing pools of light made the shadows judder so it seemed a whole host of ghosts had assembled for conclave. Perhaps they had, de Craon ruefully reflected. King Philip had good cause to fear the multitude of souls he had despatched into the silence of eternity. De Craon swiftly crossed himself as he recalled how he had been Philip's accomplice in the French king's most subtle schemes and crafty plots. Men and women had died by their thousands, sacrifices made to slake Philip's thirst for glory and his lust for power. The present situation was no different. Philip was plotting. De Craon watched as his master walked up and down, a favourite habit when the French king was preparing to draw together the threads of some tangled web.

'You, Amaury, and your dagger man Malpas, are off to England together with my brothers and their retinues. You will take the Sacred Six, those skilled clerks of our Secret Chamber. Now, once in England, you will lodge not at Windsor Castle with the rest, but at a nearby Benedictine abbey, St Michael in the Woods, under the rule of Abbot Maurice. The abbey holds one item I certainly want, and you know it – that lustrous diamond, the Glory of Heaven. The jewel was seized by the English Crown from the Templar Treasury in London. This diamond, once the property of the great Charlemagne, belongs to me, and I shall have it. Amaury, you know the history of that stone. Your task is to bring it home, which should not be hard, should it?' Philip paused in his pacing and stared down at this most cunning of henchmen. 'And how will you do that?'

'Edward of England needs you, sire, he will be amenable.'

'He certainly might be,' Philip mused. 'The Scots under Bruce threaten his northern borders. They make ferocious incursion into those shires along the Scottish march. However, the enemy within is much more dangerous. As you know, Edward has fallen madly in love with a Gascon nobleman, Peter Gaveston. Edward has promoted his darling Peter to be Earl of Cornwall, the King's principal and only councillor. The other great lords hate Gaveston and have sworn to hunt him down. They will show no quarter, it will be to the death. True, you can see what advantage this gives us over the diamond, but you can also detect the danger, yes?'

'Of course, your Grace. King Edward and Gaveston might be swept away, leaving your one and only daughter Isabella prey to the noble wolfpack.'

'Precisely, my friend.'

De Craon sighed with relief at the lighter tone in Philip's voice, but then started once again as the King grasped his shoulder in another steely grip.

'Isabella,' Philip breathed. 'My darling, darling daughter is Queen of England and is expecting a child.' Philip released his grip. 'I believe the child will be a boy. Indeed, I know it will be.'

Amaury repressed a chill. Philip of France could process up and down the central aisle of Notre Dame. He could make offerings to this church or that. He could kneel on his silk-cushioned prie-dieu and have statues and medallions around his bedchamber, but Philip was also a practitioner of the dark arts. Outside in the gardens of the Louvre there was one plot sealed off from the others. So, when Philip wanted to know the future, the King would go there to meet Paris's most skilled sorcerer, simply known as Tenebrae – Darkness. She would perform the midnight rites, sacrifice a cock hen to the dark and, if necessary, human blood. She would throw the dice then sit rocking herself backwards and forwards as she whispered in a language de Craon could not understand. Nevertheless, her predictions were invariably true. She had promised Philip that Isabella would give birth to a stout, merry boy, and so enhance the power of France and the glory of the Capets.

Philip abruptly released his grip on de Craon's shoulder as he bent down, his face only inches from that of de Craon. 'Think, Amaury, my grandson, a Capet, will wear the crown of the Confessor and sit on his throne at Westminster. Isabella will then have a second son, and he will be created Duke of Gascony, and in time this province will be returned to its rightful owner, the French Crown. Oh, yes.' Philip continued his pacing only to pause and stare at a painting which adorned the far wall, of Philip's ancestor, the sainted Louis. This depiction reminded him that the House of Capet was not only regal, but sacred, and he had to enforce that. 'No dream,' he muttered loudly. 'Oh no, Amaury, no dream but the return of empire! I will be a new Charlemagne. My writ shall run from England, east to the Rhine and south to the Middle Sea. God's will be done.'

Philip sat down in his chair and closed his eyes as he became lost in the dream of empire. He seemed asleep but then opened his eyes abruptly and lunged across, grabbing de Craon's arm.

'Amaury, Amaury,' he whispered. 'All is ready. Tomorrow you must take the road to Dieppe. I talk of grandeur and glory, but you will confront dangers both within and without. Your retinue houses a veritable Judas, yes?' De Craon groaned at the pain in his arm. Philip released his hand. 'You yourself,' the French king pointed at his henchman, 'believe that's true, yes? One or more of your clerks, the Sacred Six, is a traitor bought and bribed by that legate of Satan, Sir Hugh Corbett, Keeper of the Secret Seal. It's true, isn't it?'

'I believe so, your Grace.' De Craon chose his words carefully. 'I have established,' he continued slowly, 'that Corbett appears to know more than he should.'

'Such as?'

'Your Grace, I have already informed you. Remember?' de Craon continued hastily. 'We are to lodge at the Abbey of St Michael in the Woods, and so, I understand, will Corbett.'

'Is that a coincidence?'

De Craon shook his head. 'I don't think so. Corbett is the King's representative. He should, according to all protocols, lodge close to the Queen at Windsor Castle. I am intrigued that he isn't. In addition, your august brothers, the leaders of your embassy to the English court, will also be staying at Windsor. Corbett should join them. We have also learnt that Corbett has demanded all keys to the chantry chapel, the Silver Shrine and its tabernacle in St Michael's Church be handed over to him immediately upon his arrival. Corbett must be assuming custody of the diamond, the Glory of Heaven. So, what does he intend?'

'It certainly means,' Philip replied, 'that Corbett and his royal master must know we want that diamond back. We could take it by force or we could offer troops to assist King Edward against those great lords who are intent on destroying Gaveston. One of our conditions for doing so would be that Edward hands over the Glory of Heaven to its rightful owner, namely myself. Two choices,' he murmured. 'A quid pro quo or we just take it and face the consequences.'

'Indeed, sire. Corbett may well have learnt of your secret instructions to me that, if necessary, I seize the diamond on the legal principle that it is our rightful property.'

'Yes, yes,' Philip replied. 'It is more than a coincidence that Corbett has decided to pitch camp in St Michael's.'

'He may even know more.' De Craon rubbed his bruised shoulder. 'We have Thomas Didymus under close guard. We have used him to advance our cause. Now, because of Thomas Didymus, we have a spy in Corbett's entourage: Reboham. You and I know all about that. Who he is and what he will do for us?'

'And?'

'Your Grace, Corbett seems to have discovered that we have such a spy.' De Craon laughed quietly. 'Our English clerk has made enquiries whether the community at St Michael's knows anything about Reboham or a sect or coven known as The Apostles. They do not, but we certainly do. Corbett is like a dog, he is snouting about looking for a scent and, I believe, someone in our service has given him a lead. I shall find out who.' Once again, de Craon pointed across to the chessboard. 'Your Grace, Corbett seems to sense our moves before we make them. One of the Sacred Six, or even more, could be in Corbett's pay, deep in his pocket. So, your Grace, the board must be swept clear.'

'So it will, so it will.' Philip pushed back his chair and got to his feet. De Craon hastened to follow. Philip rubbed his hands together and pointed at de Craon. 'Once back in England you will also meet your long-lost brother, yes? He may well help you at St Michael's.'

De Craon just stared bleakly back.

'Ah well, we are finished here.' Philip stretched out bejewelled fingers. De Craon knelt and pressed Philip's hand against his lips before getting to his feet. He bowed and was about to leave when Philip called out. De Craon turned.

'Your Grace?'

'My friend,' Philip pointed to his henchman, 'whenever you can, wherever you can, however you can.' Philip fell silent.

'Yes, your Grace?'

'Kill Corbett.'

'Of course, your Grace.'

PART ONE

'How full of perils is avid discord.'

Matthew Barclay, master of the single-masted cog, *The Swallow*, out of Harwich, stood high in the prow of his ship as she cut through the turbulent waters just off the Thames Estuary. The sea roads were fairly deserted, most mariners still waiting for spring to reach its ripeness. Barclay, however, was industrious and daring; there were still profits to be made. He stared up at the sky; at least March, the month of spring, had come. Barclay just prayed that softer weather would soon follow. Winter was receding and he could soon resume full, profitable trading between the Cinque ports along the Narrow Seas and those ports of south-east England, Harwich, Walton and the rest, a string of safe harbours. The year of our Lord 1312 might well prove to be profitable. However, like other merchants, Barclay was growing deeply concerned at the news he had received from London. How the young King Edward was refusing to give up his beloved favourite, the Gascon Peter Gaveston. Indeed, the king had continued to shower honours on his friend, whom others openly called his catamite. The great barons, led by the king's blood cousin Thomas, Earl of Lancaster, were arming for war, and that meant the likes of Barclay had to be most vigilant. If the king was busy elsewhere, all kinds of monsters slunk out of the darkness. Sheriffs and other royal officials, busy collecting troops for the king, would neither have the time nor the energy to enforce penalties against the wolf-heads – those outlaws who constantly prowled the roads. Matters would grow even worse if the king's ships were ordered to stand off this port or transport troops to that harbour or the other. The pirates would seize their chance. They would slip out of their inlets and hoist the red and black banners of anarchy. This blood-drinking pack of sea wolves would be only too quick to prey on the likes of *The Swallow*.

Barclay stared out across the foaming waters, bracing himself against the biting salty breeze. Above him the seagulls whirled and shrieked hungrily, their clamour almost hidden by the creak and groan of cord and timber as *The Swallow* plunged through the waves, tipping from side to side now and again, shuddering as the sea clawed at her hull. Barclay pulled up the muffler to protect his face. He would love to go back to his little cabin beneath the stern. He would warm his hands, wipe the sweaty salt from his face and sip mulled wine carefully prepared by Ignato the cook. However, Barclay had been alerted by cries from the falcon's nest where

Delit, the lookout boy, had sighted something in the water. Barclay just hoped it was nothing threatening while he prayed that the mist would continue to thin. *The Swallow*, sail billowing, cut through the water as sharp and as swift as the bird she was named after. They were making good progress.

'Again, I see something.' Delit's cry carried strong and clear, stilling all sound on the deck below.

'I see it too!' Barclay, crouching in the prow, gripped the taffrail tighter. He stared and sighed in relief as the mist abruptly shifted and thinned like smoke against the sky. Barclay blinked and stared again at the devastation the mist had concealed. Large sections of some unfortunate ship bobbed and moved on the water; a battered mast with trailing rope and netting, a huge rail which must have topped some majestic stern. Other pieces of wreckage tipped and turned as the waves crashed into them, sweeping them backwards and forwards. Barclay glimpsed a damaged figurehead with shards of sail. He turned and shouted orders at the tillermen and sail trimmers. Delit was yelling about what he could see. Other pieces of the ill-fated ship were being swept up and hurled back again. Eventually Barclay imposed order. The sail was loosened so it could only flap bravely against the wind while the tillermen found it easier to guide *The Swallow* slowly forward to nose her way through the debris. Matlock, Barclay's henchman, joined his master.

'What do you make of it?'

'Heaven knows, Matlock. Some unfortunate ship, no

doubt, but look, open the weapons chest. Distribute swords and clubs, as well as bows and arrows for those who can at least loose straight.'

'You fear attack?'

'I don't know, Matlock. Just what is this? The result of some pirate attack? Is it a trap for us to loosen sail and tread water?' Barclay wiped the spray from his face and grinned at Matlock in a display of rotten broken teeth. 'Or is it something else? An accident? The aftermath of a storm? In which case, there must be salvage, and if there is . . .'

'It's ours,' Matlock shouted. 'Finders, keepers!'

'Mist clearing completely,' Delit shouted out. 'More flotsam in the water.'

Barclay urged Matlock to hurry and open the weapons chest as he went up onto the last step in the prow. He caught his breath. More debris from the stricken ship now clustered close. One piece of timber hit the bow of *The Swallow* causing her to turn. Barclay glimpsed the painted scrollwork along the other side of the plank. He could clearly see the name *The Ragusa*, the letters picked out in glaring red against a snow-white background.

'Matlock!' The henchman came hurrying back. Barclay pointed down to the floating debris. 'It's *The Ragusa*,' he said. 'Out of London; a Venetian galley. Heaven knows what happened here, but there must be salvage. A rich cargo ship, *The Ragusa*'s holds would have been crammed with goods.'

'Master, be prudent, be cautious. Ask yourself what

truly happened to *The Ragusa*, a powerful Venetian galley, well provisioned and armed? Most pirates would steer well clear of it – true?' Matlock scratched the stubble on his chin and stared up at the icy-blue sky. 'We had a storm last night, but the weather's now settled.'

'You're saying the wreck is a mystery?'

'I am. Look.' Matlock pointed to the rolling waves. 'The surge of the sea hides whatever is out there. God knows, master. We need to find out more. We must be careful; but we should take a closer look.'

'We should lower the bumboat?'

'Yes, master . . .'

'Body!' Delit screamed from the falcon's nest. 'I see a body in the water! To port, to port!'

Barclay and Matlock hurried across the water-soaked deck. Barclay grasped the rail, Matlock holding on to him as he leant over to view the bloated corpse which the sea and wind kept nudging towards *The Swallow*.

'By the rood,' Barclay hissed. 'Matlock, get the bumboat ready.'

Eventually the two-oared boat was lowered. Barclay and three of the crew clambered down the thick rope ladder, balancing themselves quickly. Barclay sat in the stern, Ignato the cook perched in the prow, whilst the two oarsmen took their seats. Barclay, gripping the boathook, ordered them to push away. The rowers bent over their oars, trying to keep the boat as steady as they could. Barclay could now see other items shifting about on the water, but he was fascinated by the corpse. They drew closer just as a wave abruptly shifted and the corpse rolled over. Barclay yelled at the rowers to ship their oars as they closed in. The master used the boathook to pull the corpse nearer, then stared in horror at the gruesome sight. The dark-haired, dead man's face was bloated; Barclay had seen hundreds like him before; the flesh of the drowned always showed this grisly swelling. What horrified him, however, were the malignant black buboes that peppered the dead man's flesh. It seemed the blackness had seeped to the hands, neck and feet of the corpse. Barclay, who had seen service in the Middle Sea, recalled sighting similar horrors. He recognised what some called the 'Fiercest of Fevers' or the 'Perpetual Plague'.

'A real demon out of hell,' he whispered.

'Master, what do you mean?' one of the rowers asked. 'What is this?'

'Hell's own offering,' Barclay replied. 'We do not touch anything. We must return.'

Once he'd clambered over the taffrail and the bumboat had been raised and stored safely away, Barclay beckoned Matlock to stand by him.

'We do not look for salvage, master?' Matlock asked.

'We certainly do not. We don't take anything from that wreck. *The Ragusa*,' he continued, 'truly became a plague ship. I suspect the crew died violently.'

'But why was that corpse naked?'

'One of the effects of the raging fever: that poor man must have stripped, desperate for coolness. He was not weighed down which is possibly why he floated. The rest of the crew, thank God, must have sunk to the bottom.'

'So, what happened?'

'*The Ragusa* must have become a living hell. Her master, officers and crew were stricken by the plague and left too weak to do anything. Once free of the estuary, the galley must have been hit by a storm. I suspect when she left port there were still people able to do something but, by the time they had reached the estuary, they were incapable of helping themselves. Once out in the open sea, the vessel was battered by both wind and wave. There was no one to man her, no direction given. One furious wave or a surging wind would topple her over, and the angry sea did the rest.'

'There may be survivors.'

'There are never survivors from the pestilence; if there are, let the sea have them and may the good Lord rest their souls. Believe me, Matlock, we cannot touch those unfortunates or their property; that is one lesson I learnt from the physicians. Death at sea is a mercy. I just wonder . . .'

'What?'

'Who else confronted this living death? But,' Barclay turned and glanced up at the falcon's nest before turning back to his henchman, 'when we dock, my friend, be it in Harwich or Dover, say as little as possible.' Barclay pushed his face closer. 'I do not wish to be questioned. Something hideous occurred here, but all we saw was wreckage floating in the water. Nothing more, yes?'

Matlock raised a hand. 'I swear,' he grated. 'But what will happen now? It's finished, isn't it? The ship's been wrecked and that's the end of it.'

'It never ends, Maltlock, never! Remember, if Satan could fall from heaven, believe me, he can crawl from the sea!'

Brother Felix, prior and physician at the Benedictine house of St Michael's in the Woods, crossed himself then dismounted. Brothers Odo and Aelred, who had accompanied their prior from the Abbey, followed suit. All three Blackrobes, swathed in cloaks of the purest wool, pulled their cowls up as they surveyed the hideous devastation stretching before them. The Wodewose, a small yet prosperous wayside tavern, had once fronted the coffin path that snaked on until it met the main route to St Michael's, then led on to the royal castle of Windsor. On that bitterly cold morning however, The Wodewose had apparently disappeared. Everything had been reduced to a black smouldering ash. The tavern was nothing more than a scorched huddle of ruins, with crumbling stone and blackened timbers, and the same was true of the outhouses which had once stood either side of the main building. Thankfully the fire, which had caused such destruction, had now died, though the occasional flame still flickered and flared. All three monks stood and surveyed the ruins as plaster, wood and stone crackled and crashed down. Prior Felix, hiding his fears, anxieties and remorse, walked slowly forward, pulling up his muffler against the acrid smoke that swirled around them. He stood comforting himself, recalling the time he had worked in a hospital outside Salerno.

'All we do,' Prior Felix murmured to himself, 'is for

the good of all. Death is inevitable, but disease is not.'
He wondered what was the real cause of all this destruction? Did evil constantly swirl beyond the veil and, when
it could, force an entrance into the world of men? Some
of the brothers whispered that the immortal diamond,
the Glory of Heaven, may be sacred, but it also brought
misfortune. Had not the diamond once been the property
of the Templar Order, now itself a smoking ruin, its
former proud knights and squires locked up in prisons
and dungeons the length and breadth of Christendom?
Some of them had faced torture followed by a hideous
death. Now the abbey of St Michael's had its own shrine
to the diamond, a chantry chapel which housed a tabernacle containing God's own precious jewel. Perhaps the
diamond should be handed over to some holy man or
woman for safe-keeping?

'Brother Felix!'

The friar forced a smile, turned and gestured at his
two companions. 'There is little if anything we can do
here,' he declared.

'Father Prior, how did this happen?' Aelred pointed
at the ruins. 'Look at it, not one stone left upon another,
as if it's been laid waste by some demon from hell who
rose up to wipe it off the face of the earth.'

'Fire is like that,' Prior Felix answered testily. 'We
forget that. The Wodewose undoubtedly contained vats,
sacks of oil and wine, its timbers would be old and
dried. Yes, fire is a demon, it can leap merrily and swiftly
and that's what happened here.'

'But, Father Prior,' Aelred replied. 'Didn't anyone

escape? Both Odo and I have visited this tavern many times on our journeys here and there on behalf of yourself and Father Abbot. The tavern was part of our parish. We visited them, they visited us. So what happened to mine host, his wife, two sons and three servants? All killed? Not one managed to escape either through window or door? Then there was the horse boy, who lodged in the small hayloft above the stables. He too is gone, as are the stables. Nothing but blackened ash and filthy smoke.'

'And the horses!' Brother Odo declared. 'There's no sign of the horses.'

'I am sure they will be close by,' the prior replied. He had now walked as far as he could. He felt caught and trapped, drawn in by the baleful sight stretching before him.

'Father Prior?' Aelred insisted. 'There are no survivors, none!'

'True, true.' Shaking himself free of his own dark thoughts, the prior turned and walked back to his comrades. 'Aelred, swift as you can. Notify the sheriff at Windsor Castle. Odo, hasten back to the abbey. Tell Father Abbot we were correct. The fire we glimpsed from the abbey was no forest conflagration or woodman's fire burning out of control. No, it was a truly hideous blaze which has consumed The Wodewose and all within it.'

The two brothers, eager to be gone, assured their prior they would deliver his messages. He watched them mount, and they were about to leave when Odo leant over to whisper heatedly to his companion, then turned his horse and rode back to Prior Felix.

'Brother Odo?'

'Father Prior, two questions. This fire was no accident, surely? Yet who would perpetrate such a horrid crime, and why?'

'God only knows.' Prior Felix grabbed the harness of his comrade's horse as he glanced up. 'I don't know,' he whispered. 'But sometimes God wills things which, in this vale of tears, remain a true mystery. Why did God allow this? Remember the reading from yesterday? Why did God urge the prophet Samuel to place Agag and all the Amalekites under the ban? Why did that man of God order the total destruction of an entire tribe?' Prior Felix smiled thinly. 'That's all I can say. The ways of God are most mysterious. Mine host and his wife were jolly, merry people. I never heard an ill word spoke against them. But I can say no more. Now go, and God protect you.'

The prior watched the two brothers leave. As he stood for a while listening to the raucous cawing of the rooks and crows, he rubbed the trackway with his heavy riding boots, which he had pulled on before leaving St Michael's. He then walked towards the burnt-out tavern, totally gutted from cellar to loft, a tangle of black, scorched wood and stone. He went through where the main door had stood and entered what must have been the taproom. He took the pomander from his pocket and covered his nose and mouth against the foul acrid smell wafted by the still-rising wisps of dirty smoke.

He tried not to gag at the sickening odour of human flesh, fried and burnt by the heat. This was a place of true destruction. The oilskins and other combustibles in the cellars had turned this tavern into hell's own furnace, a gruesome slaughterhouse. Prior Felix fought to control the terrors seething within him. He stared around. Now and again, he could make out human remains, a scorched ribcage, a lolling blackened skull or a claw-like bony hand pushed through the debris as if still beseeching help.

'But none came,' Prior Felix whispered. 'God dispenses as he did with King Agag.' The prior's voice faded away. He walked forward, his heavy boots crunching the mounds of hard, burnt ash. He paused and shivered at the silence. 'No sound here,' he murmured. 'Nothing but death.' He stared down at a small skull close to the toe of his boot, burnt completely to the bone. Prior Felix could take no more. He turned and fled from what he considered hell's own pit.

'You will not fear the terror which crawls by night, nor the arrow loosed by day, nor the plague which prowls through the darkness, nor the scourge which lays waste at noon.'

Sir Hugh Corbett, Keeper of the King's Secret Seal as well as the king's justiciar, with the full power of oyer et terminer, listened as the words of the lector echoed around the majestic stalls of the choir in the abbey church of St Michael's in the Woods. Corbett closed his eyes and leant back against the stall, its seat raised to display the sinister face of a wodewose, that devil-creature that lurked deep in the forest. Corbett had already noticed how many of the gargoyles, bosses, plinths, ledges and other carvings in and around the abbey church celebrated the green darkness of Ashdown Forest which surrounded St Michael's.

'Day is darkening at the window,' the lector intoned. 'The doors are shut. The silver cord has snapped. The golden lamp has broken. The pitcher shattered at the well.' The reader's powerful intonation of the warnings by the prophet Job deepened the silence along the choir stalls. A ghostly place. The Blackrobes gathered there were no more than cloaked and cowled shadows in the fitful, flitting light of torch and candle.

Corbett closed his eyes and tried to breathe in the peace of the place. He had arrived at St Michael's just as the bells tolled for compline, the last office of the monastic horarium. Abbot Maurice and Prior Felix, who was also the abbey infirmarian, had met and greeted Corbett in the great cloisters. Both monks were highly nervous, eager to inform Corbett about the great disaster that had probably occurred only a short time before Corbett's arrival. How the fortified chantry chapel, the Silver Shrine of the Glory of Heaven, had been sacrilegiously violated. The shrine's guardian or keeper, Brother Mark, had been stabbed to death and the beautiful diamond, the Glory of Heaven, stolen. Abbot Maurice and his prior, clearly agitated, added how they had secured all doors and gates whilst a cohort of lay brothers prevented anyone from leaving. Corbett had patiently heard them out. True, a great crime had been committed, a felony which bordered on treason but, there again, the diamond could be easily hidden and he doubted if even a thorough search would discover it. He also insisted that he and his retinue were exhausted and needed to rest. He would attend compline and relax. Corbett's henchman Ranulf atte Newgate, the red-haired, sharp-eyed Principal Clerk of the Green Wax, was already ensconced in his bed in a guest house chamber, whilst Chanson, Corbett's moonfaced Clerk of the Stables, had found a bed of straw close to his beloved horses. Corbett's liveried escort, Captain Ap Ythel and his company of a dozen Tower archers, had insisted on making their own camp in the abbey's gardens, sheltered by the nearby orchards.

Corbett, however, realised the full gravity of the situation. He had said as much to the Benedictines but he needed to rest and reflect. In Corbett's eyes, nothing could be gained by running around in the dark like hapless chickens whilst the melodies of plainchant provided balm to the soul. Corbett loved to chant the divine office. Even in his own manor at Leighton, he, the Lady Maeve and their two children always recited the evening office of the church. Corbett opened his eyes, took a deep breath and stared across at where Abbot Maurice and his prior sat in their ornately carved stalls. He knew both Blackrobes by reputation. Abbot Maurice, granite faced, narrow eyed, with a stubborn mouth and chin, was a former soldier, a knight of the body in the old king's household. He had tried his vocation with the military orders before being admitted to the Benedictines.

Sitting beside his abbot, Prior Felix, smooth faced and hollow eyed, enjoyed the reputation of being an excellent leech and the most skilled physician. The prior had studied at the great medical schools of Montpellier and Salerno before becoming a monk. Prior Felix was an interesting soul, made even more so by his family ties, which Corbett had been fascinated to learn about.

These two clerics and their abbey were trusted and patronised by both court and crown, one of the principal reasons for King Edward entrusting the gorgeous diamond, the Glory of Heaven, to its keeping. Now this jewel had been stolen and its guardian murdered. Corbett startled at the harsh clatter of choir seats being lowered. He now realised compline had finished and the brothers were silently filing out. Corbett waited where he was, only getting to his feet as two shadows emerged from the murk.

'Sir Hugh.' Prior Felix raised the small lantern he carried, its golden glow illuminating the prior's sharp features. 'Sir Hugh, you seem distracted. Father Abbot and I think we should show you now.'

'My apologies,' Corbett muttered, leaning against the choir stall. 'You are correct. I was lost in my own thoughts, almost drifting into sleep. But come.' Corbett picked up his war belt and cloak from the empty stall next to him then followed both monks out across the sanctuary, down into the cold darkness of the nave. Abbot Maurice, using a stout walking cane, walked carefully, following the bobbing pools of light created by the prior's lantern. The abbot paused to explain how he had ordered all torches and candles in the nave to be doused so as to conceal the abominations it now housed.

'Sir Hugh,' he murmured, leaning forward so Corbett could see his furrowed lined face. 'Night has its uses; it covers our sins.'

'But not for long, Father Abbot,' Corbett replied. 'Dawn comes, the sun rises and God's justice will be done. And if not his, the king's.'

'Sharply said,' the abbot replied before continuing on his way.

They left the nave, moving into the broad north transept. Both abbot and prior now became busy lighting the multitude of sconce torches as well as to fire the lantern horns placed close to the round, drum-like pillars. Once finished, they beckoned Corbett forward out of the shadows. Corbett did, only to stop and stare in amazement at the singular chantry chapel, the Silver Shrine, the place where the Glory of Heaven had been kept. Corbett had heard about this unique chapel yet he was still surprised by its appearance. Fashioned not out of wood or shielded by the usual ornately carved trellis, this shrine was more like a cage. It stood about four yards high and the same across, its steel, silver-like bars glittering in the strengthening light. Corbett crossed himself and walked slowly towards it and peered through the bars. Abbot Maurice murmured how these were about nine inches apart, each bar stretching up to meet those across the top where they had been expertly soldered together. Only then did Corbett glimpse a corpse clothed in the black robes of a Benedictine. The victim lay sprawled in a wide pool of blood that had surged out of some wound to drench the costly Turkey rugs which, sewn together, covered the grey flagstones. The light was dim; nevertheless, the more he stared, the more Corbett could make out the outline of the corpse and the back of the dead monk's head. The body lay before the small alabaster stone altar that stood on a dais built against the outside wall of the transept. From where he was standing, Corbett could also see that the tabernacle in the centre of the altar stood open, its small door flung back.

He stepped closer, wanting to capture the very essence of this remarkable chantry chapel, used to enshrine the world's most beautiful and costliest diamond. He also tried to memorise the details of what he was seeing. The shrine, in truth a three-sided cage, was pushed up against the outside wall of the transept, cunningly placed so as to include two oval windows. These were still intact, their beautiful stained glass glinting in the light. Corbett believed the floor underneath the luxurious carpets was of hard, freezing stone now smothered by thick Turkey rugs. The shrine was a work of art, the creation of Hanse merchants and their craftsmen who had brought the bars from Lubeck. Indeed, it would be hard to find a more secure arca or strong room. Corbett reckoned that, if his first impressions were correct, the bars were at least four yards high, placed close together with a gap of probably no more than nine inches. The upright bars were embedded firmly in holes dug deep into the paving. They rose then tapered, sharp as any battle spear; those across the top had then been soldered fast to the upright bars. Corbett narrowed his eyes.

'In God's name', he whispered to himself, 'what do we tell the king? How do I resolve this?'

Abbot Maurice and Prior Felix tried to draw him into conversation but Corbett held a hand up for silence. He needed to concentrate: time passed, certain items would disappear or be changed. Corbett had to be sure about what he was staring at. He walked down the side of the cage to its narrow entrance. Both door and lintel were of the finest oak, skilfully inserted into a gap created by shortening a few of the steel bars. Corbett pushed his hand between the bars to where he guessed the lock would be.

'Impossible,' he whispered, withdrawing his hand.

'Impossible indeed, Sir Hugh. Look.' The abbot plucked at Corbett's sleeve and led him to the other side of the steel-barred shrine, which afforded a clear view of the inside of the door. 'You see?'

Corbett nodded. On the other side of the cage, Prior Felix now stood holding a lantern pushed close to the bars beside the door and so created a pool of light. Corbett gasped in astonishment as he glimpsed two locks, the keys still in them, as well as heavy bolts at top and bottom, both pushed firmly into their clasps.

'Enough is enough,' Corbett said softly. 'A tangled mystery indeed.' He turned. Abbot Maurice was now resting on his walking stick with its bright red leather grip. The abbot held this up and smiled.

'I don't like to use this, Sir Hugh, so I hide it away.'

He tapped the cane against his sandalled foot. 'An old wound, the scar still pains. Now, you want . . .?'

'I want, I *need* urgent words with you, Father Abbot and Prior Felix. But first . . .'

'All men walk to their death, the grave opens, the tomb beckons!'

Corbett, startled by the powerful echoing voice and dramatic words, walked forward and stared into the darkness which stretched down beyond the light to the main door of the abbey church.

'Reboham!' exclaimed the abbot.

'Who?' Corbett tried to hide his surprise.

'Our anchorite. He has an ankerhold down near the baptistery.'

'Can he glimpse the Silver Shrine from there?'

'No. In fact, when Prior Felix made the discovery, apparently Reboham was fast asleep. He does fast and pray but, now and again, he likes his jug of wine. And why not?'

Once again Corbett walked around the cage before returning to its narrow entrance. He leant against the door but it held fast. 'No wonder,' Corbett declared. 'Locked and bolted from the inside. Who had the keys?'

'Brother Mark did. He held a key to each of the two door locks as well as to the tabernacle.'

'And?'

'I hold a second key to one of the locks,' the abbot replied. 'Prior Felix has the other, whilst Simon the Sacristan keeps a copy of the key to the tabernacle, which houses, or did, the Glory of Heaven.'

'And none of these keys were used?'

The abbot lowered his muffler and yanked at his robe, pulling out a piece of cord tied around his neck, a key dangling from it. Prior Felix did the same.

'Good, good,' Corbett breathed. 'Neither of you would give up your keys. This abbey,' he continued, 'was chosen specially. Our king and his queen love you Benedictines. St Michael's is close to one of the most formidable royal fortresses in the kingdom. Windsor Castle is also a royal residence, the king can stay there as well as make swift pilgrimage to this abbey, yes?'

'Of course, Sir Hugh. So, you can imagine our distress at what has happened?'

Corbett nodded understandingly and led both monks across to sit on a wall bench.

'Sir Hugh?' The prior turned and stared at Corbett, peering at him as if he was seeing him for the first time.

'My friends, good brothers,' Corbett replied. 'Listen and listen well. The diamond is gone. Brother Mark is slain. So, who could be responsible? Well, Monseigneur de Craon, the French envoy, has arrived. He lodges here, yes?'

'And has for the last few days. He, his henchman Malpas, together with his household clerks, the so-called Sacred Six, are in the main guest house.' The prior allowed himself a brief smile. 'Far enough away from you, Sir Hugh. You and your henchmen have been given good lodgings overlooking the petty cloisters.'

'Fine, fine,' Corbett replied, stifling a yawn as he fought off a surging wave of sheer tiredness. 'The hour is late,' he continued. 'Night has fallen. The nave is dark and I need to pay greater attention to all of this.'

'What about Brother Mark's corpse?'

'Father Abbot, I understand your concern, but waiting for daylight is the wisest measure. Tomorrow morning, I want you to close the abbey church. Celebrate the divine office either in your chapter house or wherever else you think fit. Now we will leave together. Once we have, every door must be locked and made secure. Captain Ap Ythel and his archers will control all approaches to and from the abbey church. Tomorrow, at first light, I need a company of lay brothers, good strong men armed with mallets. I'm afraid there is no other course to follow.' Corbett pointed across at the Silver Shrine. 'We must pound that door, buckling both the clasps and the locks, then I shall begin my investigation in the most rigorous fashion.'

The following morning, Corbett rose very early and roused a sleepy-eyed Ranulf to wash, shave and, once he was ready, to prepare the nave. Corbett fully intended to sit as the king's own justiciar of oyer et terminer and he believed that the abbey church was the most appropriate place. Corbett also informed his henchman how matters were proceeding and what he had accomplished already, saying he had risen hours before Ranulf to take care of certain pressing matters. At first the Principal Clerk in the Chancery of the Green Wax found it difficult to understand as he staggered around full of sleep. Once fully awake, however, Ranulf roused his comrade Chanson who was fast asleep on a bale of hay in the stables. He then returned to break his fast before hurrying across to the abbey church where Abbot Maurice and Prior Felix had already cancelled the singing of morning office as well as the Jesus mass. These would now be celebrated in the Chapel of St Bruno next to the great chapter house.

Ranulf, garbed in Corbett's livery of dark blue and black, soon made his authority felt, fully supported by Ap Ythel and his company of Tower archers. A long trestle table covered with a green baize cloth was set up close to the Silver Shrine. In the centre of the table Ranulf placed Corbett's war sword, a Book of the Gospels and an array of seals including that of the king as well as the different letters of accreditation drawn up and despatched by the Royal Chancery at Westminster.

Candles flamed on a row of silver-chased spigots placed judiciously down the centre of the table. A high-backed bench was set up before the judgement place where those summoned could sit whilst Ranulf appropriated the great sanctuary chair for his master and another for himself. He ordered all the sconce torches to be lit and despatched an untidy, sleep-soaked Chanson to inform Sir Hugh that all was ready. Ranulf placed his own chancery tray close to where he would sit and smoothed out the sheets of creamy vellum he would use to record the proceedings. Once finished, Ranulf had words with Ap Ythel then strode across to the battered shrine, its door forced open hours earlier. Sir Hugh, or 'Old Master Longface', as Ranulf secretly described him to Chanson, had risen long before first light. He had come down here accompanied by Abbot Maurice, Prior Felix and two burly lay brothers armed with metal-headed mallets. Ignoring the protests of the anchorite, they had smashed both locks and clasps until the heavy narrow door to the shrine crashed loose. The corpse of the murdered monk, now beginning to stink, had been placed in the abbey death house under strict guard. Corbett had then scrutinised the shrine. The blood-drenched Turkey rugs were torn up and Corbett inspected both the altar and its tabernacle. Nevertheless, as he had informed Ranulf once his henchman was fully awake, Corbett had not discovered one item to explain the murder of the guardian or how the Glory of Heaven had been stolen. Ranulf walked through the door. He too studied the paving stones, all laid neatly and strictly in line. He crouched down to peer closer but he could find nothing amiss.

'Old Master Longface is correct,' he whispered to himself. 'Nothing. Nothing to explain what happened here!' He rose and scrutinised the only contents of the chancery chapel – its altar and tabernacle. Nevertheless, search as he did, Ranulf could find nothing, either in the transept wall with its two windows full of painted glass, or the firmly laid flagstones beneath his boots, that provided any indication about the dreadful crimes perpetrated here. He walked out of the shrine then paused as a shout echoed down the nave.

'The snares of the grave have engulfed me. The horrors of the tomb await me. Now is the season of darkness . . .'

The sombre words rang like a funeral bell through

the stone-hollowed nave. Ranulf, as Corbett had instructed, ignored the anchorite's rantings. He went and sat on a wall bench, wrapping his cloak firmly about him. The abbey church, however, proved too cold. Ranulf, quietly cursing, got to his feet. He walked up and down before pushing two of the wheeled braziers closer to the judgement table and retaking his seat. He stared up at the carving that embellished the top of one of the rounded pillars. It depicted a wild man with peg-like teeth and evil squinting eyes, pierced by tendrils of twigs and sprouting gorse. Ranulf shook his head. The gargoyle reminded him of that journey through Ashdown Forest, that ocean of green darkness which seemed to circle this abbey. He himself was a child of the dark cellars of Whitefriars, a true dagger man, quite at home prowling the runnels of London. In a word, Ranulf hated the countryside, especially that silent yet watchful forest with its chilling sounds and sudden bursts of noise. Such eeriness would shatter his calm, disturb his horse and make his hand drop to the dagger in his war belt. Ranulf was pleased when they'd reached the abbey, even with the ever-present mist which shrouded its buildings and dulled the sounds of the Blackrobes. Those cowled, hooded figures moved so silently through their world of stone, with its labyrinthine passages, hollow-sounding galleries and steep, sharp stairs which stretched up into the darkness. The chambers provided, however, were comfortable enough, whilst the kitchen served tasty food. Ranulf had expected to meet Sir Hugh's constant adversary Sir Amaury de

Craon, but the French envoy had left for Windsor two days previously. In doing so, as Sir Hugh had caustically remarked, de Craon apparently rendered himself free of any suspicion that he was involved in the theft of the Glory of Heaven and the murder of its guardian.

'I have seen Satan's own envoy, if not the Lord Satan himself, prowl the wet woods. I know what the darkness holds and what lurks high in the branches of those ancient trees.' The anchorite's voice faded away. Ranulf was tempted to walk further down the gloomy nave and question the recluse, but Corbett had made himself abundantly clear. The only real interrogation of all or any involved in the dark deeds perpetrated in or around St Michael's Abbey would be through Corbett's commission of oyer et terminer. Ranulf stretched out his legs to ease the cramp of this cold hard place.

'Master Longface, where are you?' he whispered.

As if in answer, he heard the devil door crash open as Corbett led Abbot Maurice and the prior up the nave towards the judgement bench. Once there, Corbett winked at Ranulf then lightly touched the items on the table as he proclaimed his title and status as the king's own justiciar, empowered to hear and determine all cases brought before him. Abbot Maurice, grey faced and visibly agitated, lodged the usual protests about himself and Prior Felix claiming benefit of clergy, so they should not answer to any secular court. Corbett retorted that this was not a court but a legal and legitimate inquisition with which the abbot and his monks must cooperate. These were the usual conventions and references made whenever any cleric was summoned to answer, and the abbot fully knew that. Once Corbett had established his commission, the abbot crossed himself and, followed by his prior, touched the Book of the Gospels to indicate that he was now sworn to the truth. Abbot Maurice then repeated his own rights and those of his abbey, which Corbett must respect. The king's justiciar simply slumped in his chair, eyes half closed, with Ranulf slouched beside him impatient to begin. Once the Abbot had finished his litany of what was due to him and his community, Corbett made the conventional reply: how he would discharge his duty and fully respect the rights of Holy Mother Church who, Corbett added, better not come between him and the task in hand.

The anchorite, the recluse or whatever the People of God wished to call him, sat on his high stool peering through the squint hole, which gave him a clear view of the nave. However, because of the row of pillars, the judgement table, the royal clerks and, above all, the Silver Shrine, were obscured from view. The anchorite, who called himself Reboham, was most attentive. He could clearly hear the claims and counter claims being made between Sir Hugh Corbett and the abbot. Reboham knew all about the justiciar. He'd glimpsed him before and certainly knew of his reputation. Corbett was here to retrieve the Glory of Heaven, that exquisitely beautiful yet eerie diamond which had so mysteriously entered human history to become the most coveted jewel on earth. This was a hurling time. The diamond had been stolen, murder had been committed; no wonder Satan and his demons prowled this abbey. The anchorite had fought to control himself. Nevertheless, ever since these proceedings had begun, he had felt the urge to declaim, to issue those dark warnings from scripture. Reboham closed his eyes, leaning forward to rest against the hard wood of his ankerhold, a perfect box of polished timber built opposite the baptistry and close to the main door of the abbey church. He went back in time to another life, another era, one so different from the path he now trod. Once he had been Etienne de Crotoy, Knight Templar, a lord in his own right and keeper of that same diamond, the Glory of Heaven, now stolen from this abbey. The former Templar had been entrusted with that precious object when the Mamelukes attacked Acre in the fateful year of our Lord 1291.

Acre! The last great fortress of the Templars in Outremer, once a stepping stone into the Holy Land and the roads to Jerusalem. The anchorite could still vividly recall that fateful, final day. At the time he had thought it was the end of the world. He almost expected, even prayed, that the heavens would open and Christ descend in glory! But no! That day was a day of danger, of anger, of wrath. The armies of Islam massed around the great fortress, kettledrums rolling, green, gold-edged banners snapping in a hot dusty breeze. Above the city, the darkening sky was scorched by a torrent of fiery missiles loosed by the attackers' massive war machines. The roaring war cries grew louder as the Muslims forced a breach in the walls, their elite troops, the Janissaries, pouring through like a deadly yellow flood. The city was lost. The fortress came under close attack. The Templars, the last of the garrison, had no choice but to fall back to the quayside and the waiting war galleys. Reboham and his comrades could do little to prevent the hideous massacre of the women and children who had fled into Acre for refuge and protection. They expected mercy and quarter. None was given on that day of great slaughter. Both defender and attacker had to walk through blood that swilled above their ankles, drenching the ground so the rooms, galleries and stair-cases reeked like a slaughterhouse.

Reboham and the others, including Father Abbot, then a young acolyte in the Temple of Order, were entrusted with the sacred treasures of the temple. The Shroud, the Mandylion and, of course, the diamond. Reboham had held the precious jewel strapped close in his war belt as he and others, back to back, shields locked, swords flickering out like the tongues of vipers, hacked their way through until they reached the gore-strewn quayside and the war galleys moored alongside. Behind them a true disaster. The screams of the women and the plaintive yells of the children they had deserted still echoed through the nightmares which plagued Reboham's soul.

'So much,' he now whispered to himself, 'such a deadly wound to the spirit.' He opened his eyes and crossed himself. Now the past, like some prowling wolf, lurked close by ready to spring. Reboham shook himself free of his feverish imaginings to loudly declaim the psalm,

'The lord is the light of my life', not really a prayer but a desperate plea to God to forgive him the past.

Amaury de Craon, Philip's envoy to the English court, was also dwelling on the past. He sat on a log in a glade just off the main thoroughfare, in truth nothing more than a glorified coffin path which wound through Ashdown Forest to the Abbey of St Michael's. A cold brittle morning, the hardy hoarfrost still clinging to where it could. They had camped on the forest fringe only a few paces into the trees, yet the darkness still embraced them. Such a dense place it would be so easy to lose your bearings and become lost. De Craon's retinue, the Sacred Six, as well as their escort and guide, four burly lay brothers from St Michael's, had made themselves comfortable. They had lit small fires using the kindling and oil in a sack tied to the saddle horn of one of the lay brothers' horses. They were busy roasting strips of meat; the smell made de Craon slightly sick. He tried to ignore it as he bit into a manchet provided by the royal buttery at Windsor. However, the bread was so hard de Craon took a gulp from his small wine skin. He cleaned his mouth and stared across at Malpas, who had now finished his food and walked over to the horse line.

'Good,' de Craon murmured to himself. 'All is in place.' He raised a hand in greeting and Malpas replied in kind. De Craon, reassured that all was proceeding to plan, returned to his own twisted thoughts. He had landed in Dover after a frenetic voyage across the

Narrow Seas. The royal French war cog *The Temeraire*, despite its considerable bulk, had been tossed like a piece of flotsam on waves whipped up by a constantly adverse wind. From Dover de Craon had travelled on to St Michael's Abbey. He had set up camp in that gloomy abbey before hurrying to Windsor to join Prince Charles and Prince Louis, also recovering from seasickness, to present themselves to the now heavily pregnant queen. De Craon believed all was well. Everything was unfolding like a well-rehearsed mummers' play. He recalled his own mother cooking in the stone-flagged kitchen of the family manor house outside Dijon. She would have the ovens either side of the deep hearth fully fired, their shelves stacked with all she wanted to cook or bake. She would then tend the flames that danced merrily around the heavy iron bowl hanging from its tripod. Once satisfied, she'd move back to the fleshing table to cut, slice and grind meat, vegetables and spices. De Craon had always admired his mother's consummate skill in tending so much and bringing it to such a delicious fruition. He allowed himself a smile. To a certain extent, this was no different to what he was doing. All the plots of his intended strategy were vigorously flourishing. The young queen was well placed at Windsor. Hale and hearty, Isabella would in time give birth to Philip's first grandson. In addition, Reboham, his secret spy, had received his instructions, whilst matters at St Michael's Abbey were well in hand and the same was true here. Once again, de Craon recalled his mother's sweet face then sighed at the spurt of deepest anger such memories always provoked. How could he think of Maman without recalling her favourite, that holier-than-thou son, Raoul, his parents' firstborn? Raoul the scholar! Raoul the learner! Raoul the holy! Now Raoul the monk!

'I suppose I will have to meet you at the abbey,' de Craon whispered through gritted teeth. 'God knows I have to.' A burst of laughter made him glance towards his household clerks, the Sacred Six, clustered together around their meagre fire. De Craon curbed his anger. He stared towards Malpas, crouched beside one of the horses, examining its hoof. De Craon looked away, determined not to be smug; not everything was in order. Both Malpas and he believed that one, or even more, of the Sacred Six was a Judas, a traitor, the minion of Sir Hugh Corbett whose legion of spies stretched like a net across Paris, the Île-de-France and even the cold, dark places of the Chambre Noire. Most of Corbett's minions were snappers up of mere trifles, but Malpas believed, and de Craon likewise, that one of Corbett's spies had broken into the circle of the Sacred Six. Information known only to them was being passed to Corbett and the English Secret Chancery. De Craon had ordered Malpas to bring all six clerks under the closest scrutiny but, so far, he had discovered nothing. No evidence that would fasten the noose around the neck of the Judas being nourished and favoured so close to the power of France.

'Root and branch!' de Craon hissed. 'And, if need be, the wheat with the chaff.' He got to his feet and stared around. It was time! He clapped his gauntleted hands. Brother Peter, leader of the escort, blew hard and long on his hunting horn, summoning all to the horse lines. Eager to be moving, de Craon's retinue doused fires, adjusted war belts and drew their cloaks close about them. Suddenly the camaraderie of the camp was shattered by what sounded like a whistle, followed by the most piercing scream. One of the Sacred Six, his cloak still half clasped, staggered then turned, mouth and nose spraying blood, head back to show his exposed throat ruptured by a feathered, long shaft.

'Sebastian,' de Craon shouted. 'What is happening?' His hand fell to the hilt of his sword as he went to a half-crouch, staring wildly around. All was confusion. Sebastian had collapsed, choking and gurgling on his life-blood. De Craon made to move towards him when a second shaft hissed through the air to strike another clerk, Lavelle, a killing cut direct to the heart so he toppled over to sprawl across the corpse of the first victim. De Craon screamed for order, gesturing at the horse lines, ordering his escort to use their mounts as a shield against the mysterious, murderous bowman.

At last, some order was imposed. The horses were quietened, de Craon and his retinue waited. Another shaft was abruptly loosed but this smacked into the trunk of an ancient oak which stood along the forest edge. De Craon waited some more; he then hurried across at a half-crouch, eager to discover what was clearly tied to the shaft just above its goose-feathered flight. He took this off and hastened back to his horse. Malpas called out, raised a hand and pointed to the fringe of trees bordering the forest edge. De Craon nodded, gesturing with his hand. Malpas slipped away from the horses into the line of trees. De Craon and his retinue stood listening. However, apart from the constant cawing of the crows and rooks, they could hear nothing untoward. Malpas emerged from the treeline shaking his head.

'Monseigneur,' he called out. 'Nobody. Nothing. But the archer must be English, skilled in the use of the war bow.'

'Perhaps not,' de Craon shouted back, holding up what he had taken from the third arrow. He again examined the rough, hard waxen seal and the crude insignia it bore.

'It shows two poor knights. They ride the same horse,' he exclaimed. 'That is the seal of the accursed Templars.' He pointed to the two corpses. 'The Temple and its coven are responsible,' he proclaimed in ringing tones. 'They have the blood of our comrades on their hands.'

Sir Hugh Corbett sat back in his throne-like chair before the judgement table. He sifted his Ave beads through the fingers of his right hand as he stared at Abbot Maurice and Prior Felix sitting on the bench across the judgement table. Corbett deliberately maintained a silence. Other monks waited in the sacristy in case Corbett decided to call them, but they too would have to wait. Ap Ythel's men now guarded all entrances, whilst two archers had been placed on guard to silence the anchorite if he started to bellow imprecations down the church. Corbett glanced at the Silver Shrine and the tabernacle where the Glory of Heaven had been stored. The Turkey rugs had now been replaced back on the paved floor of the shrine. Corbett had decided that he wanted to see things as they had been. Nevertheless, he openly conceded, the shrine held no secret passageway or hiding place, certainly nothing to explain the great mystery perpetrated there. Perhaps this inquisition might shed some light on the gathering dark. All was now ready, or nearly so. Ranulf, pen poised, was waiting to transcribe. The Clerk of the Green Wax kept his head down to hide his smile. Old Master Longface was not in the best of humours, having to face one petty obstacle after another. Now it was time.

Corbett rose to his feet, read out his commission in a clear, carrying voice, then sat down, pointing at Abbot Maurice.

'You have heard the king's proclamation. You are on oath. You and Prior Felix will answer my questions. So, Father Abbot, your baptismal name is Thomas Brienne, born in France, a subject of the French king?'

'And first and foremost,' the abbot testily retorted, 'a Benedictine monk. My vows to the Order supersede all others.'

'We shall see, we shall see,' Corbett replied. 'Your family had close ties with the now disgraced Templar order?'

'As we did with the Benedictines, Franciscans and—'

'You entered the Templar Order as a novice, an acolyte, a man-at-arms in Outremer. A member of the garrison of the last Templar stronghold.'

48

'Acre!' the abbot intervened, face slightly suffused, his snapping voice betraying his hostility.

'Pax et Bonum,' Corbett soothed, holding up his right hand. 'Father Abbot, all I am doing is putting matters into perspective.'

'True, true,' the abbot murmured. He slumped slightly on the bench, crossed himself and glanced up. 'Do continue, Sir Hugh.'

'The beautiful diamond, the Glory of Heaven, was brought from Acre and handed over to the Temple in Paris.'

'I had nothing to do with that. Question our anchorite, the one who calls himself Reboham.'

'Oh, I shall do. Yet you know the diamond's history?'

'Of course.'

'Then tell me.' Corbett half smiled as he pointed at Ranulf. 'Tell me, at least just for the record of these proceedings.'

'The Glory of Heaven,' Abbot Maurice replied, 'is a miracle. The Virgin Mary, Mother of Our Lord Jesus Christ, spent her last days with John the Evangelist in their home at Ephesus. The beloved disciple had moved Christ's mother to a safe place well away from the chaos and confusion in Jerusalem. Rebellion and revolt were in the air, a very bloody confrontation between the Jews and the occupying Romans. Anyway, the Virgin Mary grew frail. Some theologians talk of the Dormition . . .'

'That the Virgin Mary died and that her soul went to heaven, her body to some sacred secret site in Ephesus.'

49

'Precisely.' The abbot's face creased into a smile. 'You are quite the scholar, Sir Hugh.'

'My mother, God rest her,' Corbett replied, 'nourished a deep devotion to the Virgin. She read and learnt whatever she could, whenever she could.'

'So, you will know the second proposal?' Abbot Maurice declared.

'That the Virgin did not die,' Corbett replied. 'That her body and soul were glorified and she was assumed both body and soul into heaven. What we call the Assumption.'

'Yes, Sir Hugh, the Assumption. A teaching we Benedictines fervently encourage.' The abbot drew a deep breath. 'The Glory of Heaven is part of this tradition, according to which, the Virgin, before she was assumed, said that she would leave a small token of the glory awaiting her. Now the apostle John had left a pewter goblet of water beside her bed. He returned to discover the Assumption had taken place. The goblet no longer held water but an exquisitely beautiful diamond: a glorious jewel we now call the Glory of Heaven.' The abbot spread his hands and sat in silence for a while.

Corbett glanced swiftly at the prior and wondered if the arrival of his brother, Amaury de Craon, had disturbed him. During his collection of information about St Michael's and its monks, Corbett discovered that Prior Felix's baptismal name was Raoul de Craon. Corbett knew very little about the private life of his arch rival and this discovery had set him wondering, his curiosity and suspicion sharpened further by the violation of the shrine and the theft of the famous diamond. He must not forget the hard political facts. The Glory of Heaven was claimed by Philip of France, and that king did have a number of his subjects holding high office in the Abbey of St Michael's. Was there a connection between Philip, the diamond and its keepers here at St Michael's?

'Sir Hugh, Sir Hugh.' Corbett broke from his reverie and smiled at Ranulf, who'd leant forward, tapping his quill against the table top.

'Abbot Maurice,' Corbett declared. 'I do apologise for being distracted. Do continue.'

'The Glory of Heaven became a great treasure of Holy Mother Church, being passed from hand to hand. It was owned by Charlemagne and eventually by the House of Capet, the sacred line of the kings of France.'

'But one of these gave it away?'

'Only in trust, Sir Hugh. King Louis of France entrusted the diamond – and I repeat, *entrusted* – to the Templar Order. Now that Order has been dissolved by the Holy Father—'

'And by Philip of France.'

'Whatever, Sir Hugh. Yet the Order is now gone and King Philip demands the diamond's return. Of course, the King of England claims it was given as a gift to him and his successors "in perpetuity" by the now defunct Templar Order. King Edward has many such items given to him and he has no intention of returning either these or the diamond.'

'And you? What do you think?'

'Sir Hugh, I am French by birth but a Benedictine

by choice. Our Order always accepts the rule of the kingdom which shelters them. Accordingly, Edward of England is my master on this issue.'

'And you, Prior Felix? Do you think the same? Even though you are the brother of Monseigneur Amaury de Craon, Philip of France's most loyal henchman.'

If the prior was startled, he did not show it. He just leant slightly forward, smiling to himself.

'Well?' Ranulf demanded.

'Sir Hugh, I realise you have discovered the blood-tie. Yes, I am Amaury's brother. I was baptised Raoul but assumed another name, as is customary, when I became a Benedictine. I fully support what my abbot has said on this matter. True, the Book of Proverbs claims "that brothers united are as a fortress", but sadly that is not the case between myself and Amaury.'

'You mean, more like Cain and Abel?'

'No, Ranulf-atte-Newgate.' Prior Felix's voice cut like a lash. 'I am no blood-drinker. I do not desire my brother's life. I just want him to leave me alone. I want to serve God, not Caesar.'

'Very well,' Corbett intervened hastily. 'Let us now turn to the crime, the theft of the diamond.' He rose and walked over to the Silver Shrine. 'This,' he declared grasping its bars, 'is the chantry chapel built to house the diamond, yes? Come.' Corbett gestured. 'Join me.'

The monks and Ranulf rose to follow Corbett down the side of the shrine, now greatly battered. They went through the ruined doorway onto the soft, though blood-stained, Turkey rugs. Corbett went and stood with his back against the snow-white altar. He gestured around. 'When was this built?'

'It was completed three years ago,' Prior Felix answered. 'Around Michaelmas. The diamond being installed in the tabernacle behind you on the feast of St Stephen.'

'And the design?' Corbett asked.

'I know a little about it. The gift of the Hanseatic League. Their merchants in the steelyard in London wanted to please our king. They proposed what you see now. Costly steel bars, which would shimmer and shine in the glow of hundreds of candles and fiery sconce torches. A fitting tribute to the brilliant beauty of the diamond. I understand,' the prior scratched his chin, 'that a similar shrine can be found in Lubeck. Our king was certainly delighted with the proposal. The royal masons saw no problem. The shrine would be embedded on one side, deep into the outside wall of the transept. The rest of the bars would be soldered together to form this square. The door would be reinforced and held secure by two locks, each with its own unique key. Further security would be provided by clasp bolts at both top and bottom. Of course, the masons also made use of the small roundel windows. As you can see, these were brought into the design and permanently sealed with thick panes of painted glass depicting scenes from the Assumption.'

'True, all true,' Corbett declared. 'I am convinced no secret entrance or any such other device exists here. So how?' He paused and pointed at the prior. 'You discovered the guardian's corpse?'

'Yes, I came down here as customary to ensure all was well as we approached the end of our horarium. Compline would be sung and the abbey church locked and bolted—'

'Pause there,' Corbett instructed. 'Brother Mark, the guardian, was murdered between vespers and compline, yes? Would he leave the chapel to join you?'

'Oh yes, and then return. He could sleep here. The sacristy holds all he needs. Food would be brought to him from the refectory as it was to the anchorite.'

'And Brother Mark was a good and trusted monk. Yes, Father Abbot?'

'Brother Mark was much loved by us all,' the abbot replied. 'A simple soul; a former soldier. He was greatly honoured to be the guardian of the diamond.'

'And during the day, what would he do?'

'Well, he would join us for divine office. Sometimes he would come to the refectory or study in the library. During such occasions another monk would take over his responsibilities, but outside the Silver Shrine, not within.'

'And how was Brother Mark during the days before his death?'

'As far as I could see,' Prior Felix replied, 'as happy as a spring sparrow.'

'He had no enemies? No unexpected visitors? He didn't leave the abbey, I mean in the days before his murder?'

'Sir Hugh, nothing untoward occurred.'

'And until you discovered the murder, nothing unusual had taken place either here or elsewhere in the abbey?'

'There was the conflagration which totally destroyed The Wodewose.'

'Rest assured, Prior Felix, we shall come to that by and by. But again, I ask you – nothing occurred in the abbey, in or around the Silver Shrine, which might explain the heinous crimes perpetrated here?'

'No,' Prior Felix retorted. 'Nothing until I came down here yesterday between vespers and compline. Darkness was falling.' The friar spoke slowly, emphasising each word. 'Torches flared, candlelight floated through the darkness. All was quiet. Not even rantings from our anchorite. Anyway, I approached the shrine. Torches flamed either side of it, with a lanternhorn near the door. Nothing exceptional in that. I called for Brother Mark. Of course, there was no answer. Then I noticed our guardian sprawled just close to where you have your feet, Sir Hugh. He lay in a pool of widening blood, splashes of which . . .' He gestured at the great ugly stains on the Turkey rugs.

'And nothing else?'

'Nothing.'

'And so, we now come to the question of locks and bolts,' Corbett declared. 'When we broke through this morning,' he tapped the wallet on his belt, 'I took three keys, two from the locks on the door and one from the tabernacle. I withdrew all three keys despite the door being ruptured. I found the keys still went in and out of their lock easy enough. The tabernacle key was no different. I drew it in and out, closed the door and locked it. But there must have been copies.'

'There is only one copy of each,' Abbot Maurice

replied. 'Sir Hugh, we have already explained this. I carry one on a cord around my neck. A key for the top lock on the chantry door. I assure you, that has never left me.' The abbot pulled down the muffler of his robe, plucking out the string with the key tied there.

Corbett peered close: it looked identical to one of those he now held.

'I carry the second,' Prior Felix declared, pulling out the cord around his neck. 'And I would swear a solemn oath that this key has never left me.'

'And the third?'

'The tabernacle key is held by Brother Simon. He waits in the sacristy.'

'Fetch him,' Corbett replied. 'Please tell Captain Ap Ythel to let him through.'

A short while later the sour-faced sacristan shuffled in. He explained how he had been busy in the stores checking recently acquired purveyance, particularly candles, when the crime had occurred, and yes, he assured Corbett, there were other brothers who would swear to that. The sacristan, eager to be gone, also pulled out the cord carrying the tabernacle key. He too declared that it had never left him.

'Why the interest in the keys?' the abbot asked once the sacristan left. 'The door to the shrine was bolted securely at top and bottom: the keys are only one defence, the bolts are a second.'

'And these bolts cannot be reached by anyone pushing their hand or any implement through the bars?' Corbett asked.

The prior shook his head. 'The Silver Shrine,' he declared, 'was most secure, tighter than a hunter's trap.'

'So how?' Corbett declared. 'How did the assassin enter that locked and bolted shrine, stab Brother Mark, steal the diamond then vanish like a mist, leaving the door both locked and bolted? In which case I must go back to Brother Mark – could he have been an accomplice in this crime, then murdered when his associate no longer needed him?'

'Sir Hugh, with all due respect, that is nonsense. Brother Mark took his duties as guardian most seriously.' The prior half smiled. 'He adored Father Abbot. No no.' He waved a hand as the abbot made to object. 'He truly did, Maurice. He was ever so proud that you'd appointed him as guardian of the shrine.'

'Why did you?' Corbett asked.

'Mark was of middle years. Strong, active, a former man at arms with a deep devotion to our abbey. He was the perfect choice.' The abbot spread his hands. 'I never had any occasion to regret my decision.'

'So, he was an able-bodied man who could defend himself?'

'Of course, and I follow your logic,' the abbot replied. 'There is little or no evidence of Brother Mark defending himself. He had a sword and club stored in the sacristy along with a palliasse, goblet, jug and bowl. As I have said before, Brother Mark lived for this shrine. He was as happy as a monk should be. Kind, obedient, dutiful to his brothers and his superiors. And when visitors or pilgrims did come –' the abbot pointed across the darkened nave – 'prayer stools are stored there which the lay brothers would pull across so the faithful could kneel and pray before the Silver Shrine. Such pilgrims were not allowed into the shrine itself of course.' The abbot sighed. 'If the King or any member of the court visited, the shrine would be opened, the prie-dieu set up before this altar and the Glory of Heaven exposed for veneration.'

'And when was the last time that happened?'

The abbot closed his eyes, lips moving soundlessly.

'Ten days ago,' Prior Felix interjected.

'Of course, yes, of course,' the abbot breathed, opening his eyes. 'These present troubles have greatly disturbed my humours.'

'You've had visitors?' Corbett demanded.

'Her Grace the queen, accompanied by certain French guests; her uncles Charles and Louis, together with other notables.'

'Including Monseigneur Amaury de Craon.' Corbett pointed at the prior. 'Your esteemed brother?'

'Esteemed indeed,' the prior mocked. 'We glimpsed each other from afar but we did not meet or talk.'

'Our last important visitor,' the abbot declared, 'was in fact Monseigneur de Craon. He paid the shrine a second visit a few days ago, just before he left for Windsor.'

'Will he be greatly troubled by the theft?'

The abbot forced a smile. 'Of course he will be. The French crown claims the Glory of Heaven as its rightful property. Come, Sir Hugh, you know that.'

'True, very true.' Corbett grinned. 'I was being a little

mischievous. So, I'll ask the obvious question, even though it might provoke great insult or hurt in certain quarters. To be blunt, could our French visitors be involved in this mayhem?'

'But how?' Prior Felix spread his hands.

'How indeed?' Corbett retorted, getting to his feet. 'How did the assassin enter and leave that shrine? The door was locked and bolted four times over. How did they murder an able-bodied man who appears not to have resisted or raised the alarm? The assassin opens the tabernacle, takes the diamond and leaves. Yet the door remains bolted, the keys still turned in their locks. Oh yes,' Corbett added in a whisper as if to himself, 'Satan has walked here and practised his sly and subtle ways. Look,' he continued, 'when we broke into the shrine this morning, I examined Brother Mark's corpse. I must do it again formally as part of this inquisition.'

Corbett glanced quickly at Ranulf and winked. What he had said about the corpse was true, but he also believed further scrutiny was required. Abbot Maurice agreed and, leaving Ap Ythel on guard, they left the church, making their way around the great cloisters. Corbett pulled his hood up. A weak sun had broken through, but it was a truly cold day, the freezing frost still staining ledges and cornices. The abbey was certainly busy. Torch-flare glowed through half-open doors; lanterns shed rays of faint light. Candles glowed, as did coloured lights before statues and grim-faced gargoyles who glared down in stony terror. A place of shifting shadows and flickering lights. The air was fragrant with sweet cooking odours, which mingled with those of incense and candle smoke. The abbey was a sacred place, Corbett reflected, but one which also housed horrid crimes, rank treason against both God and the king. They left the main abbey building with its soaring walls, arches and pillars and crossed a field still frozen white under a hard hoarfrost.

At last, they reached the abbey death house. This stood close to the curtain wall, a morbid, barn-like building, reeking of pinewood, candlewax, pitch and incense, which did not quite conceal the fetid, mouldering stench of death. All the mortuary tables were empty except for one just beneath a stark, black crucifix. Abbot Maurice distributed pomanders before pulling back the shroud cloth to reveal Brother Mark's naked corpse. Corbett crossed himself, murmured the requiem then scrutinised the lean muscular body stretched out before him.

'Certainly a strong man,' Corbett murmured. 'Notice the muscles in the arms and calves? A former warrior. See the scars and marks, old wounds from his fighting days.' He turned the corpse over then shook his head, before placing it back in its original position. 'Nothing,' he declared, 'except this.' Corbett asked for one of the many candles placed in pots around the room and used this to cast a pool of light over the dead man's face. He ran his finger along the brow then down to his nose.

'Ah, I see,' Ranulf murmured. 'Slight bruising to the top of the nose and forehead.'

'Yes, that's what I glimpsed this morning. Father Abbot, can you explain this?'

'I don't know . . . Perhaps in his death throes poor Mark clattered against the bars of the shrine?'

'Possible,' Corbett replied. 'But come, this is a cold, dark place. I have seen what I wanted.'

The abbot offered his own lodgings for Corbett and Ranulf to relax in for a while. Corbett thanked him but insisted they return to the judgement table for he was not yet finished. Once they arrived, the prior ordered fresh braziers to be fired and wheeled close. More candles were lit. Corbett recited a 'Gloria Patri', then pointed at the abbot.

'Father, does the name Reboham mean anything to you?'

'Of course.' The abbot half turned on the bench, peering into the darkness. 'Our anchorite has taken that name. In the Old Testament, Reboham is the son of King Solomon who built the temple in Jerusalem, which became the fief, the very heart, of the Templar Order. Philip of France has destroyed that Order and slaughtered many Templars: those who survived have fled. They have gone into hiding; they have assumed new names. Both church and crown have turned against them. These fugitives wish to remain deep in the shadows. I believe our anchorite is one of these, but you should ask him yourself.'

'Oh, I will!' Corbett smiled bleakly. 'I certainly shall. Secondly, does the term "The Apostles" mean anything to you? By the way, I am not referring to the twelve men chosen by Christ.'

'Of course.' The abbot cleared his throat before he continued. 'Sir Hugh, acting troupes, mummers and masquers, move across the shires of this kingdom. They perform whenever and wherever they can. Many of them, genuine and skilled, are patronised by merchants as well as the lords of the soil.'

'And you are both,' Corbett replied.

'We are a very rich and prosperous abbey; I cannot deny that. We till the soil, tend our herds, plant produce and reap a very rich harvest. We work for what we have. We also,' the abbot hurried on, 'have a duty of care to the many faithful of the shire who view this abbey as a most sacred place as well as a heavenly mansion of great wealth. We have many obligations, including a duty to preach the Gospel in whatever way we can.' The Abbot pointed into the darkness. 'The walls of this church preach Christ's teaching in the many paintings we have commissioned. Go and look at them, Sir Hugh. You will see angels falling from heaven, Mary and Joseph journeying to Bethlehem, Christ turning the water into wine and, of course, we celebrate His passion, death and resurrection. In addition, we have paintings celebrating the life and virtues of our founder, St Benedict, as well as those of his holy sister, Scholastica. Jesus spoke in parables. He preached divine truths through them. So do we.'

'And The Apostles?'

'Correct, Sir Hugh, we patronise a troupe of mummers who call themselves The Apostles. They move across the shire but always return here for the great liturgical feasts and festivals; Christmas, Easter and Pentecost.'

'And they cause no trouble or pose no threat?'

'Heaven forbid,' the prior exclaimed. 'They are most

law abiding and keep the king's peace more faithfully than their so-called betters.'

'Such as?'

'The great barons, Sir Hugh. We hear constant rumour, the threat of civil war. How the great lords want to do away with both the king and his cat—'

'Favourite,' the abbot swiftly interjected.

'And where are The Apostles now?' Corbett kept his face impassive, as he knew full well where they lodged.

'Bloody Meadow,' the prior replied, scratching his face. 'A broad stretch of grassland beyond the abbey walls, though owned by us. It also contains derelict granges, barns and outhouses. We lease all this to The Apostles. The local villagers and forest people do not like such an arrangement. They claim Bloody Meadow is haunted by the ghosts of Vikings massacred there hundreds of years ago. The Apostles, however, appear to revel in such stories and legends but, of course, that's their meat and drink. Sir Hugh, I assure you they are most peaceful.'

'And very skilled,' the abbot added. 'During Holy Week they plan to stage one of my most favourite masques, "Pilate's Wife". Anyway, Sir Hugh, why the interest in them?'

'Well, Father Abbott, it is no secret what has happened here.'

'Oh, The Apostles would have nothing to do with the theft. They are innocents. More importantly, they would never be allowed to wander through the abbey. Do you entertain such suspicions, Sir Hugh?'

'I speak as I find. Human nature always surprises me.'

'*Concedo*,' the abbot whispered. 'I concede that. Is there more?'

'There certainly is,' Ranulf abruptly intervened. 'The total destruction of an entire tavern, The Wodewose.'

Corbett glanced at his companion. Ranulf had been strangely quiet, intense and now that unease was showing in his blunt questioning. Ranulf was eager to hasten proceedings along.

'Ah yes, The Wodewose,' the abbot replied, turning to his prior. 'A true mystery, yes?'

'So, tell us what you know,' Ranulf insisted.

'It has little to do with our abbey or the theft of the Glory of Heaven.'

'With all due respect, Father Abbot, I will decide what falls within the remit of this inquisition. My learned colleague's question still stands.'

'The Wodewose,' Prior Felix replied slowly, 'was a forest tavern on the road to this abbey, which then winds its way on to Windsor.' He paused to collect his thoughts. 'The tavern was built out of red brick with a black slate roof and it rose three stories high. It had no curtain wall or fortified gate but fronted the trackway. On either side of it stood storerooms, stables and other outhouses.'

'And its owner?'

'Crispin. He lived there with his wife Mathilda, their two sons, Matthew and Luke, three servants and the horse boy, Robert.'

'You knew them well?'

'Of course, Sir Hugh. They bought our produce. The

Wodewose was not only a wayside tavern, a journey-man's inn, but in many ways was a small market in itself. Master Crispin sold goods to those travelling the roads, as well as to the forest people, those living in the small hamlets and farmsteads scattered across Ashdown.' The prior, head down, abruptly crossed himself. 'God give them good rest,' he murmured.

'Crispin and his family, they were honest Christians?'

The prior lifted his head and Corbett noticed the tears brimming in his eyes. 'The Wodewose enjoyed a pleasing reputation, yes, father?'

The prior nodded his agreement. 'Yes, and it was busy enough,' he declared. 'Once winter passed, spring returned and the trackways opened.'

'But at other times such as these, before spring broke?'

'As you can imagine, Sir Hugh, it was deserted, quite lonely,' the prior replied. 'Crispin and his household were regular visitors here. They would attend the Jesus mass on Sundays and holy days. As I said, they bought produce and supplies from us, some of which was for their tavern, the rest for sale. We encouraged that.' The prior shrugged. 'We are an abbey, a house of prayer, not a market. Moreover, it was easier for people to flock to The Wodewose than to come here.'

'So, your relations with them were good?'

'Very much so,' the abbot replied. 'Crispin was left handed and so am I. He would often tease me about what we had in common.'

Corbett noticed the look of absolute sadness which flitted across the abbot's face, and he wondered yet again what secrets this abbey held. He had no proof, no evidence, but Corbett sensed that all was not well here and he was determined to find the root cause. The king would insist on that. He had made it very clear that the Glory of Heaven was to remain at St Michael's Abbey. However, Corbett's task had abruptly changed. Recently, he had received secret orders from the king himself to seize the diamond and keep it safe, but someone had struck before he could.

'And now?' Ranulf tapped his quill pen against the table. 'I mean before the fire took place, when did that occur?'

'On the morrow of the Feast of St David, the first of March, and to answer your question, Ranulf-atte-Newgate, as far as we know, nothing untoward occurred in or around The Wodewose.'

'No!' The Abbot abruptly waved a hand, sandalled feet tapping the paving stones. 'On the night of the great fire at The Wodewose, and it erupted after the early sunset, our anchorite, as you will learn, was wandering outside. Under the indenture he signed, he has the freedom of the abbey church and God's Acre. No more than that. Anyway,' the Abbot continued excitedly, 'our anchorite maintains he glimpsed the Lord Satan, or some high-ranking demon, striding through God's Acre, a figure with a hideous, horned face, a black cloak billowing all about him.'

'How could he be so certain?' Ranulf asked. 'I mean, darkness had fallen . . .'

'A small bonfire lit by the gardener still burnt, fitfully

casting a light through which the demon strode before disappearing into the dark.'

'Was this before or after the conflagration at The Wodewose?'

'Oh, hours before, Master Ranulf. Now that is what our anchorite claims he saw, but I am not too sure about his wits and whether his perception of what is real is true. However, to be fair to him, I cannot see why he should lie. True, he likes to trumpet quotations from Holy Scripture that all is doom and gloom. He warns that the coming judgement will find us all wanting. However, proclaiming verses from scripture is not the same as saying you had a vision of the Lord of Hell walking around your abbey. More than that,' the Abbot blew his lips out, 'I cannot say.'

'And the fire at The Wodewose, how was the alarm raised?'

'Sir Hugh,' Prior Felix replied. 'We have watchmen along our walls as well as on the top of the church tower. They glimpsed the first flames shortly before midnight. They rang the tocsin. Of course, it took some time to decide what could have happened. Father Abbot, myself and other brothers eventually assembled in our chapter house. We wondered what the cause of the fire might be. We realised the flames came from the direction of The Wodewose, but there again fires do break out in the forest, though not so much during the wet months of the year. True, we strongly suspected it was The Wodewose and, naturally, we wondered about the cause. Perhaps some nasty accident.'

'Or outlaws,' Corbett interjected.

'To be honest, Sir Hugh, the outlaws of Ashdown are few and far between.' The Abbot pulled a face. 'There is no organised or well-led coven of wolfsheads, no band prowling like a pack of wild dogs. If there were, we have lay brothers, former soldiers who would show them no mercy. Moreover, we have excellent relations with the sheriff as well as the Constable of Windsor Castle. Both would give us every assistance.'

'And what did you decide at that chapter-house meeting?'

'I offered to investigate at first light,' the prior replied. 'Myself and two lay brothers, Odo and Aelred. Once dawn had broken, we rode out to view what was a total annihilation. We reached where the tavern once stood. Both it and, to a greater extent, the outhouses on either side had been reduced to a smoking, crumbling mess of scorched brick and blackened timbers. In fact, nothing remained. The fire must have roared like hell's own furnace.'

'And no survivors?'

'None, Sir Hugh, just a hideous mound of scorched bone. Nor were there survivors in the outbuildings . . .'

'Were human remains found there?'

'No, no, the remnants were clustered together.'

'All of them in one place?'

'Sir Hugh, that's what I discovered both in my visit and when we removed what human remains we could find.'

'So, the corpses of all the victims were close together

as if gathering in one room? In this case it must have been the taproom.'

'Yes, Sir Hugh, I would say they were.' The prior crossed himself. 'Nothing remained. Nor could we find any evidence of violence, of an attack of any sort. The only survivors were the horses.'

'The horses?'

'Yes, they had been released from their stables. They were found wandering about, terrified of the fire, but they still clustered close to what they regarded as their home.'

'So,' Ranulf demanded, 'you do not know why, when or how The Wodewose was destroyed, or, most importantly, who was responsible?'

'That is true,' the abbot confirmed. 'We, or rather Father Prior, who cleared the site with his lay brothers, discovered nothing which could explain this heinous attack. If you want, when you want, do question Brothers Odo and Aelred. They will simply confirm what you already know.'

'Tell me,' Corbett declared, 'when you sifted amongst the remains, did you find, albeit scorched or burnt, anything of value, be it coins, rings, a bracelet?'

'Yes, we did, different items.'

'And the horses had been cleared from the stables?'

'Yes.'

'And, as you have said, there is little or no evidence of any coven of outlaws lurking in the area?'

'That is correct.'

'So, the motive for the crime could not have been

theft. Valuable items were not taken, good horses released and ignored. So why?'

'And why, Sir Hugh, is the king's justiciar in these parts so interested in a tavern fire?'

'Because, Father Abbot, at least eight of our king's most loyal subjects were foully murdered, or so it would seem.'

'Sir Hugh, please,' the prior spread his hands, 'worse things occur in other parts of this kingdom. We have heard the most terrifying stories about what is happening along the Scottish March.' The prior joined his hands as if in prayer. 'We have tried to be honest with you. My question still stands.'

Corbett glanced at Ranulf who simply shrugged.

'Very well, listen.' Corbett sipped from the small cup of morning ale. 'I do not know who was actually in that tavern when it was attacked and burnt, those within cruelly massacred. However,' he tapped the manuscript in front of him, 'one person we believe was there was Stephen Filliol.'

'Who?'

'Prior Felix, Stephen Filliol is, or rather was, a royal squire, the king's own courier. A young man of noble family, much loved by both the king and queen. We do know that Stephen left London two days before The Wodewose was destroyed. He was carrying important messages for the queen at Windsor.'

'And you are sure of this, Sir Hugh?'

'Oh yes, Father Prior. In fact, you proved that Stephen

visited The Wodewose.' Corbett smiled as the prior startled in surprise. 'Remember you submitted a report to the Royal Chancery; a brief summary of the damage caused? You said no worthwhile treasure or valuables survived the blaze except for the horses. You then, as the shrewd prior you are, listed each of these with the briefest description.'

'Of course.' The prior smacked the heel of his hand against his forehead. 'I remember it, a fine, sturdy, brown-dappled garron.'

'The same, Father Prior, as the one Filliol took from the royal stables on Westminster fields. So, Filliol must have lodged at that tavern.'

'He was also a fighting man,' Ranulf murmured. 'If the tavern was attacked, Filliol would have organised a defence, despatched someone for help.'

'Anyway,' Corbett intervened, 'now you know our interest. True innocent people were cut down in the most barbaric way, but Stephen Filliol was much loved by our king, his queen and the Lady Beatrice. More importantly, as you well know, my friend, an attack on a royal courier is regarded as high treason. Such a crime is viewed as a malicious assault on the royal privilege, its status and its power. So you can . . .'

Corbett broke off as the tocsin bell tolled deep and sombre. They all rose to their feet. Doors further down the nave crashed open, voices shouted. The bells kept up their insistent tolling, almost drowning the cries and sound of pattering feet. Captain Ap Ythel emerged from the darkness.

'Sir Hugh,' he gasped. 'My apologies, but Monseigneur de Craon has arrived. Two of his clerks were killed on their return here. Arrows loosed from the trees . . .'

PART TWO

'What does it profit to resist the king?'

Corbett snatched up his war belt and cloak and, accompanied by the others, hurried out of the church. They hastened around buildings, garden plots and cloisters. The bells still tolled. Blackrobes, disturbed from their duties, hurried about armed with torches and lanterns. At last, Corbett and his party reached the great stable yard stretching down to the high crenellated curtain wall and its massive fortified gateway. Dusk was gathering, deepening the confusion, as men tried to soothe horses or push through the throng carrying flaring torches and lanterns. At last, Abbot Maurice, assisted by Ap Ythel and his archers, imposed some order. The crowd in the great stable yard thinned as people now hurried away. The clamour died. Corbett and Ranulf, accompanied by both abbot and prior, walked across the yard to the group now waiting in the shadow of the gatehouse.

Corbett glimpsed two corpses thrown over the saddles

of their horses, made fast with pieces of rope. The monks who had accompanied de Craon were dismissed. Corbett waited until they had gone and walked towards the French envoy, his face wreathed in a smile as false as the one de Craon swiftly assumed. They met, clasping hands, exchanging the kiss of peace and, as they did, Corbett thought of Judas, because the man he now embraced was just as traitorous. Once the introductions had finished Corbett stepped back and bowed.

'Amaury, so good to see you.'

'Sir Hugh, believe me, my heart leapt like a deer in spring when I glimpsed you.'

On any other occasion Corbett would have burst out laughing, instead he stared over his shoulder at Ranulf to ensure that he did not. He turned back to de Craon.

'You've suffered a great mishap?'

'Murder, Sir Hugh. Two of my clerks from the Sacred Six, slaughtered like hapless hogs. Some archer skilled in the war bow. No such archer is to be found in my company.'

'Nor a murderer in mine, Monseigneur. Be careful what you say, what you imply.' Corbett stared at this most inveterate of enemies, a man who truly hated him. De Craon was not ageing well. Perhaps the rancour he nourished now stained his body as well as his soul and spirit. The Frenchman's moustache and beard were sparser and streaked with the white of age: his face had become more lined and furrowed, though his eyes still held that baleful glare. Dark and menacing, as Ranulf once remarked, 'like two piss holes in the snow'.

'Two men killed,' Ranulf, standing behind Corbett, intoned. 'God rest them and pardon their sins. Do you need help with the corpses?'

De Craon lifted a gauntleted hand. He glanced back towards where the abbot and prior were helping with both the horses and their gruesome burdens. De Craon exuded a deep sigh, letting his hand drop. He then turned abruptly on his heel and strode across to join the Benedictines. Corbett was about to speak to Ranulf when one of the horses, screaming in terror, reared up on its hind legs, sharpened hooves scything the air. The corpse draped over the horse's saddle slid off onto the cobbles as the men around the wounded animal scattered like leaves before the wind. Corbett just froze at a half-crouch. He then heard the whirr of an arrow, piercing the air to strike another horse in the rump. Chaos descended. De Craon and the Benedictines hastily doused torches and retreated into the protection of the early dusk. Corbett and Ranulf followed. They crouched, staring across the stable yard. The cobbles glistened with piss and blood from the two injured horses, which now lay on their sides, whinnying hysterically at the pain from their wounds. The yard was very broad. On either side were outhouses, storerooms and other sheds.

'You could hide a small army here,' Ranulf whispered. He then paused as Corbett pointed across the yard. Ap Ythel and his archers had now gathered deep in the shadows between two barns. They were about to deploy. The archers seemed to shrink deeper into the darkness, but then three of them abruptly darted out, running across the yard to take up a new position. They had barely crossed the yard when one of the stable doors crashed open and Chanson, Corbett's Clerk of the Stables, came hurrying out, waving his arms and shouting, 'Pax, pax, pax!' He abruptly stopped.

'Over here, Chanson.'

Slipping and slithering, the Clerk of the Stables hurried across the cobbles.

'Sir Hugh,' he explained, 'whoever is responsible has fled.' Chanson pointed back. 'There's an old forge room. When the arrows were first loosed, I hid there – I glimpsed a figure, hooded and visored. He carried a war bow. He loosed a second shaft then fled.'

'I am sure he did.' Corbett patted his clerk on the shoulder. 'Chanson, take care of the wounded horses. If the animals are beyond help then advise their owners to give them the mercy cut. Now, you,' he pointed at his henchman, 'prepare yourself. Remember we, together with de Craon, are to be the abbot's honoured guests at supper in his refectory.'

'When was that announced?'

'As soon as we arrived at St Michael's, Ranulf. Abbot Maurice said he expected de Craon's return later today and that he would invite both envoys to celebrate together. Believe me, my friends, this is something I cannot afford to miss.'

Despite the chaos and sorrow, Abbot Maurice and his brothers worked hard to entertain the royal envoys. The abbey kitchens and buttery served up delicious food in the abbot's splendid private refectory. Of course, it was Lent, with Holy Week fast approaching, so red meats were not served. Nevertheless, delicious dishes such as oysters, pigeons, potage with beans, brie cheese and white manchet loaves wrapped in napkins streamed from the kitchens along with mustard and other sauces, savoury or sweet. After the main courses were cleared, oranges, lemons, pomegranates, dates, figs and raisins, specially imported for the abbey by Italian merchants, were presented in silver dishes and bowls. The best of wines from Bordeaux and the Rhine poured out from gold-edged jugs into deep, jewel-encrusted goblets. The banquet finished with a carafe of the most exquisitely delicate hippocras. Corbett and de Craon sat together either side of the nef, a golden model of a cog studded with jewels and full of the most savoury sauce. Torchlight and candle glow brought the luxurious chamber to life, dazzling the precious goblets, mazers and jugs carefully placed along the table. The light also illuminated the array of gorgeous tapestries adorning the pink plastered walls. These exquisite drapes portrayed scenes from the Apocalypse, in particular Archangel Michael's war against Satan. In the gaps between these tapestries were hangings of embroidered silk damask and extraordinarily costly Florentine velvet. The floor of the refectory was tiled, each one boasting a colourful heraldic device which caught the light from the great Catherine wheel crammed with beeswax candles on its spikes.

Sitting on a throne-like chair with cushions of flame-coloured silk and gold tissue, Corbett could only smile to himself. As a reminder to both envoys that they were about to enter the most holy season of Christ's passion, Abbot Maurice had installed in the refectory a life-size wooden statue of Judas. The statue held niches for the twelve paschal candles which would be snuffed out, one by one, to symbolise the apostles abandoning Jesus. Most appropriate, Corbett thought, especially in a place like this where treachery and treason swirled like a cloying mist around them. He also wondered if the reference to the apostles held any real significance for de Craon as it did for himself. Was this just a coincidence, Corbett wondered? That the desertion of the twelve apostles be brought to his attention and that of de Craon, or did it hold a special significance for the abbot and his monks? Corbett leant back in his chair. He truly wished to be away from here. He was tired and needed a rest from the constant hunt for the king's enemies. Once he had finished at St Michael's, God willing, he would return to the Lady Maeve and his two children. He would celebrate Easter with his own beloved family and let the world go hang.

Corbett opened his eyes as Abbot Maurice rose to deliver a blessing. The banquet was now drawing to an end. Corbett and de Craon were invited to meet in the small buttery, which adjoined the refectory, a most comfortable chamber, its walls delicately panelled with gleaming wood. Turkey cloths warmed the floor and a sweet-smelling fire roared in the hearth built against an outside wall, whilst the windows, full of painted glass, reflected the delicate light of the candelabra. Abbot Maurice ensured more hippocras was brought in, then bade the royal envoys and their henchmen a wholesome good night.

Corbett and Ranulf made themselves comfortable on their cushioned chairs. De Craon and Malpas did likewise on the other side of the polished elm-wood table. The French envoy had drunk deeply and exuded a false bonhomie, insisting that he serve the fresh jug of hippocras. Corbett left him and Ranulf to arrange this. He glanced quickly at Malpas, de Craon's loyal henchman, a mailed clerk and the most skilled of dagger men. Malpas was dressed as he always was in a dark blue sleeveless cotehardie over a cambric white shirt, which emphasised the clerk's narrow, sallow features. His straw-coloured hair was cut close above his ears, one of which sported a dangling silver ring. Malpas had that mock devout look a supercilious priest assumed when addressing the not so sharp-witted of his parishioners. He lifted his head, caught Corbett's gaze, half smiled and glanced away. At last, de Craon finished his fussy preparations, lifting his own cup to toast Corbett and Ranulf.

'Good to see you, my friends,' he rasped.

'I would love to respond in kind,' Corbett laughingly replied. 'Though, in truth, it's good to gather here.' Corbett lowered his goblet. 'You lost two men today.'

'Good men.' De Craon's voice betrayed a quaver. 'Good men,' he repeated. 'Two of my dearest clerks, members of the Sacred Six.'

'Why do you think they were killed?'

'Sir Hugh, God knows, I certainly don't.'

'The assassin must be an experienced archer,' Malpas declared. 'Skilled in the longbow, an English weapon.'

'Welsh, to be correct,' Ranulf countered. 'But I will swear to this, no one from our company was out in the forest today.'

'Nor in the shadows of these buildings,' Corbett added, supping his wine. 'Well, Amaury, here we are. I do not know why your men were slaughtered, but to turn to other matters. Why are you in England?'

'To pay my royal master's compliments to his most beloved daughter.'

'And you have done this?'

'Yes and no. We would like to return. Of course, we would love to wait until the child is born, then I will leave along with Lords Charles and Louis.'

'Have you brought help to the English crown? You know the challenges my lord king now faces.'

'Of course, Hugh! We will do anything we can to bring peace to this poor, benighted kingdom.'

'Not so poor or benighted, Amaury, as you might discover to your cost should your master, or any other foreign prince, decide to meddle in matters which do not concern them.'

'Sir Hugh, Sir Hugh. Let us be blunt and honest. We interfere in each other's kingdoms. We are like swordsmen on the tournament field. But in truth, King Philip wants peace in Europe as well as the most close and holy alliance with this kingdom. We are here to help.'

'But it comes at a price, the Glory of Heaven being part of that price?'

'Not really, Sir Hugh. We believe the Glory of Heaven is the rightful property of the French crown.' De Craon spread his hands, his face all anxious. 'We merely seek its return.' He rapped the table. 'I emphasise the word *return*. So, let me make this very, very clear, and I would take an oath on the Book of the Gospels, we had nothing to do with the theft of that diamond from its shrine. We were far away from this gloomy abbey when the crime was perpetrated. Oh yes, on our return Father Abbot told us all the details, mysterious and tragic, murder and sacrilege in God's own house. Certainly, a strange place, Sir Hugh, surrounded by this sea of greenery. Oh yes, it is certainly a maze of mystery.'

'St Michael's also houses your brother.'

The false smile faded from de Craon's flushed face.

'Monseigneur de Craon,' Malpas spoke up, 'looks forward to meeting his beloved brother, but that, Sir Hugh, is a personal matter, nothing to do with the politic behind monseigneur's visit here.'

'Of course, of course,' Corbett replied. He then fell silent, staring at a point above de Craon's head. The French envoy used this opportunity to study his adversary. Corbett certainly looked the same: his raven-black hair, tied behind his head, was now streaked with small lines of silver, his smooth olive-skinned face slightly lined, the nose sharp above full lips, but Corbett's eyes had not changed, deep set and hooded. He reminded de Craon of a powerful hawk watching and waiting for its prey. De Craon wondered just how much Corbett really knew. He felt a slight spasm of panic in his belly

83

so he hid his nervousness behind a noisy slurp from his goblet.

'Talking of politic,' Corbett's voice was almost a drawl, 'Amaury, do you know anything about The Wodewose, a nearby tavern recently burnt to the ground?'

'Of course,' de Craon replied. 'We have heard the chatter, the gossip of the good brothers. However, apart from that, what does it have to do with us?'

'Does the name Reboham hold any significance for you?' Corbett hid his pleasure at needling his adversary. De Craon, however, remained impassive, pulling a face and gazing blankly as if bored by the whole proceedings.

'Reboham?' Ranulf repeated.

'I understand it is the name of the anchorite here, but why the madcap calls himself that, God knows?'

'And The Apostles?'

'Weren't they the first followers of Christ?'

Corbett held de Craon's contemptuous gaze. The French envoy was quietly mocking him, which meant that de Craon believed he was in charge of the game, the dice rolling the way he wanted. Was it a game of hazard? Mere chance, luck, good or bad fortune? Or was it more calculated, a game of chess? De Craon was moving his pieces, waiting for Corbett to respond. Corbett conceded he was playing a dangerous game and he had to be careful. He did not want to expose his spy in de Craon's household. He pushed back his chair, meaning to rise. He needed to think, to reflect and to plot. He was about to leave the buttery when there was a hurried rap on the door, which was flung open and Prior Felix bustled into the buttery.

'My apologies,' he gasped, 'but Father Abbot said you must see these.' The prior undid the small pouch he carried and emptied the two battered wax seals onto the table. De Craon immediately grabbed these and studied them carefully before pushing them towards Corbett. He then turned to the prior.

'Well?' he snapped. 'Where did these come from, though I can hazard a guess? The two horses?'

'Yes, monseigneur, the two horses wounded in the arrow attack. They had to be put out of their misery. Our stable boys were stripping them of all their harness as well as removing the shafts embedded deep in the horses' flesh. Those seals were fastened to each of the arrows just above the flight feathers. Father Abbot told me to give them to you.'

Corbett studied the battered pieces of hard wax. The Templar arms, two poor knights sharing the same horse, were clear enough.

'We found the same after the arrow attack in the forest,' de Craon slurred. 'It's quite obvious.'

'So it would seem,' Corbett interrupted, 'that former Templars . . .'

'Fugitives from my king's justice, Sir Hugh.'

'As I was saying, former knights of the Templar order are waging a secret war against the French crown, that's logical enough.' Corbett warmed to his theme. 'Philip of France destroyed The Temple, he hunted down members of the Order and, I understand, tortured and killed those he caught in the most barbaric way. Templars are renowned bowmen, skilled archers, men used to fighting in any terrain, be it the hot sands of Outremer or the rain-drenched forests along the Rhine. They would be at home in Ashdown.'

'But, Sir Hugh,' Malpas declared. 'I have made careful search. I have not heard even a whisper about the Templars, be it here or at Windsor Castle. Moreover, if they do lurk in the forest, who shelters them? Who gives them food? Is it possible they were responsible for the fire at The Wodewose? Templars are ruthless enough—'

'Why should they fire a tavern?' Ranulf demanded.

'Why indeed, Master Ranulf? Perhaps they wish to hide something.'

'And let us not forget,' de Craon intervened, 'Philip of France has moved against the Templars, but he did so with the full authority of the Holy Father.'

'Who's now in your king's power at Avignon,' Corbett retorted.

'The Holy Father has approved my master's actions, and his redoubtable son-in-law, Edward of England, has done likewise. So, Sir Hugh, take the matter up with him. Edward of England has seized Templar property, including the Glory of Heaven, a priceless diamond, which should really be returned to its proper owner, Philip of France.'

Corbett decided to remain quiet. He drew a deep breath and glanced at Prior Felix who now stood in the shadows close to the door. 'Now is not the time,' he whispered as if to himself. 'The candle flame burns; time is slipping away.' He half smiled at de Craon. 'Monseigneur, you must do what you must do. I have my own business to pursue and will do so at first light tomorrow morning.'

Corbett kept to his word. He rose long before dawn and roused his companions as well as sending messages to Abbot Maurice and Prior Felix to meet him at the judgement table. Once they had, Corbett ordered Ap Ythel to fetch the anchorite out of his cell which, as Corbett expected, provoked more loud ranting. But at last, the anchorite, garbed in a black robe, sandals on his feet, was invited to take his seat on the bench between the abbot and prior. Once he was settled, Corbett just sat and studied him carefully. Unlike many recluses, Reboham, as he insisted in calling himself, was clean shaven, his hair closely shorn. He was squat, thick set with the long arms of a born swordsman. The recluse's face was lean with high cheekbones, slightly slanted eyes, a hook nose, his thin lips slightly pursed. He had certainly served in Outremer, his skin burnt dark by the relentless sun. Despite his ringing proclamations, the anchorite seemed calm and poised, and he steadily returned Corbett's gaze.

'You are Reboham, the recluse, the anchorite?'

'I am,' the man replied in a strong voice. 'I am all those things here in this abbey, and have been—'

'Since the diamond, the Glory of Heaven, was placed here?'

'That is correct. I have devotion to it.'

'And before the present time?'

'I was born and baptised Etienne de Crotoy in a small village outside Poitiers.'

'In the kingdom of France?'

'Unless they have moved it.'

Corbett laughed softly. 'You are a Templar?'

'I am, or rather I was, for that Order is no more. I am what you see, a recluse. Look,' the anchorite drew himself up, taking in a deep breath, 'I was born Etienne de Crotoy. I entered the Templar Order, I served in Outremer and I fought in the rearguard when we had to flee Acre. A ferocious fight, Sir Hugh, along the quayside. We were desperate to reach the galleys. It seemed as if all hell had erupted. We were not only fighting for our lives, but for the sacred relics kept in Acre.'

'Including the Glory of Heaven?'

'Including the Glory of Heaven, Sir Hugh. The Muslim lords knew about the diamond. They offered us terms if we surrendered that diamond to them. Of course we did not. During our flight, I was entrusted with the Glory of Heaven. I kept faithful guard until I surrendered it to our Grand Master at the Temple in Paris. This was some decades ago. Five years ago, Philip of France attacked our Order. I wanted peace and safety. I wanted to spend the rest of my life in prayer and reparation. I heard about the diamond being housed here.' The anchorite paused, turned and sketched a bow towards Abbot Maurice. 'I approached the abbey and Father Abbot kindly inducted me into the community.' He raised his eyebrows. 'And why not? Abbot Maurice knew of me, when he served as a novice, an acolyte in our Order. He too was at Acre – yes, Father Abbot?'

'Another life, another life,' Abbot Maurice murmured. 'It seems, well,' he stumbled over his words, 'a complete lifetime away, but yes, Sir Hugh, I was only too willing to welcome a former comrade here. He's in sanctuary, he's kept safe.'

'And many thanks indeed,' the anchorite declared. 'I like St Michael's. I live in my ankerhold; I am served food from the buttery—'

'And who brings that?' Corbett interjected.

'Sometimes I do,' Friar Felix answered. 'Sometimes Father Abbot, but there again anyone who wants to.'

'And yesterday, when the theft took place?'

'The kitchener, Brother Aidan,' the anchorite replied. 'I clearly remember that as he likes nothing better than to chatter about cooking and the use of certain herbs. The man never shuts up about them.'

'Very good, very good,' Corbett whispered, glancing down at the notes he had made in his own secret cipher. 'And you saw or heard nothing amiss when the sacrilege was committed?'

'Sir Hugh, on my honour and on the Gospels, I swear I did not.'

'And you assumed the name Reboham because of your links to the Temple?' Ranulf asked, pausing in his transcribing.

'Of course.'

'And the destruction of the tavern, The Wodewose?' Corbett asked.

'I heard about it. God save the poor souls caught up in such a blaze. The devil surely stalks. He prowls through the shadows.'

'And you saw him?' Corbett asked. 'You claim to have seen Satan, a figure with the most hideous face, striding through God's Acre.'

'I am allowed to go there. According to the indenture I sealed, I am granted the freedom of the abbey church and God's Acre. I sometimes go for a stroll. I did so on the night the fire broke, before the alarm was raised. I was praying, threading my Ave beads, when I glimpsed it – a creature out of hell. A figure wrapped in a cloak striding through God's Acre, making his way around the funeral plots and gravestones. He did not see me, but I glimpsed him in the light of a bonfire the gardener had left to die down. Then he was gone.'

'Where to?'

'Perhaps back to hell.'

'Are you sure you saw what you claim?'

'As sure as I am seeing you, Sir Hugh.'

'And that was only the once?'

'Did you see where he came from, what direction?' Ranulf asked. The Clerk of the Green Wax was genuinely intrigued. He recognised the recluse for what he was, a former Templar, God's own warrior, not some troubadour given to fanciful musings. 'Did you see where he came from?' Ranulf repeated.

'Master Ranulf, I can only say what I saw. Perhaps he came up from hell. The ancient ones claim that certain graves, certain tombs are really passageways into the underworld. Perhaps he used one of these. Only God knows. The figure was truly hellish with his swirling cloak and hideous face.'

'Is there anything,' Corbett emphasised his words, 'anything you can tell us about the sacrilege committed here or the destruction of The Wodewose?'

'No.'

'Do you know anyone else who has assumed the name Reboham?'

'No.'

'And The Apostles. Does that term have any significance to you?'

'Only that they were the first followers of Christ.'

Corbett sat back in his chair. He sensed he was finished here. There was, for the moment, no loose thread in the tapestries of lies confronting him. Corbett had made secret moves, plotting a possible way forward. Unbeknown to Ranulf, Corbett wanted to confirm an important link between himself and de Craon's retinue and he had achieved that. A scribbled note in a special cipher had been pushed under the door to his chamber. Corbett had found it as soon as he rose. To most people it would look like a scrap of dirty parchment, the fragment of a tavern bill or the scribblings of some ill-educated scribe. Corbett, however, immediately translated the cipher and became deeply alarmed by the message it contained. He needed to reflect on that as well as summoning Megotta, that woman of many parts.

'Sir Hugh?'

'Lord Abbot, my apologies.'

91

'Sir Hugh, I understand Prior Felix is going to accompany you to view the ruins of The Wodewose but I must prepare to celebrate the requiem for Monseigneur de Craon's two slain clerks. They are to be buried here.'

Corbett gently urged his horse onto the blackened mass of what had once been The Wodewose tavern. It was hard to imagine that such a dwelling had once stood here. The site was nothing but scorched earth sliding down into what were formerly the narrow tavern cellars. The outer buildings both to the right and left of the main tavern had also been gutted by what must have been a veritable inferno.

'Mine host,' Prior Felix declared, urging his horse alongside Corbett's. 'Mine host, Crispin, stored wine, wood, kindling and all he needed for his tavern. However,' he pulled up the muffler as a bitter breeze blew into both their faces, 'he also served the forest folk. We supplied him with some of this produce so the abbey was not plagued by families wanting this or that.'

'Of course, of course,' Corbett replied, patting his horse's smooth neck, soothing his mount who could still detect the acrid smell of fire. Corbett gently urged his horse forward to the far rim of the lake of ash, then turned, staring to his right and left where the stables and storerooms had once stood. He urged his horse around and stared back at where he had come from, memorising the lay of the land. 'The main building stood here,' he whispered to himself, 'with outhouses to the right and left. There's the trackway, then the forest edge, a broad swathe of copse and bushes, stretching up to trees densely packed together.'

'Sir Hugh, you are well?' Ranulf, who had stayed on the trackway called out. 'And you too, Chanson?' Ranulf gestured at his comrade who had dismounted, picking his way carefully across to where the stables had stood. 'Sir Hugh,' Ranulf called. 'Chanson wants to know what happened to the horses.'

'They were freed,' Prior Felix replied. The Blackrobe had now dismounted to grip more firmly the reins of his agitated horse. 'They were freed,' the prior repeated, 'and were found wandering nearby.'

'No harness or saddle?'

'None whatsoever, Sir Hugh. We could only submit to the Royal Chancery the number of horses and their description.'

'And that's how we discovered Master Filliol must have lodged here. God rest the poor man.'

Once again, Corbett stared around. The day was cold, the sunlight weak and the strengthening breeze was making itself felt. He shivered. The weather was harsh, but this scorched stretch of land truly was a place of misery, haunted by the devastation that had so swiftly swept it off the face of God's earth. Corbett could only imagine the ferocity of the flames. He'd seen the effect of such blazes, fed by oil, dried timber and other materials. The fire would gather like a storm to rage and roar beyond control, the flames leaping and dancing like demons.

'But how did it happen?' he murmured. 'Why and by whom? This could not have been chance or some unfortunate accident. No, no, no,' Corbett shook his head, 'this was the work of an arsonist.' Yet there were contradictions. Why hadn't the residents, mine host and his family, fought back? Squire Filliol was a mailed clerk who had campaigned along the Scottish March. He would fight dearly for his life. Why hadn't one of those who had been living here escaped? It would have been fairly easy. The Wodewose must have had enough windows and doors to clamber through. Any why? Corbett reflected. If it was murder, why did the killer wipe out fellow human beings, some of them young, all of them innocent, yet spare a stable of horses? For how else could they have been free to wander close to where they had been kept? And the fiery tempest had been so sudden, so unexpected. On their ride here from the abbey, Prior Felix and the two lay brothers had confirmed there was no outlaw band, no roaming wolfs-head plaguing Ashdown or its trackways.

Corbett gathered up the reins of his horse. The day was beginning to fade. The baleful silence of the forest was making itself felt. Ranulf was turning his horse, allowing it to move, to break free from what his henchman called 'the terror of the trees clustered so close'. Ranulf claimed they were like ancient sorcerers plotting the destruction of any soul who ventured into their dark kingdom. Corbett abruptly started as a flock of crows, black as souls from hell, burst from the trees to wheel and swoop above him. Corbett certainly agreed with Ranulf, this was a fearsome place. He could see the effects of the hideous violence but not the cause. Had he been misinformed? Did the forest hide a coven of blood-drinking wolfsheads? Had they dealt out death and destruction to The Wodewose and all the souls it housed? Corbett tapped the hilt of his dagger, so many questions, such murky mysteries. Who might be responsible for all of this? Was de Craon involved in the theft of the Glory of Heaven, the murder of its guardian, and did that most sinister envoy have a hand in what happened to The Wodewose? But why stop with de Craon? What about the monks of St Michael's and their anchorite? Were they all just innocent spectators? Whatever! Corbett recalled the cryptic message he had received from his spy. De Craon was certainly brewing mischief, but Corbett had to analyse it, reflect and then act. 'It's time,' he murmured. 'Time to spread out my own net.'

'Sir Hugh,' the prior called. 'Have you seen enough?'

'Yes and no.'

'Meaning?'

Corbett urged his horse across the scorched plot, reining in beside the prior.

'A place that suffered brimstone and fire from heaven, eh, Sir Hugh?'

'Why was there so much oil and wine in the cellars? There must have been to cause such an eruption.'

'Sir Hugh, as I informed you, The Wodewose supplied the forest people and, more especially, the mummers troupe, The Apostles, who returned to St Michael's for Holy Week and Easter. So many souls, all in constant need of purveyance.'

Corbett studied the anxious-faced prior.

'You seem troubled, brother, agitated, vexed in spirit?'

'And why not, Sir Hugh?'

'Of course, Father Prior, I understand.'

The prior leant closer, eyes brimming with tears. 'Sir Hugh, I knew these good people; I truly mourn for their deaths. I feel guilt, remorse. Perhaps I could have done more.' The prior's voice trailed away as he steadied his horse, then he said, more firmly, 'We should be gone from this place.'

'I agree, Father Prior, but one further question, perhaps more.'

'Yes?'

'You removed the remains from here?'

'Well, yes, together with Brothers Odo and Aelred and a few servitors from the abbey. We brought carts and sifted amongst the ruins. At times it was difficult to identify human remains. They were nothing more than tangles of bone, scorched, brittle and easy to break.'

'And?'

'We took all we could identify back to St Michael's. The few bones we could recover were laid out on the mortuary tables. Other items are now kept in the storeroom next to the death house.'

'And you dressed the remains for burial in God's Acre?'

'Yes. Odo and Aelred assisted. A grisly, gruesome task. We sprinkled the remains with holy water, incensed them, prayed the requiem and committed their souls to God's mercy.'

'Did you or your assistants notice any violence to

the remains? I appreciate the fire must have wreaked hideous damage, yet—'

'You mean cuts, slashes to the bone or skull?'

'Yes.'

'Sir Hugh, you can question Aelred and Odo but, to my best recollection, I noticed nothing which could have indicated assault or injury but, as I said, the remains were badly burnt. We did what we could. We placed the remains in waxed shrouds, celebrated a requiem mass and buried them in God's Acre. Now, Sir Hugh, we must return, it's getting colder and the darkness is fast creeping in.'

Corbett agreed. They made their way back through the greying light to the warmth and cheer of the abbey. Corbett was pleased to be out of the biting cold, away from the brooding balefulness of the forest. Ap Ythel, who sensed his master's mood, did his best to gladden both him and Ranulf, cheerily pointing out the first beginnings of a late spring. Corbett allowed himself to be drawn into the conversation about the seasons. However, once back in St Michael's, Corbett immediately asked to be taken to the mortuary storeroom, a gloomy chamber with its unadorned walls and meagre lights. The room was cold and clammy. Prior Felix, grumbling under his breath, fired braziers and lit candles. He then picked up a sack knotted and sealed at the neck. The prior opened this and emptied the contents onto a shabby table.

'What we found at The Wodewose,' he explained. 'Pathetic though it seems.'

Corbett thanked the prior and, once he'd left, drew his own dagger and used it to sift amongst the meagre remains of that murderous fire. He pulled across brace-lets, a ring, a metal button, two medals and a pilgrim's badge, all badly scorched. He searched and eventually found the thick copper tube which would have held the letters Filliol was bringing to Windsor. The tube was badly scorched and burnt but not as ruined as other items. He noticed how the cap still sealed the tube tight, as if the fire had soldered the two together. Corbett, using his dagger, eventually prised the cap off. He shook the tube then thrust his fingers into it. 'I expected fragments,' he murmured. 'But the tube holds nothing.' He returned to his scrutiny but could find nothing at all, not even a wisp or fragment of burnt, scorched parchment. Mystified, he put the copper letter scroll to one side and continued with his search. He found nothing remarkable except for a thick, leather dagger sheath, the blade still thrust in, both it and the sheath ravaged by the flames. Corbett pulled across a tallow candle and, using its dancing light, peered at the remains of the heraldic device embossed in the thick leather. Of course, it was now colourless, the paint had been scorched away, but the deep inden-tations formed to present the insignia still remained, the gules and chevrons of some noble family.

'Undoubtedly Filliol's,' Corbett whispered to himself. He tried to pull the dagger from the sheath but it was nigh impossible, and the ivory handle crumbled under his grip. Corbett pushed it away and scrutinised the other items. 'Nothing comes from nothing,' he murmured. He turned at a knock at the door. Prior Felix came into the chamber.

'Are you finished, Sir Hugh?'

'Yes, yes, I am.'

Corbett gestured at the pile of ruined objects he had examined.

'You'll keep these for a while?'

'If you wish.'

'I do wish,' Corbett replied. 'But I also want to find some solution to the mysteries.'

'Did you find anything of Filliol's?'

'A few scraps.'

'Poor man,' Prior Felix murmured. 'Young, in love, riding from Queenhithe to meet his beloved at Windsor. God knows, Lady Beatrice must deeply mourn him.'

The prior fell silent at the sound of running footsteps. Ranulf, catching his breath, came in.

'Sir Hugh, Prior Felix, you must come.'

'What is the matter?' the prior demanded.

'The guest house,' Ranulf gasped. 'Something's amiss. I heard shouts. De Craon is there. I tried to go up the steps to the gallery but Malpas blocked my way. Sir Hugh, you must come and I'll take care of Malpas.'

By the time Corbett and Ranulf reached the guest house, which overlooked the great cloisters, others had also gathered: monks, servitors, all clustered fearfully around their abbot. Malpas and one of the Sacred Six guarded the steps up to the gallery. Corbett could hear the knocking and clattering which echoed from the floor above them. He paused before Malpas and bowed mockingly.

'Sir,' he exclaimed, 'stand aside. Stand aside,' he

repeated, raising his voice. 'I am the king's justiciar in these parts. You, sir, are an obstacle. I shall—'

'Let him through.' De Craon came to the top of the stairs. 'Let him through,' he repeated.

Malpas and his companion stood aside. Corbett and Ranulf roughly brushed past them, clattering up so swiftly de Craon almost jumped to allow them through. The gallery was well lit by lanterns hanging on hooks between the doors on either side. Three of the Sacred Six were gathered before a room at the far end of the gallery. Ignoring the protests of Prior Felix, they continued to punch the door, kicking and pounding. De Craon shouted for silence and the clerks stood aside.

'Sir Hugh,' de Craon declared, coming up behind him. 'One of my henchmen, Ambrose of Amboise, retired for the evening. Jean-Claude came to visit him. He knocked and shouted and, when there was no reply, he made a swift search of the guest house. To cut to the quick – we believe Ambrose is still in his chamber and we strongly suspect, as you must, that some evil chance has befallen him—' He broke off as the abbot came up the stairs shouting at de Craon to call off his ruffians, which de Craon did, telling them to go and stay below.

'The doors to these chambers can be both locked and bolted from the inside,' the abbot gasped, coming along the gallery. He pointed back down the stairs. 'I have brought Brothers Odo and Aelred. Clear the gallery; they will force the door.'

'Very good,' de Craon retorted. 'Only I will stay.' He then tapped Corbett on the chest. 'And you as the king's justiciar. You can remain on one condition, and you would do the same if it was one of your henchmen. I need to ensure our secret chancery boxes and pouches are safe.' Corbett nodded in agreement.

Ranulf and the rest went downstairs. The two lay brothers, armed with heavy mallets, clattered up. As they passed, one joked that breaking down doors now seemed part of the abbey's horarium. De Craon beckoned them on. The brothers, pulling back the sleeves of their gowns, set to work. Corbett stayed at the top of the stairs. He only approached when the door splintered sickeningly to crash back on its leather hinges. De Craon, shouting at the brothers to stand aside, hastened into the chamber, exclaiming at the dark as well as the foul smell. Corbett immediately followed him in. De Craon, holding the bar, pulled the shutters aside. Corbett was grateful, the room was dark with a nasty stench. De Craon politely asked him to stand on the threshold whilst the French envoy hastily scrutinised what was on the chancery table. He then swept up the sheets of vellum into a coffer before hurrying across to the corpse slumped in a shadow-filled corner.

'Poor Ambrose,' de Craon murmured. 'Come, Sir Hugh, look.' Corbett crouched next to his inveterate enemy and gazed pityingly at the corpse of the balding Ambrose; his life cut cruelly short by a killing blow to the heart. He tapped the bone handle of the common dagger driven deep into the left side of the man's chest. A deathly thrust right to the hilt.

'God have mercy on him.' Corbett crossed himself.

'The only consolation is that he must have died swiftly. Such a deep cut to the heart.' He tilted back the dead man's head. The blood which had bubbled out and stained the dead man's tunic, was now drying to a dark crust. Corbett noticed the clasped fingers of the right hand. He prised these open and plucked out a dirty wax seal, hard as stone, though the Templar insignia was very clear to see. He handed this to de Craon, who cursed and slipped the wax into his own purse.

'The Lord accept his soul,' Corbett whispered. 'But how was that soul despatched?' He rose and walked over to the door. At a glance, he could see the lock and bolts had been recently splintered, though he could detect nothing suspicious, no subterfuge or trickery.

'How?' de Craon demanded.

'How what, my dear Amaury?'

'Ambrose was a truly strong man, skilled with a dagger and a garrotte. How could he . . .' Once again, de Craon crouched by the corpse, murmuring a prayer. Corbett kept his face impassive. He hadn't the slightest feeling of regret or guilt at the death of Ambrose of Amboise. He knew all about him. A veteran member of the so-called Sacred Six, Ambrose enjoyed a most sinister reputation as a torturer, a sadist, a true blood-drinker. Instead, Corbett recalled those of his company, men and women, who had spied for Corbett and the English Crown, faithful retainers caught up in the constant power struggle between England and France. Trapped and unmasked, some of these loyal servants had experienced hideous torture at the hands of

Ambrose and his coven. Men and women abused so cruelly, they begged for the mercy cut, but no clemency was shown. Corbett had, in his early years, acted as a spy, an agent of the old king. He knew and accepted the price for failure. Death came soon enough to everyone so why not make it simple and swift? Why revel in the pain of another God-created human being?

'Again, I ask how?' De Craon blessed himself and got to his feet. 'How, Hugh, you have seen this chamber . . .?'

'The window?'

'Sealed and shuttered. I had to lift the bar; inspect it yourself.'

Corbett walked over to the window. The shutters hung open. De Craon had placed the bar just beneath the sill. Corbett examined this before he returned, walking around that narrow chamber. He beat the heel of his boot against the floor, pressing his hand repeatedly along the walls, but there was nothing except hard plaster.

'Not a crack, gap or crevice for even a mouse to crawl through. Very strange, Amaury. How was a mailed clerk locked and bolted in his room, the window shuttered, stabbed to death? Why was it so swift? Why isn't there any sign of resistance by Ambrose? I agree it's as if the assassin slipped like a ghost through the wall or door, stabbed your clerk to death and vanished the same way. But of course, we know that's fanciful. Our assassin was of flesh and blood. So yes, like you I ask how?' Corbett was tempted to point out the similarity between the murder of Ambrose in this chamber and that of Brother Mark in the Silver Shrine but he decided to hold his peace.

'Well, at least we know who was responsible.'

'Amaury?'

'Sir Hugh, the waxen seal? The insignia? The Templars! God knows how many of those degenerates lurk in and around this abbey. Fugitives, desperate men, waging their own secret struggle against my master.'

'I doubt it.'

'What?'

'Amaury, reflect. If the Templars are fugitives, men like Reboham, why crawl out into the light where they can be caught and punished?'

'Revenge is a powerful motive, Corbett. These Templars lived high on the hog, they regarded themselves as the masters, favoured by Crown and Church. King Philip, however, knew them for what they were: a rotting tree which had to be pulled up. Most Templars are cowards, renegades more concerned with their bellies than anything else. All their wealth and luxury has been seized. I am sure there are some who hold my master responsible for their downfall, who would love to do great damage to the French Crown and everything we represent.'

'I hear what you say, Amaury. I suppose that's your perception and I must leave you to it.' Corbett sketched a bow. 'I bid you adieu.' He gestured towards the corpse. 'And God have mercy on him, for I think he'll need it . . .'

Megotta the moon girl, a child of the sun, had quietly settled down in the mummers' company. She was now one of the community, a liveried member of the travelling acting troupe who called itself The Apostles. Sir Hugh Corbett, Keeper of the Secret Seal, was Megotta's master in all matters considered sub rosa. He had used his influence with both Abbot Maurice and Lord Janus, leader of The Apostles, so Megotta could join the mummers' group. Corbett had also warned Megotta that she would enter a world of shifting shadows. She was to trust no one and be vigilant at all times. Megotta had sworn that she would. She had become immersed in the clandestine and highly dangerous world of secret politic. That twilight world, as Corbett had described it, concealed from the eyes of men, but, as Sir Hugh concluded, not hidden from the eyes of the God or the king. Whatever happened, whatever occurred, she must keep fealty and honour her vows to the Crown. Megotta had agreed. She had eagerly taken the oath of fealty, her long fingers pressed against the Book of the Gospels in Corbett's private chamber at Westminster. Megotta had no qualms about her role. She was a born masquer, a true mummer. She could assume, then discard, any character she had to play, be it a highborn lady, a devout nun; she could even assume the raucous appearance of a foul-mouthed harridan from the Kingdom of Midnight, the sordid slums and kennels of Whitefriars. Now, however, she had no part to play but, as Corbett had instructed, Megotta was to join The Apostles then simply watch and wait. When she'd asked, wait for what? Corbett gave that lopsided smile and replied she would know when she saw it.

Here on Bloody Meadow, Megotta had certainly

waited. She had settled down very well amongst The Apostles, who deeply admired her innate skill at mimicry and mummery. Megotta was all things to all people. She acted the pleasant newcomer, but as she sat and watched, she memorised names and appearances. However, that was becoming increasingly difficult. On the troupe's return to their great patron the Lord Abbot of St Michael's, Janus, their leader, hired others to join the group. He was busy recruiting more members in preparation for staging a series of mystery plays during the great feasts of Holy Week and Easter. Janus explained how they needed more labourers, skilled craftsmen as well as those who could be used in a mob or crowd scene. Consequently, strangers now flooded the camp, spread out on Bloody Meadow. So many had arrived it was difficult to distinguish between individuals, especially the men who, because of the weather, went around hooded and visored or allowed moustache and beard to grow unkempt.

In addition, Corbett had sent her a cryptic message asking Megotta to discover if there was any other group known as 'The Apostles' and did the name Reboham have any special significance for anyone in the troupe? Finally, Corbett asked if there was any sign of former Templars amongst those camped out in Bloody Meadow? Megotta had become intrigued. Even though Corbett's questions meant little to her, nevertheless she kept them in mind as she walked the camp and listened to the fireside chatter. She could find no answer for Corbett, but she had remained vigilant for anything untoward and her patience was richly rewarded. Two nights previous, Megotta had glimpsed a cowled figure hurrying through the dusk, taking the solitary path which wound round the abbey buildings into the forest. On the following nights Megotta had set up close watch, but the figure she had glimpsed never re-emerged. Perhaps tonight! Megotta was certainly prepared. She was dressed like a man, her black hair deliberately shorn as she had been playing the role of Daniel in the miracle play *The Magi of Persia*. She was cloaked, hooded and booted whilst the war belt strapped beneath her cloak carried a sheath dagger and a small hand-held arbalest. She had eaten and drunk and was, as she comforted herself, ready for any mischief.

Megotta kept her eyes on the trackway even as she reflected on what might be happening. She had heard about the theft of the precious diamond and the murder of its guardian. Such news had swept through the community, as did rumours of the dreadful destruction of The Wodewose and the death of all who lodged there. Megotta knew a little about that. Janus had often despatched her there to buy purveyance and she was on cordial terms with mine host and his household. She was definitely intrigued.

On the afternoon before the fire broke out, she had, at Janus's request, sent that imp of impunity, Osbert the owl boy, a young boy with a gift for imitating birdsong, to the tavern. Megotta regarded him as fey witted, but Osbert was sharp enough to take messages to mine host at The Wodewose asking if he had any salted ham or sausage meat. Megotta distinctly remembered that because another member of the troupe had pointed out that it was Lent and they should not be eating red meat. Janus replied that Lent was made for man, not man for Lent, and people should shut up and mind their own business. Osbert the Owl had been despatched, racing along the trackway. Megotta would have forgotten all about the incident except that Osbert returned with a very strange story. He had reached The Wodewose to find the outhouses empty and the tavern all shuttered and boarded up. He had banged and banged, shouting and scurrying around, 'like a duck with its tail on fire', as he said, but he could rouse no one. He thought that mine host may have taken his household and any guests to some market or fair.

At the time nobody gave Osbert the owl boy's account any consideration. However, once the fire broke out, Megotta, in accordance with Corbett's strict instructions about reporting anything untoward, had questioned the Owl most closely. The boy, his eyes all round, assured Megotta of the truth of his story. So, Megotta wondered, what had happened at that tavern? Boarded up, shuttered, all silent until the fire erupted, wiping the tavern and whoever lodged there off the face of God's earth?

Megotta chewed the corner of her lip as she stared across the meadow. She wondered again what the solution to these mysteries might be and if Sir Hugh Corbett could resolve the tangle. Megotta was wary of the Keeper of the Secret Seal. Corbett was chivalrous, generous, open and kind. He was not a bully; he did not play the great lord or abuse her as if she was some tavern wench or street slattern. He treated her like a lady, yet Megotta sensed a darkness in Sir Hugh: a brooding watchfulness, which could erupt if he discovered that the king's peace had been cruelly violated. Megotta had watched him hunt down a coven of outlaws who had terrorised the byways and highways of Epping. Corbett had eventually brought them to judgement, sitting in a tavern listening to the evidence, and then hanged all six out of hand. Corbett showed no mercy or compassion. He declared that the world was a better place for their departure and they could take up the argument with God, because the king was finished with them. Corbett had then moved deeper into Essex to a small village outside Chelmsford. He had hunted down a gang of rapists who had violated a number of women in the village. They had resisted, fortifying a house and, armed with long bows, drove the sheriff and his small comitatus away. Then Corbett had arrived. He asked the men to surrender and stand trial. They had replied by loosing a shaft, which narrowly missed the king's justiciar. Corbett reacted. He ordered no more talk but Ap Ythel's archers to loose fire arrow after fire arrow at the house. Corbett then stood and watched both the building and those within be caught up in the hideous conflagration. So, what might happen here, thought Megotta, when Corbett moved to judgement? Sometimes he didn't immediately. Sometimes the mysteries perplexed him, but Corbett never gave up. His sharp mind would gnaw at a problem for weeks, even months, before he reached a resolution. So, what would happen here and could she help the king's justiciar?

Megotta breathed out noisily and repressed a shiver. Night was fast approaching. She was about to end her vigil when she glimpsed a figure flitting through the mist-hung twilight. Another followed. Megotta watched then rose and raced at a half crouch towards the trackway that was no broader than a snaking coffin path. She passed beneath the soaring abbey buildings, all cloaked in darkness, silent and lonely except for the occasional flare of a cresset torch or the glowing light of a window candle. She turned, racing along the curtain wall following the trackway as it turned and swerved towards the forest edge. Megotta had no fear of woods or any such dark place. She had been in more dangerous places. Matters now turned easier as one of those she was pursuing stopped to strike a tinder and light a shuttered lantern. Megotta immediately crouched, waited for a while then moved on. All she had to do was to keep that bobbing light in view. Megotta reckoned that they were about a few hundred yards into the trees when the light disappeared. Megotta cautiously made her way forward. She glimpsed the glow of a fire then abruptly crouched behind a thick clump of gorse. The reason for the lantern light disappearing was that the ground suddenly fell away to create a fairly deep dell bordered by trees and sprouting vegetation. Megotta had a good view of the situation. The two men she had followed joined others camped around a fire, its flame burning merrily beneath what Megotta thought must have been a rabbit, skinned and skewered, above the flames.

She studied each of the men carefully and felt a spurt

of excitement. Despite the hoods, visors, long hair and beards, she was certain that the group, about twelve in number, were former Templars. They were garbed in the robes of that Order, albeit stained and dirty, yet still displaying the black and red crosses of the Templars, the insignia quite distinctive in the light of the dancing fire. There was another individual, but he or she had a deep cowl and, like his companions, a visor over his face. Nevertheless, Megotta suspected that this individual was a Blackrobe, a monk from the nearby abbey. Or, perhaps, someone who had just borrowed a robe so as to steal more easily through the dark. Straining her ears, Megotta heard scraps of conversation, though most of it was unintelligible, whilst she dare not move any closer. Certain words and phrases caught Megotta's attention, especially as the group began to rejoice over the slaughter of the French clerks.

Corbett had informed Megotta of what awaited him at the abbey, how he would encounter a mortal enemy of many years. Megotta had heard rumours that all was not well with the French clerks lodged at St Michael's. Rumours of some of them being killed by shafts loosed in the forest. From her conversations with Corbett, Megotta knew the justiciar truly hated the Chambre Noire and always believed that his struggle was '*Un lutte* à *l'outrance*' – a fight to the death! So, was the slaughter of those clerks Corbett's doing or, more probably, the men sitting around this campfire? Megotta also knew about the Templars, their dissolution and destruction. Corbett had given her a brief history of the Order and the assault Philip of France had launched against it. Megotta had direct experience of some who had followed the Piebald standard. A few of the servitors, acolytes and novices from that Order had been left with nothing; turned out on the road like beggars. They would ask, for safety's sake, to join the mummers' group where they would work for food, drink and warmth. Once comforted, they would disappear as swiftly and silently as they had emerged from the dark. Such men must nurse deep grievances against King Philip and the power of France. So, Megotta wondered, had this group before her been responsible for the yard-long shafts loosed through the green darkness? Certain details about the attack had seeped out like water from a cracked pitcher. Gossip and chatter were Megotta's meat and drink and many of the company had openly shared what they had learnt. They were certain that a longbow had been used, but Megotta was sure that the company, The Apostles, had no skilled archers amongst them, whilst no one owned a war bow, which was nigh impossible to conceal.

A sharp breeze rose, rustling the leaves and driving the cooking smoke towards her. The conversation around the campfire now paused as the meat was removed from the fire, cooled and passed round, each individual plucking a piece to place on some makeshift platter. A bulging wine skin was also produced. Megotta's interest quickened. She truly believed the old proverb, 'in vino veritas' – in wine there is truth! Such drink might loosen tongues. Megotta was not disappointed. The conversation began again. Then the most puzzling ceremony took place. One of the coven began to go around the circle of companions. It looked as though he was fastening their boots or wiping them with a cloth. This produced some merriment and laughter, the man performing the action being pushed and shoved. The group grew more excited. Voices were raised but the conversation continued in a different tongue. Megotta recognised it though she could not understand the lingua franca of the Middle Sea, still used as common speech along the quaysides of London. Megotta, however, knew some of the words. She listened intently and wondered about the constant reference to what sounded like 'mandatum'. The discussion abruptly ended when the figure who was garbed like a Blackrobe rose and intoned a prayer in Latin, crossing himself on a number of occasions, before slowly bringing something out of the pocket of his robe. As he did, the rest of the group knelt with their heads bowed. The Blackrobe raised two hands, like a priest did with the consecrated host, only this time, no circle of snow-white bread but a brilliantly hued diamond which caught the fire flame so it dazzled like a light through the dark. The Blackrobe then intoned the 'Salve Regina, the Hail Holy Queen', the church's evening hymn to the Blessed Virgin Mary. Megotta, who had heard all about the diamond they called the Glory of Heaven, gaped in astonishment at the sudden appearance of this magnificent stone, completely captivated by its sheer beauty. Megotta was tempted to leap forward, to rush and seize this truly exquisite object. However, the celebrant of the mysterious ceremony raised the stone three times in blessing over the group then slipped it away. Megotta, curbing her excitement, realised the group were beginning to disband, so she crept back, turned, and hurried through the trees towards Bloody Meadow.

Corbett was eager for work the following morning. He and Ranulf had risen early and attended the Jesus mass celebrated in the chapter house chapel. The purification of the abbey church still had to be completed, the removal of all signs of the violence perpetrated there. The church would be purged, blessed and consecrated. Amaury de Craon and the abbot had also arranged the requiem mass for the three slain clerks who were to be buried in a special plot in God's Acre. Once this was completed, the monks tried to return to their usual horarium as Corbett had promised the abbot that, at this moment in time, there was no further need for questioning. Instead, both clerks had withdrawn to Corbett's chamber, concentrating on writing up everything they had seen, heard or discovered.

Seated at Corbett's chancery desk, Ranulf finished sharpening a quill pen and declared he was ready.

'Good good,' Corbett murmured. '*Procedamus in Christo*; let us go forward in Christ. *Primo*.' Corbett began his usual pacing. Now and again he'd pause, head slightly to one side as if listening to the faint sounds of the abbey: the clatter of dishes, the slamming of doors, the patter of sandalled feet and the sweet sound of plainchant, the choir being rehearsed by the master of novices. '*Primo*,'

Corbett repeated. 'We are caught up in the game of kings. Our prince now faces civil war with his barons over his favourite Peter Gaveston. Edward, God bless him, loves Gaveston with a love beyond all others. He has created him Earl of Cornwall and, on occasion, even appointed him as Regent of the Kingdom. Gaveston doesn't help matters. He is beautiful, charismatic, a born jouster and a man of sharp wit. The barons do not appreciate the many nicknames he has created for them. They will never forgive him for who he is or what he has done. They want his head. Lancaster, the king's cousin, leads this unholy alliance. He and his coven lead a vast array of retainers; knights, men at arms and archers. Edward is not so fortunate. He can summon up the shire levies, but when he does, will they come to his aid? He can unfurl his banners and declare all who oppose him are traitors. Consequently, anyone caught in arms against him will be executed. However, that is all straw in the wind. On the field of battle, the only thing which counts is the victor. At this moment in time, Lancaster would sweep all before him. Wouldn't you agree, Ranulf?'

'It's obvious and it's logical, Sir Hugh.'

'The situation here in this kingdom,' Corbett continued, 'is rendered all the more dangerous by the malicious, mischievous interference of Philip of France. As I have said before, Philip dreams the imperial dream. Sovereign lordship over all the kingdoms of the west, by marrying his children off to leading families. At this ring on Time's hour candle, Philip flies on eagle wings. He believes his sons will inherit the territories their wives brought as dowry. Philip intends to bring all of these under the iron-hard domain of the golden lilies, the power of France and his royal family, the Capets. Nowhere is this more true than here in England. Philip's one and only beloved daughter Isabella is now with child by our noble prince. The common rumour is that the child will be a boy.'

'How do they know?'

'Wishful thinking, Ranulf, helped by soothsayers and fortune tellers. If this is true, Philip will be beside himself with glee; his grandson, a Capet, will wear the crown of the Confessor and be enthroned at Westminster. Philip views himself as both pope and emperor. Nothing more, nothing less than God's own regent on earth. If that were true, God help us all. *Secundo*,' Corbett continued. 'A very valuable and sacred diamond, the Glory of Heaven, once owned by the Templars who gave it to our king, was placed in a specially built chantry chapel, the Silver Shrine, here at St Michael's. This diamond was kept in a locked tabernacle on the altar of the Silver Shrine. The shrine itself is protected by steel bars, which are impenetrable, and a heavily reinforced door secured by two special locks as well as bolts at both top and bottom. Brother Mark was appointed the guardian of the diamond, a former soldier, strong, capable and, from what we gather, fiercefully loyal to both his abbot and the diamond. Now of course, anyone would love to have such a jewel and top of our list of suspects must be Philip of France. He views the diamond as his rightful property. He demands everything seized from the Templars, especially the Glory of Heaven, to be handed over to him. The Glory of Heaven, in Philip's eyes, would greatly enhance his imperial ambitions.'

'But as you said,' Ranulf interrupted, 'anyone would love to own that diamond. There are others besides Philip.'

'Such as?'

'The Templars.'

'No, Ranulf, they gave it to the English Crown, a deliberate act to both deny and defy King Philip.'

'Outlaws then? No!' Ranulf shook his head. 'Sir Hugh, I take that back, I am not being logical.' He smiled at Corbett. 'Never mind the who, but the how, yes?'

'Very true, Ranulf, that's the key to this mystery. How did someone pass in and out of what is essentially a steel-bound cage with no other aperture or gap available? Someone entered and silently slew a strong and vigorous man who, despite what was happening, appears to have offered no resistance. The tabernacle was opened, the diamond removed and then the assassin left the shrine, its doors were still bolted at top and bottom as well as locked with unique keys, each firmly in its specific lock.'

'It is strange.' Ranulf paused in his transcribing.

'What is?'

'That no one heard or saw anything. I mean, didn't Brother Mark glimpse the felon with his dagger? Didn't he see him approach the Silver Shrine? Didn't he call out? And, is it a coincidence that when the robbery took place, our anchorite was asleep? Was he, Sir Hugh? Or was he wandering the church again looking for devils? Is he the thief? He is a Templar, or a former one. After all, didn't he once carry the diamond when the Templars fled Acre? Perhaps he thought he should be its sole guardian?'

'I cannot answer for the anchorite. Nevertheless, I agree with you, Ranulf, the assassin did risk being seen or heard, if not in the act, at least approaching and leaving the Silver Shrine.'

'And again,' Ranulf declared, as he continued his transcribing. 'Brother Mark's corpse sprawled quite a distance from both the bars and the door. How could he be stabbed so expertly when he was, in fact, deep in the shrine, far from any opening? Though, there again,' he continued, 'it's possible he could have staggered towards the altar. Perhaps the poor man was lost in some last thoughts about protecting the tabernacle and what it contained.'

'Or,' Corbett added, 'was he pushed over there? But how?' He paused in his pacing to take a sip of morning ale. 'Let us leave that for the moment. *Tertio*!' He put his blackjack down on the table. 'We have The Wodewose tragedy. A wayside tavern burnt to the ground, totally annihilated and at least nine souls despatched most unjustly for judgement. We know the fire must have been ferocious. Mine host Crispin had oils and wine stored in his cellars for the forest people and of course the mummers' group, The Apostles, camped close.' Corbett continued his pacing. 'The Wodewose, I understand, was an ancient tavern, its wood dry, excellent kindling for the flames. All that is no mystery. A fire took place and, given what the flames fed on, it is hardly surprising the buildings were devastated. However, my first question must be, how did that fire begin?'

'An accident?'

'Possible, Ranulf. Such accidents do happen, they are a daily occurrence in London. On most occasions people get out. At The Wodewose no one did. Why? Think of a fire in this abbey, Ranulf. We might hurry to find the source, help fight it, but we would keep one eye on the flames and the other on any window or door we could escape through. During such conflagrations, people are burnt or strangled by the smoke but some get out. I can't understand why there were no survivors at The Wodewose.'

'They could have been murdered before the fire started.'

'A very strong possibility, Ranulf, but that poses another problem. Those lodged at The Wodewose were fairly young and vigorous. You've seen tavern kitchens and taprooms, there is no shortage of knives, hammers, mallets, iron bars and other implements. They could easily defend themselves. They certainly had the means. More significantly, one of those lodging there was a royal squire, Stephen Filliol, an experienced mailed clerk who would have definitely fought back. According to all the evidence, he did not – why?'

'And mine host and the others would have certainly helped.'

'Yes, Ranulf. And there's another puzzling paradox. If a killer or a coven of killers annihilated the inhabitants of The Wodewose, why did they show compassion for the horses? Moreover, if the assassins were a coven of killers, where did they come from? Why did they attack The Wodewose? Why didn't they strip the dead of valuables – because they certainly did not, I have seen their pathetic remains. Furthermore, if they were outlaws, why not steal the valuable horse-flesh?' Corbett sat down on a stool watching Ranulf's quill pen race across the cream-coloured parchment: his henchman finished writing and glanced up.

'Sir Hugh, there's also nothing to indicate anything untoward happened in or around The Wodewose, be it outlaws or any other miscreants.'

'True, true, Ranulf. What is significant is what Reboham the anchorite claims he glimpsed in God's Acre. Who or what was that dire-looking apparition striding through the abbey cemetery hours before the fire at The Wodewose broke out? I agree.' Corbett sighed. 'Satan walks, yet why should he visit St Michael's? When there are so many on God's earth eager to do his dreadful work for him?'

'So, you suspect that dreadful apparition had something to do with the fire?'

'I suspect, Ranulf, nothing else. I have no real evidence. Not even a hint, just a feeling that I cannot properly express.' Corbett went and stared at a gaily painted wall-cloth. 'Quarto.' He spoke over his shoulder. 'We have the Templars and the slaughter of the clerks amongst de Craon's so-called Sacred Six. Now the idea of former Templars killing Philip of France's servants and retainers is logical enough. Indeed, their Order's grievances against Philip of France and the Chambre Noire are known to all.'

'And what better occasion and place to settle such grievances than England, where the high and mighty of the French court are more vulnerable.'

'I agree, Ranulf. A matter I shall return to.'

'Sir Hugh, you do not seem very concerned, in fact not at all, about the murder of de Craon's clerks.'

'Why should I be? I cannot mourn for men I have no respect for. I would show them or their master no mercy simply because that is the way matters have turned out.'

Ranulf stared hard at Corbett who simply winked and returned to his desk. Ranulf sat back in his chair, eyes half closed. He did not know Corbett's mind; his master was far too secretive and kept his thoughts to himself. Nevertheless, Ranulf knew that Corbett deeply cared for those he had hired in France to defend the rights of the English Crown. Ranulf had opened letters informing the Secret Chancery that such a person had been found horribly wounded, his corpse floating in the Seine. Others talked about English spies being hanged on the great gallows of Montfaucon near Saint Denis. These same people had also informed Ranulf that de Craon had taken a solemn vow to kill Corbett, given the opportunity. As Sir Hugh had often said, dealing with the likes of de Craon really was a fight to the death. Ranulf picked up his pen, but Corbett was still lost in his broodings.

'You do have your own spy in de Craon's household, Sir Hugh? You made reference to it in some of our whispered conversations.'

'True.' Corbett glanced up.

'Master, who is it?'

'Not yet, Ranulf. Please.' Corbett lifted a hand. 'I trust you but I always fear that de Craon may seize you even here in England and put you to the question. Sometimes a man can take only so much pain. It's not a question of trust, just a matter of what you don't know you can't tell. Yes, I have a spy in his retinue. But, what concerns me, is who and where is de Craon's spy?'

'In your household?'

'Oh, Ranulf, who would betray me? You, Chanson, my Lord Chancellor? No!' Corbett clapped Ranulf on the shoulder. 'Oh yes, I am sure de Craon has his spies at Westminster and elsewhere who gather tittle-tattle or gossip. I wager such men and women are neither efficient nor effective. They collect mere trifles, snapping them up like a dog does scraps of stale meat. This is different. I truly believe de Craon has a spy either here in St Michael's Abbey, in Windsor, or in both. I also know his name – Reboham!'

'The anchorite?'

'No, I am certain it's someone else. I have learnt that from de Craon's secret whispers and scribblings. Ranulf, he has bought, enticed or suborned someone who's deeply involved in this present business. My spy also tells me that both Philip and de Craon refer to a coven known as The Apostles, and I know they are not talking about a mummers' group. Whoever these Apostles may be, I am certain they are part of de Craon's secret designs on behalf of his royal master. At first, I was very surprised. We know who Reboham and The Apostles are so why does de Craon use the same names about his spy and a coven of malignants who, perhaps, nestle deep in the shadow of de Craon's right hand?' Corbett caught Ranulf's look of puzzlement. 'You're probably asking yourself why my spy can't be clearer, more certain about what he reports, but he has to be careful. Philip and de Craon often discuss matters between themselves and no one else is involved. So, what my spy learns is from listening at keyholes or the odd word in some whispered conversation. If he's really fortunate, de Craon may scribble something on a scrap of parchment then not destroy it. As I have said, my spy must be most prudent. If he is trapped and caught, de Craon would show him no mercy: the poor man would be literally skinned alive.'

'So, what does de Craon intend by using the names Reboham and The Apostles? Are there people in this kingdom ready to betray both you and our royal master?'

'Ranulf, the answer is simple. De Craon is intent on mocking us and confusing us. He fervently hopes that we will lash out, spend time and energy questioning that mummers' group out on Bloody Meadow and, when we've finished with them, that hapless anchorite sheltering in his narrow cell!'

'You think he's innocent?'

'I am not too sure, Ranulf, but our anchorite was a Templar so I doubt very much whether Philip of France could suborn him.'

'So, what is our response to all this?'

'At this moment in time, Ranulf, let us wait and see.'

'As we are waiting for Megotta?'

'We certainly are and, while we do, I want to dictate a letter under the Secret Seal.'

'To whom?'

'Her Grace the queen. So, let's prepare.' Corbett waited until Ranulf had smoothed out an ivory-white sheet of the costliest vellum, choosing the sharpest quill pen as well as preparing the wax for sealing. He declared he was ready and Corbett began to dictate. Now and again Ranulf would pause in his transcribing to exclaim or ask a question but Corbett simply shook his head and pressed on. At last the letter, short and terse though courteous enough, was finished to Corbett's satisfaction. He had just finished pressing the seal on the letter as well as the pass or licence which his courier to Windsor would need, when there was a sharp knock on the door. Ranulf hastened to answer. Brother Aelred stood in the gallery outside, almost shielding the hooded figure behind him.

'My apologies,' Aelred gasped in a gale of ale-drenched breath. 'But this courier has arrived for you. Our chief porter, Brother Norbert, admitted him and inscribed his name in our visitors' book. He says you know him.'

'Welcome, Master Daniel,' Corbett shouted. 'Brother Aelred, thank you. Ranulf, show our visitor in.'

Aelred stomped off as Megotta slipped into the chamber. She pulled back her hood and lowered the visor.

'Sir Hugh, Master Ranulf, good day and God's grace be with you.'

'Daniel!' Ranulf exclaimed, returning to his chair. 'Why Daniel?' He grinned. 'Though by the cut of your hair and the way you dress, perhaps you are a true Daniel.'

'Hold your tongue,' she mocked back. 'I am Daniel in the play and,' she shrugged prettily, 'I am Daniel in this masque.'

Ranulf decided he would hold his tongue. Megotta was a truly attractive woman but Ranulf was very wary of her. He had never met her like before. She could be extremely cutting with her tongue or with a swift, sharp slap of her hand. A formidable woman, Megotta had admitted that in Corbett's service, she had killed men who had tried to rape her. Nobody ever took liberties with her. Ranulf watched as she exchanged the kiss of peace with Corbett, then he did likewise. Megotta teasingly pulled Ranulf closer but then pushed him away.

'Very well.' Corbett could see Ranulf was a trifle embarrassed, a rare mood for the Clerk of the Chancery of the Green Wax. In order to divert attention from this, Corbett busied himself. He pulled across a stool, insisting Megotta take her cloak off, then served them all morning ale, before taking a seat himself.

'Megotta,' he exclaimed. 'It's good to see you. And what news do you bring?'

The moon girl told him all she had garnered. How she believed she was being watched on Bloody Meadow so she had decided to lie low and move cautiously. She felt at peace, but at other times, as she strolled through the camp, she was certain she was being followed, though, try as she might, she could not detect anyone or anything suspicious.

'Just a feeling,' she concluded. 'Like a cold blade against sweaty skin.'

'Be careful.'

'Sir Hugh, I am and it has borne fruit.' Megotta then told him about that strange meeting in the forest, what she had seen and heard. As she talked, Ranulf exclaimed in surprise, whilst Corbett whistled under his breath, a common mannerism when he was truly startled. Once Megotta had finished, Ranulf asked a few sharp questions to clarify matters. Corbett just sat listening, intently staring at the floor.

'Sir Hugh?'

'Megotta, you have done well.' Corbett rose and walked over to the door. He unlocked it, peered out, then, satisfied no eavesdropper lurked, locked it and returned to his chair. 'What you have told me comes as a great surprise. It certainly refutes some of the hypotheses I was forming. Yes, you have done refutation as sharp and as clear as any master in the schools. First, it certainly appears that the Templars are a presence in and around the abbey of St Michael's and, I wager, quite a powerful one. They don cloaks and meet at the dead of night. More importantly, this group may well be The Apostles and their leader, the black-garbed figure, is Reboham. He undoubtedly killed Brother Mark and stole the diamond, which he now keeps in his possession. He dresses like a monk and acts like a priest with the host.'

'So he's a Benedictine?' Ranulf interrupted.

'Not necessarily, Ranulf. Remember the old adage "the cowl doesn't make the monk and the Blackrobe doesn't make a Benedictine". It could be anybody. So,' Corbett continued, 'we now know that a group of Templars, who probably are The Apostles, led by Reboham, have not fled the area. They haven't taken the diamond and slunk off to some other hiding place. They still wait around St Michael's. What is their secret design? What do they conspire to do? What subtle web of mischief is being secretly spun? And of course, the mystery of how they seized that diamond has to be resolved.' Corbett played with the quill pens on the chancery table. 'What else? Several other matters intrigue me. First, what do they mean by "mandatum" or some such word? Secondly, what was that strange ceremony they performed? The individual going around that circle of Templars. Thirdly, who is the prime mover behind all this mischief? De Craon? Yet this hardly fits with what we have just learnt. The Templars by themselves? Or is there some other secret coven hiding deep in the shadows? If so, why, who and for what purpose? All these questions, my friends, assume an even more pressing importance as the days pass. The Glory of Heaven is not far away. What you learnt, Megotta, proves that, but such a situation won't last for ever. The hour candle burns, the light goes and darkness descends.'

'And there's more,' Megotta declared. 'We all heard about the conflagration at The Wodewose. Janus, our leader, bought purveyance from the tavern, especially wine and oil. Now through sheer gossip I discovered that Janus sent one of our urchins, Osbert the owl boy, to ask something of mine host Crispin. Intrigued, I questioned Osbert closely. He was quite clear about what happened. He said he reached The Wodewose, hammered on the tavern door and banged at the shutters but no one appeared. He then wandered across to the outhouses and found the horses stabled but again there was no one about. He said it was very quiet, strangely so, more like a graveyard than a merry wayside tavern.' She shrugged. 'That's what he told me.'

Corbett sat staring at a crucifix nailed to the wall, that of San Damiano, before which St Francis had his vision about reforming the Church.

'Sir Hugh?'

'Yes, Ranulf?'

'Your thoughts?'

Corbett breathed in deeply. 'Everything we think, everything we say, everything we do either strengthens the light or deepens the dark.'

'Meaning?'

'Meaning, Ranulf, the darkness is spreading and, as it does, it deepens. Here before that crucifix,' Corbett crossed himself, 'I truly believe de Craon lies at the heart of most of what is happening. So, I thank God I have a spy close to that most malignant man. Megotta, you said there is more and there certainly is. I have learnt from my spy that de Craon has invited the great English lords, Lancaster, Hereford and Warwick, to Windsor to meet their French counterparts, Philip's brothers, Charles and Louis.'

'Isn't that just court etiquette?'

'No, Ranulf, such invitations lie only in the hand of our king or indeed our queen. De Craon is being clever. Now at first I did wonder if de Craon was nursing some madcap notion of seizing the queen. De Craon would get Philip's daughter and her son, the heir to the English throne, out of this kingdom to set up a rival court in Paris. On reflection that would be very, very foolish. Lancaster and the earls, the so-called Lord Ordainers, would simply ignore it. They would still move against Edward then God knows what might happen. Would they execute Gaveston and then turn on the king? After all, Lancaster is Edward's blood cousin. He may nourish and nurse his own secret ambitions.'

'A most arrogant man,' Ranulf agreed. 'Lancaster has bounding ambition without the talent to match. So, Sir Hugh, what mischief is de Craon really plotting?'

'Think, Ranulf, think of Windsor: one of this kingdom's most impregnable castles, a redoubtable fortress fully provisioned and well situated within striking distance of London and the Thames, as well as the east and southern ports.'

'I would agree with that,' Megotta intervened. 'The Apostles, the mummers' group, recently visited Windsor Castle to present our play *The Prodigal Son* in the Great Hall. A truly impregnable fortress, well armed and equipped for war.'

'And so,' Ranulf pointed to the letter Corbett had just dictated and sealed, 'you are asking the queen, despite her pregnancy, to leave Windsor and lodge here. But for what purpose?'

'Let's say, Ranulf, that Lancaster and his fellow earls, with their swollen retinues, sweep into Windsor. They set up camp together with France's most powerful lords. They are now united to control one of this kingdom's most powerful fortresses. To cut to the quick, I do wonder if de Craon is trying to establish a foothold in England as well as create a powerful alliance between the great lords of England and France. They would control Windsor and all its appurtenances. Above all, they would have the young queen in their power and, in the very near future, the heir to the English throne.'

'And that is why you invited the queen to move here. Is that wise, given her condition?'

'As you know, Ranulf, on our journey here we first made a brief secret visit to Windsor. I spoke to the queen about possible dangers. I admit, at the time I did not know about de Craon's machinations. Nevertheless, I impressed upon Isabella the real danger of the deepening rift between her husband the king and his great lords. Isabella, God bless her, assured me she would take refuge here with me, the king's justiciar. She would seek sanctuary on consecrated ground where no one would dare trespass, let alone violate. St Michael's is a prestigious Benedictine abbey, not only protected by the Crown, but with all the power, both temporal and spiritual, of Holy Mother church. Holy Week and Easter are fast approaching. The magnificent liturgical celebrations can be staged here. Isabella would be the honoured guest of Abbot Maurice. Moreover,' Corbett grinned, 'just in case people started to feel for their swords and daggers, St Michael's is a fortified abbey, well provisioned and well prepared for any siege. Oh no, the queen must move from Windsor, and the sooner the better. She need not bring an extensive retinue, just the ladies and squires of her chamber. Once she has refuge here, she will be safe. Prior Felix is an accomplished herbalist and physician. If Isabella gave birth here at St Michael's she would be in the best possible hands. Furthermore, time will pass. Edward the king would not be happy at such an assembly of English and French magnates. He would hasten to help us. No, no, we shall play a waiting game, but one where we are all protected, particularly the queen.'

Corbett turned to Megotta. 'My friend, you have done well. I now know Templars do lurk close by and are deeply immersed in some plot. They are probably The Apostles and their leader could well be Reboham. They apparently hold the Glory of Heaven, though I would dearly love to know how they seized it. I am also intrigued by those constant references to the "mandatum"?' What is it? That's the word you heard from their whispered conversation, yes?'

'It was, Sir Hugh. I am sorry it is so unclear.'

'For the time being, my friend, for the time being. Then of course, there is that strange ceremony where one of them moved round the circle kneeling before the others. What's the significance of that?' Corbett shrugged. 'Heaven knows.' He leant over and patted Megotta on the shoulder. 'I also appreciate your questioning of the young Osbert about his visit to The Wodewose. What you learnt truly mystifies me. Why the silence? All I conclude is that Osbert's visit, and what he reported back, is proof enough that something dreadful occurred in that tavern before the fire.

'Now I have another great favour to ask of you, Megotta. You must journey with all speed to Windsor. You will be furnished with a special licence issued under the Secret Seal as well as a letter for the queen.' Corbett picked up both sealed documents from the chancery table and thrust them into Megotta's hand. 'The licence will give you immediate access to the queen's presence. She will grant you an audience. Once there, give her the letter and impress upon the queen the need to be immediate and swift. She must accept what I have written and what you say. I pray she will. If so, Isabella will gather her retainers and leave Windsor accompanied by you and her chamber people. You must travel as swiftly as you can back to St Michael's.'

'Why not send me and Chanson, or just one of us?' asked Ranulf.

'No, no.' Corbett shook his head. 'De Craon and his dogs roam this abbey, I need both of you with me. If de Craon believed that I was alone and vulnerable, he would strike. Oh yes.' Corbett forced a smile. 'That is the constant message from my spy in his retinue. Now come.' Corbett clapped his hands gently. 'If it's to be done, then it's best done swiftly.'

PART THREE

'The whole land was much
desolated by such a tumult.'

Megotta spurred her mount along the trackway. Noonday had come and gone and the light was beginning to fade. The forest on either side was falling quiet, the constant rustle through the undergrowth almost hidden by the clatter of her horse's hooves, a sturdy garron Chanson had selected from the abbey stables. Corbett's sealed letters were in her belt pouch. Megotta had donned her finest travel cloak, a thick woollen gown Corbett had given her from his own wardrobe.

'I wore it along the Scottish March,' he murmured. 'Better protection than a fire against the cold.'

Megotta was booted and belted, as well as armed with a small arbalest and a Welsh stabbing dirk, both of these looped over the horn of her saddle. She wanted to be in Windsor within the hour and quietly prayed for a peaceful journey. She was glad to be out of St Michael's, where she still felt she was being watched.

And yet, she had that same feeling even out here, along this lonely trackway with the crows circling above her and the mist seeping through the trees. Now and again, she'd pause and look over her shoulder, then glance quickly at the treeline either side. But there was nothing.

She cantered on, rounded a bend and frantically reined in as her horse reared. A man lay sprawled across the trackway close by a pool of thickening blood. Megotta quietened her mount and swung herself out of the saddle. She'd hardly done so when she realised her mistake. The blood was too congealed and spread a little distant from the body! She quickly grasped the bridle with one hand and the horn of the saddle with the other, but it was too late. The man on the trackway rolled over and sprang up as other wolfsheads burst out of the trees on either side. They swiftly surrounded her and her horse, grabbing her fiercely, pulling her away, keeping her arms pinioned so she could not even draw her belt knife. She struggled, kicking out at the men milling around her until a blow to her head sent her toppling into the darkness.

She awoke to pain and biting cold, her hands tied above her to a branch. She blinked and stared at her four attackers, bearded and hooded, faces scarred and weathered. One had lost an eye whilst another had the 'F' for felon branded deeply on his forehead. They were outlaws but, Megotta suspected, they had been hired by someone to plan and carry through this ambuscade. They shouted at her, poked her body, one of them ran an appreciative hand over her breasts. Another crouched down and began to undo the points on her hose. Megotta, her desperation drowning out all the pain of her attack and capture, stared desperately around. She glimpsed her war belt with its dagger and pouch on the ground nearby. She swallowed hard, clearing her mouth, pulling at her bonds, struggling to break free.

'We'll ride her,' one of her tormentors slurred. 'Look at those graceful legs and full breasts. A good mount for a hearty ride.' This provoked laughter from the others. The wolfshead, undoing her points, thrust his hand in beneath her clothing, feeling her belly and kneading her skin. 'The bitch will ride better unharnessed.' He got to his feet and in one slash cut the rope, freeing her hands. Megotta tumbled to the ground and deliberately rolled closer to her war belt and the ivory-handled dagger. She was unable to reach it, being pulled to her feet and shoved and pushed. One of the attackers closed with her, dragging her towards him in some clumsy embrace. Megotta tensed to fight then she heard the whistling whirr of a long shaft piercing the air. The wolfshead dragging her closer abruptly stopped, his gaping mouth full of blood. He sighed, eyes rolling backwards, then he toppled forward, the arrow shaft deep between his shoulder blades. More whirring shafts pierced the air to shatter the face, chest and belly of Megotta's attackers.

She could only crouch and stare in bewilderment until a shout from behind made her turn. A fifth wolfshead, who had been lurking deeper in the forest's edge, burst out from the trees and ran screaming towards Megotta, an axe in one hand, a club in the other. Megotta moved quickly. She grasped her war belt, sprang to her feet and swung the belt, catching her assailant full in the face. An arrow whistled through the air between her and her assailant only to smack into a tree. For a few heartbeats, this distracted the wolfshead. He turned then twisted back. Megotta struck: a well-aimed slash, which tore open the man's swollen belly. He just stood swaying, dropping both weapons as he clutched the deadly wound as if trying to seal in the blood bubbling out. He took a step forward, groaned, then crumpled to the ground.

Megotta stared around. One of the wolfsheads who had taken an arrow to the chest still moaned and quivered in his death throes. Grasping her dagger, she gave the man the mercy cut, a deep slash which opened his throat. She watched the life-light fade in his close-set eyes, then rose to her feet. The glade had fallen deathly quiet, no birdsong, no frenetic bustling in the undergrowth. Turning slowly, Megotta glimpsed her horse hobbled between the trees. The corpses of her attackers lay stiffening. She stood still expecting her rescuer to emerge from the darkness of the forest, but there was nothing. She shivered, collected her clothing and dressed. She opened her belt wallet to find both parchments intact. She now understood what the attackers intended. She was to be brought down, abused, plundered then killed, whilst anything like the parchments was to be kept intact – but for whom? Who had planned this ambuscade?

'De Craon!' Megotta whispered. 'It has to be.'

The Frenchman must have hired these reprobates and issued strict instructions on what to do. They would have found it easy enough, despite her best efforts, to watch her move around the abbey, leaving the guest house then dealing with the stables, before leaving on the only possible route to Windsor. The man she found lying sprawled out on the trackway, pretending to be dead – that was a favourite trick and she had fallen for it. Megotta vowed that would never happen again. She stared into the darkness of the forest. Where was her rescuer? Lurking amongst the trees? Or had he gone? She knew whoever it was meant her no harm, but why did they not show themselves?

'Who are you?' she shouted. 'Where are you? Why did you save me? For that I give heartfelt thanks. Answer me!' Her voice echoed across the small clearing. 'Answer me!' she repeated.

There was no reply. Nothing but the silence of the forest, broken only by the chatter of the birds and the usual crackling of the bushes and coarse grass. Megotta waited for a while then began to inspect the dead, going through their meagre possessions. There was no indication of who her attackers were or where they came from. The weaponry they carried was crude: axe, hammer and battered knives. They had been on foot with no horses, food or any sustenance. That was logical, they planned to rape her, cut her throat, bury her in some forest marsh and return to the abbey only a short distance away. They would re-join that growing group of people milling about Bloody Meadow, merging in with the mummers, offering to do jobs in return for food and drink. Megotta continued her search. The personal items she found were paltry, along with a few coins, which would not amount to much. Feeling a little better now, she simply heaped the money and the other items beside one of the corpses.

Once again she stared around. Had her saviour left? Megotta cupped her mouth. 'Are you still here?' she called with all her might. 'Are you close?' Her voice echoed back, there was no reply. Megotta walked over to her horse, untied it and mounted.

'What is left,' she shouted, rising high in her stirrups, 'is rightfully yours, pathetic though it might be. Once again I thank you and bid you adieu.' Megotta urged her horse back onto the trackway, digging her heels to move to a gallop, determined to reach Windsor before twilight.

After the meeting with Megotta, Corbett and Ranulf spent the rest of the day going through their schedule of questions. Frustrated at not being able to clarify matters, Corbett returned to the abbey church. Once more he inspected the shattered Silver Shrine, its bars, locks and clasps. He had instructed Abbot Maurice not to repair the damage but to leave it until he had resolved the mystery surrounding both the burglary and the murder of Brother Mark.

He then wandered across to the ankerhold and had a brief conversation with the anchorite, but the recluse had very little to say. Corbett strongly suspected that he was more than partial to a full goblet of Bordeaux, something to provide warmth and ease the pain of his lonely vigil. The anchorite slurred his words, yawned and said it was time to sleep. Corbett recalled that the recluse did exactly the same on the evening when the robbery took place. Perhaps that had played some little part in what had happened? Was the anchorite telling the truth? Or did he know more than he confessed? Corbett inspected the Silver Shrine once more then, accompanied by Ranulf and Chanson, rode out to the scarred, crumbling ruins of The Wodewose.

Ranulf and Chanson became deeply immersed in a conversation about Megotta, Chanson arguing that the young lady was a good judge of horseflesh. Ranulf began teasing Chanson, asking him whether he found the lady more worthy of his attention than his horse.

Corbett left them to it. He dismounted and walked slowly across the crumbling ash and black charred wood. He could still smell the acrid smoke as his boots crunched the cinders. On one occasion he slipped, then he crouched down. The ruined timbers were wet, and he ran his finger along them. At first, he thought the dampness might simply be the water of the frost as it thawed. However, when he sniffed what he rubbed between his fingers, he detected oil. Corbett got to his feet and walked slowly forward. He found another few streaks of the same; rubbing it between his fingers, sniffing carefully, he was sure it was oil, but that did not make sense. All the oil had been consumed in the raging fire, but this was fresh, as if someone had brought oil to the ruins to create a second fire. Corbett continued his search. Ranulf and Chanson, now intrigued by what was happening, dismounted and came over to assist him.

'What I found,' Corbett declared, 'is fresh oil splattered across the ruins.'

'Impossible,' Ranulf replied.

'I am telling you what I found, my friend. Can you find any more?'

They did, though neither of them could explain why fresh oil had apparently been poured out over these ruins. Intrigued, Corbett mounted his horse and, with Ranulf and Chanson riding beside him, they cantered back to the abbey. Once there, Corbett went out into God's Acre. He stood for a while beneath an ancient yew tree, staring around this haunted, lonely place. He came across the ruins of the fire the gardener had lit which had illuminated what the anchorite claimed to be Satan striding through God's Acre. A lay brother, who had come out to see if all was well, showed him where the abbot had decided to bury the remains of those burned at The Wodewose: a mound of earth surmounted by a simple wooden cross. Corbett watched the lay brother leave, walking quickly around the headstones, plinths and all the other items found in any garden of the dead. Corbett crouched down and ran his hand across the mound of earth, digging deep with his fingers. He then pulled his hand away and half smiled; oil had also been splattered here, just as it had on the ruins of that tavern. Corbett cleaned his hands as best he could and got to his feet. Darkness was beginning to fall, the ever-present mist beginning to thicken. Somewhere deep in the trees an owl hooted to greet the dusk.

'I must remember that,' Corbett whispered, staring up at the sky. He tested his own hypothesis, walking back across God's Acre to the Devil's Door. He tried to walk purposefully, as the lay brother had, striding like that eerie figure whom the anchorite had glimpsed here in God's Acre.

'Yes, I am certain,' Corbett whispered. 'The devil knew where to walk.'

He entered the abbey church and made his way to the ankerhold, tapping on the hatch until the recluse angrily pulled it back and glared out at Corbett.

'Sir Hugh, I am busy about my prayer.'

'My friend,' Corbett retorted, 'I too am busy about God's work, and that of my king. I have a question to ask you. On that evening before the fire at The Wodewose, you claim to have seen Satan, garbed in a swirling cloak, his face all hideous, striding through God's Acre.'

'I have told you that,' the anchorite retorted.

'Tell me again. Did he walk purposefully as if certain about where he was going?'

'Of course.'

'He didn't slip or slither?'

'No.'

'Or stumble at any time?'

'Satan never stumbles.'

'No, he doesn't,' Corbett agreed. He walked away from the ankerhold and stared at a vivid painting on a pillar close to the main door, again depicting the clash between the Archangel Michael and the powers of hell. 'Satan never stumbles,' Corbett repeated to himself. 'But, there again, nor does a Benedictine monk who knows the cemetery very well and which paths to take through God's Acre.'

Corbett returned for a quiet evening in his chamber. He wrote a brief but warm letter to the Lady Maeve, sending her and his beloved children every grace and blessing. He sat for a while listening to the different sounds of the Abbey, letting his mind float. Closing his eyes, he recalled the shattered Silver Shrine, those narrow bars, Brother Mark's corpse, then The Wodewose and those strange oil marks he'd discovered. He wondered how Megotta was faring and how soon the queen would travel the short distance between Windsor and St Michael's. Eventually he decided to retire early.

He slept well, rose at sunrise and, joined by Ranulf and Chanson, heard the dawn mass in the Chantry Chapel of St Scholastica in the abbey church. An ancient Benedictine celebrated the mass, the old priest speaking slowly, hesitatingly. Corbett soon found that he was distracted by this problem or that, including the question of who might take his letter to the Lady Maeve. He stumbled over the responses to the Agnus Dei, so he forced himself to concentrate on taking the Eucharist.

He had just finished his prayer of thanksgiving when

the nave rang with shouts, heavy footfalls and the clatter and clash of weapons. Abruptly the noise and clamour grew as the main door to the abbey church crashed open. The rasp of steel against steel echoed shrilly. Corbett and his companions collected their war belts from a bench and hurried down the nave. The clatter of weaponry rang as ominously as any tocsin. The anchorite was also alert, bellowing warnings about the Day of the Great Slaughter. Monks, all fearful, bustled about.

The light was still poor, but when Corbett reached the baptistery, he stopped in amazement. One of the Sacred Six, de Craon's personal clerks, stood with his back to the baptismal font, sword in one hand, dagger in the other. He used the stone column to protect his back as he confronted de Craon, Malpas and the remaining two of the Sacred Six, who, also armed with sword and dagger, edged nearer then darted forward in a furious whirl of steel. Corbett recognised their quarry: the fair-haired Jean-Claude who had tried to rouse the clerk stabbed to death in his own chamber. The sword and dagger play paused as the combatants, gasping for breath, prepared for a second clash. Corbett made to intervene but de Craon turned, still at a half-crouch, sword and dagger out.

'No, no, Sir Hugh,' he snarled. 'Don't interfere; this is my business, my service to the French Crown.'

'And this is mine,' a voice bellowed.

An arrow whipped through the air to smash against a pillar. Corbett and de Craon turned as Abbot Maurice, flanked by four other monks, emerged from the shadows. The abbot carried a powerful yew bow, a long shaft already notched and pulled back. One of the abbot's companions carried a quiver of deadly looking, goose-quilled arrows; the other three were armed with small, handheld arbalests, primed and ready for use.

'This is my abbey,' Abbot Maurice grated. 'The House of God and the Gate of Heaven. Although a priest and a monk, I am sworn to defend this church, and I will.'

'You surprise me, Father Abbot.'

'Don't be surprised, Sir Hugh, I am of knightly birth. I have served in the royal array and I am skilled in the war bow. But enough of that – what is happening here?'

Standing back, de Craon gestured to his companions to do the same. Jean-Claude, however, immediately turned and, before anyone could intervene, knocked Corbett aside and ran as swift as a whippet up the nave. He reached the soaring, intricately carved rood screen and turned.

'I claim sanctuary,' he yelled. 'I claim sanctuary in accordance . . .' he stumbled over the words, 'in accordance with common law and the rights and privileges of this abbey.'

'Then put down your weapons,' the abbot shouted, lowering his war bow. 'All your weapons – no knife, no blade, nothing. Otherwise, you forfeit sanctuary.'

Jean-Claude hastened to comply, dropping both sword and dagger in a clatter of steel before the entrance to the rood screen.

'Go through,' the abbot shouted. 'Grasp the horn of

the altar, the right-hand corner as you face it. You must make the pledge then go into the sanctuary enclave behind the high altar.'

Jean-Claude nodded, crossed himself and went through into the sanctuary.

'Now, gentlemen.' The abbot handed the war bow to one of his assistants. 'For the moment, this matter is closed. May I remind you this sanctuary is sacred, it has been approved by royal charters, sealed and signed by successive kings. Any attempt to drag out a claimant, be he French, English or from beyond the great Silk Road, would mean immediate and total excommunication by Holy Mother Church. The person who committed such sacrilege would feel the full force of bell, book and candle, cursed in everything he did, unable even to enter a church. Now, to be blunt, I do not care about politic. The Glory of Heaven has been taken. Our community has been disrupted, our horarium turned upside down. We have had men murdered in our guest house. Satan walks our cemetery whilst dagger sword-play shatters the peace of this church. So, gentlemen, I shall leave you alone. I understand . . .' Abbot Maurice caught Corbett's glance and fell silent.

'I can speak to him, of course. There is no bar in canon law against talking to someone in sanctuary?'

'Of course, Sir Hugh,' the abbot replied sharply. 'You knew that before you asked, but you must first ask him and he must agree. Please heed my warning, both of you, English and French, otherwise I must ask you to leave.'

'Do what you want,' de Craon growled, gesturing at the nave. 'Our sanctuary man is one of yours anyway, isn't he, Corbett?'

'What do you mean?'

'Oh, don't act the innocent.' Malpas, who had been standing in the shadows, strode forward. 'I repeat, Sir Hugh, don't act the innocent.' De Craon's henchman sheathed both sword and dagger.

'Innocent of what?' Corbett insisted.

'Oh come.' De Craon adjusted his own war belt and pulled his cloak around him. 'I'll not stand in this freezing church bandying words with you, Corbett. Take your filthy little Judas.'

'If you do speak to him,' Malpas declared, 'advise him that he'll be watched as close as a cat does any mouse hole. I'll set up strict guard on this church so the traitor cannot run like the vermin he certainly is.'

De Craon and his party then swung on their heels and clattered out through the Devil's Door.

'You'll speak to the sanctuary man, Sir Hugh?'

'Of course, my Lord Abbot, and now is as good a time as any. So yes.'

'Then God be with you, Sir Hugh.'

Corbett watched the abbot and the other monks leave. Only when he was sure they were out of earshot did Ranulf pluck at Corbett's sleeve.

'Hush now.' Corbett smiled. 'I know what you are going to ask. What you might suspect.'

'Sir Hugh?'

'We've now learnt that Abbot Maurice is a master

148

bowman. He possesses, and certainly carries, both the bow and a quiver of arrows. He is a most accomplished soldier, a skilled archer. However,' Corbett sighed, 'I would wager there's quite a few of those in St Michael's. Look at the guardian of the Silver Shrine, Brother Mark, a former soldier, possibly a bowman. Certainly, our abbot made no attempt to hide his skill. Of course, he may well be our mysterious archer, but we shall see, we shall see.'

They reached the entrance to the rood screen. Kicking aside the fallen weaponry, they went up to the sanctuary, a place of dappled light as a weak sun rose higher and pierced the stained-glass windows to bathe the exquisitely tiled floor in light. The strengthening sun brought to life the different motifs painted there: snarling griffons, fire-breathing dragons, four-winged eagles and other strange creatures. The choir was empty except for the sacristan, busy around the high altar. Brother Simon greeted them with a false smile and promised Corbett that the weaponry the Frenchman had dropped would be collected and placed in the abbey armoury. The sacristan then gestured towards the altar, a majestic table of costly stone and marble.

'Our visitor,' he sighed, 'has already made himself at home. I will bring him victuals soon enough.'

Corbett murmured his thanks as he and Ranulf went round the altar and into the apse. The Frenchman was sitting in the cushioned enclave, a rolled-up palliasse lying next to the small lavarium. Jean-Claude glanced up at the two English clerks then gestured to the wall bench placed against the back of the altar.

'I expected you, Sir Hugh.' Jean-Claude rubbed red-rimmed eyes. 'So suddenly,' he murmured, 'so strange.'

'What was? And why were you expecting to see me?'

Jean-Claude wiped the sweat from his face on the sleeve of his bottle-green jerkin and ran a finger behind the slightly stained collar of his cambric shirt.

'Oh, I'll tell you,' he said. 'In a word, de Craon has taken leave of his senses.'

'Why do you say that?'

'He accused me of being your spy, Sir Hugh. He and the others searched my belongings. They found a wax cast of your seal, scraps of parchment with secret cipher notes, as well as a purse of freshly minted English silver coins. I suppose I expected it. I've always been an outsider. My mother was English, my father French. I attended the halls and schools of Cambridge as well as the Inns of Court. So, I am skilled in the English tongue.'

'Why did they accuse you?'

'As I said, I am vulnerable because of my birth, my parentage, my upbringing.' Jean-Claude shrugged. 'God knows what.'

'No, come,' Corbett urged, 'there must be more.'

'Well, Sir Hugh, you can tell the truth, here at least in this sanctuary. Am I your spy?'

'How can I agree with that or disagree? A spy by very definition is someone hidden in the shadows. What makes you think the English Crown even has a spy in de Craon's service? And, if we did, why would you think that we would know his or her name?'

'Well? Do you have a spy?'

'I can't and won't answer that.'

'Oh, come on, Sir Hugh – do you have a spy? Yes, or no?'

'As I have said, I won't answer that. What do you think?'

Jean-Claude plucked at a loose thread on his hose.

'De Craon thinks you know more than you should.'

'Such as?'

'Well, he comes to this abbey; you come to this abbey. He is keen to acquire the Glory of Heaven, you appear equally zealous to make sure it's found again.'

'But there must be more than that?' Corbett asked.

'To put it bluntly, Sir Hugh, I do not want to make the situation worse. I cannot give you chapter and verse, but you do seem to be constantly one step ahead of de Craon. As he turns and twists, so do you.'

'So, what do you offer?' Corbett declared. 'I mean, you are in sanctuary now. You can stay here for forty days but once those days are spent you have to leave. And where do you, a Frenchman, go? Where do you lodge? What job do you take? Who will hire you? What will you do for clothing, food and drink? You are used to the finer things in life, Jean-Claude. I am sure you are well acquainted with the luxurious *auberges* of Paris and the comfortable, well-furnished chambers of the Louvre. You receive payment four times a year. You accompany your master to the most splendid banquets and feasts. You'll not find the same in Ashdown Forest. So, if you wish to be patronised and protected by the

English Crown, you must sell something to us.'

'De Craon hates you.'

'We know that.'

'He plans to kill you.'

'We know that as well.'

'Ah, Sir Hugh, but your death could be closer than you think.'

Corbett patted Ranulf on the arm then gestured over his shoulder to where Chanson stood on guard.

'Believe me, sir,' Corbett continued, 'I trust my henchmen as I do my own self. No traitor lurks close by in my retinue. Does de Craon trust you all?'

'You have a spy in Monseigneur's household?'

'That is not a matter for you and certainly not for de Craon. Though he seems to believe it's you, doesn't he?'

'In which case, Sir Hugh, am I your spy?'

'I didn't say I had one.'

'But de Craon certainly believes that you have, and it would explain why you are here talking to me now.'

'Enough, sir, of this parrying,' Corbett snapped. 'I'm here to ask the questions and, if you value your life, you must make worthy answers. You talk of de Craon planning my murder and that the assassin might be close by, but, as I've said, there is no traitor here.'

'No, Sir Hugh, listen. One of the Sacred Six, Gaston Foix, is not only a trained chancery clerk but a most skilled assassin, be it with the knife, the garrotte or a pot of poison. You recall Gaston? He has close-cropped black hair, is clean shaven with pointed features, of medium height, he walks with a slouch—'

'Yes, yes,' Corbett interjected. 'I recall him clearly.'

'I hope so, sir.' Jean-Claude breathed out. 'Because Gaston Foix has one task and one only – to kill you. To my recollection, Gaston never fails!'

'But that's in Paris,' Ranulf rasped. 'Not here in England.'

'Let him try,' Corbett murmured. 'But what else can you tell me? Why should Edward of England admit you into his peace?'

'I can talk, Sir Hugh. I can chatter about all the secret, subtle dealings of the Chambre Noire . . .'

'Hush now,' Corbett retorted. 'Let us move to matters in hand. Does de Craon have the Glory of Heaven, that priceless diamond stolen from this abbey church?'

'No, Sir Hugh, Monseigneur is as mystified as anyone.'

'Surely not?'

'Surely so. We had no dealings, no involvement with that theft.'

'Yet de Craon seems pleased.'

'True, true,' Jean-Claude conceded, 'but I do not know the reason.'

'And The Wodewose?' Ranulf demanded. 'Did you and yours have a hand in that?'

'No, we did not.' Jean-Claude's voice took on a note of desperation. 'I am here,' he continued, 'because Monseigneur believes I am your spy.'

'And as I have said, sir,' Corbett replied, 'I can do nothing about that. What do you expect?' He leant forward, his face only a few inches from Jean-Claude's.

'If I say you are not my spy, if I say you *are* my spy, in truth they mean the same. I am conceding that I do have a spy in Monseigneur's retinue. Denial or approval simply doesn't apply here. De Craon believes you're the spy and he's determined on your death. So why should I save you?'

Jean-Claude rubbed his face. 'I can talk,' he declared. 'But I must be taken to a safer place. Then I shall tell everything I know. Sir Hugh, I hail from the Vexin, only a short march from Paris. Whenever we meet to confirm and seal a pact or pledge, we do so in a church and drink a goblet of wine as a symbol of agreement. Can we do that here? Can I have your word at least that I will be taken to a place of safety? It won't hurt anybody, a goblet of the finest Bordeaux.'

Corbett gazed steadily back at Jean-Claude. He had heard of such a practice. Agreements reached in a church, confirmed and sealed with a goblet of wine.

'It will be,' Corbett answered slowly, 'as you so wish. We shall confirm our pact and seal it with the finest out of Bordeaux.' He got to his feet and patted Jean-Claude on the shoulder. 'Until we drink the wine, keep safe, be on your guard. De Craon will certainly try to kill you.'

Jean-Claude peered up at Corbett fearfully.

'You will leave a guard?' he stuttered.

'My Clerk of the Stables, together with some of the good lay brothers, will mount strict watch. I shall return.'

Corbett and Ranulf left the abbey church. Corbett

pressed a finger against his lips as a sign to keep silent. They returned to his chamber, where Corbett unlocked the door and immediately crouched down to pick up a small square of parchment. Ranulf realised it was no mere scrap. Corbett undid it carefully and took it over to the narrow window to read it more clearly.

'Sir Hugh?'

'Matters progress, my dear friend, matters progress – look.' Corbett went over to a brazier, dropped the scrap of paper in and watched it turn to ash. 'Look,' he repeated, 'go and tell Chanson to keep guard close to the main door of the church. Once you've done that, make a visit to the buttery.' Corbett undid his belt purse and handed Ranulf a silver coin. 'Give that to the kitchener or whoever is in charge. I want a jug of the best Bordeaux and two goblets.'

'You are going to seal the pact?'

'I am going to seal the pact, Ranulf.'

'Do you think he's telling the truth?'

'Pilate asked what is truth and didn't wait for an answer. For the time being, Ranulf, I am suspicious, but,' he smiled, 'that's my nature.'

'Do you have a spy in de Craon's household?'

'Ranulf, you have asked me that before and I will give you the same answer. I trust you completely, but because of my love for you, I cannot tell you everything. We have just left Jean-Claude in sanctuary. I know about his dealings. Oh, he looks all frightened and subdued, but I wager, like the rest, he's a born mummer, a man who can act many parts.'

'And this Gaston, is he a threat?'

'Ranulf, my friend, think and reflect. Of course. Gaston is a killer, so is Jean-Claude. You don't blame a wolf for howling, or foxes for killing chickens: the same is true of de Craon's retinue. They are all blood-drinkers just like their master. If Gaston decides to strike then we will watch the roll of the dice. He won't be the first one to try, nor will he be the first one to fail.' Corbett laughed and patted his chest. 'As you can see.'

'Is Jean-Claude valuable?'

'Yes and no. We'll take him to an abbey like this or some fortified manor or castle along the Welsh March. We shall provide him with comfortable lodgings, good food and other diversions. Then we shall invite him to talk. We will encourage him to chatter like a sparrow on the branch. Once he has finished, we will go through the transcript of everything he's told us. You would be surprised at the real pearls you can find amongst the most sordid rubbish. Oh yes, Jean-Claude could be valuable. If he proves his worth, we shall reward him with an appointment at some castle where he can act as clerk to the constable and dream of his glory days. Now, let us move on.'

Ranulf left to carry out his master's instructions. Corbett stood listening to his henchman leave, then knelt on the prie-dieu before a painted wall-cloth bearing the image of Our Lady of Walsingham. For a while, Corbett just knelt silently before slowly reciting three Aves, fervently asking for protection as he approached the trap set up for him. By the time he had finished, Ranulf had returned with the jug and goblets. Corbett poured a little of the wine then tasted the delicate yet tongue-tingling Bordeaux.

'*Parfait!*' Corbett drained the goblet and handed it back to Ranulf. '*Procedamus in Christo*,' he declared. 'Come, Ranulf, let us drink wine with our enemy and, as always,' Corbett added enigmatically, 'act the innocent!'

They returned to the abbey church. Corbett noticed how de Craon's men were keeping the doors to the nave under guard. Corbett had a few cautionary words with Chanson, who was lounging in the porch, before going up into the sanctuary.

Jean-Claude rose to greet them, clapping his hands as he glimpsed the goblets and jug. He insisted on pouring the wine. Corbett let him as he led Ranulf into the sacristy where Brother Simon was busy folding altar cloths to place in the great aumbry. Corbett was just about to ask where Abbot Maurice might be when a noisy altercation broke out along the nave. Chanson, standing just within the main doorway, was shouting whilst others were yelling back.

Corbett immediately returned to the sanctuary enclave where Jean-Claude had placed both goblets, brimming with wine, on a wall ledge. The Frenchman thrust one of these into Corbett's hand and then raised his own in toast. Corbett, however, apparently distracted by the clamour, shook his head and put the goblet back on the ledge, indicating that Jean-Claude do likewise. The Frenchman did so. Corbett clapped him on the shoulder and pointed to the enclave.

'Stay there,' he ordered. 'I will see to this. Ranulf, go halfway down the nave, keep an eye on both side doors. I will see what's bothering our friend Chanson.'

Corbett picked up one goblet, gave the other to Jean-Claude, toasted him and walked out of the sanctuary, hurrying down to the main entrance. Chanson stood blocking the threshold, shouting at de Craon who, surrounded by his clerks and other retainers, was trying to gain entry. Chanson, equally vociferous, yelled that this was a matter for the king's justiciar. Corbett went to stand by his Clerk of the Stables.

'Monseigneur.' Corbett, still clutching the wine goblet, bowed mockingly at de Craon. 'What is the matter?'

'We wish . . . we want to ensure that the sanctuary man is still where he should be.'

'We have that right,' Malpas insisted, stepping closer, one hand falling to the hilt of his dagger.

'Take your hand away,' Chanson bawled.

'Yes, take your hand away from your weapon,' Corbett declared in a ringing voice. 'I am the king's justiciar. I ask you to withdraw. Jean-Claude, who has sought sanctuary here, remains ensconced behind the high altar. I give you my solemn word on that. The word of the king's justiciar: Jean-Claude still lies in sanctuary at this abbey church.'

De Craon looked as if to object, then shrugged, turned on his heels, snapping at his escort to follow. Corbett watched them go, paying particular attention to Gaston, the dark-haired would-be assassin.

'Oh yes,' Corbett whispered to himself, 'I shall

certainly remember you and let heaven and earth witness it.' He tossed the wine from his cup onto the gravel path and stared up at the sky. 'The hour candle burns quickly,' he murmured, 'night follows day follows night. The queen should be here tomorrow and Abbot Maurice must be informed . . .' Corbett paused in reflection as a scream, followed by a shout of alarm, rang down the nave. He hurried in to where Ranulf was waiting, even as the anchorite began to recite the death psalm, 'Out of the depths I cry to thee, oh Lord . . .'

'For God's sake,' the sacristan shouted as he hurried down the nave. 'Hold your peace. Sir Hugh, the sanctuary man lies dead. I think he's been poisoned.'

Corbett turned, telling Chanson to continue to guard the door. He then hurried up to join Ranulf in the sanctuary enclave where Jean-Claude lay sprawled against the wall. The Frenchman's face had turned a vivid hue, eyes popping, mouth hanging slack, a dirty white foam slipping through his lips. Corbett felt for the life beat in the man's neck and wrist. The victim's flesh was clammy cold and Corbett could find no sign of life.

'He's definitely been poisoned,' Corbett exclaimed.

'I'd best fetch Father Abbot and Prior Felix.'

The sacristan, all flustered, fled the church. Corbett let him go. He picked up the goblet the dead man had used. He sniffed it but could detect no evil odour. He then inspected the jug. Some wine still remained but it too seemed untainted.

'In heaven's name,' Ranulf breathed, crouching down

on the other side of the corpse. 'How was this done? Sir Hugh, you drank wine from the same jug.'

'I certainly did, with no ill effect whatsoever.'

Abbot Maurice and Prior Felix arrived. Both men looked tired and depleted.

'More deaths!' the abbot exclaimed, biting his lips. 'Is this God's punishment?'

'For what?'

'Nothing, Sir Hugh, nothing, except my abbey has become a battleground, a tourney field where the likes of you, Sir Hugh, and de Craon can joust in the lists. The war between England and France takes many forms. Not just battles on land, or conflicts at sea, but in men's hearts and souls – such men are now in my abbey.'

'We do the king's business,' Corbett retorted. 'The theft of the Glory of Heaven, the murder of Brother Mark and the burning of The Wodewose cannot be laid at our door. The same is true of the slaughter of these French clerks.'

'Let me see, let me see.' A rather dishevelled Prior Felix crouched by the corpse, asking Corbett and Ranulf to step away. Once they had, the prior scrutinised the cadaver, paying particular attention to the foam between the dead man's lips. 'Poisons come in many forms,' he declared. 'Some of the most deadly can be found in a cottage garden. Certain potions take hours, even days, to kill, others strike as swift as an arrow to the heart. The poison that killed this poor soul was most vicious.' The prior sniffed at both goblet and jug. 'I'll feed what's left to the rats in the cellars. But I suspect this poison was the rare, costly type without taste and odour.'

'I had a goblet from the same jug,' Corbett retorted, 'with no ill affect. Brother Simon,' he called, 'Brother Simon, I need you.' Furtive and frightened, the sacristan came fearfully around the altar into the enclave. 'What did you see,' Corbett demanded, 'when you were alone with him? What happened?'

'I saw him.' The sacristan flailed a hand towards the corpse. 'I saw him come into the sacristy. He was carrying his goblet – the one you gave him. He walked in and out, sometimes standing by the door to listen to the confrontation between you and de Craon. Eventually he left, going back to the enclave. I distinctly heard him put down the goblet hard on the floor. I am sure he sighed but I thought nothing of it. Time passed. I suppose . . .' The sacristan's fingers fluttered to his mouth. 'It was the silence which intrigued me. I grew curious so I came round the altar, and then I realised what had happened.'

'Prior Felix, would you please go through the dead man's pockets and pouches?' Corbett asked, and the prior did so deftly, bringing out small innocuous items, which he immediately handed to Corbett. They did not amount to much: Ave beads, a piece of sealing wax which bore the colours of the French Royal Chancery – blue and gold – a small seal and a narrow-bladed chancery knife.

'Nothing of real interest,' Corbett murmured. 'Not even a Templar seal. Ah well.'

He collected the items and handed them to Ranulf. 'Anything else?'

'Nothing, Sir Hugh.' The prior got to his feet. 'I will see to the removal of the corpse to the death house—' He broke off at the clamour coming from the main door.

'I suspect de Craon has discovered what has happened,' Corbett declared. 'Ranulf, tell Chanson to let them through.'

A short while later, shouting at his escort to stay in the nave, de Craon, accompanied by Malpas, swept into the sanctuary and around the high altar. He brushed aside the two monks and glared down at the corpse.

'Poisoned!' he exclaimed. 'That's what one of the brothers told me. Poisoned! Well, let the devil take his soul. Father Abbot, I would appreciate it if he could be buried here. One last gesture to a veritable Judas.'

'Bury the bastard deep,' Malpas, standing behind de Craon, exclaimed. 'Bury him deep,' he repeated, 'so he'll soon be forgotten.'

'And who is responsible for this outrage?' de Craon asked.

'God knows,' Corbett replied, holding de Craon's stare. 'God knows what is going on. Jean-Claude drank from the same jug as I did. I carry no poison, nor did the victim.'

'Oh, for God's sake, just bury him,' Malpas exclaimed. 'Father Abbot, we shall pay any fee.' De Craon made to leave but Corbett held up a hand.

'Monseigneur, Father Abbot, I have news for you.

Her Grace the queen is travelling from Windsor with every intent to lodge here. I suspect she wishes to celebrate the liturgy of Holy Week at St Michael's.' On any other occasion Corbett would have burst out laughing at de Craon's expression, his face turning slack with astonishment.

'How, when . . . what?' de Craon spluttered.

'Heaven forfend,' the abbot exclaimed. 'Prior Felix, come, we must prepare.' The two Benedictines hurried off, followed by a woebegone de Craon, muttering furiously to Malpas.

'There goes a group of truly astonished men,' Ranulf chuckled. 'Sir Hugh, you fair set the fox amongst the chickens.'

'Oh, more than one fox, my friend,' Corbett replied, gripping Ranulf by the arm. 'More than one. Anyway, our moon girl is on the way back with Her Grace the queen so we must keep to the business in hand. Go and collect Chanson so we too can stage our own little masque about the deceased.' Corbett pointed at Jean-Claude's body. He was about to continue, but paused as the sacristan called out that Prior Felix had sent lay brothers to remove the corpse.

'Let's be gone,' Corbett whispered. 'Ah well, it will be good to see Her Grace. I will be even more pleased to greet Ap Ythel and his archers. I despatched them earlier today to greet the queen. I think we are going to need her and them to push matters through. But, as I said, let's stage our own little masque.'

They returned to Corbett's chamber. Ranulf fired up

the brazier and lit candles whilst Chanson served ale from a jug sent up by the buttery. Once settled, Corbett gently clapped his hands.

'Now, my friends, let us go back through the events of this day. Chanson, you – Ap Ythel being absent – were guarding the main door of the abbey church. Ranulf, you went to the buttery to collect a jug of Bordeaux and two goblets. You brought them back to me, yes?' Both henchmen murmured their agreement. 'Now, to take note of every action. You, Ranulf, gave the jug and the cups to me. I took them to Jean-Claude. He insisted on pouring so I let him. I understand that is customary in the confirmation of a pact; the one who requested the agreement serves the wine. We did so in this church. Jean-Claude understood that he would be taken to a place of safety and, at the appointed time, tell us everything he knew. Anyway, Jean-Claude served the wine but then the altercation between Chanson and de Craon broke out. I took Jean-Claude to the sanctuary enclave, thrust a goblet into his hands, then left. The Frenchman stayed with Simon the sacristan who, at this moment in time, is above any suspicion of wrong-doing.'

'I would agree,' Ranulf declared. 'Simon is a monk totally immersed in his own small world of the sacristy.'

'Very well. Jean-Claude stays in the sanctuary. He may have wandered about. He is certainly sipping the wine, drinking the poison, though God knows how it got there. He suddenly feels ill, crouches down to squat against the wall and dies.' Corbett paused. 'Have I omitted anything?'

'No,' Ranulf replied. 'I was on guard halfway down the nave in order to watch the two side doors.'

'So, the problem is,' Chanson declared, 'how was Jean-Claude poisoned and by whom, bearing in mind that you, Sir Hugh, drank the same wine from the same jug?'

'Very perceptive,' Ranulf teased.

'Very perceptive indeed,' Corbett declared. 'A telling question, Chanson. At this moment in time, I can offer no solution. Anyway, I ask both of you, who were in constant attendance whilst all this was happening, did you glimpse anything untoward?' Both henchmen replied they didn't. 'In which case,' Corbett continued as he rose, 'let me know if you do. But come, Her Grace the queen is approaching and we must prepare.'

The imminent arrival of the queen turned the abbey into a beehive of frenetic business. Monks, lay brothers and servitors scurried about like rabbits through a corn-field. Chambers were cleaned, fresh hangings brought out from store, the laundry became busy, charcoals fetched for braziers, logs chopped for the hearth and a stream of freshly slaughtered flesh despatched to the abbey kitchens. Abbot Maurice vacated his private lodg-ings, as did other leading officers of the abbey. Corbett and his henchmen kept to their rooms, apart from the occasional walk down to the buttery where they made sure they kept well clear of de Craon and his cronies. Corbett wrote another letter to Maeve and decided that both missives would be taken by one of Ap Ythel's mounted archers as soon as they returned to St Michael's.

For the rest he stayed in his chamber, drafting his own notes.

Ranulf became deeply intrigued, as he realised Old Master Longface kept drawing three concentric circles on sheets of parchment, making his own special notes along the rim of each one.

'What is this, master?'

'My attempt to impose order, to create some form of logic.'

'But why the circles?'

'Well, that's what they are, Ranulf. They are not interlocked – well, I don't think they are – but each holds its own mystery. Perhaps if I can solve one, the rest might follow. You see, this –' Corbett tapped the outer circle – 'is the theft of the Glory of Heaven. Remember, Ranulf, the important items of that mystery. The door of the Silver Shrine remained intact. No other entrance existed. The bolts of that door were clasped shut, the unique keys rested firmly in their special locks, yet the jewel was stolen and its guardian foully murdered. So how was that, eh? Even more mysterious, no one heard or glimpsed anything untoward.'

'And the second circle is the mysterious fire out at The Wodewose?'

'It certainly is, Ranulf. Reflect. We have a merry wayside tavern housing eight souls – nine if we include the royal courier, the mailed clerk, Squire Stephen Filliol. Now, I have learnt that in the afternoon before the fire, Osbert, a boy from the mummers' group, was despatched on an errand to The Wodewose only to find the entire tavern shut and locked. Horses still stood in their stables but, apart from that, there was no other sign of life. No reply to Osbert's constant knocking. In addition, earlier in the evening, just before that dire event, our anchorite in the abbey church claims to have seen Satan, hideous in appearance, walking through God's Acre. I ask myself, was that macabre event connected to the ferocious fire which broke out later that night? And when it did, why didn't anyone escape? Were they murdered beforehand? If so, by whom? True, there are many lawless men, but to attack a tavern like The Wodewose would require a cohort of determined killers with no regard for God or man. Now, no such group has been detected in the area. Moreover, if the tavern was attacked, why didn't some of those lodged there fight back, or escape?'

'Squire Filliol certainly would have done.'

'Too true, Ranulf. So, it's hard to accept that they were murdered beforehand. Even if they were, why did their cold-hearted assassin loosen the horses so they could wander the nearby fields? Finally, I went down recently to view the tavern remains, as you know. I discovered fresh streaks of oil splattered on the charred timbers and stones. Why was that, eh? The Wodewose had been destroyed, the fire extinguished. Was someone trying to restart the flames? I found the same on the burial pit in God's Acre where the remains of those who were killed lie buried.'

Ranulf pointed to the third inner circle. 'And this circle concerns the death of the French clerks?'

'That, my dear Ranulf, must, for the time being, remain a secret. But you are correct, it includes the slaying of the clerks.'

'And do you have any solution that would break one or all of these three circles?'

'At this moment in time,' Corbett smiled up at his henchman, 'I only have supposition, nothing on a firmly grounded hypothesis; that is a matter of time, our cunning and God's good grace.'

Corbett continued with his studies until late in the evening. On the following morning, Queen Isabella arrived just before the Angelus bell. Her outriders, carrying stiffened pennants and proceeded by a trumpeter, clattered through the wide-open gates of the abbey, followed by a line of carts, wheels rattling, their contents protected by waxed sheets. A host of sumpter ponies followed, supervised by officials of the queen's household: the pantry, buttery, chancery, kitchen, wardrobe and the rest. Ap Ythel and his archers came next, followed by the young queen in her luxurious carriage pulled by four chargers, black as night.

The carriage stopped in the abbey bailey and Isabella, assisted by her ladies, climbed elegantly out to be greeted by the abbot with Corbett and de Craon in close attendance. Isabella was resplendent. She was dressed in a pellicom, a voluminous, fur-lined mantled gown, with slits at the front for her arms and a great cowled hood which she now pulled back to reveal hair the colour of the sun. She moved back the white gauze veil fluttering about her beautiful face. She then thanked the abbot in a pretty speech and allowed herself to be led off to her lodgings. The cavalcade now broke up, horses unhitched, carts emptied.

Megotta emerged from the company of Ap Ythel's archers. She glimpsed Corbett's startled expression when he saw the bruises and cuts to her face, putting a finger to her lips as a warning for silence. Corbett had a few words with Chanson then plucked at Ranulf's sleeve.

'My chamber!' he murmured.

They went back through the abbey to Corbett's lodgings. Megotta joined them a short while later. Corbett ordered Chanson to stand guard outside, where Ap Ythel and some his archers would join him. Megotta made herself comfortable, accepting the morning ale Corbett poured. She sipped carefully, favouring the bruise on her mouth. She then informed them, in terse, clipped sentences, about the ambuscade on the road to Windsor; the attack by the wolfsheads and the emergence of her unexpected, mysterious saviour.

Once she'd finished, Corbett sat in silence for a few moments before getting to his feet. He paced backwards and forwards, asking Megotta a few questions. Ranulf noticed how his master did not seem so concerned about Megotta's rescuer but, rather, how did people learn that Megotta was in his service, on an important errand which would take her to Windsor? Corbett conceded that her attackers were wolfsheads, probably recruited by de Craon from the horde of landless, former soldiers who roamed the roads and country lanes.

'Nevertheless,' he declared, 'how did de Craon know about you and your task?'

'He must have spies all over this abbey and Bloody Meadow,' Megotta retorted.

'No, no,' Corbett murmured almost to himself. 'I must think. Ah well.' Corbett returned to his chair. 'And Her Grace the queen?'

'In very good spirits, Sir Hugh. Once I reached Windsor I was ushered into her private chamber.' Megotta grinned. 'Your pass opened doors more quickly than any key. The queen received me graciously, she asked about the cuts to my face. I told her I had taken a fall. She then accepted the letter and read it.' Megotta sighed deeply. 'The queen lost no time. Within the hour her household were loading the carts, readying both horse and harness for the journey.' Megotta shrugged. 'I waited until all was ready and joined the royal procession to St Michael's.'

'Good, good.' Corbett rose. 'Megotta, you truly are a *mulier fortis et audax* – a bold and courageous woman. Now is the time for you to rest. Re-join your own people and we will meet soon enough.'

Megotta and Corbett clasped hands, and the moon girl had hardly left when Chanson knocked on the door and opened it.

'Sir Hugh, Her Grace the queen wishes to see you now.'

A chamberlain, armed with a white wand of office, chest all puffed out like a pigeon, escorted Corbett into the royal presence. Isabella and her ladies-in-waiting had been provided with the abbot's lodgings and its ante-chamber was a spacious, most luxurious and comfortable room. Multi-hued Turkey cloths covered the floor, painted cloth hangings and vivid triptychs adorned the walls. Clusters of well-placed beeswax candles provided both light and perfumed smoke. The queen's chamber ladies occupied a cushioned settle in a large window embrasure. Isabella herself was enthroned in an ornate chair before a roaring fire. The chamber smelt sweet with the fragrance of the ladies, now relaxing after their journey, breaking their fast from the platters of food laid out on the shiny elm-wood table. Corbett genu-flected before the queen and took the proffered chair placed so Isabella could see him directly.

'Madam,' Corbett made himself comfortable, 'you are well lodged here?'

'*Parfait, Monsieur, tout parfait.*' Isabella grinned and Corbett smiled back. She had removed her veil, letting her long golden hair hang free. Corbett considered her to be a truly beautiful woman with her heart-shaped face, lustrous large blue eyes and almost perfect features. The young queen reminded Corbett of the paintings he'd seen of sun-haired, silver-bodied angels. Nevertheless, the queen, despite her tender years, had already acquired a reputation for being shrewd, cunning and capable. She had a fiery temper but she also had the sharp mind and keen wits to conceal this. Isabella had proved herself a source of good counsel for her errant husband and Corbett just prayed that his royal master would accept her advice.

Corbett glanced swiftly at the Queen's stomach – her belly must be distended although any swelling was well concealed by her thick cambric gown. Isabella was undoubtedly pregnant and Corbett knew she was desperate to produce a living male heir to please both her father and her husband. Corbett had his coven of spies amongst the royal physicians as well as the cohort of 'wise women' who attended the Queen. Stories floated through the court only to disappear as others emerged. How the young Queen had false pregnancies. How she may not be as far gone as she declared. How she had suffered miscarriages and other mishaps. At times Isabella could be highly erratic, acting with great vigour whilst at others she would declare herself '*tout fatiguée*' and retreat to her private chambers. No one could say what was the truth of the matter or when the birth would occur. Perhaps October around the feast of Edward the Confessor? The King would love that.

Whatever rumours swirled, Corbett was convinced of one important fact: Isabella was intent on using her pregnancy to win the support and sympathy of everyone for herself and, above all, for her benighted royal husband. In Corbett's eyes the Queen was succeeding brilliantly.

'Hugh.' Isabella smiled dazzlingly and gently laughed. 'I can never pronounce the H.'

'Madam, my lady, who cares as long as I can bask in your smile.'

'Silver tongued as always, Hugh; silver tongued.' Isabella leant over, her hands mittened in pure velvet set with tiny white stones, and gently cupped Corbett's face. She then sat back. 'Well, Sir Hugh, your courier Megotta informed me about what was happening here. Am I safe?'

'Safer than being at Windsor, your Grace, you must not allow—'

'I know what you're going to say, Sir Hugh. I must not be used by anyone, fair or foul, against my husband the king.'

'There is that danger, madam, but you are also safe here. The abbey is well stocked, well provisioned and is as formidable as any fortress. Your presence here keeps you safe from being used in any game of catspaw. Moreover, you can also celebrate the festivals of Holy Week and Easter in this house of prayer. Despite what's happening here, it is a truly holy place.'

'Yes, yes.' Isabella patted the quilted armrests of her chair. 'But matters have changed. From the outset, my husband the king was to join me at Windsor for the holy festivals of Maundy Thursday, Good Friday and Holy Saturday. In particular, he was going to celebrate Maundy Thursday – the institution of the Eucharist. He had also agreed to participate in the ceremony of the washing of the feet, as Christ did to his apostles at the last supper. My husband was to act as Christ, an example to us all, to serve and look after each other.'

Corbett kept his face impassive. Apparently, the queen did not appreciate the real contrast between her pampered, luxurious living and the sheer misery of the lives of many of her subjects.

'Now, however,' Isabella continued, her voice turning very harsh, her eyes and face suffused with anger, 'now,' she repeated, forcing a smile, 'my husband cannot join me. So, it will not be at Windsor, it will be here and I have a favour to ask you, Sir Hugh – or rather, Father Abbot has. Would you act as Christ at the mandatum, the washing of the feet?' Corbett just stared back. 'Come, Hugh, you are the Keeper of the King's Secret Seal, his justiciar south of the Trent. My husband's envoy and most trusted councillor.'

'Of course, your Grace, of course,' Corbett replied. 'If that's what you wish.'

'It is.'

'Then your will be done.' Corbett rubbed his hands together. 'And the twelve apostles?'

'I believe Lord Abbot was going to choose these from abbey servants or wherever he can.'

Corbett sat back in his chair, nodding in agreement, trying to hide his surprise at the cascade of thoughts, words and images stirred up by such a simple conversation about people attending a religious ceremony.

'Hugh, are you well?'

'My lady, as I said, I rejoice to bask in your smile. I also plead for two favours. First, you keep to the advice contained in my letter. No English lord, be it Lancaster or anyone else, must be allowed to bring their retainers into this abbey. They are in conflict with your husband.'

'And your second request?'

'Despatch urgent messages to the Constable of Wallingford Castle. Order him, on his sworn allegiance to the Crown, to assemble and, if necessary, bring his entire garrison here to St Michael's. We may not need such a comitatus but, my lady, we are drifting towards civil war. You are *enceinte*, and in time our young prince will be born. There are many in this kingdom who would love to seize both you and the child and use you as pieces in a deadly game of hazard.' Corbett was tempted to add that Isabella's father was just as much a threat as Thomas of Lancaster, but he realised he must hold his peace. Staring at the young queen, Corbett was sure Isabella's sharp wits would warn her that her esteemed father was not above playing the same game.

'I have one further request, my lady. I need to speak to one of your ladies, Beatrice Saveraux.'

'About what?'

'The death of her beloved, the squire, the royal courier, the mailed clerk Stephen Filliol.'

'Ah yes, Stephen was expected at Windsor. He never arrived. We then heard news that he stayed at a tavern which was burned to the ground killing everyone within, Stephen included.'

'It was a tragedy, my lady, in so many ways, but Stephen was a servant of the Crown carrying important letters. If his death was murder, arson, then the perpetrator is guilty of high treason. An attack upon a royal official is an attack upon the king himself.'

'I know, Hugh, I know. Your questioning will certainly awake bitter memories for Beatrice, but it must be done.' Isabella twisted in her chair and raised a hand, snapping her fingers. The chamberlain guarding the door hurried over. He listened to the queen's instruction then hastened across the room to the ladies gathered around the window embrasure. He escorted one back and introduced her. Lady Beatrice Saveraux was a tall, willowy young woman garbed in dark colours, her black hair pinned under a simple veil, her face pinched and unadorned. She sat on a stool between Corbett and the queen, nervously twisting the napkin she clutched.

'My lady.' Corbett smiled and stretched across to pat her gently on the wrist. 'I need to talk to you about your beloved Stephen. I appreciate it is difficult but I must establish what he was doing at The Wodewose and what caused the terrible fire which killed him.' Corbett withdrew his hand. Beatrice's eyes filled with tears. She half turned to look at her mistress who just stared back. Beatrice composed herself, dabbing her eyes with the napkin.

'Stephen and I . . .' she began haltingly, 'were hanfasted, betrothed. We were to make our vows at the church door. We looked forward to our marriage day. He was young and ardent. He wrote to me saying that he was to bring messages from Westminster to Windsor. However, he intended to stop at The Wodewose to compose himself and make himself presentable.' She laughed sharply. 'Stephen was very ambitious. He wanted to become a Batchelor Knight in the king's own household. He could be ever so particular about his appearance, especially when he appeared at court.'

'I would certainly agree with that,' Isabella intervened.

'Especially after travelling,' Beatrice continued. 'He

would want to wash and change. At the time, I thought nothing of it. Stephen did what Stephen wanted and he would tolerate no gainsaying.'

'So, he was travelling from Westminster?' Corbett paused. Something had jarred his memory yet he could not place it. Something about Filliol – but what?

'Sir Hugh?'

'I am sorry, your Grace. So, Stephen left Westminster and took the road to The Wodewose. Now, did he say anything else about what he might be doing? Was he meeting someone? Was he going to travel somewhere apart from The Wodewose and Windsor? My lady, anything out of the ordinary?'

'Yes.' Beatrice opened the pouch on her snow-white cincture and took out a small scroll. She offered this to Corbett who shook his head and smiled.

'A love letter, mistress. Stephen's last love letter to you, yes?'

Beatrice nodded as the tears ran down her face. She paused to dab at these.

'Just read,' Corbett pressed on, 'just read what lies outside his loving outpourings.'

Beatrice nodded and undid the scroll. 'This . . .' she declared, tapping it and lifting it closer, screwing up her eyes. '"As a symbol of my love I intend to bring you a gift the like of which you have never seen before. I must visit Queenhithe to secure the casket and all it contains. A rare gift, my beloved, from far beyond the Silk Road."' Beatrice glanced up and smiled between her tears. 'And then Stephen returns to the verses he had composed.

God knows,' she continued, 'what he was bringing, yet, Sir Hugh, that's all I can tell you.' Corbett thanked both her and the queen, who promised she would despatch the messages he had asked her to. He bowed his thanks, kissed the queen's ring hand and bade her adieu.

Lost in thought, Corbett walked the cloisters, arms folded, staring down at the hard paving, his mind teeming with possible solutions. He took out his Ave beads and threaded them through his fingers. He was bemused and slightly surprised at how his conversation with the queen and her lady-in-waiting had begun to dent that circle he had drawn around The Wodewose and the murders committed there. Corbett was now certain of that: Filliol's death and those of the others was no accident, but murder. All he had to do was find the cause and he was sure this would lead him to the perpetrator. In the meantime, he needed to do some study as well as reflect and prepare for the next step forward. Corbett glanced up at a gargoyle fixed above a rainspout, a devilish monkey face, its mouth gaping as if the gargoyle was constantly laughing at the ways of men.

'Satan can appear as a lord of light,' Corbett murmured, staring at the carving. 'He can appear most beauteous and he can most certainly walk the hallowed precincts of an abbey. Nevertheless, the real lords of light watch him and I ask them to guard me.'

'Are you well?'

Corbett broke from his reverie and stared at the lay brother.

'I have seen you walking, sir, can I help you?'

'The library,' Corbett retorted. 'The abbey has a library, yes?'

The lay brother beckoned at him to follow. They went down hollow-sounding corridors and narrow, gloomy passageways. Corbett kept a wary eye out for de Craon and his minions but the Frenchman nor his coven were to be seen. At last, they reached the library, built like a small chapel overlooking the abbey gardens, a rich stretch of herb pots, grassy verges and vegetable plots. The lay brother took him up some steps and into a world Corbett truly loved; books, folios and manuscripts stood stacked on shelves. Capped candles glowed on the polished tables glinting in the fine oak used to set the library up. Baskets and hampers arranged along the wall contained loose-leafed pages of some books, each of the containers being tabulated, with what they held, on lists pinned to the side. Caskets, coffers and chests stood carefully stacked. Above all, there was the perfume, which Corbett always welcomed, the sweet smell of learning: leather, ink and sealing wax. Corbett was introduced to the librarian, Brother Henry, who sat down and listened intently to what his visitor needed to study. He made careful note and brought these items to Corbett. Manuscripts and books containing chronicles of the east as well as treatises on diseases, their containment and, where possible, treatments using potions and philtres as prescribed by the leading masters of medicine. Darkness fell; the librarian's assistant began to extinguish lanterns and candles.

'Sir Hugh?'

'Brother Henry?'

The librarian placed a thin, calfskin-covered tome on the desk.

'Sir Hugh, you might find this interesting. I understand you are here about the Glory of Heaven. I think you should read that.'

Corbett thanked him and opened the tome. It contained a schedule of documents, memoranda, indentures and letters surrounding the Templar's transfer of the Glory of Heaven to the English Crown. Corbett read these and sensed how the Templar Order really believed that the English king, on receiving such a precious relic, would afford them every protection. In the end, he hadn't. Oh, the young king had sworn oaths. These documents carried both his signature and his seal yet they proved to be nothing but dust in the breeze, quickly forgotten as Edward turned to protect himself from his father-in-law's spiteful anger.

'Sir Hugh.' The librarian came out of the dark. 'You found that interesting?'

'Yes, yes I did.'

'And now night has fallen.'

Corbett took the hint and returned to his chamber. He was hardly there before Ranulf and Chanson rapped at the door. Both clerks looked highly anxious.

'Sir Hugh, we searched high and low for you.'

'Ranulf, I have been high and low myself, immersed in the library, but more of that later perhaps. Chanson, fetch Captain Ap Ythel. Ranulf, I have a letter to dictate.'

Chanson left Corbett and Ranulf drafting a letter to Sir Miles Kynaston, Admiral of the Seas from the mouth of the Thames and Chief Harbourmaster of all the ports and quaysides along London's river. Ranulf finished the letter. Corbett signed and sealed it and, when Ap Ythel arrived, ordered the captain to give that letter to one of his bowmen and to a second, the letters for the Lady Maeve. Ap Ythel and Ranulf left. Corbett spent the rest of the evening in his chamber, turning over in his mind what he had learnt from his conversation with the queen and the Lady Beatrice. Words such as 'apostles' and 'mandatum', along with other sentences he had read in the library, rolled through his mind like dice in a cup. Nonetheless, Corbett was pleased. He was beginning to break into two of those circles that contained such taunting mysteries.

The next morning, the Saturday before Palm Sunday, Corbett rose early and went down to the abbey church, which the good brothers had prepared for Holy Week. All lights were doused. Statues, crucifixes and paintings had been hidden behind purple, gold-edged cloths. During the coming week, the church and its chantry chapels would be stripped of all finery and decoration until the Gloria was intoned during the Festival of Light on Holy Saturday. Corbett attended mass in the chantry chapel. The only other person present was the anchorite, wrapped in a heavy brown blanket against the cold. After the final blessing, the anchorite followed Corbett down to the Silver Shrine. The bars around the door were still battered; the door itself lay on the ground with one of the bolt clasps close by. The anchorite went into the chapel, wandering round, gaping at the altar and ruined door. He picked up the bolt and clasp.

'Look, Sir Hugh, strong and sturdy. Yet still the assassin passed through that door like a wisp of smoke. Look.' The anchorite crossed and, pressing himself against the bars, thrust his right hand through so Corbett could take the broken bolt. He did and stared open mouthed at the anchorite. 'Sir Hugh, are you well?'

Corbett continued to stare at the anchorite.

'I . . .' Corbett couldn't find the words, his surprise was so sudden and unexpected. 'I . . .' he stammered then broke off at the tolling of the tocsin. He placed the clasp bolt on the ground and hurried down the nave.

Ranulf and Chanson were waiting in the Galilee porch. Corbett stopped as a blast of trumpets cut through the morning air. He half guessed what was happening.

'We have visitors?'

'We certainly have, Sir Hugh,' Ranulf retorted. 'Faucomburg and two heralds.'

Another trumpet echoed stridently.

'Oh dear. Let's go,' Corbett urged. 'After all, we cannot keep Squire Faucomburg or his master waiting.'

They left the church, hastening across the great bailey, pushing aside the monks, then up steep steps to the parapet above the majestic gatehouse. Prior Felix was already there and Abbot Maurice, grumbling under his breath, joined them. Corbett, standing between the crenellations, stared down at their visitor.

'Faucomburg!' Corbett exclaimed. 'Principal squire, mailed clerk, henchman and bully boy of no less a worthy person than the king's cousin, Thomas, Earl of Lancaster. Lord Thomas, as you may know, Abbot Maurice, is the leading light of the Ordainers who are implacably opposed to Gaveston, the king's favourite, and, *ipso facto*, to the king himself.'

Corbett braced himself against the crenellated wall, letting the wind whip his hair and face. He glanced up at the icy-blue sky. The day would be bright but freezing.

'What do they want?' Abbot Maurice pleaded. 'No more violence, surely?'

Corbett just shook his head as he stared down at Faucomburg, dressed in the royal red and gold livery of Lancaster, the tabards of the heralds either side displaying the same insignia. Lancaster's squire, head shaven, slouched arrogantly on his warhorse, one hand on the saddle horn, the other holding a stiffened pennant depicting the roaring lions of the royal house.

'Very well, very well,' Corbett murmured. 'So you represent the king's blood cousin and I know what you want.'

As if in answer, the heralds either side lifted their trumpets and blew a short piercing blast. Once finished, Faucomburg stood high in his stirrups.

'I am,' he shouted in a powerful, carrying voice, 'the personal herald of Thomas, Earl of . . .'

Corbett turned to Ap Ythel who had joined him on the parapet.

'Captain, three strong blasts on your hunting horn.'

Ap Ythel did so immediately, the strident noise almost deafening Faucomburg's proclamation. The final horn blast trailed away. Silence descended. Corbett, leaning between the crenellations, took a deep breath.

'Faucomburg!' he shouted. 'I know who you are and you should recognise me.'

'Of course I do – Sir Hugh Corbett. It would be very good to meet.'

'And so we shall,' Corbett shouted back. He then went along the parapet and down the steps, indicating that Ranulf and Ap Ythel should follow him. Corbett led both henchmen into the gatehouse, ordering the porter to open the small postern door built into the main entrance. He then turned. 'Ranulf, you come with me. Tell the porter to keep the door open just in case. Ap Ythel, my friend—' The captain stepped closer, his deep hood pulled forward against the sharp breeze, his wizened nut-brown face transformed by a mischievous grin.

'I know what you are going to ask, Sir Hugh, as I know who Faucomburg is. You have crossed swords with him before.'

'In more ways than one, captain. However, he now has a more healthy respect for us all which, I hope, he maintains today.'

'And just in case,' Ap Ythel exclaimed in his sing-song voice, 'I and my six men will be standing on that parapet, war bows notched.'

'Excellent, my friend.'

Corbett shook hands with Ap Ythel then walked towards the postern door and, followed by Ranulf, stepped through onto the trackway.

Faucomburg urged his horse forward. He then abruptly reined in as two yard-long shafts smacked into the ground only a short distance from his destrier. The warhorse whinnied and twisted until Faucomburg, displaying considerable skill, brought his mount back under control.

'Far enough, Faucomburg,' Corbett warned. 'What do you want?'

'Admission.' Lancaster's henchman stroked his horse's neck, quietening it further. 'Admission to the Abbey of St Michael for my master, Earl Thomas of Lancaster, and the Lords Ordainer . . .' He paused as Corbett slowly walked forward, coming up so close to Faucomburg's horse he could grasp its bridle and stare up into the envoy's harsh, wine-flushed features. Faucomburg leant down, forcing a smile. 'Hugh, Hugh,' he whispered, 'all I am doing is bringing you my master's message.'

'And you know, I know and he knows what's behind it. Which makes us all very knowledgeable. So, my reply is as follows. Inform Earl Thomas that the queen is *enceinte*. She does not wish for further excitement or disruption. She wants to immerse herself in the silence of this abbey and celebrate peacefully the great feast of Holy Week.' Corbett squinted up at Faucomburg. 'Take that message to your master and this. God forbid the queen's pregnancy be harmed, be it her or the child. If that happened, the world would not forget those responsible for such a dire event. Do you understand?'

Faucomburg nodded and gathered up his reins.

'And this is the queen's wish?'

'It is.'

'In which case, Sir Hugh, I bid you adieu.' Gesturing to the two heralds, Faucomburg turned his horse and rode away.

Corbett stood and watched them go.

'Master, what was that all about? I mean, I know the great earls would like to be close to the queen.'

'Yes, they do, Ranulf. That is the world of politics; power and who controls it. However, I have learnt something else. Faucomburg's arrival proves that Philip of France and his minion de Craon desperately wanted a great meeting, a coming-together of the French and English lords at Windsor. Once gathered, they could preside over and control both the young queen and the king's heir from one of this kingdom's most powerful fortresses. They failed. However, they are desperate. They are trying to do the same here at St Michael's Abbey but, again, they have failed, so the chessboard has to be rearranged.'

'And now?'

'And now, Ranulf, I am to act as Jesus Christ, and I wonder what de Craon will make of that.'

Megotta the moon girl was also thinking of de Craon as she sheltered in her covered cart surrounded by all the necessities of her trade. She had been pleased to return; the journey to and from Windsor was like a sleep plagued by nightmares. On her arrival there, she had been shown into the queen's presence. She had knelt on the cushions, delivered her message, answered her questions and had been favoured by the queen's smile, then gifted with a silver coin.

On dismissal Megotta had waited silently, trying to overcome the abuse she had suffered in that forest glade. The cruelty, the pain, the humiliation and the shame clung to her like a rash. Today she felt different, like a swimmer breaking free of the water. Megotta now raged at what had happened to her and she had made her decision. She would kill de Craon, the author, 'the *fons et origo*', as Corbett would say, of the hideous abuse heaped on her. Megotta was no stranger to violence. She had killed and killed again in self-defence. She had sat in the bleak hole of Newgate and faced the prospect of a hanging. She had carried out legitimate execution of those found guilty by Corbett. Megotta felt no guilt over such deaths and the same would be true of de Craon's. She knew from conversations with Ranulf that the French envoy hated Corbett with a passion beyond all telling. He was determined that Sir Hugh be removed. Well, if Corbett would not solve the problem, then she certainly would.

Megotta had spent the night plotting every step forward, reflecting on everything she had learnt about St Michael's Abbey, the plan of the buildings and what paths and corridors to take. She had opened her small wardrobe chest and taken out what she would need.

Megotta had devised a plan. She had noticed how the laundrywomen of the mummers' group could wander into the abbey precincts close to the main gate where the washtubs stood in a row of outhouses. The mummers' washerwomen would also do the monk's laundry, for which they were paid and blessed; the good brothers were grateful that such an onerous task was completed by others. In the main, these old crones, weighed down by heavy sacks, crawled like snails across the great abbey bailey towards the different doorways. Megotta now transformed herself into one of these. She adopted the guise of the Witch of Endor, a role she had played time and again in the miracle play *King Saul and David*. Garbed in dusty, feather-light clothing, a great straggling wig pulled tight over her head, her face transformed by a yellow cream, Megotta looked the part. She put on a false hooked nose, fastening it securely, then splattered her teeth with black spots. She looked at herself using a shiny piece of metal as a mirror. Satisfied, she climbed out of the covered cart then pulled out a bulging sack. She positioned this on her back and, at a half-crouch, staggered across Bloody Meadow and through the postern door of the abbey gateway. Brother Norbert, chief keeper and porter, was standing in the doorway to his narrow chamber. He hardly gave Megotta a second glance but simply turned to the ledger on the table beside him and recorded her name and state – 'Richolda; washerwoman' – and let her through.

Megotta slipped into a deserted washhouse, a bleak

damp chamber with massive tubs standing on stone plinths. She glanced around, the place was empty. She had deliberately chosen this time because the washer-women usually did not gather until after the Angelus bell. The moon girl hastily removed her disguise and donned the black robe of a Benedictine monk, wrapping the cincture cord around her slim waist. She then took the Welsh stabbing dirk from the sack and placed it carefully up the voluminous sleeve on her right arm, positioning it carefully in the sheath strapped to her wrist. Megotta glanced down at her sandalled feet and pulled over the deep cowl, which almost hid her face and head; the broad muffler across her mouth virtually completed her disguise. She took Ave beads from a pocket in her robe and sifted them through her fingers. 'Well, well, Brother John,' she whispered to herself, 'here you are in a living masque, a monk intent on murder.'

Satisfied that all was well, Megotta left the washhouse and crossed the bailey into the maze of narrow stone passageways. She had familiarised herself with the abbey precincts, especially the guest house and de Craon's large chamber on the ground floor. Thankfully, only a few brothers pattered about on this early-morning task or that. The horarium of the abbey was marked by the tolling of bells and Megotta knew that she had plenty of time before the monks were summoned from their chambers and cells to sing the divine praises in the abbey church. She went unchecked.

She reached the guest house and paused on the steps outside, peering around. She half expected a guard, at least some of de Craon's liveried retainers lounging about, but there were none. Megotta felt a cold prickle of fear. She sensed something was very wrong. Corbett had guards, Ap Ythel's archers, not to mention Ranulf and Chanson. De Craon knew he was a marked man. Corbett would not weep to see him go. De Craon had enemies both within and without, surely he would take special guard? Megotta leant against the wall, trying to control her breathing. She had seen de Craon swaggering about the abbey but he always had his dagger men to his left and right, hands constantly on the hilt of sword or dagger. Perhaps, she wondered, de Craon had left, going back to Windsor on his own secret business.

Megotta took a deep breath and entered the guest house. She stood outside de Craon's room and put her hand on the latch then abruptly paused, turning her head to listen more carefully. At first, she thought they were tricks to her hearing. However, the longer she listened the more certain she became of the loving noises coming from within, moans, groans and cries of pleasure. Two voices, both men. Megotta hastily withdrew. She left the guest house and stood in the yard outside, head bowed like any obedient monk reciting his Aves whilst threading prayer beads through his fingers. She pretended to be lost in meditation, immersed in matters spiritual. She moved slowly, positioning herself so she could watch the door to de Craon's chamber, and her patience was soon rewarded. The door opened. She heard de Craon shouting farewell, then Malpas, distinctly dishevelled, came out. He stood on the steps, wrapped his cloak about him then, head down, quickly left the guest house.

Megotta waited before slowly walking back through the abbey precincts. She reached the washhouse and, still immersed in her thoughts, was startled by footsteps outside. She immediately retreated behind one of the great water vats. A Blackrobe entered the room; he pulled back his hood and Megotta recognised Prior Felix. The monk seemed agitated. He returned to the doorway, looked out furtively before returning to the sack he had brought in, hurriedly emptying its contents into a vat of water. The prior then grasped the long wooden ladle and stirred the water-soaked robes. Eventually he stopped, peered into the vat and hurried out of the washhouse. Intrigued, Megotta listened to his fading footsteps then crossed to the vat. She seized the ladle and drew out two robes and two undershirts, the latter both heavily blood-stained. She also examined the black robes but the bloodstains were not evident due to the colour of the cloth. Nevertheless, Megotta noticed that both hoods were of the costliest wool and lined with expensive fur. Megotta laid the robes out on the floor. She had been correct in her guess. The two robes were of different sizes so each must belong to a particular individual and, given the costly texture as well as the fur trimmings, Megotta concluded that the robes probably belonged to the abbot and prior. She hastily thrust the robes back into the vat, completed her own preparations, then fled the washhouse.

Once she had returned to her covered cart, she again

changed and, using Corbett's seal, entered the abbey. She found the Keeper of the Secret Seal busy in his chamber. He welcomed her in, offered a quilted stool for her to sit, then served morning ale in leather-bound blackjacks. Megotta drank greedily as Corbett closely studied her.

'My friend,' he murmured, 'you seem agitated. Are you troubled?'

'No, no, Sir Hugh, let me explain.'

Megotta drained her blackjack then informed Corbett about all that had happened from the moment she had decided to kill de Craon to the business of the robes in the washhouse. Corbett heard her out, not wishing to break the flow of words as he could see Megotta was full of surprise at the sharp, twisted turn of events. Once she had finished, Corbett began pacing up and down the chamber.

'Sir Hugh, you do not seem as surprised as I am, I mean about de Craon.'

'That's because,' Corbett smiled at her, 'with all due respect, nothing surprises me about de Craon, nor any other human being on the face of God's earth. Though such wisdom,' Corbett hastily added, 'is simply the legacy of my many mistakes. Yes, Megotta, I cannot lie. I do know a little about de Craon's sexual proclivities, just crumbs of gossip, rumour. However,' he came to stand over Megotta and stared down at her, 'Megotta, promise me, and I mean solemnly promise me, that you will leave de Craon well alone. He is a true snake of a man; even in destroying him, you could do yourself a mortal injury. Promise me.' He held her gaze. 'Promise me or we are finished.'

Megotta held up her right hand. 'You have my solemn word, Sir Hugh.'

'Now,' Corbett declared briskly, wanting to divert her, 'as for those bloodstained robes you found.'

'I am sorry, Sir Hugh, but the information on de Craon, can't you use that?'

'Oh yes, I could, Megotta. Philip of France views himself as a saint amongst sinners. He is the most righteous ruler in Christendom. He is a princely prig; he is so full of himself he has no room for God. If he discovered what you have, de Craon would be torn to pieces on the scaffold at Montfaucon. So yes, the information about his relationship with Malpas is something I have watched and let grow, at least for a while. Now, as for the bloodstained undershirts, I believe flagellation is practised by both the prior and the abbot, and it does seem to me as if both monks have whipped each other. Some spiritual writers regard such a practice as an act of penance for sins of the flesh. Others argue that it is a fitting spiritual exercise, imitating and honouring the torture of Jesus before his crucifixion. Hence the well-established rite of creeping to the cross on every Friday in Lent. The person who performs this strips his back bare and crawls along the cold flagstones of a church, up the steps to the sanctuary towards the cross, which is placed prominently on the high altar. During this journey, he is flogged three times as an act of remembrance for Jesus's falls on his journey to Calvary.'

'But this?'

'I agree, Megotta, this is different. Like you, I strongly feel that. After all, as I have just said, flagellation is a spiritual exercise so why is Prior Felix being so secretive. Why does he bring the stained robes down to the wash-house? He has a legion of helpers. Why the haste? I don't know. All of this may well be connected to the mysteries which challenge us. Or, there again, it may have nothing to do with it at all. In the meantime, Megotta, remember what you promised about de Craon.' He stretched out his hand and clasped hers. 'All praise to you and thank you.'

Megotta left with Corbett's praise ringing in her ears.

PART FOUR

'For whatever happened to the king,
his party would surely perish.'

B ack in his chamber, the Keeper of the Secret Seal
sat in his chair staring at a triptych extolling the
life of famous Benedictines, though his mind was
elsewhere. Corbett truly believed he had broken through
those three circles but he needed to resolve certain
nagging questions. He recalled his conversation with
Megotta. He just prayed that the very capable but
hot-headed young woman kept her word. De Craon,
despite his many crimes, had to live, that was essential
in the great game being played out between England
and France. The Chambre Noire in the Louvre and the
Secret Chancery at Westminster both collected scandalous information about each other. Only a month
ago, Corbett had received interesting news from his spy
in de Craon's household that not all was well at the
Court of France. Philip had one daughter, Isabella, and
three sons, all married but apparently not happy.
Scurrilous stories were being whispered about how the

wives of Philip's three sons were glad eyed at the attention being shown them by leading squires of the Court. Now Corbett knew this was part of any Court. Isabella loved to be praised and had a hunger for compliments. However, the chatter coming from Paris claimed what was happening breached established etiquette. Corbett had promised himself to dig a little deeper here and see what effect this might have on England's relationship with the French Court.

At the same time, he despaired at the veritable torrent of scandalous chatter being stirred up about his own king's friendship with Gaveston. Some people claimed that the relationship was simply that of two brothers, like that of David and Jonathan in the Old Testament. 'How they had a pure love surpassing that of a man for a woman.' Corbett was not so convinced. Edward's Court could, at times, become a deep cesspit, leaving the king vulnerable to his enemies, in particular the leading bishops of the realm. In the meantime, however, all such matters would have to wait.

Corbett rose and walked to the door. He had not forgotten what Jean-Claude had said about de Craon's henchman, Gaston Foix, a skilled assassin entrusted with the sole task of killing Corbett. The Keeper of the Secret Seal turned the key in the lock, ensured the window shutters were secure and returned to his reflections. One minor matter Megotta had mentioned now intrigued him. Her description of how she entered the abbey as a washerwoman, her arrival being recorded in a ledger. 'This I must see,' Corbett murmured to himself. He pulled on his boots, strapped on his war belt, collected his cloak and left the chamber.

He asked the guard, one of Ap Ythel's archers, to summon Ranulf. Then he went downstairs into the small garden to wait for his henchman. Corbett, still thinking of the threat posed by Gaston Foix, kept in the shadows. He quickly noted what windows overlooked the garden and if they were well placed for any assassin to lurk there with war bow or arbalest. He was satisfied it was safe. All the windows were shuttered. Any sudden attempt to open them would be alarm enough. Eventually Ranulf joined him, breathlessly announcing how he had been entertaining the queen's ladies with stories of the horrors of Whitefriars.

'I am sure,' Corbett grinned, tapping his henchman on the side of his face, 'that they were well and truly entertained. So come.'

They walked out of the garden and across the great bailey, now very busy as the grooms brought sumpter ponies in and out of the stables. Carts and barrows full of feed trundled across. The ground underfoot had turned slippery, as dirty water swilled and shifted across a carpet of horse dung. The noise was deafening; the shouts of stablemen, the neighing of horses and the constant beating of the blacksmith's hammer drowned all conversation. At last, they reached the porter's lodge. Brother Norbert rose to greet them. Corbett asked to look at the ledger of visitors. The Blackrobe was only too willing to help. He laid out on his chancery table a leather-bound ledger, explaining how there was a page for each day. Corbett recalled the date of the fire and sat down on a stool while Ranulf took up guard just within the narrow lodge.

'Sir Hugh. I can help you, yes?'

'Of course. Tell me, what does your rule say about visitors?'

'Well, it's not so much the rule but the ordinances of each abbey—'

'Yes, I understand,' Corbett hastily intervened, not wanting to receive a lecture. 'So, any visitor here, be it prince or pauper, is carefully recorded?'

'Agreed, Sir Hugh. The entries are swift and precise.'

'And who are your most regular visitors?'

'Oh, the common people, the mummers, travelling chapmen, tinkers, pilgrims.' Brother Norbert waved a bony hand.

'And people from The Wodewose?'

'Oh yes, a fairly regular occurrence. We enjoyed good relations with mine host. Poor Crispin.'

'And on the day of the fire?'

'Sir Hugh, I am not too sure. You see, as I said, The Wodewose did business with us and they were fairly regular visitors. We sold them produce and now and again they were our guests here at the abbey.'

'But when they came here for business, who dealt with them?'

'Prior Felix, of course.'

'And on the day of the great fire at The Wodewose?'

Brother Norbert pulled a face and scratched his stubbled chin.

'Oh yes, that fateful day, I remember it well.' The porter turned over the yellowing leaves of the ledger. He reached one page and looked down. 'What in God's name!' he exclaimed. 'How's that?' He handed the ledger to Corbett. 'Look,' he exclaimed. Brother Norbert tapped the page and Corbett saw one of those entries just before the Angelus bell had been crudely scratched out.

'Why would someone do that?' he murmured, glancing up. 'Brother Norbert, who holds this ledger?'

'Sir Hugh, how many angels can dance on the point of a pin? The ledger is not some valuable document. As you can see, it consists of yellowing pieces of manuscript stitched together with stout lacing and kept between two covers of battered leather. It's definitely not valuable so I just leave it here on the chancery desk. However, I must admit that scratching out is curious. I cannot explain it.'

Corbett just nodded, leafing through the ledger. He could detect no further entries deleted. Yet there was something else which caught his attention. He was about to return to the ledger when the bell beside the postern gate outside began to clang noisily. Mumbling under his breath, Brother Norbert pushed by Ranulf and hurried to answer the raucous summons.

'Sir Hugh?' Ranulf turned. 'I think this visitor is for you.'

Corbett rose and went out to meet the new arrival. Brother Norbert, gesturing beside him, was all afluster.

'Sir Hugh, I don't know who he is, but he insists on speaking to you.'

'It's me, Corbett.' The muffled, hooded figure pulled back his cowl and lowered the muffler over his mouth.

'God be thanked,' Corbett exclaimed. 'It is good to see you, Kynaston.' He and the admiral clasped hands before Kynaston glanced over his shoulder at Brother Norbert.

'If you could open the gate, brother, my squire will take care of our horses.'

'He will, he will,' Corbett soothed. 'Brother Norbert is most competent.' He then bowed to the Benedictine and led Sir Miles across the bailey. They had to watch their step; the stables were now frenetically busy, the number of horses greatly increased due to the arrival of the queen. The noise was deafening and Corbett was glad to enter the abbey precincts, where he stopped and turned to his guest.

'Sir Miles, I do appreciate your coming here. I did not intend that. You could have sent a letter.'

'Ah, Hugh, for heaven's sake. These are important matters and it is good to see you. You are the king's justiciar south of the Trent. You have some authority over the London harbours and the movement of cogs.' The admiral scratched the dome of his balding head, his weather-beaten face creased in a smile which reflected the merriment in his light blue eyes. 'To cut to the quick, Sir Hugh, I thought it best if I came myself. The ride was short and sharp. The trackways and paths are sound and hard underfoot. Good travelling weather.'

'I do appreciate it,' Corbett replied. 'Come, we will talk in my chamber.'

Once there, Corbett made his visitor comfortable, wheeling a brazier closer whilst Ranulf left to bring goblets of steaming posset from the buttery. Kynaston shook off his heavy military cloak and revelled in what he called 'the warm comfort of the room'. At first, he and Corbett discussed friends in common as well as the health and welfare of their families. Kynaston eventually drained his goblet and placed it on the table.

'Sir Hugh, I can only imagine what you are involved in. Rumour and gossip like water seep through our lives. But enough of that.' The admiral rubbed his hands together. 'Let's turn to the business in hand. I studied your letter and the blunt answer to your question is yes. The harboumasters and port reeves have recently dealt with an infected ship. A Venetian galley, *The Ragusa* out of Sicily, intended to berth at Queenhithe but stayed midstream, dropped the anchor stone, reefed their sails and put up oars. My port reeve clambered into a bumboat and went out as far as he could, just within shouting distance. The master of *The Ragusa*, standing by the taffrail, declared there was infection aboard. The port reeve replied that *The Ragusa* could not berth: there was no remedy for it, the ship would have to turn and go back to sea.'

'Is that common practice?'

'Of course, Sir Hugh. Woe betide any ship's master who tries to deceive us. He would be arrested, imprisoned, even hanged. The ship would be seized, the crew left to fend for themselves. *The Ragusa* obeyed the port reeve's instructions and our harbourmaster ordered two of our men to watch the ship constantly to ensure our edict was enforced. It was, except for one occasion. The crew of *The Ragusa* soon realised she would not be allowed to berth. There seemed to be something wrong on board because they moved slowly but then with great haste. They intended to hoist sail and make for the open sea. Now, during those final preparations, a ship's boat was seen approaching the Venetian galley. A shadowy, cloaked figure went aboard, then, a short while later, clambered off and came back to the harbour. The port reeve's men made to intervene when the stranger abruptly rose and, keeping his balance, opened his cloak to display the royal tabard—'

'Filliol,' Corbett exclaimed. 'Squire Filliol going to collect the gift for his beloved.'

'Whoever it was,' Kynaston replied, 'a humble port reeve is not going to interfere with a royal official displaying the arms of the Crown and probably carrying a seal which allowed him to go wherever he wished whenever he wanted.' The admiral spread his hands. 'A short while later *The Ragusa* hauled up its ropes and made for the estuary, but it does not end there.' Kynaston sat back on his chair, shaking his head. 'At first I could not believe it, but there's rumour, and we shall not know the full truth for many a month, that *The Ragusa* went down. Some storm along the Narrow Seas. There is no real evidence, just stories about scraps of timber, cordage and rope which might have belonged to *The Ragusa*.'

'Surely a storm?'

'Possibly, it's the season. Anyway, on that I can say

no more. However, there is something else. Sir Hugh, I know about the Lords Ordainer, the presence of a powerful French embassy here, and our king's growing frustration with his barons. Consequently, I thought I should inform you that English cogs report a mustering of French war vessels around the ports of Honfleur and Calais.'

'Yes, yes,' Corbett replied. 'Something was being planned though I suspect it has now been brought to nothing. The French would love to fish in troubled waters and there is a great deal of nonsense being planned about a meeting at Windsor, but that will not happen. Is there anything else?'

'No.' Kynaston shook his head and got to his feet. Corbett did likewise. They clasped hands. The admiral collected his belongings and followed Ranulf down to the stables. Corbett stood listening to them chatter as they went along the gallery and down the stairs. Eyes half closed, he reflected on what Kynaston had told him. He was certain the truth was beginning to emerge and some of it was connected with what he had read in that visitors' ledger. Corbett put on his cloak and hastened down to the porter's lodge. Brother Norbert, half asleep in his chair, handed the ledger over with a sigh. Corbett ignored him and sat on a stool, going through the pages listing the visitors since Michaelmas last. He glanced up.

'Brother Norbert?'

'Sir Hugh?'

'This abbey is visited by a number of your brothers

from Benedictine houses in and around Paris. Why is this?'

The porter was now awake and Corbett could see the question had startled him.

'Why, Brother Norbert? Why are there so many visitors, Benedictines, from that part of France?'

'I don't really know,' Norbert stammered. 'I can't really say.'

'So, whom do they visit?'

'Why, Father Abbot. Why not ask him? He will tell you.'

Corbett put the ledger down. He closed the door and moved the stool so that he could stare squarely at the Benedictine.

'Brother Norbert, I am asking you. I have come to this abbey where mortal sin has been committed. One of your brothers, Mark, was brutally murdered in the Silver Shrine. The lustrous diamond, the Glory of Heaven stolen. So, when I ask questions to clear the murk and mystery, I expect an honest answer. Now tell me, why?'

'I, I can't. I don't want to.' Brother Norbert flailed a hand. 'Sir Hugh, I beg you. Let me think. Let me reflect, then I will come to you, I promise.'

Corbett nodded and got to his feet.

'I look forward to meeting with you, brother. Make it sooner rather than later. I do not want to have to return with my henchman to force it from you, but I will have the truth. *Pax et Bonum*, brother.' Corbett tapped the porter on his shoulder, opened the door and left.

Brother Norbert sat listening intently to the sounds outside. Corbett's acknowledgement of one of the brothers faded away. Horses neighed. Carts rattled across the cobbles. Norbert breathed in deeply, mopping his brow with a rag. He was truly fearful of Corbett. The king's man was well named: *Le Corbeau* – the crow. Corbett was persistent, pecking at a man's soul and the secrets it contained. Should he inform Abbot Maurice and Prior Felix? The latter was not so involved, but the abbot certainly was.

Norbert, like other monks, recognised the Templar Order was finished, ruined. To quote Holy Scripture, 'the Templars had built their house on sand and when the tempest came, what a fall, what a ruin'. The fortunes of the military order had been devastated by the fall of Acre, the last great Christian outpost in Outremer. Yet the conquest and defence of the Holy Land, the capture of Jerusalem, were the main reasons for the Templar's existence. They had retreated back into Europe to become what? Merchants? Bankers? The Order grew fat and lazy. The Templars were no longer God's warriors but merely shadows of what they had once been. Little wonder Philip of France had turned on them. And yet many Benedictines had a close affinity with the disgraced Order. The abbeys and monasteries of the Blackrobes housed many former Templars. St Michael's was no different. Lay brothers, priests, even ordinary servants, were former Templars. But, Norbert thought as he pushed the ledger away, what was he to do about the present problem? Corbett, like the hunter he was, had swooped on juicy scraps of information, seizing items which should have been destroyed months, if not years, ago. Secrets could then be kept hidden well away. So, what was he supposed to do now? St Michael's was caught up in murder and theft. Poor Brother Mark killed on holy ground, and there had been other deaths too. Brother Norbert closed his eyes and willed himself to sleep, away from the scruples nagging at his soul, trying to remove the memory of Brother Mark's murder from his mind.

Megotta the moon girl was also intent on murder, or at least its prevention. She had given Corbett her solemn word that she would leave de Craon alone, but Gaston Foix was a different matter. She knew all about Jean-Claude's revelation. How Gaston Foix was a professional assassin entrusted with the task of killing Corbett. Megotta believed that if that were so, Gaston Foix would not give up. He would try to achieve what his master de Craon wanted. She had thought deep and hard and eventually decided to bring the would-be assassin under close watch. It was not so difficult. De Craon had a daily routine, and when he appeared, Foix and the remaining of the Sacred Six, along with that dark shadow Malpas, were never far behind. Megotta was truly puzzled by what she had observed and what she had reflected on. De Craon was easy to follow around the abbey and beyond, yet, for the life of her, Megotta could not understand his forbearance over the slaughter of some of the Sacred Six, royal clerks, members of his own private chamber. Surely any envoy, especially one like de Craon, would be incandescent with fury at such murderous attacks on envoys held to be sacred? Any other ambassador would make a complete nuisance of themselves. They would appeal to the king or the likes of Corbett for justice and reparation. They would, even if it was hypocrisy, mummery like that of a miracle play, be acting all aggrieved and stricken. De Craon had done nothing of the sort. Just as curious, Corbett, who was the king's justiciar, had made no attempt to investigate these murders. She had raised such concerns with Ranulf, who simply made a face and declared how their master kept his own counsel. Corbett himself, whilst breaking his fast in the buttery earlier that day, had heard her whispered questions. Once she had finished, he just shrugged and murmured something about the mills of God grinding very slowly.

Other mysteries nagged at Megotta. She had now fully recovered from that brutal assault on the road to Windsor but she was also deeply perplexed by who her saviour could be. He had not appeared at the time, nor since. No attempt to meet her, so how had all that happened? Who was it? Corbett? Ranulf? Had they despatched Ap Ythel or one of his bowmen? Again, when she tried to discuss the matter with Sir Hugh, he had given the grim reply that angels must hover close to her for he had no explanation to offer. Megotta, confused, returned to a much simpler problem: watching Gaston Foix.

On that particular day, long after she had met Corbett in the buttery, Megotta noticed Foix appear by himself

PAUL DOHERTY

and then, in the shadows of an abbey building, don a
black robe. He carefully disguised himself as a
Benedictine and began to walk the length of the curtain
wall of St Michael's. Megotta, recalling her own disguise
when hunting for de Craon, smiled at the irony of the
situation but then grimly concluded that Foix must also
be intent on murder, and his quarry must be Sir Hugh
Corbett, the one man Megotta truly loved. Her convic-
tion deepened, as she watched the Frenchman inspect
the curtain wall then pause near marshy ground where
the wall was not so firm and strong. Foix's circuit had
taken at least two hours. Megotta was convinced the
Frenchman must be preparing to strike.

'You're not trying to get out,' she whispered to herself.
'You are looking for a place to get in, but why? Why?'
Megotta kept to the deep shadow of the abbey wall as
she followed Foix to the edge of Bloody Meadow. She
watched the would-be assassin, still cloaked in the black
robe of a Benedictine monk, hurry across into the great
noisy throng milling about there. Once amongst the
carts and all the impedimenta of the mummers' camp,
Megotta found it easy to follow her prey. The assassin
walked swiftly. He reached a battered cart and knocked
on the wood until a man appeared, climbing over the
tailgate to meet his visitor. Megotta watched as both
men stood deep in conversation. She dare not move any
closer but decided to wait. At last Gaston Foix turned
and strode back across Bloody Meadow. The man he
had been talking to moved to squat before a campfire.
He was alone, fixing a makeshift grill over the flames

as he prepared for the evening meal. Megotta swiftly adjusted the small handheld arbalest she carried in the large pocket of her robe. The moon girl also checked the long stabbing dirk in its sheath deep in the voluminous sleeve of her gown. Satisfied that she was ready, Megotta strolled across and sat down beside the stranger.

He was so surprised he could only gape as Megotta carefully adjusted her cloak so, if necessary, she could seize the arbalest. She then drew out the dagger and placed it on the ground beside her. She smiled at the man.

'Who in the devil's name are you?' he stammered. He peered closer. 'I am sure I have seen you before.'

'Of course you have, but that is not important.' She picked up the dagger and thrust the blade into the hard ground between them. 'What is important, my friend, is that I have this dagger close by as well as a small arbalest already primed with a small but jagged barb: it would tear your face apart.'

'And I will just sit and wait for you to do that?' the man snarled, recovering from his surprise. 'Just like that, eh?' He snapped his fingers, even as his other hand dropped to the dagger in his belt.

'No,' Megotta warned. 'Please do not do that, and you might live. You might escape from here with your life, your health and any silver your patron Gaston Foix . . . Yes?' She saw the man's surprise. 'Yes, that's his name. He gave you good silver, didn't he? One piece, two? You and he are accomplices to murder. You have been plotting someone's death. You kill as easy as you do kindle this fire. You couldn't care. You have no soul. You can be bought and sold for less than thirty pieces.'

'Go to hell.' The man leant forward, his bewhiskered face twisted in anger, bloodshot eyes glaring, lips curled back on his yellowing rotten teeth.

'Hell can wait,' Megotta retorted. 'You must listen now and you may live. You are a former soldier. You served along the Scottish March or on the Narrow Seas. You have been hired to kill Sir Hugh Corbett, the king's Keeper of the Secret Seal, a royal justiciar in these parts. You are to return to the abbey under the cover of darkness and enter through a gap in the wall caused by the marshy ground nearby. Monsieur Foix has just visited you. Now,' Megotta edged closer, hand on the hilt of her dagger, 'I could spring to my feet.' She plucked the blade from the ground. 'Yes, I could brandish this and scream "Harrow! Harrow!" and raise the hue and cry. Lord Janus, master of the mummers, would come hurrying along with his henchmen. I am a member of his group. They would believe me. I would tell them what I know. I would accuse you of treason. For that is what you are guilty of: conspiring with a foreigner to murder the king's own justiciar. I would claim I overheard you and watched you pocket the silver your patron gave you.'

Megotta leant so close she could smell the man's foul breath, but she also glimpsed the fear in those bloodshot eyes, the wariness of an old fox frustrated in its hunt. 'Do you know what would happen then, my friend?

You would be summarily tried before the same Sir Hugh. True, you could lie, but I would bear witness against you. Do you know the punishment for treason? You would be half hanged, your body cut open from throat to crotch. They would pluck your innards out and toss them into a fire. Then they would cut off your head, your body quartered and tarred. Afterwards all the bloody remnants of yourself would be displayed above some town gate or out at a desolate, ghost-ridden crossroads where your damned soul could mingle with others of its kind.'

The man hawked and spat before turning back to face Megotta. She could tell he was convinced. He would talk.

'Of course,' she continued softly, 'I could let you go so that you vanish and we never, ever meet again. You could take whatever coin you have been given along with your battered cart and try your fortune elsewhere, far from this abbey meadow. So, my friend, let us roll the dice. Let's finish this game of hazard.'

The man glanced away. He closed his eyes, drew a deep breath and then looked back at Megotta.

'You'll keep your word, woman?'

'I do and I will.'

'I was hired to kill. I was to meet my *patron*,' he spat the word out, 'if that's what you call him. He told me where the place was – as you say, near some marshy ground which has damaged the curtain wall. I was to go there tonight, soon after dark.' He stared up at the fading sky. 'Once there I would be given a lantern, a black robe and a small purse of coins. I was to enter the abbey, but –' he paused and grinned – 'you had it wrong, woman.'

'What do you mean?'

'Not Corbett.' The man repressed a shiver. 'I am not stupid, I would not agree to kill a king's man, not him, he would be too well guarded.'

Megotta hid her surprise. 'Then who?'

'Why, mistress, a Frenchman, Philip Malpas.'

'No, never!'

'Yes, that's what my patron told me. I was to meet him close to the wall. Once ready, he would guide me to Malpas's chamber. He would entice him into a trap, then I must strike.'

Megotta stared at the man and sat shaking her head.

'Why?' she demanded.

'He never told me, mistress, and in truth I don't really care. I am a soldier. I have fought against the French both on land and at sea. I am a stealth man, an archer, despatched to crawl into the enemy camp at night and slit as many throats as I can, particularly their captains and other leaders. I have killed Frenchmen, so many I cannot count, one more doesn't concern me.'

'By daybreak tomorrow,' Megotta replied, 'be gone from here. And I mean be gone, disappear. We shall not talk again.'

Megotta rose to her feet and hurried through the camp back to her own cart. She took a sip of wine, made herself presentable and, using Corbett's seal, entered the abbey buildings and walked up to his chamber. She noticed how the stairwell and steps up were guarded by Ap Ythel's archers. Corbett answered her persistent knocking on the door, ushering her in and insisting she had a goblet of hot posset from the jug. Megotta gratefully accepted and sipped it, watching the clerk intently over the rim of her cup.

'You look tired, Sir Hugh.'

'Little wonder.' Corbett pointed to the parchment strewn across the chancery table. 'But never mind,' he murmured, 'soon we will deploy. The murk and the mystery are thinning fast. I await some further pieces of information, but . . .' He pulled up a stool close to hers. 'Megotta, the flame burns time as well as wax. What brings you here?'

Megotta told him all about Gaston Foix, what she had seen and heard, what the Frenchman was plotting.

Corbett heard her out and whistled beneath his breath.

'When I talked about de Craon, Megotta, I also meant his entourage. Gaston Foix in particular. But,' he leant over and squeezed her hand, 'you have done very well, Megotta, very well indeed.'

'And?'

'I will not be drawn. Let our enemies destroy each other.'

Corbett glanced longingly back at the table. From where she sat, Megotta could see that they apparently carried the one theme. The same message: circles within circles with scribbled notes around them.

'Sir Hugh, you do not seem concerned.'

'Megotta, why should I be? As I have said, if de Craon's coven wish to kill each other, what can I do? What do I want to do? Nothing but leave them to their own twisted devices. Yet I do thank you.' He pointed a warning finger at her. 'Stay away from de Craon and his entourage. So far, you have been fortunate, but do not roll the dice again. De Craon has marked you down, Megotta. Keep in the shadows. Keep close to me. You have done enough.'

Megotta left the chamber as mystified as she had entered it. She went down and stood in the small garden, lost in her own thoughts. She glanced up.

'The hour of the bat,' she murmured. Dusk was gathering, soon it would be nightfall. She recalled that long stretch of curtain wall and made her decision. She had to see this matter through, but first she had to prepare. She hastened to the buttery for something to eat and drink, keeping a sharp eye on the window, watching it darken. She begged the kitchener for a hand warmer, a metal casket with fragments of sparkling charcoal, as well as a small wine skin and a linen napkin containing strips of bread and meat. She went outside, sat in an alcove to eat and drink before leaving the abbey precincts, slipping through the dark to that particular stretch of curtain wall. The night was clear, the moon heavy and full of light. She took up position in the shadow of a buttress. Even from where she stood hooded and muffled, clasping the hand warmer, Megotta could clearly see that damaged stretch of the abbey wall with the wetlands or marsh close by.

'A good night for the hunter,' she said softly. 'But will my quarry appear?' She glanced up at the Easter moon hanging like a lamp in the sky. The abbey had settled down for the night. The psalms and hymns of compline and the gentle chimes of prayer bells now stilled. Blackrobes moved about, flitting like ghosts, the patter of their sandalled feet fading to silence. Megotta moved to ease the cramp in her legs then she started, gasping in surprise. A figure had suddenly emerged from the darkness, darting across the open space stretching down to the wall. He carried a shuttered lantern. When he reached the gap, the shutter was quickly lifted up and down repeatedly. The figure waited. Another shadow appeared in the gap. Both shadows met before moving a little away. Megotta could not see exactly what was happening, but she almost cried out when one of the shadows abruptly keeled over. She was sure she had heard the sharp carrying clash of weaponry followed by a short groan of agony. Megotta watched fascinated as the killer moved swiftly, dragging the body of his quarry through the gap in the wall. He paused halfway and Megotta realised he was picking up stones to place under the clothing of his victim. He then pulled the body completely through the gap. Megotta heard splashing and realised the assassin was burying his victim in the deep marshy waters beyond the wall.

She crouched and waited. She wondered who the assailant was and who his victim might be? She tried to catch a glimpse of the assassin but she had little chance. The killer suddenly reappeared in the gap in the wall then raced, swift as a shadow under the sun, across the open ground and into the abbey buildings.

'In sweet heaven's name,' Megotta whispered, 'what gives here? Where, as Sir Hugh would ask, is the logic behind all of this?'

Megotta was no longer certain about anything. She decided it would be best if she kept her counsel at what she had just witnessed. A man had been murdered and only tomorrow might reveal who it could be. But, even then, it would be best to hold her tongue. Megotta felt a spurt of icy fear – what if the murder victim was Sir Hugh? After all, she had told him what she had learnt earlier in the day. Indeed, only four people knew about Gaston Foix's intent: the Frenchman himself, the hired assassin, Corbett, 'And me!' she whispered. Or was there someone else? Had Corbett informed Ranulf? Had Sir Hugh's henchman decided to take the law into his own hands? Megotta fought to control her turbulent fears, to quieten the curdling in her belly and the fear in her heart. She must wait. She must remain patient and prudent. Tomorrow would shed light on those deeds carried out in the dark.

Ranulf-atte-Newgate, Principal Clerk in the Chancery of the Green Wax, was also busy as darkness descended like a shroud over St Michael's. Ranulf ruefully conceded to himself that he felt he was travelling a road both strange and threatening. St Michael's sprawled, a maze of dark stone, with towers and roofs soaring up against the sky, a brooding mass which seemed to cast a lasting shadow over him, whilst beyond the abbey stretched that sea of greenery, close-clustered trees which bent and rustled under the early spring breezes. Ranulf wished they were gone, though he was also alert to the very real danger confronting his master. The abbey housed assassins and Corbett's presence, both within and without, was regarded as a real threat to these malignants. Corbett was now closing fast with the mysteries which had entangled their lives. Soon, Old Master Longface would challenge the sons of Cain. Ranulf's duty was to protect Sir Hugh both now and in the coming confrontation. So far, he had succeeded. Corbett's chamber and the approaches to it were strictly guarded by Ap Ythel and, when Sir Hugh left his chamber, those same bowmen shadowed him, a cohort of zealous guardian angels. Nevertheless, murder still lurked, like the demon it was, not so much in the shadowy corners of this abbey, but deep in the darkness of the human soul. True, they had allies. Ranulf knew that Megotta was busy on her own affairs, so he had left her well alone. She was a law unto herself and, as Corbett often said, she tilled her own furrow. Instead, Ranulf had decided to help clear a way forward.

Corbett tended to dismiss the anchorite but Ranulf disagreed. The recluse had, in some strange way, been connected with the mysteries that challenged them, even the fire at The Wodewose. After all, the anchorite had glimpsed the demon stalking through God's Acre heading in the direction of that ill-fated tavern. If the dreadful apparition had nothing to do with the fire, what other explanation could there be? Moreover, both the appearance of that demon and the consequent destruction of The Wodewose had occurred sometime before the theft of the gem, although there seemed to be no link between the two crimes except, once again, for the anchorite. He had seen the apparition on the day of the fire. He had also been in the abbey church when Brother Mark was murdered and the diamond stolen. There were other connections, tenuous though they may be. The anchorite had been a Templar, a member of the Order which once owned the diamond. The recluse had also been in the great Templar retreat from Acre when the diamond was entrusted to his care and later handed over by him to the Temple in Paris. Finally, because the Glory of Heaven had been housed in St Michael's, the anchorite had petitioned the abbot to be anchorite here.

'Oh yes,' Ranulf whispered into the darkness, 'the anchorite has a great deal to answer for. And I believe, despite the late hour, answer he shall.' Ranulf left his chamber and quietly visited Corbett's. He did not disturb his master but simply ensured that Ap Ythel and his guards were alert and vigilant. They were. Satisfied, Ranulf hurried down across the great cloisters only to abruptly pause when he glimpsed de Craon and Malpas close together, questioning one of the brothers. Ranulf stayed in the shadows until both men strode away, the French envoy gesticulating angrily to his henchman. Once they had gone, Ranulf approached the Benedictine. The monk turned and Ranulf recognised the lean, hollow-eyed chief porter, Brother Norbert. The Blackrobe peered closely at Ranulf.

'You're Corbett's man, aren't you?'

'Yes, brother. I just wanted to ask what was worrying our French friends.'

'French, yes; friends, no, Master Ranulf. But, nothing much. They are looking for a colleague, Gaston Foix. Have you seen him?'

'No,' Ranulf replied. 'Nor do I want to. Good night, brother.'

Ranulf walked on, entering the abbey church by the corpse door. The nave was icy cold and grim as if the very stones were part of the bleak preparation for the litany of Holy Week. Abbot Maurice and Prior Felix were there with some of the other brothers setting out twelve high stools in preparation for the mandatum during the mass of the Last Supper on Maundy Thursday. They were working as swiftly as they could for the cold was biting and their breath hung like mist in the air. Ranulf raised his hand in salutation and Abbot Maurice replied, sketching a blessing. Ranulf crossed himself and walked further down the nave to the ankerhold. He rapped hard on the narrow wooden door. Inside, the anchorite loudly moaned about both the hour and the cold, yet the door creaked open. The bleary-eyed anchorite, wrapped in a thick horse blanket, waved Ranulf in. He gestured at a stool then pulled another one up close to it. He offered some ale but Ranulf shook his head as he stared around. The anker-hold was a truly bleak chamber containing only the bare necessities: a cot bed, battered stools, a scruffy table, a broken chest, lanterns and lavarium. Crucifixes, black and bleak, adorned the white plastered walls. The floor was of hard stone, the cold fended off by small braziers and pots of fire laced with herbs to perfume the air.

'You are curious, Ranulf-atte-Newgate.'

'Yes, I am. Very curious about the evening you glimpsed the devil stalking across God's Acre.'

'What about it? I have already spoken to Sir Hugh on that matter.'

'No, no, listen.' Ranulf opened his purse and took out a silver piece. He held this up so it glistened in the dim light of the two lanterns the anchorite had lit. Ranulf saw the greed start in the anchorite's eyes.

'What do you want?'

'At this moment in time, I want you to reflect on what you can buy with this silver piece. Some delicacy, or even better.' He pointed to the small wine skin hanging on a nail driven into the wall. 'Some fine Bordeaux. You are partial to red wine, are you not? Truly delicious, the full, mouth-cloying richness of the finest from Gascony.'

'What do you want?' the anchorite repeated.

'Very little indeed, my friend. But listen.' Ranulf, still clutching the silver piece, leant forward. 'I want to talk about the devil appearing in God's Acre, but let's leave that for a while. You remember the fall of Acre, yes? You were there. You saw the blood swilling ankle deep. The flames scorching the sky. The roar of the kettledrums and the war cries of the attackers. You do remember the fall, don't you?' Ranulf was both surprised and intrigued by the recluse's swift change of expression.

'I'll not talk about that.' The anchorite's voice was so thick Ranulf suspected he had already drunk deep from the wine skin. 'I'll not speak about that,' the anchorite said again. '*Sanctum secretum* – a sacred secret.'

'What is?'

The recluse blinked, quickly reasserting himself and chewing the corner of his dried lips as if he had realised that he had stumbled into something he shouldn't have.

'Ah well, ah well,' he mumbled. 'Nothing. What is it you want?' The anchorite crossed his arms. 'I won't talk about that,' he said slowly. 'But the demon, yes.'

'Very well. If I ask you just to imagine the fall of Acre and your part in it, you could do so, yes?'

'Yes.'

'And you would recall every detail?'

'I think so. That day is seared on my soul.'

'Then do the same for that evening when you glimpsed the devil. Recall what you actually saw – do so and this coin is yours.'

The anchorite closed his eyes, rocking himself backwards and forwards on the stool. He murmured a few words, chatting to himself in the lingua franca of the Middle Sea. Eventually he opened his eyes and grinned at Ranulf.

'Well?' the clerk demanded.

'It was dark. Tendrils of mist were already crawling

over the gravestones and crosses. Not a full moon, but no rain. The beginning of a frost. I glimpsed a dark figure because of the fire the gardener had left. The demon was fantastical. He had something like a horn jutting out from his face.'

'And what else?'

'Ah yes, he had what looked like a chancery satchel across his shoulder. Yes, yes, he did so,' the anchorite declared, all excited.

'And what would the devil need with a chancery satchel?'

'Why not ask him? Perhaps the devil is a clerk?'

Ranulf grinned at the sly insult.

'You are doing very well, my friend. What else can you remember?'

'He had a thick cloak, boots, oh yes, and what looked like gauntlets on his hands.'

'Gauntlets?'

'Yes, Master Ranulf, gauntlets. Thick leather ones such as a master mason would wear when he inspects some wall or building. I remember that because he held a hand up against the light from the fire.' The anchorite opened his eyes. 'That's all I can remember. It was only a brief moment.'

Ranulf sat listening to the sounds echoing from further down the nave.

'And what is the *sanctum secretum*?'

'I cannot say. I will not say,' the anchorite snapped. 'Sir, you must believe me. A slip of the tongue, I can tell you no more.'

'On that, yes. But what about the evening the Glory of Heaven was taken?'

'I was fast asleep.'

'Don't lie,' Ranulf countered. 'Don't you think it strange how, on that fateful occasion, you were so fast asleep you saw or heard nothing untoward?'

'What do you mean?'

'You drank wine earlier that day?'

'Yes, I did.'

'And did it ever occur to you that your wine must have contained some sleeping potion to dull the senses and sink you into a deep slumber? After all, Brother Mark must have groaned at being stabbed. There must have been footsteps, even voices.' Ranulf watched the anchorite carefully. He knew he had struck home. 'Do you know, my friend,' Ranulf continued, 'some people might even begin to wonder if you do know something about that sacrilegious, murderous occurrence. However, you choose not to speak and, of course, the next question would be why?'

'Don't frighten me, clerk. I may be an anchorite now, but once I was a fighting knight, skilled in combat, strong enough to bring an enemy down.'

'In which case, isn't it strange that on that particular occasion you seemed to lack all the qualities of a warrior and all the vices of a toper.'

'I like my wine, I drank deep that day, but I put no potion in, I swear.'

'Who brought you the wine?'

'Brother Aidan, the kitchener.'

'You are sure?'

'Of course I am.'

'In which case, who controls the jars and philtres of sleeping powders here at St Michael's? Come, come, you have been a member of this community, albeit a distant one, for a number of years. You must have needed physic, this potion or that potion. Who would dispense that?'

'Why, Prior Felix. He is also the infirmarian. He would be responsible for such powders. And of course, Abbot Maurice must have keys to the cabinets.' The anchorite rubbed his face. 'That's all I can tell you, Master Ranulf. I am in a holy place even though it's one violated by hideous sin. I swear by all that is sacred, I know nothing. I had nothing to do with Brother Mark's murder or the theft of the diamond.'

Ranulf realised he could learn little more from the anchorite though he was intrigued by what he had garnered during his visit. He thrust the silver coin into the man's callused hand and quietly left the abbey church. He went straight to Corbett's chamber where he informed his master of everything he had learnt. Corbett slouched in his chancery chair and nodded.

'Soon,' he declared. 'Very soon, Ranulf, we will close with our enemy.'

'Sir Hugh?'

Corbett glanced up. 'We are ready, Ranulf. However, be vigilant. You and I and all whom we hold dear and protect in this abbey face great threat. I need one final piece of information. You have referred to it in your discussions with the anchorite and I greatly value what you have told me about your visit. It confirms my suspicions. As for the *sanctum secretum*? I suspect that is a key which unlocks one of my circles. I pray to God we find it soon.'

Corbett's prayer was answered a few days later, on Spy Wednesday in Holy Week, the day the Church recalls Judas arranging to betray Christ. How he offered the Pharisees his services as a spy against the Saviour. Corbett opened his psalter and read the verses for that day. He then washed and shaved before going down to the abbey church. For a while, he just knelt and prayed. He begged for help and wisdom. He commended to God the Lady Maeve and all whom he loved. He then finished with a plea that on the morrow, Maundy Thursday, he would bring these murderous mysteries into God's own light and that of the king. Corbett knew that Maundy Thursday was the fatal day and the mass being prepared for that evening was when the danger would fully emerge. He blessed himself and returned to his chamber, pleased to find Brother Norbert waiting in the shadowy alcove outside.

'God bless you, Sir Hugh,' Brother Norbert declared. 'Your guard let me through. I believe you have been waiting for me. I need to speak to you, and the sooner the better.'

'And for that, brother, I thank you and I assure you I will be your most attentive listener.' Corbett ushered the monk into his chamber, showing him to the most comfortable chair. He also offered morning ale, which was politely refused. Corbett took off his cloak and sat down on a stool close to the Benedictine.

'And so?' Corbett demanded.

'And so, Sir Hugh, let us deal with the business in hand. I am a Benedictine. I was, like so many of my brothers, not a Templar, but a hospitaller serjeant-at-arms. I was with the cross-bearers in Acre when that fortress fell and the darkness descended. I met Abbot Maurice there, known then by his baptismal name Thomas Brienne. He had an identical twin brother, also called Thomas but with the title Didymus which, as you may know, is the Greek word for twin. Now the fall of Acre was truly dire. Hell on earth. The end of a dream, the beginning of a nightmare. The chroniclers and the poets depict it as a glorious epic like the great battle at Roncesvalles with those magnificent knights, Roland and Oliver.' Brother Norbert snorted with laughter. 'Nothing of the sort! Men were desperate, thirsty, hungry, wounded and terrified of the Mamelukes who showed no mercy. Acre was ablaze, its poor inhabitants driven like sheep to the slaughter. Oh, we fought but with one eye on the enemy and the other on the swiftest path to the quayside. In the panic and the chaos, horrific mistakes were made . . .'

'Such as?'

'Oh, gates and posterns were left unguarded so the enemy poured in like a swollen river. Thomas, our present abbot, was only an acolyte, a novice in the Templar Order. Thomas Didymus, his twin brother, was a fully fledged knight. To be brief and blunt, during the last hours of our retreat down to the quayside, the brothers quarrelled violently over an unguarded postern leading to Acre's greatest and tallest tower, our last defence. The quarrel was most violent; weapons were drawn, blade against blade, awful curses exchanged.'

'And who was the innocent?'

'Sir Hugh, none of us were innocent! Why do you think I am here, a Benedictine monk, praying, fasting, working? I am trying to live a life of atonement. We failed the Cross at Acre. We failed our Church, we failed each other and we failed our God. Nobody was innocent. We are all as guilty as sin.'

'You are too harsh on yourself.'

'Perhaps that will save us from the harshness of God, Sir Hugh. Read the chronicles. Discover what truly happened after we abandoned Acre. God help you if you were a woman or child.' Brother Norbert sighed. 'Anyway, Acre fell, we retreated, our anchorite carried the Glory of Heaven. Even then the two brothers were still quarrelling. We reached the galleys and made our return to France. However, before we separated, all the survivors of the Acre garrison gathered in a ruined church on the road from Paris to Provins. Overcome by guilt, we swore a great oath on the sacrament never to reveal what truly happened at Acre. This is our *sanctum secretum* – our holy secret. Even then, we were liars. It is not really holy and it's not truly a secret. It's just that the truth has been cleverly hidden beneath layers of romantic stories and heroic ballads. Anyway, Thomas left to enter the Benedictines. Thomas Didymus continued with the Templars, achieving a prominent position in the Order's main house in Paris.'

'And then King Philip struck?'

'Yes, he did. Many Templars fled to lose themselves in this wilderness or that. A few changed their names and sank into obscurity. Others were housed with other religious orders, the Blackrobes in particular.'

'And Thomas Didymus?'

'He appealed for help to his brother, Abbot Maurice. At first, his brother refused to help and then Thomas Didymus disappeared. Now at the beginning of the suppression of the Templars, everyone thought Philip would act with great dignity and justice.' He paused as Corbett laughed sharply. 'Precisely, Sir Hugh. Stories began to seep through of the most hideous torture and hellish abuse.'

'Those stories are all true,' Corbett interjected. 'We know that.'

Brother Norbert wagged a bony finger. 'Don't become so righteous, Sir Hugh. Matters did not go so well in England. Local lords turned on the Templars in their particular shire. Houses were plundered, stock taken, crops seized, treasures pillaged. You know that.'

'We tried to stop it, but our young king had other things on his mind: marriage to Isabella, and of course his love for Peter Gaveston.'

'Whatever,' Norbert retorted. 'The Templars in this country were abused but,' he spread his hands, 'I concede nothing compared to what happened in France. We heard stories about Templar prisoners being hung over slow fires so the flesh on their feet fell away. Others were stripped and thrust into the icy waters of the Seine, nothing about them but a coarse rope so they could be hauled in and the questioning continued. Philip of course was after treasure.'

'And the Glory of Heaven in particular.'

'Oh yes! You know the history of that diamond, Sir Hugh. Philip regards it as his own personal property. From what I gather, and I am sure you have learnt the same, Philip was furious when he discovered that the Glory of Heaven had been handed over to the English Crown to be enshrined here at St Michael's. My perception of the situation –' Brother Norbert pulled a face – 'and it's only conjecture, but I suspect Thomas Didymus was responsible for getting the Glory of Heaven out of Paris and safely to London. Now, as the months passed, the news about the treatment of the Templars became more and more dire. Stories of real horrors being heaped on men who'd once defended Christendom. Abbot Maurice broke down, overcome with guilt at his treatment of his own blood brother! Stricken to the heart, he was! He despatched messages to all the Benedictine houses in and around Paris, desperate for any information about his brother. The Blackrobes, fearful of King Philip, did what they could, sending what information they had.'

'Which was?'

'That Thomas Didymus had been taken by Philip's henchmen, that he was imprisoned in a secret cell in the Chambre Noire at the very heart of the Louvre

Palace. Of course, such news made matters worse. Thomas Didymus had become entangled deep within Philip's web. I know all this because our Father Abbot took me into his confidence. Indeed, he had no choice. He needed to explain why this abbey despatched so many messengers to France and received so many in return.'

'Is Thomas Didymus still alive?'

'Perhaps.' Norbert scratched his balding head. 'I know Abbot Maurice whips himself in reparation for neglecting his brother. Both he and Prior Felix strongly advocate flagellation as a means to subdue the flesh and make reparation for sins committed.' Brother Norbert laughed harshly. 'I am not too sure. We all have to walk different paths, Sir Hugh. Abbot Maurice walks his and I have to walk mine. I must confess the truth before God. I am deeply perturbed. Brother Mark was foully slain, the Glory of Heaven stolen.' He shook his head. 'Something is very, very wrong with our abbey. I am not too sure what, I cannot say who is responsible. All I do know is that the ghosts of the past, the ghosts of Acre and else-where, have caught up with us. I won't . . .' he stammered. 'I cannot say any more. I will not point the finger of accusation; that is for you, Sir Hugh, and I leave you to do it.' Brother Norbert made his farewells and left.

Corbett sat for a while collecting his thoughts. 'It's time,' he whispered, 'yes, it's time.' He rose, went to the door and summoned Ap Ythel.

'I want you, my friend, to collect Ranulf and Megotta and return with them here as soon as possible.'

Once what Corbett called his 'secret council' had gathered, he described what would happen on the morrow. All three sat in astonished silence.

'You think this is the way, Sir Hugh?'

'You've heard what I said, Ranulf. It's the only way. We cannot have a confrontation with the young queen, heavy with child, sitting only a few paces away. Nor do I want de Craon interfering. Ap Ythel, once we leave for the church, I want you to bring four archers with you, but the rest are to guard de Craon's chamber and that of his henchmen. The French must not be allowed to leave.'

'They'll object. They will claim they are envoys, that they are sacred.'

'Oh yes, of course they will. De Craon can lie with the best of them.' Corbett's face creased into a grin. 'But tell them that we are confining them to their quarters because they are sacred envoys surrounded by privilege and every right under the sun. Indeed, they are so sacred, we want to keep them safe. They will object, they will ask what is happening. You will reply that it is a secret, but that Sir Hugh Corbett's only concern is their safety and well-being. You will ask them if they want something to eat or drink. They will refuse, of course. They will demand to know when what they call this nonsense, will finish. You will tell them that in time the truth will manifest itself. For the rest, you've now caught the drift of what I said. Just keep that fox and his henchmen safely caged until we are finished. When this happens tomorrow, Ap Ythel, prepare your archers; Megotta, you will stand close to me. Ranulf, I want you to scrutinise the length and the breadth of that abbey church, just in case.'

'And when does this begin?'

'Tomorrow.'

'At what hour?'

'Three hours after noon, as the abbey prepares for the mass of the Last Supper. So,' Corbett rubbed his hands together, 'I have told you what I can and what I plot. Have a good night's sleep and pray that God assists us.'

Corbett rose very early that Maundy Thursday. He dressed carefully, once again donning his light chain mail jerkin under his shirt and sleeveless cotardie. Corbett felt the chain mail was his best protection, light but impenetrable, the creation of skilled artisans in Milan. He pulled on thick woollen hose and riding boots without the spurs. He then strapped on his war belt. For a while he knelt on the prie-dieu before the crucifix. He crossed himself, closed his eyes and murmured a prayer for divine help.

Ranulf arrived and both clerks went down for the dawn service in the abbey church. Afterwards they broke their fast in the buttery before making their way to the quarters of the young queen. Isabella, attired in dark blue velvet, was already preparing herself for the evening service. The queen's chambers were noisy with squires, retainers and household officials bustling about. Corbett and Ranulf were shown into the queen's presence and bent the knee. The Keeper of the Secret Seal then pleaded for a personal meeting in the queen's private chamber. Isabella agreed. Corbett whispered to Ranulf to stand guard outside. Once he was alone with Isabella, Corbett genuflected before taking the offered chair facing her.

'Sir Hugh.' Isabella leant forward, one hand on her swollen belly, the other pointing at Corbett. 'You said we would be safe here. You are here to warn us, are you not? Something is wrong, I can sense it.'

'Yes, your Grace, something is wrong. But I cannot tell you for the moment. However, I do assure you that you are safer here than at Windsor, where there was a plot to assassinate your husband.'

'Never!'

'Your Grace, that is the truth. Believe me, so I swear by the Holy Rood, that you are much safer here. However, dangers still confront us. Now the mass of the Last Supper is to be celebrated early this evening. You and yours must not attend. The danger we face has not yet emerged, but it will, and we must be ready.'

'But, Sir Hugh—'

'Your Grace, I will reveal all later. Please, please,' Corbett clasped his hands together as if in prayer, 'when the bells ring out the summons for the mass, you and yours must not leave for the abbey church. You must confine yourself to your chambers, lock yourselves in and order your squires to be armed and harnessed for war. Once your doors are securely shut, do not open them unless I or my henchman Ranulf demand it. I shall, as I promised you, in God's good time, tell you all. In the meantime, I shall have food and drink brought discreetly to your chamber. Your Grace, you must trust me.'

'I do.'

'Very well.'

'Sir Hugh, you are confident? Is help on its way?'

'Oh yes, your Grace.' Corbett smiled. 'Put your trust in myself, Ap Ythel and, God willing, the Constable of Wallingford Castle.'

The queen moved to ease her discomfort, gesturing with her hand that Corbett remain seated.

'Sir Hugh, there is one further problem. You have told me to lock myself in and not to open the door to anyone except for you or your henchman.' The queen drew a deep breath. 'But matters are complicated.'

'How so, your Grace?'

'One of my ladies, Beatrice Saveraux – you met her?'

'Yes, she is, or rather she was, the beloved of Squire Filliol, the royal courier who was killed with the others at The Wodewose.'

'Sir Hugh, Lady Beatrice is still distraught. She mourns poor Stephen and she feels confined here. She has taken to going for long walks in the abbey grounds; it is safe enough for her, yes?'

'For her, yes, your Grace. I would say it was safe enough. So, what has happened?'

'Well, she's been gone for at least three hours and I am growing concerned. I worry where she is.'

'Your Grace, I shall order a search. However, Lady Beatrice's disappearance must not prevent you from doing what I ask. You will remember what I have said and act swiftly on it?'

The queen assured him she would.

Corbett genuflected and left. He asked Ranulf, walking quietly beside him, to check on Chanson, then he returned to his own chamber where he asked Ap Ythel to organise a search for the Lady Beatrice. The Captain of Archers said he would. He also assured Corbett that the courier he had sent to the Constable of Wallingford, despatched the evening before, would have delivered Corbett's message and be on his way back by now.

Once Ap Ythel left, Corbett busied himself with drafting what he called 'the final indictment', which should shatter two of the circles. The third one, he reasoned, would have to wait for the other two to be resolved. Ap Ythel returned to report that he could find no trace of the Lady Beatrice and that perhaps she had left the abbey precincts? The Captain of Archers added how the French were also looking for someone, one of the Sacred Six, Gaston Foix, who had apparently disappeared without trace.

'Leave the dead to bury their dead,' Corbett enigmatically replied. 'Keep searching for the Lady Beatrice, do what you can and remember to bring four of your best archers to meet me here at three o'clock in the garden below. The others will join us there.'

Corbett then rested, lying down on the bed, eyes half closed as he went through once again what he had prepared. Ranulf eventually roused him with a knock on the door. It was time!

Corbett hastily put on again the jerkin of chain mail. Once he had finished dressing, he strapped on his war belt, collected his cloak and went down into the small garden where Ranulf, Ap Ythel, Megotta and four bowmen waited for him. Corbett had a quick word with them, insisting that, however strange they might appear, they should carry out his orders even, as he wryly added, in the teeth of opposition from Holy Mother Church. Once satisfied they understood what was to happen, Corbett led his group through the maze of stone galleries and passageways to the abbey church. They entered through the Devil's Door. Corbett was relieved to discover that the nave, choir and sanctuary were busy as the good brothers bustled about preparing for the mass of the Last Supper in all its gorgeous liturgy. Corbett and his comitatus were largely ignored, regarded simply as lay people wanting to crowd into the nave in readiness for the mass later that day. Corbett, however, led his group into a chantry chapel just to the left of the main sanctuary, next to the resplendent Lady Chapel, although most of that now lay hidden between the purple and gold-edged Lenten drapery. Corbett waited for a while. He and his coven just stood listening to the sounds from the nave. Corbett then turned to Ranulf.

'Chanson is in the stables, yes?'

'Of course, Sir Hugh, where else? I have impressed upon him the need to keep a sharp eye on any stranger, be it on foot or on horse, who might unexpectedly arrive.'

'That's good.' Corbett drew a deep breath. 'Go to the sacristy, those we are hunting should now be assembled there. Yes, they must be. If they are, come back to me, it will not take long; a swift glance will suffice.'

Ranulf slipped out of the chantry chapel. He returned a short while later, grim faced, nodding at Corbett. 'You are correct, Sir Hugh. The men chosen to be the twelve apostles are assembled. Abbot Maurice has apparently ordered them to stay there until they are needed.'

'Are they harnessed for war?'

'Difficult to say,' Ranulf replied. 'But they are well cloaked and hooded.'

'Anything out of the ordinary?'

'Three of them are sitting on the floor with their backs to a rather grubby wicker basket. One of those strong, sturdy creations often used to carry weapons.'

'Thank you, Ranulf. Come.' Corbett raised his voice. 'Let us do the king's business.'

They left the chantry chapel, walking quickly up the steps and through the yawning entrance of the rood screen, its two doors pulled fully open. They continued on through the choir and into the sanctuary proper. The sacristy stood to the left of this. Corbett opened the doors and led his party in. The room was well lit with candles and lanterns and it smelt sweetly from the wax and incense stored there. Simon the Sacristan sat nervously on a high stool just within the door. Across the cavernous room along the far wall lounged a number of men. Corbett did a quick count; twelve in all. They looked indistinguishable with their shaggy hair and thick, unkempt moustaches and beards. Nevertheless, Corbett sensed who they were. Garbed in long heavy cloaks, they looked and moved like soldiers, alert, quick to action. They clambered to their feet as Corbett, flanked either side by two archers, war bows notched, walked towards them. He rapped out an order and the war bows swung up. Corbett then paused, as did the archers. The clerk threw back his cloak to display his war sword, and Ranulf and Megotta did likewise.

'What is this?' One of the men, tall with iron-grey hair and a red-purple scar that deeply furrowed his brow, walked forward. He kept his cloak close about him but Corbett suspected that, like the rest, he was harnessed for war. Corbett held a hand up for silence as he quickly scrutinised this sinister-looking battle group. They were all dark faced, skin burnt by the fierce sun of Outremer.

'I saw them in the forest, I am sure,' Megotta, who had come up close behind Corbett, whispered hoarsely.

Corbett walked forward. All pretence was forgotten. The twelve men, the so-called Apostles, now threw their cloaks back to reveal war belts and the long daggers fastened to them. One of the twelve made to move towards the wicker basket but the leader, the man with the scarred forehead, growled a warning and his comrades drew back.

'Gentlemen.' Corbett sketched a bow. 'I am Sir Hugh—'

'I know who you are.'

'Of course you do,' Corbett snapped back. 'You

planned to murder me. The mandatum being arranged here wasn't going to be a sacred ceremony but a blood feast where deep treachery and the murder of an innocent would walk hand in hand.'

'You are no innocent, Corbett.' The leader stepped forward and then hurriedly drew back as one of Ap Ythel's bowmen loosed. The arrow whistled through the air and smacked noisily into the plaster on the wall above The Apostles.

'No further, gentlemen,' Corbett warned. 'No further. I know who you are. You are former Templars. You came dressed as the Twelve Apostles to have your feet washed in imitation of Christ. But the truth is, you are assassins, intent on murder. Your first victim was to be our king. You have been foiled in that plot. Circumstances changed, so I was to be your next sacrificial victim.' Corbett heard Simon the Sacristan moan in terror.

'Do not worry, brother,' Corbett soothed without turning. 'You are safe. They have no quarrel with you or yours. Moreover, they are no longer a threat. These gentlemen are going to surrender their weapons together with all their impedimenta, be it on their war belts or in that basket.' Corbett pointed at the self-proclaimed leader of The Apostles. 'Why?' he demanded. 'Why are you so intent on murder, first our king and then me?'

'You know full well, Corbett. Philip of France has destroyed our Order. He has tortured, maimed and killed our brothers. Edward of England, his son-in-law, is no better. Both kings are killers. We, in the name of the Temple, would have culled them all. But then you intervened. Windsor was warned, the queen removed, whilst Edward of England is away, busy with his catamite.'

'Watch your tongue.'

'Sir Hugh, what do you want?'

'Your surrender. Hand over your weapons and you can stand trial for your crimes.'

'No, I don't think so.' The leader of The Apostles shook his head like a magister in a school showing his disapproval for a not-so-bright scholar. 'We shall do nothing of the sort. We must be gone. Yes, time is passing. So, listen and listen well. We planned for this possibility. We are soldiers. We must expect the unexpected. So, the Lady Beatrice Saveraux?'

'What about her?'

'We have her, crying and pitiful.'

'Where?'

'Not yet, Sir Hugh. We really must go. If you prevent us, the Lady Beatrice will surely die, her lovely, swanlike neck will be cut, that soft throat slashed, those lovely eyes dulled in death. If you let us pass through, once we have reached the forest edge, we will leave a message about the Lady Beatrice, but you must not move until . . .' The man turned and walked over to the tall candle on its stand in the corner. He beat his fingers against it. 'When the flame reaches the fourth ring, then you will find the Lady Beatrice. We intend her no harm but we really must be gone. Corbett, make your choice.' He drew his long dagger.

Corbett turned and stared at his henchmen. Ranulf

imperceptibly shook his head. Ap Ythel did the same whilst Megotta, chewing the corner of her lips, just shrugged. Corbett knew what he had to do. He turned back to his opponent.

'In God's name, leave,' he said. 'The sooner the better, but I warn you, when that flame reaches the fourth ring, I expect to find Lady Beatrice hale and hearty. Once I have, I am going to hunt you down.'

The leader almost ignored Corbett. He turned to his companions, shouting out orders in the lingua franca. The basket was opened, daggers, crossbows and war axes were taken out and pushed into war belts. The Templars milled around, chattering amongst themselves almost as if they had forgotten about Corbett, who studied them closely. These men were born soldiers, either knights or squires, who had campaigned and won their spurs on the battlefield. Nevertheless, he sensed an arrogance about them and Corbett recalled that ancient Irish prayer, 'Oh Lord, make my enemies proud'. At last, the Templars were ready. Their leader turned to Corbett, raised his hand in salutation and they left, going through the door leading into God's Acre. Corbett heard a few sounds as they hurried away, then silence.

He turned at a knock on the sacristy door and snapped his fingers at Ranulf.

'Lock it. Bolt it once the sacristan leaves. Brother Simon, you are our envoy to the abbot. Tell him what you saw. Tell him what you heard but, above all, tell him we will be back.' Corbett walked over to the hour candle and stood transfixed by the flame.

'What do you think will happen?' Ranulf came up beside him.

'A clever trick, my friend,' Corbett laughed softly. 'I did not think they would do that: take Lady Beatrice hostage and hold her for ransom. I had no choice. I cannot sacrifice a young woman, the queen's lady-in-waiting, simply to seize a group of malefactors. But those Templars have made a dreadful mistake.'

'Sir Hugh?'

'They are going to flee to the forest, Ranulf. They have no other choice. If they cling to the highway, we will ride them down. They think they can hide deep in that maze of greenery and never be found. But, Ranulf, I have fought in such places. The forest outside is like those of the Welsh valleys: a veritable barrier, but you can still find a path through. More importantly, Ap Ythel's bowmen were born in forests like Ashdown. They are hunters, verderers, the Templars are not. I wager a silver piece to a silver piece that we will catch up with them soon enough. But first, watch the candle, watch the flame. As soon as it reaches the fourth ring,' Corbett clapped his hands, 'then we leave, so prepare! Once we are ready, Ap Ythel, collect two more of your bowmen. We will take six into the forest.' Corbett stood for a while, fascinated by the candle flame. 'Very good. It's time,' he declared and led his company through the outside door into God's Acre.

'Sir Hugh, look.' Ranulf pointed to his right and there, fastened with cords to a stone plinth, a gag thrust into her mouth, stood the Lady Beatrice Saveraux.

Corbett hurried across, removed the gag from her mouth, cut the ropes and for a while held her. She simply cried quietly, clinging to him.

'I was walking,' she whispered. 'These men appeared, a sack was pulled over my head, a dagger pricked my throat and I was told to remain silent.'

'Did they do you any harm?'

'No, no, none at all. They gave me some food, a little wine and told me not to fear. They were hiding in God's Acre, then they brought me out and fastened me here. They said they would leave me for you, Sir Hugh.'

Corbett stared across the mist-hung cemetery.

'So, you were kept prisoner?'

'Yes, Sir Hugh. Let me explain.' Lady Beatrice, despite her courtly ways, was resilient, swiftly recovering from her ordeal. She glanced quickly at Corbett, her mouth tightening in a stubborn line. 'As I said, I was walking. Men appeared, a sack was pulled over my head. I was taken to some ancient vault down some steps under a great slab. The gap was narrow. I bruised my side.' Beatrice blinked. 'I could tell it was dark, as I heard them light lanterns and candles. It was cold, very cold, but they brought me a small brazier and a hand warmer.'

'Did they ill treat you in any way?'

'No, no, Sir Hugh, as I said, they did not,' she stammered, 'dishonour me.'

'And did you hear them talk, any conversation?'

'No, apart from telling me what to do, where to go, where to sit, what to eat, I heard nothing between them.

245

Sir Hugh, that's all I can tell you. I am cold, tired and not one to disgrace myself with tears.'

Corbett beckoned to Ranulf and Megotta.

'Take Lady Beatrice to the queen's quarters then return to me. Ap Ythel, while we wait, send out your best huntsman.'

'Brancepeth,' the captain retorted. 'He's as good, if not better, than any lurcher. He'll find a way.'

Corbett watched them leave then beckoned the rest of his comitatus back into the shelter of the porch. He stood reflecting on what had just happened. He felt elated, excited by the progress he was making, one of the reasons he loved such work. It was not just the thrill of the hunt but the stripping away of lies and falsehoods which assassins hid behind, a shield for their wickedness.

'And so it is,' he whispered to his unseen enemy. 'So it is. You have made a dreadful mistake and you will pay the penalty.'

Ranulf and Megotta returned. The Clerk of the Green Wax was grinning from ear to ear, as Megotta said, like the cat who'd supped the cream.

'It's de Craon,' Ranulf explained, 'he's bawling like a babe in its basket, loudly complaining about being confined to his chamber. About losing his henchman, Gaston Foix, who cannot be found. He says he will appeal to the King . . .' Ranulf broke off as Ap Ythel came hurrying across into the porch.

'Sir Hugh, I was right, it didn't take long. Brancepeth has found the path. Our quarry has fled into the forest.

They are following an ancient trackway. It's best if we leave now.'

'They outnumber us,' Megotta warned.

'They do indeed,' Corbett retorted. 'But not for long, just for the moment. Good, let the hunt begin.'

Led by Ap Ythel, they left the abbey church, hurrying across God's Acre, out through a narrow postern gate which Ap Ythel hacked open and on to the forest edge. Brancepeth was waiting for them further along the treeline.

'Sir Hugh,' the archer declared proudly, 'I have found the path, look.' He took them along the forest edge, stopped and pointed. At first Corbett could detect nothing, then Brancepeth gently pulled aside a clump of fern to reveal a narrow, snaking trackway, nothing more than a coffin path. He stretched down and plucked a piece of cloth from a trailing bramble. 'Sir Hugh, they will be easy to follow. Come.' Brancepeth led them single file into the cold darkness. Deeper in, the forest truly was an eerie place, ancient yet freshening as spring approached. The ground underfoot was turning damp. Bramble and gorse were sprouting more vigorously. The briars caught their cloaks as they went deeper and deeper into the sombre greenery. Corbett followed Brancepeth. Behind him Ranulf quietly cursed at all the strangeness around him. The forest lay silent except for a sudden rustling in the under-growth or the strident cry of some bird. There was a watchfulness, a feeling of menace in the brooding silence as if the very trees were spirits studying them closely. They hurried on until Brancepeth paused, lifting a hand.

'Listen, Sir Hugh.' Corbett strained his hearing. At first all he could hear was the call of a bird, the creak of branches and the rustling of leaves under the strengthening breeze. Corbett listened intently then he heard it. A voice calling, distant yet clear enough to conclude it was no forest sound.

Brancepeth led them on. They crossed narrow woodland streams and climbed small hills, pushing away the rich vegetation. Corbett felt he was back in those deeply wooded valleys of south Wales. As then, he was moving through a world of dappled darkness and shifting shadows. Now and again, they would stop in alarm as shadows moved, only to relax when they realised no danger lurked. Nevertheless, Corbett was wary, waiting for the arrow loosed from some hidden place, or the enemy springing out as if the earth had spat them up. Corbett knew he must concentrate on what was before him, and listen for that sound out of place amongst the trees clustered so closely together. They breasted a small hill and stopped, Brancepeth exclaiming in surprise. The ground fell away, sweeping down to a broad glade clear of any vegetation or trees. In the centre was what Corbett had suspected, an old hunting lodge: a two-storey house of plaster and wood on a blood-red brick base. The chimney stack, built on the side, was already trailing white smoke. They crawled closer. Corbett could see the Templars busy opening doors and pulling back shutters. One of them suddenly put down the logs he was carrying and stared up the hill.

'He's seen something,' Brancepeth hissed. 'A colour,

a movement, something out of place.' The man was now shouting at his companions. Corbett turned to Ap Ythel.

'Notch and loose as fast as you can,' he ordered. 'Do so.' The captain and his bowmen obeyed. Bows were swiftly strung, arrows notched and, at Ap Ythel's command, the yard-long shafts were loosed. Three of the Templars went down, spinning and staggering as the arrows smacked into chest, belly or face. The rest of the group, taken by surprise, could only draw their swords. Again, Ap Ythel's archers loosed in a deadly macabre ritual of notching, aiming, then loosing the feathered death. Corbett had witnessed the real power of these war bows in Wales and, in the hand of a skilled archer, the weapon was truly lethal. Many did not realise how it could deal out death so swiftly and the Templars below were certainly not aware of it. The only real defence against Ap Ythel's shafts was to take immediate shelter. The Templars, however, had been caught by surprise. Exposed and startled, they lost half of their company before they fully realised what was happening. At last they retreated into the house, shutting the door and pulling fast the shutters.

'What do we do now?' Ranulf demanded. 'Shall we storm the lodge, Sir Hugh?'

'No, I do not want to lose good men. They'll not surrender.' Corbett continued, 'I suspect some of them are French. If we take them prisoner, Philip of France will demand their extradition. He has a hatred for the Order and wishes to seize as many of its members as he can. If Philip gets his hands on them, God help the poor bastards. No, it will be a fight to the death.' Corbett wiped his mouth on the back of his gauntlet and repressed a shiver. He had sweated during the chase and now his body was beginning to cool. 'Light fires,' he ordered. 'Eat and drink whatever we have brought with us.'

'And then?'

'And then, Ranulf,' he gestured down at the old hunting lodge, 'we shall burn them out. So, God have mercy on all our souls.'

Within the hour, two fires were burning, the flames leaping merrily. Fashioning a cross from some thick twigs, Corbett despatched an archer to ask, under the sign of the crucifix, for the Templars' surrender. If they did not, as Corbett made the archer repeat, they would face total and utter annihilation. The archer left, going down the hill. Corbett watched the door open, a man came out. He shouted to the archer to proclaim his message. He did so, but the man standing on the threshold simply went back inside, slamming the door shut behind him.

'We have received their answer.'

'So we have, Ranulf. It's what I expected. Ap Ythel, burn them out.'

Ap Ythel led his archers to the brow of the hill, safe from any crossbow bolt. At his command, the archers unleashed a firestorm, skilled bowmen loosing shaft after fiery shaft. All of them found their mark either on the shabby roof or the wood and plaster walls. The fire soon caught hold, flames bursting out of windows, shutters clattering loose. One Templar tried to escape through a rear door. Ap Ythel, however, had placed Brancepeth there who brought the man down. The firestorm soon had the old building flaming like a torch in the wind. Corbett watched it burn. Once the flames began to subside, he despatched two archers to quickly circle the lodge to ensure no one had survived. They reported back, Brancepeth accompanying them, that no one had escaped the conflagration.

'Very well.' Corbett stared pityingly down at the corpses strewn before the building, those Templars cut down in the first arrow storm. 'Ap Ythel,' he declared. 'Tomorrow morning, I want you to send Brancepeth and two archers back here with spade, pick and mattock. Bury the corpses in this quiet place where their souls left their bodies. Fashion crosses to mark their graves. Ask a Blackrobe to accompany you to deliver the rite of burial and so give the dead a blessing. They deserve that.'

'And those caught up in the flames? They'll be little more than charred remains.'

'Do what you can, captain. Tell Brancepeth to bring corpse sheaths with him. Prior Felix, the infirmarian, should have a good stock of these. Collect whatever remains can be found and bury them alongside the corpses with as much dignity as can be mustered.'

'Of course, Sir Hugh, but one matter bothers me.'

'Only one?' Corbett asked.

'One amongst many,' the captain replied.

'Which is?'

'I know what you are going to say,' Megotta declared.

'Tell us, battle maiden.'

'Well, we do not know this place,' Megotta replied. 'Though it must remind you of the narrow dark valleys of Wales. Yet the same is true,' Megotta pointed to the lodge, now a smouldering ruin, 'of our enemy. Those Templars were strangers here. Yet they seemed well acquainted with this part of the forest. How did they know about the old hunting lodge? Who advised them, providing both support and sustenance?'

'Oh, I agree,' Corbett replied. 'But,' he crossed himself, 'God willing, by this time tomorrow we should be wiser and know a little more about what happened here. Well, Ap Ythel, you have my orders.' The Captain of Archers assured him he had. 'In which case, let the flames burn themselves out. There is nothing more for us here. Go through the dead men's clothing, take anything valuable. Ap Ythel, you can share that amongst your men. But, for the rest, we are finished.'

PART FIVE

'He who hunts two hares together
will lose now one, or else the other.'

On his return to St Michael's, Corbett found that the Constable of Wallingford had arrived with a comitatus of thirty men-at-arms and twenty archers. The entire battle group had camped out on Bloody Meadow, eager to mix with others during the coming Easter festival. Corbett met the constable in his chamber. The Keeper of the Secret Seal knew Ralph Swinburne of old; a veteran soldier who did his duty for God and the king and couldn't give a fig about anything else. They clasped hands, Corbett assuring the constable that his presence was needed as a shield against any danger to the queen. He insisted that the constable stay close to St Michael's and, if the queen moved back to Windsor, he must escort her there. Swinburne promised he would, before loudly announcing he was famished and that he was off to the buttery.

Corbett then arranged to meet his secret council. As soon as they had gathered, Ap Ythel declared he was already beginning to organise a return to the forest the following morning where, under the direction of his henchman, the dead would be cared for. Corbett asked Megotta to assist the burial party whilst Ranulf would keep an eye on proceedings in the abbey.

A short while later, with Ranulf and the archers guarding the door, Corbett had his private audience with the queen. Isabella sat stroking her belly. She looked a little tense, eyes red rimmed, face not so blooming as it was the last time they'd met. However, she stoutly declared that she was in the best of health, whilst the baby within was vigorous and, the queen added with a smile, making his presence felt. She assured Corbett that the short journey back to Windsor would be feasible. She just prayed that her husband would join her there. She then listened to Corbett's report, raising her eyebrows at what he told her. Yet the queen, despite her indisposition, was shrewd enough to accept Corbett's advice. She professed that Monseigneur de Craon's imminent departure to Windsor would, in the circumstances, be most desirable.

'Indeed,' she declared, 'it would be best if dearest Amaury journeyed back there with all speed. After all,' she added, 'there is little for him to do here at St Michael's.' Once she had finished speaking, she summoned her steward, who led Corbett over to a window recess where he could have private words with the queen's lady-in-waiting. Once he had, and received Lady Beatrice's assurances that Corbett could use her kidnapping and imprisonment in whatever way he wished, Corbett made his farewells and, escorted by the archers, left the royal quarters for the guest house.

The archers on the door reported that the French envoy was within and not at all happy with the turn of events. Corbett smiled his thanks, winked at Ap Ythel and pounded on the door. De Craon, wrapped in a fur-edged robe, flung the door open and glared like some angry fishwife at Corbett.

'This,' he yelled, 'is most unacceptable.'

'You mean your manners?' Corbett retorted. 'Why do you stand half-naked yelling at the king's representative, the personal envoy of our queen?'

De Craon, face twisted in anger, stepped forward. Corbett tensed as the French envoy's hand went beneath his robe. Malpas, however, intervened, grasping his master by the shoulder, gently squeezing, warning him to be careful. De Craon spun on his heel and strode back into the chamber. Corbett followed, keeping the door wide open so Ap Ythel and his archers could crowd in behind. Corbett stared around. The room smelled stale. It certainly looked untidy with chests and coffers flung open whilst the bedding lay all dishevelled and heaped in a pile. De Craon, still breathing heavily, now lounged on the window seat. The one survivor of the Sacred Six stood close by, as did Malpas; the henchman seemed wary, glancing sharply at Corbett then back at de Craon. Corbett ignored him and walked slowly towards the French Envoy.

'Monseigneur,' he declared. 'There has been some

excitement here, but please do not trouble yourself, that is my concern.'

'It's mine as well, Corbett. The mass of the Last Supper has been cancelled. In this abbey nothing is as it should be and I hold you responsible for that.'

'No, what happens in this abbey is Father Abbot's decision.'

'I would like to know what is happening and why,' de Craon snapped. 'I am not a child.'

'Then don't behave like one. If you have questions to ask, see Abbot Maurice. But, there again, you will have to do that swiftly because tomorrow morning, monseigneur, Her Grace the queen wishes you to be gone. You are to join her uncles at Windsor.'

'Why? W-what?' de Craon stuttered.

'I cannot say, monseigneur, but Her Grace will also be journeying back to Windsor. Once there you can seek an audience and ask whatever questions you want. Whether the queen deigns to give you a reply is a matter for her. However, the message I now bring comes directly from Her Grace. Tomorrow morning, you and yours must be gone. Do you understand? Do you accept Her Grace's decision? More importantly, will you follow our queen's very clear instruction to you and,' Corbett waved a hand languidly, 'your entourage? You must leave this abbey tomorrow.' Corbett snapped his fingers. 'As swiftly as that.'

The Keeper of the Secret Seal kept his face impassive but he secretly enjoyed every word he spat out. De Craon was his enemy, a man who would take his head without a second thought. The French envoy certainly looked as if he was ripe for murder, on the verge of the most ferocious rant.

'You are well?' Corbett asked. 'You would like some wine, perhaps some ale to clear your throat?'

De Craon, breathing heavily, just shook his head.

'All of you must be gone,' Corbett sang out. 'Except you, sir.' He stepped forward and grasped Malpas by the arm. De Craon leapt to his feet. Ap Ythel, who had been informed about what would happen, stepped forward, drawing his sword, and his archers did likewise. Corbett pulled Malpas closer. Ap Ythel and two of his bowmen hurried to assist, grasping Malpas roughly, pulling him towards the door and into the custody of the other archers. The prisoner, recovering from his shock, abruptly lunged at Corbett, throwing off the grip of one of his captors. Corbett retaliated with a stinging slap across Malpas's face.

'Why?' Malpas shrieked, trying to break free of the archers who had pinioned him.

'Yes, why?' de Craon echoed, leaving the window embrasure and walking as close as he dare. The French envoy now looked drained of all anger, his face slack, mouth gaping, eyes staring plaintively at Malpas. 'Sir Hugh,' de Craon pleaded, 'what is all this?'

'I am not too sure, monseigneur. One strange incident among many here at St Michael's. However, to be brief, one of the queen's ladies-in-waiting was mysteriously abducted.' Corbett held up his hand. 'No, no, nothing to worry about. The lady has now been safely returned to Her Grace's tender care. The woman in question, Lady Beatrice Saveraux, claims that during the abduction she heard a voice. She believes it was French and thought it was Malpas, whom she had heard speaking in the queen's presence on a number of occasions.'

'Nonsense, utter nonsense,' Malpas gasped.

'A mistake, surely?' de Craon shouted.

'God willing,' Corbett replied, 'it is a mistake, monseigneur.'

'Philip is an envoy. He is sacred.'

'And he will be treated as such,' Corbett retorted. 'Provided he does not lunge at me again, in which case his face will be well and truly slapped. Oh, I know well, monseigneur, an envoy is sacred, but so is Lady Beatrice, in herself and as a principal lady in our queen's household. As you well know, an attack on a royal retainer is an attack on the Crown itself. I am sure there is a satisfactory explanation for all this and I do look forward to hearing it.'

'But what is this abduction? Why the Lady Beatrice? Why should Malpas be involved in such a crime?'

'Why indeed, monseigneur, that is what I want to know. I cannot provide you with more details because this is a matter kept under the Secret Seal and I am its Keeper. The Lady Beatrice, if you wish to ask her yourself, was abducted. She has now been found and the circumstances around her kidnap are being closely investigated. She has maintained that she clearly heard Malpas's voice, and we must investigate that.'

'I shall appeal to the king, and to Her Grace too.'

'Monseigneur, you can appeal to the Holy Father for all I care. I shall detain Monseigneur Malpas and when I have discharged my duty to both the Crown and Her Grace the queen, not forgetting the Lady Beatrice, your clerk, hopefully, will be released. Until then he shall be accorded every rightful honour. Now,' Corbett bowed, 'you must prepare to leave. You should be gone by noon tomorrow.' Corbett again bowed then turned on his heel, snapping his fingers at his escort. Once outside the guest house, he turned on Malpas. 'You, sir, will be confined in a chamber close to mine. Any nonsense, any attempt to escape, will be treated as an admission of guilt. One of these archers, who will guard you day and night, will bring you down with an arrow should you attempt to leave us unexpectedly. Now,' he poked the prisoner in the chest, 'be gone.'

Malpas, cursing and protesting, was dragged away. Corbett, still fighting the laughter bubbling within him, told Ap Ythel to ensure the prisoner was confined in a small chamber above his. He watched the captain hurry away then glanced up at the darkening sky.

'You enjoyed that, didn't you, master?'

'I certainly did, Ranulf. I like nothing better than lecturing de Craon, especially when he doesn't want to listen. He will be gone but the game isn't over yet. However, the day is drawing to an end and for the moment we are done. So, first to the buttery for a platter of food and a goblet of wine.'

'And then, Sir Hugh?'

'Let us sit and chat in my chamber. Let us plan carefully for the morrow.'

The next morning, Corbett prepared for his visitor. He
washed, shaved, dressed, then swept the different sheets
of parchment from his chancery desk. He met Ap Ythel
and gave the captain fresh instructions. Ranulf appeared
and Corbett asked his henchman to be ready for anything.
Abbot Maurice eventually arrived just after the Angelus
bell finished pealing: the very last bell to be rung until
the Festival of Fire, the celebration of Christ's resurrection
just around midnight on Holy Saturday. Corbett made
sure his visitor was comfortable and then sat staring at
the severe-faced monk who was responsible for such
murderous mayhem in his own abbey.

'Sir Hugh, you are staring.'

'Yes, Father Abbot, I am.' Corbett pointed his finger.
'I accuse you of treason, robbery and murder.'

Abbot Maurice made ready to spring to his feet but
Ranulf, seated beside the door, rose drawing his dagger.
The abbot sank back into his chair, eyes fearful as he
looked to the left and right.

'I don't . . .' he stammered. 'I want . . .'

'No, father! No nonsense about my authority or I'll
order the Constable of Wallingford to take you back
to that grim fortress where I will lay this indictment
against you and demand certain answers. At Wallingford
there are men who can make you talk, confess, admit,
indeed whatever they ask you to. Of course, you may
have a satisfactory explanation for everything, though

I doubt it. Anyway, before I begin, do you want some ale? A goblet of wine?'

The abbot shook his head.

'Then let us begin.' Corbett picked up a page of parchment. 'You are French born. Your baptismal name is Thomas Brienne. You are a twin. Your brother, when held over the baptismal font, was also christened Thomas but given the additional name of Didymus, the Greek word for twin. I understand from the Gospels that there was a Thomas Didymus amongst Christ's followers: your parents were paying homage to that saint. So, we have two Thomases, scions of a knightly family who see themselves as God's own warriors. You and your twin brother join the Templar Order shortly before the great disaster at Acre. You take part in the desperate flight from that fortress along with the likes of our anchorite, who now calls himself Reboham. In fact, he carried the Glory of Heaven, that beautiful diamond, from Acre back to the main Templar community in Paris, who later entrusted it to the English Crown. Now, during and after the great retreat from Acre, you and Thomas Didymus quarrelled most bitterly. I do not know the cause or the content, it really doesn't matter for the moment, nevertheless a deep rift was caused. Then Philip of France intervened . . .'

'I know this, Corbett.'

'Don't snap at me like a gull, Father Abbot, but listen humbly and intently. We are about to take a journey along the path to your secret sins, which, if I have my way, will be exposed to public view. So, Philip of France

suppresses the Templars but it is no honourable dissolution. Philip showed his hand and matters turned very
nasty. Templars were hunted down as if they were
vermin. They were seized, taken up and tortured to
confess to whatever Philip of France asked them: a
veritable litany of foul crimes and hideous vices. Whether
these are true or not is a matter for another court.
However, Philip persisted and his accusations were taken
as the gospel truth. The Templars were truly broken and
they fled to hide in monasteries and abbeys across
Christendom. Abbots and priors offered them refuge
and you were no different. After all, you had been an
acolyte in the Order. However, when your brother begged
for help you resolutely refused. Time passed. News about
the horrors inflicted on former Templars seeped through
Christendom. Only then did you realise the real danger
threatening your brother. You repented; you changed
your mind, but it was too late. Your brother had been
captured and flung into some dark cell in the Chambre
Noire at the Louvre. I suspect he was tortured, maltreated.
You must have become very concerned.'

'Do you have proof of my moods and state of mind,
Corbett?'

'Do you have evidence to contradict it? I refer to one
question your superiors will ask, and certainly the king's
judges likewise: why did you at first do nothing and
then begin to send messages to Benedictine houses in
and around Paris? And why do so many of the brothers
from those houses visit St Michael's? Oh yes, there will
be questions enough.'

'I can see Brother Norbert has been talking to you.'

'Yes, Father Abbot, more truth. Brother Norbert is now deeply concerned about what is happening here at St Michael's. If summoned by any court or council, he will go on oath. He will simply tell the truth, which I have already described, and there's no denying it. The horrors Philip of France conflicted upon the Templars are common knowledge. No doubt there are letters, documents, which will show your concern for your brother, there is nothing wrong with that. In fact, it is natural for a brother to care for his brother. But then matters took an abrupt turn. De Craon came hunting. He approached you, didn't he? A fellow Frenchman, all genial and persuasive. De Craon put a proposal to you. Your brother could be released, even handed over to you, on certain conditions – and with a man like de Craon, Father Abbot, there are always conditions. Most importantly, and he didn't care how, the Glory of Heaven should be given to him. De Craon would take it back to Paris where Philip of France would erect his own shrine of veneration. If the English Crown protested, Philip of France would say the diamond had found its rightful home. What could Edward of England do about that?'

'In heaven's name, Corbett,' the abbot snarled, 'what proof do you have for this? What evidence do you hold that I was responsible for the theft of that diamond and the killing of Brother Mark? You have seen the Silver Shrine, how it was when the Glory of Heaven was stolen. The door was locked and bolted with no other possible entrance.'

'Oh yes.' Corbett leant forward. 'It was almost the perfect crime.' He rose to his feet, opened the door and ordered Ap Ythel and two of his archers into the chamber. 'Take my Lord Abbot,' Corbett declared, 'down to the Silver Shrine. We will join you there.' Ap Ythel beckoned at the prisoner, who sighed, rose to his feet and joined Ap Ythel and his archers outside. Corbett waited, listening to them go.

'You can demonstrate how the theft took place and Brother Mark was murdered?' Ranulf asked.

'I can and I definitely will.'

'Then what worries you? I can see that, master – you're not too sure of something, are you?'

'Oh, I believe that Abbot Maurice is an assassin, a traitor and a thief, but I haven't really grasped why.'

'A desire to save his brother?'

'Perhaps. But there's something else. Anyway, I am worried. I ask myself, does the abbot still have the diamond, and if he does, how do I retrieve it? If de Craon has seized it then,' Corbett shrugged, 'we have well and truly lost it.'

'What we do know,' Ranulf offered, 'is that our unholy Abbot Maurice walks Murder's market. He did form a pact with the devil. Perhaps we can offer him one with the angels.'

'Too true, my friend, so let us test the water.'

Corbett and Ranulf went down to the abbey church, along the cold hard passageways and galleries where the fluttering torchlight revealed the devil-faced gargoyles staring down at them. An eerie silence seemed to have descended on St Michael's. The occasional Blackrobe passed by, his sandalled feet breaking the strange stillness. Apart from that, the sinister silence hung like a pall, an air of brooding watchfulness as if the monastic community knew only too well something dreadful was unfolding. The church was also empty. Simon the Sacristan appeared, flitting like a bird as he hurried round lighting candles. He then disappeared into the sacristy, slamming the door behind him. Abbot Maurice sat on a wall bench opposite the Silver Shrine, Ap Ythel and his archers close by.

'Very well,' Corbett began in a clear, carrying voice. 'Abbot Maurice, stay where you are. Ranulf, you are now Brother Mark and I shall pretend to be the Lord Abbot. Go into the shrine and wait for me.' Corbett approached the abbot, staring down at him. Abbot Maurice refused to meet his gaze and glanced away. 'Early in the evening when the robbery took place,' Corbett continued, 'you, Father Abbot, came down here. You had made what preparations were necessary; in a sense there was only one. You first visited the buttery where the kitchener, Brother Aidan, had prepared a platter of food and a jug of wine for our anchorite, who is probably now straining his ears to learn what is happening here. When I met with our kitchener, he assured me that, as usual, on that day a platter of food and a small jug of wine were left on the buttery table waiting to be taken to the anchorite. I am not saying you took them. Oh no. However, you had visited that buttery for a purpose. Brother Aidan distinctly remembers you coming into the buttery late that afternoon. You came to secretly pour a sleeping potion, dream powder, into that jug of wine. It certainly worked. Despite all the murderous mummery which occurred in this church a short while later, our anchorite never heard a jot or a tittle. You made certain the anchorite was fast asleep, and that he would remain so until long after you had gone.'

'You have proof of all this, Corbett? Not just the vague recollection of certain brothers. I mean, Brother Aidan is not the sharpest member of our community. Where is your proof? Perhaps I should get up and leave.'

'You'll be seized,' Corbett countered. 'Thomas Brienne, Abbot Maurice, or whatever else you want to call yourself – you will confess.'

'Evidence?'

'In time, in time. But let me return to what truly happened here. I will be honest. I am not too sure. I cannot understand what possessed you.' Corbett paused at the abbot's scoffing laughter. 'What you really intended. Was it murder from the start or a struggle that went horribly wrong? Let me demonstrate. You, Abbot Maurice, were outside the Silver Shrine, Brother Mark was within. For whatever reason you gave, you wanted to hold the diamond, a fairly logical and reasonable request. After all, you are the abbot of this house with the specific task of venerating our famous diamond. Brother Mark is a good, honest, obedient brother who, I understand, had a deep respect for his Father Abbot. He has taken vows to obey you. He sees no problem with your request. Anyone who saw the Glory of Heaven would love to hold it close, admire its sheer beauty. I have seen it before; it is well named. Anyway, Brother Mark takes the diamond from its tabernacle, but to save time, he does not leave the shrine.' Corbett walked to the glittering bars gesturing at Ranulf to join him on the other side. 'Instead, Brother Mark puts his hand through – Ranulf, please.' His henchman approached and thrust his hand through so Corbett could grasp it. 'Brother Mark does the same. He hands the diamond over without leaving the shrine. He thinks his Father Abbot simply wants to treasure it closely, but then . . .' Corbett released Ranulf's hand and walked away. Arms folded, he stared down as he tapped a booted foot against the hard paving. 'God knows what truly happened next. Well,' he lifted his head and pointed at the abbot, still slouched on the wall bench, 'God knows, and so do you. I suspect that you indicated to Brother Mark that you would not return the diamond immediately. Indeed, you had already pocketed it, clearly demonstrating that you would not be handing it back. Brother Mark would become agitated, caught in a dilemma. Conscientious, he wanted the diamond put back in its proper place, yet he was most reluctant to challenge his abbot.'

'But this is nonsense,' Abbot Maurice interjected. 'If I kept the diamond or was intent on doing so, Brother Mark would have proclaimed as much to the community. I could only keep it for a short while surely. I mean . . .' The abbot made to rise but Corbett held up a hand and the abbot retook his seat.

'Yes, yes, I agree with you,' Corbett replied. 'If you had taken the diamond from the church, Brother Mark, in conscience, would have had to inform others: that compels me to a most logical conclusion, one you have now confirmed by your own mouth.'

'Which is?'

'That you came into this church to steal the diamond and silence the only witness to your crime – Brother Mark. And this is how you did it.' Corbett turned back to the shrine. 'Ranulf, come close to the bars and thrust your hand through as if you are waiting for me to give you something. Brother Mark did the same, expecting to receive the diamond. Now watch.' Corbett, standing on the other side of the bars, pulled Ranulf close, grasping his jerkin with one hand whilst Corbett punched his henchman in the left side of the chest. Ranulf winced as he banged his head on the bar. Corbett then pushed his henchman away, murmuring his apology. 'And that's what happened,' Corbett declared loudly. 'Brother Mark approached the bars expecting to receive the diamond. Perhaps he was hopeful. After all, you had placed your walking cane on the ground so as to free your hands. You, Father Abbot, grabbed Brother Mark by the front of his gown with your right hand whilst your left, now holding the dagger hidden on your person, delivered a swift killing blow through the bars. A lethal wound to the heart. You withdrew your dagger. Mark also hit his head against the bars, as you did, Ranulf. This explains the bruising we found on his forehead. I pushed Ranulf away from the bars.

You, Father Abbot, did the same with Brother Mark, using your walking cane. The poor man staggers away, his chest wound spouting blood. He is dying, he is in shock, he can do no more. He collapses close to the tabernacle that he guarded so faithfully, and dies there.' Corbett paused. The abbot now slumped, head down. 'It's the only logical explanation,' Corbett insisted. 'The door to the Silver Shrine was locked and bolted. Consequently, the only way that diamond could be removed was if Brother Mark, and only he, handed it over to someone standing the other side of the bars.' Corbett glanced at Ranulf. 'I thought of that, Ranulf, when the anchorite handed me the ruptured bolt left lying on the floor. He passed it through the bars. Brother Mark did the same with the Glory of Heaven. I then asked myself, why would Brother Mark do that? To whom would he entrust the diamond? More importantly, who had the authority to demand it? The answer to all these questions is you, Father Abbot.' Corbett walked towards the Blackrobe, who sat shoulders all hunched, a dark sombre shadow in the dim light of the nave.

'But of course,' Corbett declared, 'the theft of the diamond was only part of a greater plot. Let me return to my indictment. De Craon and you met in secret council. Our French envoy spoke about your brother, Thomas Didymus, hidden deep in the Chambre Noire. How, if you cooperated fully, Thomas Didymus would be safe and released into your care. A deadly conspiracy was formed. You would become de Craon's man, held fast both body and soul. You took the name Reboham, a devious twist to your tangled plot. Now de Craon hoped I would be seriously misled. I would be trapped into believing our anchorite, a former Templar, who had also assumed the name Reboham, was deeply involved in all this murderous mischief, a cunning distraction from the truth.' Corbett paused in his pacing and stared around. The nave looked ghostly. The torches licked the cold darkness in a vain attempt to strengthen their light, the flames dancing and fluttering in the bitter breeze seeping through the nave. Shadows shifted; faint noises broke the sinister stillness. The nave truly had become a mummer's stage where murder and treason were being unmasked. Ap Ythel and his escorts stood like grim statues, spectators, fascinated by Corbett's indictment. Ranulf, likewise, had now left the Silver Shrine and stood leaning against one of the great drum-like pillars.

Corbett gathered his thoughts. 'And now,' he declared, 'I shall begin the second part of my indictment. I learnt through my own spies about Philip and de Craon's references to Reboham and we have clarified that. The same applies to the word "Apostles". You used that to deepen the mystery because that is also the name of the mummers patronised by this abbey, now camped close by on Bloody Meadow. You were cleverly insinuating the possibility that the mummers' group were in some way also involved in Philip's plots. Of course, that was a lie.'

'Again,' the abbot proclaimed, 'what you say is conjecture! In heaven's name, Corbett, you have studied in the schools of Oxford. You are trained and educated in the Disputatio, the construction of argument based on reason, logic and above all evidence, which is sorely lacking here.'

'Do not,' Corbett retorted, 'lose yourself in words. You talk of evidence, then let me tell you of one hard fact. Your brother, Thomas Didymus, needs me more than he needs you or de Craon. I have no real evidence for that, I simply refer to what we both know about Philip and de Craon. Think about what has happened. De Craon has failed. You are part of that failure. You and your brother will pay the price.' Corbett watched intently; he had hit his mark. For the first time since this tournament of words had begun, Abbot Maurice had suffered a blow that wounded. So swift, so sure, he could only mumble and mutter as he squirmed on the bench trying to recover his wits. 'Remember this,' Corbett declared solemnly, 'remember, Thomas Brienne, self-proclaimed Abbot Maurice, your brother's safety lies in my hands and no one else's, a conclusion I will develop much later.' Corbett watched Abbot Maurice's face even as he hid his surprise and quietly conceded his own mistake. He had totally underestimated Abbot Maurice's love for his brother and the deep guilt the abbot now felt, the cloying fear of knowing his beloved twin, whatever their differences, lay at the mercy of Philip of France and his minions. Corbett promised himself to exploit this to the full.

'You talk of evidence, abbot; I fully concede the second part of my indictment could well be dismissed as conjecture, though the crimes you attempted to commit are now clear enough. To be brief and succinct: de Craon and you conspired to steal the diamond. Philip wanted that and I have demonstrated how you did it. But there is more, with someone like de Craon there always is, and you were drawn deeper into the plotting of another crime. For that you both needed assistance and you found it amongst former Templars. You, Abbot Maurice, are well known amongst that group, you must be. You were a novice in that Order; you took part in the so-called heroic defence of Acre. You, like others, were the last to be driven out of Outremer. Above all, so was your brother. A hero of the Order, yes, who rose to pre-eminence in the principal house of the Templars in Paris,' Corbett waved a hand, 'and so on and so on.'

'I dislike de Craon.'

'Nobody likes de Craon. But your love for your twin is greater than any hatred you have for the French or for me. You love your brother deeply. De Craon, like the snake he is, a true descendant of the Serpent of Old, came and whispered in your ear. He wanted the Glory of Heaven but he also wanted nothing less than the murder of our king, the noble Edward, during the ceremony of the mandatum on Maundy Thursday. You were committed. You had agreed to the theft of the diamond. You became responsible for the murder of Brother Mark. De Craon urged you to use your ties with the Order to recruit twelve assassins from the ranks of former Templars. These would strike during the ceremony of the washing of the feet. King Edward would perform that rite. He would be unarmed, vulnerable, crouched like a penitent before his murderers. He would wear no chain mail, no armour, he would be alone. No escort, no guard. You know that's what was planned. When you met your coven out in the forest you actually practised what you plotted. Oh yes, Abbot Maurice,' Corbett half smiled at the surprise on the Blackrobe's face, 'we know more about you than you think. We do have evidence for your crimes.'

'But to kill a king,' Abbot Maurice riposted, 'and for twelve former Templars to assist in that crime? Are you saying we had a motive? Philip of France is the author of the Templars' misfortunes. He alone bears the guilt.'

'That's a lie and you know it. Of course, I also wondered about that until I visited your library. By chance, I was shown the schedule of documents drawn up when the Glory of Heaven was entrusted to the English Crown. Our young king swore a mighty oath as he took receipt of the diamond, to do all within his power to protect and defend the Templar order. The indenture, signed and sealed by the king, was drawn up in December 1307 during my absence from the Chancery. Now, that date is important because when the diamond was transferred to the English Crown, Philip of France unleashed his fury against the Templars in Paris. People soon realised a storm was coming. The Templars, in a word, tried to bribe Edward to protect them. He took the bribe and, for many reasons, he broke his oath.'

'He certainly didn't keep his word.' Abbot Maurice's voice turned sneering. 'Unlike his great father, our present king is a weak reed who would bend before any breeze. Edward and the likes of you, Sir Hugh, did absolutely nothing to protect scores of innocent men accused of the most heinous crimes. They were arrested without charge, dispossessed, some thrown out on the road, others into dungeons, whilst leading Templar officials were handed over to Philip of France to be abused, tortured and killed.' Abbot Maurice fell silent, shaking his head as he continued the conversation in a whisper to himself. Corbett hid his own growing elation. The accused was now lost in his own world. Corbett watched intently. The abbot shook himself free of his reverie, glanced up and pointed at his accuser. 'I merely describe what truly happened. That does not mean I am guilty of any crime.'

'Oh, I think it does and I will argue the same. Edward of England, in your eyes and those of your Templar accomplices, is as guilty as Philip of France. Edward made matters worse by the violation of his own sacred oath. The Templars regard this as sacrilege as well as theft of a revered sacred relic acquired under blatant false pretences. Edward took the Glory of Heaven and totally repudiated his sworn word. Now you plotted to strike during the mandatum to be held at Windsor.' Corbett paused, licking dry lips as he stared at the accused, who was now becoming more visibly agitated as the truth unfolded.

'You, Abbot Maurice, with all your ties to the

Templars, recruited hard, bitter warriors, former knights of the Order, men who had fought the infidel in Outremer. Men like yourself, desperate to punish a prince who had failed them time and time again. You assembled such a coven. You let them mingle with The Apostles, the mummers' group this abbey patronises. An easy enough task. The assassins would be virtually indistinguishable from all the others crowded there. You probably provided them with coin and sustenance. You, with all your knowledge of Ashdown, informed them about the old hunting lodge deep in the forest which they could use. You also informed them that the moon girl Megotta was of my retinue. After all, I informed you and Lord Janus that she would be joining the mummers.' Corbett paused. 'Oh yes, they were well served by you. They gained further protection because the name they had assumed was the same as that given to the mummers. So, you plotted that death-laden cere-mony, the Mandatum of Murder, a blasphemous mockery of the spiritual truths which inspired it.'

'And afterwards?' Abbot Maurice retorted. 'Afterwards, Corbett? I have left myself open to be accused as my so-called fellow conspirators were either cut down or hanged out of hand.'

'No, no, Father Abbot. The chapel at Windsor would hold enough notables, including yourself, to be taken hostage, that's precisely what The Apostles tried here. They seized the Lady Beatrice Saveraux to be their hostage so they would be able to flee unscathed. You plotted to do the same at Windsor.'

'But the French Lords would also be vulnerable, the queen's uncles; Philip's brothers. De Craon wouldn't dare countenance that.'

'Oh come, come, Father Abbot, you are a man of the world, you've visited the royal chapel at Windsor. I am sure de Craon would arrange matters so that the queen and her relatives were kept safe enough, well out of harm's way.' Corbett went and crouched before the abbot, forcing him to look up. 'You would be taken hostage,' Corbett continued, 'poor hapless Father Abbot! You and others would be seized so The Apostles could escape. Afterwards, of course, you would plead total ignorance of the plot; you would portray yourself as an innocent who recruited twelve men from those camped out on Bloody Meadow. You would claim that they were eager to do this sacred task especially for a coin and something to eat and drink. You would depict yourself as an innocent, guilty of no wrongdoing. Unfortunately, you made a mistake.'

'And the purpose of all this, Corbett? Why would such an assault be organised?' Abbot Maurice, his face ugly with hate, leant a little closer and Corbett could smell his wine-laden breath.

'You know full well, Father Abbot. The Templars wanted revenge, whilst de Craon would rejoice in the chaos and confusion such an assault would provoke throughout a kingdom already weakened by its king's infatuation with his favourite. The pieces on the chessboard would be toppled over, giving Philip of France a free hand to intervene, all dramatic, to protect his beloved daughter and, God willing, his even more beloved grandson.'

'And the English lords?'

'Oh, come, Father Abbot,' Corbett got to his feet, 'they are already divided, some for the king, others against him. A few sitting on the fence, watching and waiting. The chaos would divide and confuse them even further. De Craon was committed to ensuring Philip of France emerged as the saviour, the arbiter of this kingdom's affairs.'

'And me?'

'Ah yes, you.' Corbett jabbed a finger. 'Well, as I said, you would act all innocent. Who knows, de Craon would arrange some mummery to depict you as a man of integrity who tried to fight back. But what did you truly care? In the chaotic collapse of royal government, you would soon be forgotten. You'd have fulfilled your part of de Craon's perfidious pact. I suppose you could be transferred to some great Benedictine abbey in the Île-de-France, installed as its abbot and accorded every preference. Once that happened, your brother would join you. The Glory of Heaven would then be handed over to Philip.' Corbett paused. 'But of course, there was me. I've described what was planned for Windsor, but it didn't happen. De Craon must have been furious at the collapse of his devious design. There was to be no mandatum at Windsor, Edward the king would not be there, embroiled as he is with his great lords. Thank God he didn't come. I also advised the queen to shelter here at St Michael's. I can only imagine de Craon's fury.

He decided to settle matters with me once and for all.
I had frustrated him so he plotted, with your support,
my murder. Oh, de Craon had enough motive. I have
crossed swords with him on many occasions and I am
sure this will not be the last. He would not have found
it difficult to convince you, Abbot Maurice. Earlier,
when you were talking about Edward of England's
failure to protect the Templars, you also claimed the
blame was shared with men like me. That is simply not
true. I had nothing to do with such a decision. I was
absent from the Chancery at Westminster. When my
opinion was eventually asked, I always maintained, and
still do, that the Templars were the innocent victims of
Philip of France's voracious hunger for wealth and
power.' Corbett shrugged. 'Of course, de Craon didn't
give a whit for that and I suggest neither did you. Your
accomplice was totally intent on removing the king's
right-hand man and so deepening the chaos and confusion in this kingdom. You fully cooperated. You had
no choice; you were committed. The effect of my murder
would have been similar to what would have happened
in the aftermath of the king's murder at Windsor; utter
chaos and deep confusion.' Corbett sat down on the
wall bench next to the abbot, staring into the darkness.
He had decided to bluff and the moment was ripe.
'Father Abbot, those Templars?'

'What about them?'

'The entire coven you recruited to carry out the
murders were annihilated; you must have heard that?
I beg to differ. There was a survivor, the leader, the man

with a furrowed forehead, the legacy of some ancient nasty wound. Rest assured, he will talk. He will convict you.' Corbett got to his feet. 'I should have died yesterday, murdered here in this abbey church. I'm not being arrogant or proud, but my king would have sorely missed me as he faced a rising tide of discontent and disarray. The light would have dimmed, the darkness deepened, but,' Corbett clapped his hands, 'thanks be to God, I survived. So, Abbot Maurice, you must make a decision.' He came and stood over the Blackrobe. 'Listen!' Corbett's voice was almost a hiss. 'De Craon failed miserably. I suspect he does not have the diamond. Our king was saved; he is alive and vigorous and might follow the good counsel he is given. I too am still very much alive. The murderous forays planned for both Windsor and here have been totally foiled. Now look at me, priest.' Abbot Maurice glanced up. 'You are finished,' Corbett jabbed a finger, 'but I will tell you something else – so is your brother. The trap, the lure you and de Craon set up, may well catch you out. You have probably signed and sealed your brother's death warrant. De Craon will return to Paris full of fury, Philip's mood will be no better. You know what will happen to Thomas Didymus.' Corbett crouched down before the Blackrobe. 'Only I can save you both.' Abbot Maurice gasped. 'I could save your brother,' Corbett insisted. 'I have in custody Philip Malpas, de Craon's henchman and, I suspect, much more than that. De Craon cherishes Malpas almost as fervently as you do your brother. However, Malpas has been seized because he stands accused of crimes against the Crown.' Corbett waved a hand. 'But that is not your concern. You may have heard chatter, gossip in the abbey, but I tell the truth.'

'You will exchange Malpas for my brother?'

'Lord Abbot, for the first time in this *inquisicio* you have asked an honest question. De Craon will sorely miss Malpas. He will desperately want him back as soon as possible. And for what? The price de Craon will have to pay is your poor brother, a bruised and battered former Templar whom de Craon would only keep alive so as to vent his bile upon. Oh yes, de Craon will be most interested in such an offer.'

'Won't he be suspicious?'

'Who cares? De Craon will want the entire business forgotten as soon as possible. Of course, we shall dress up our proposal in the most appealing fashion.'

'What do you mean?'

'You do feel guilty about your past, yes?' The abbot, tight lipped, gave the curtest of nods. 'You, a priest, have the burden of many, many sins, scarlet and vivid, that's why you flagellate, isn't it? Whip your back till it bleeds? Well, I suppose you have good reason for that.'

'And what has that to do with me and my brother?'

'Oh, a great deal,' Corbett replied. 'Abbot Maurice, you could plead benefit of clergy and resist being tried before King's Bench at Westminster. You are a cleric, a priest whom only the Church courts can deal with. Nevertheless, that doesn't stop you being what you really are in the eyes of the Church; a traitor, an assassin and a thief. No, no.' Corbett held up a hand. 'Please don't be hypocritical, passionate about your status and calling. What I have just called you is the truth. Consequently, you cannot continue to be abbot here or anywhere else in the Benedictine world. You are finished. What is left for you? Some bleak anchorite cell in the far south-west? Or some lonely peel tower in the wilds of Ireland? In a word, you cannot walk away from what you have done. But, at the same time, your confession and full cooperation might win your brother his freedom as well as provide you with another purpose in life.'

'What do you mean? Explain!'

'At the appropriate time I shall consult with the king and his Secret Council. As a consequence of this, the queen will petition her beloved father for the release of Thomas Didymus Brienne. Once freed, he and his brother Maurice, former Abbot of St Michael's in Berkshire, can lead a deputation to some foreign ruler in Outremer with the glorious news about the birth, hopefully, of a lusty male heir – a joy Isabella wishes to share with the princes of the earth. You are chosen not only because of your status, but you, like your brother, have lived in Outremer. You know its customs and have knowledge of the Lingua Franca, and so on and so on. King Philip and de Craon will read between the lines, but how can Philip refuse his beloved daughter, who has provided him with his first grandson, the future King of England? Of course, Malpas' return to France would be discretely included in the offer. Philip will only be too pleased to grant his daughter's request as well as see the back of both you and your brother. De Craon would also be overjoyed.' Corbett tapped the abbot on the shoulder. 'You can make that long pilgrimage, true reparation for your sins here. Perhaps you may be given licence to visit Jerusalem where you could crawl to the Cross begging for God's forgiveness.'

'So, what do I have to do? What do you want from me?'

'A full confession to my indictment which my henchman Ranulf-atte-Newgate will witness, as well as the immediate surrender of the Glory of Heaven. Nothing more, nothing less, nothing else.' Corbett walked across to the Silver Shrine and stared through the bars. He then turned and came back. 'Think, Abbot Maurice. The path I have opened up for you is the safest and most just. Time is passing, I am becoming tired. I need to know now!'

'And I must return to my chamber.' The abbot glanced up. 'You need not guess the reason.'

Corbett waved toward the corpse door.

'Captain Ap Ythel, with one of your archers, escort the abbot back to his chamber.' The Blackrobe gave a deep sigh, rose and, accompanied by the bowmen, left the church. Corbett and Ranulf stood in silence listening to them go.

'Well, Sir Hugh, what first led you down this path?'

'The anchorite. It's so easy to overlook the obvious. When I present an indictment it seems that I am in the right, but that's only because I have spent hours revising, but not here. I made a mistake. The solution was so simple I didn't even consider it, not until the anchorite passed that broken bolt through those bars. Once he had, I then stumbled on the answer to the who, the how and the why of this crime. After that it was only a matter of logic. As for the twelve so-called Apostles? Well, Megotta's journey into the forest clarified matters. The Blackrobe figure must have been Reboham, Abbot Maurice, and again I ask the obvious: why assemble such a group for such an occasion if not murderous mischief? No, Ranulf, the real problem in all this is obtaining that confession and, above all, recovering the diamond. So let us see, let us wait and let us pray that we do.'

Abbot Maurice and his escort eventually returned to the church. The Blackrobe walked straight up to Corbett, who immediately grasped the handle of his belt dagger, Ranulf drawing his with a rasp of steel.

'Peace, peace, peace!' the abbot pleaded. He dug into his robe and drew out the diamond, holding it up so it caught the light and dazzled in the darkness. Corbett could only marvel at the jewel's sheer lucid beauty which provoked gasps of admiration from those around him. The diamond was as large as an egg, perfect in symmetry, brilliant in its light. The stone seemed to contain some sort of spiritual power and Corbett wondered how many people had died in their attempt to seize such beauty. The abbot lowered the diamond and handed it to Corbett, who slipped it into the pocket of his cloak.

He could feel its weight and, for a moment, wondered if the diamond did have a life of its own.

'Now you have it,' the abbot grated. He turned and walked back to the wall bench. He sat down, leaning forward, legs apart, hands clasping his knees as he stared at the floor. 'It is as you said,' the abbot intoned as if reading from the lectionary. 'I am not truly Abbot Maurice, a Blackrobe, a monk, a priest. First and foremost, I am Thomas Brienne, twin brother of Thomas Didymus. You know my history, Corbett, I will not deny it. My brother was taken up by the French king's minions. I heard about the hideous abuse Philip heaped upon the Templars. At first, I acted like Cain, not caring about my brother. We had quarrelled during the retreat from Acre, argued over stupid mistakes we'd both made. I was arrogant. When King Philip launched his attack, I thought nothing much would happen to the individual knights and squires of the Order. Of course I was wrong. Tales about the horrors were proved correct. My brother appealed for help but I remained hard faced, stone hearted, until,' the abbot's voice shook, 'I received a letter from our mother which deeply wounded my very soul. She said that Thomas Didymus and I had shared her womb and so we should be one in everything. I repented, determined to do anything to atone and make amends. I whipped myself until I bled but that was useless. Good perhaps for the soul, but it would not bring my brother back. Of course, I then became the abbot of the Benedictine house where the Glory of Heaven was installed. I have always been wary of that diamond. Some people claim it brings misfortune but, for me, it was a constant reminder of the Templars, their destruction, the cruelty of Philip and the complete neglect of Edward our king. Above all, it was a constant reminder of my brother. Nevertheless, I treated that diamond with respect. You have seen the Silver Shrine, and poor Brother Mark was appointed as its guardian. The years passed and, of course, there were visitors, pilgrims, the curious, and . . .'

'And de Craon.'

'True, Corbett, Philip sent his minion back and forth. He was to keep an eye on the young queen, especially during her pregnancy and he would also keep a sharp watch on the diamond. De Craon would come, all pleasant and bright eyed, like the carrion bird he is. We would meet in the buttery or my chamber, and the conversation eventually turned to Didymus. I left the path of light for one leading into the deepest darkness.' The abbot quickly crossed himself. 'De Craon was clever, subtle. He was like a merchant going through different items but then he reached his conclusion. If I returned the diamond, if I cooperated in his assault on Edward, then Thomas Didymus would be released unharmed. I agreed.' The abbot glanced up. 'Remember, Corbett, Edward swore to protect the Templars. The Glory of Heaven was entrusted to him to confirm his oath and seal the pact made between him and the Templars. I also wrote to our king begging, pleading letters, asking for his help with Didymus. He didn't even acknowledge them. Nothing! Edward of England is a liar, an oath-breaker, a prince who does not care for his flock, only for its fleece!'

'Careful, my Lord Abbot, what you say is tantamount to treason.'

'That doesn't stop it from being the truth. I know, I know. But at least it explains my full compliance with de Craon.'

'And the former Templars you recruited?'

'Easy enough, I have close ties with those warriors of God. It was not difficult to draw them into the conspiracy, first against Edward and, when you frustrated that, against you. I am sorry, Corbett, I cannot really explain what happened.' He tapped the side of his head. 'Here in my mind and heart, I just wanted Didymus released. I was caught up in the furious flood of events. Ah well . . .' he sighed, 'all is gone. What now, Corbett? You will keep your promise? Whomever you serve, you are still a man of your word.'

'My word is my bond, Abbot Maurice. You will be taken to Wallingford Castle. You will be treated honourably and given comfortable lodgings until the king makes his pleasure known. Captain Ap Ythel, take the abbot back to his chamber. Mount a secure guard. Leave two of your men there, then collect Prior Felix.' Corbett rubbed his arms. 'This nave is too cold. I will meet the prior in my chamber.' Corbett clapped his hands. 'These proceedings are now finished. Oh . . .' Corbett paused for effect. 'One thing further, Abbot Maurice. I have the diamond, but not the pyx which holds it, a beautiful work of art in itself. You have it, my Lord Abbot?'

'No, no.'

Corbett walked across and plucked at the abbot's sleeve.

'Another lie!' he hissed. 'But you know where it is and the truth will out, then I shall keep my word.'

Corbett sat behind his chancery desk, Ranulf on his right, Ap Ythel to his left. Outside, archers milled about in the gallery. The room was well lit and warm. Prior Felix, however, sitting on the other side of the desk, looked as if he was cold. He was shivering, rubbing his hands and staring over his shoulder at the door.

'You seem very nervous, Prior Felix.'

'Sir Hugh, where is Father Abbot?'

'Safely lodged away.'

'What is happening here?'

'More importantly,' Corbett abruptly leant forward, staring intently at the prior's worn, unshaven face, 'what is happening here is not so important. What I want to know is what happened at The Wodewose?'

Prior Felix tried to reply but he stammered and stuttered back into silence. He became like a child crossing his arms, turning sideways in his chair as the tears rolled down his cheeks. 'Very well,' Corbett declared. 'Let me tell you what I believed happened at The Wodewose, though my story originates thousands of miles away.' He sifted amongst the documents on the chancery table. 'I have read, I have heard, stories from across the Great Silk Road. Tales that chill the blood about powerful diseases, vicious, deadly infections which spread swift as a breeze. Now and again ships, be they fishing smacks, cogs or galleys, are found drifting, their crews all dead, their corpses swollen with great black boils peppering their dead cold flesh. Those who find such horrors stay well away and, if they can, burn the infected corpses and everything associated with them. Your library contains a number of chronicles and histories which describe in great detail how these gruesome plagues surface in history, cause utter devastation and then disappear as mysteriously as they emerged. You have read the same, Prior Felix?'

'Aye, and I have seen such nightmares.'

'Of course you have. You may be a prior, a humble monk, and I mean that kindly. You do not boast about your studies at Montpellier, Salerno and other great schools of medicine. Nevertheless, you are steeped in the world of physic, potions and philtres. You have studied the great authorities such as Galen, Hippocrates and the rest.'

'What is this?' the prior mumbled. 'A hymn to my past?'

'No, Prior Felix, a prologue to the present. More importantly, it has great bearing on the fire at The Wodewose. So let us turn to no less a person than that mailed clerk, courtly squire and royal courier, Stephen Filliol. Filliol was very much a man of the Court. He had great ambitions for himself and for his beloved, the Lady Beatrice Saveraux, one of the leading hand-maids of our queen. Life was good for both those young people; they were desperate to see each other. Filliol was despatched from Westminster with letters and missives for our queen at Windsor. Of course, he took such a task most seriously as he did his devotion to the Lady Beatrice. Filliol wished to impress his beloved so he ordered an exquisite rare gift from the markets along the Great Silk Road or elsewhere. God knows what it was, some precious nard, perfume or lotion or, there again, perhaps it was a roll of the purest silk. Filliol must have made a pact with the master of *The Ragusa*, a powerful Venetian galley out of the Middle Sea. Once the agreement was made, Filliol waited for the galley to return and when it did, he planned to meet the master when he berthed *The Ragusa* at Queenhithe. Filliol would collect his gift, pay the price and ride immediately to Windsor.'

'What is all this about?' Prior Felix sharply inter-jected. 'What does this have to do with me?'

'Oh come, come, Prior Felix, it has everything to do with you.' Corbett picked up a sheet of parchment and studied the memoranda written there in a cipher known only to himself. 'Filliol was a most unfortunate man, for *The Ragusa* was no ordinary ship,' Corbett declared. 'On its approach to London, some form of nasty infec-tion broke out. God knows its source or origin, what symptoms it presented, how many of the crew were ill; however the master had no choice but to inform the harbourmaster and port reeves. This is a very important duty, reinforced by the most stringent penalties, including the possibility of being hanged on the gallows along the river. You know that, don't you?'

The prior nodded. 'Of course,' he whispered, 'many great infections are seaborne.'

'And this was no different. *The Ragusa* was ordered to stand off and wait on developments. Of course, Prior Felix, this was no mild infection and the situation worsened. The ship was kept under close surveillance by the port reeves. No one would be allowed to disembark or board that vessel. Filliol, a haughty young man, was a different matter. He was a royal squire, the Crown's own courier. He wore the tabard and livery of the royal household. He would have carried the king's seal, not to mention a writ giving licence for Filliol to go where he wanted without hindrance or let. In a word, Squire Filliol would not be frustrated. He boarded *The Ragusa*, collected what he needed and left Queenhithe for Windsor.' Corbett paused. 'That's where you made your mistake.'

'What mistake?'

'Remember when we were talking about Filliol? You expressed sorrow over the young man's death, but then you made a reference to the squire leaving Queenhithe. How did you know that?' Corbett paused. 'Again, I ask, how did you know that Filliol left for Windsor from Queenhithe rather than from the Royal Chancery at Westminster. Well? Filliol was a royal courier. He was supposed to leave Westminster but he decided to make his own personal journey to meet *The Ragusa* at Queenhithe. I doubt if Filliol wanted many people to know that.' Corbett paused as if listening to the sounds outside his chamber. 'Ah well, Squire Filliol began his journey. He planned to stay at The Wodewose to refresh himself to make himself even more comely and handsome so as to win the admiration of his beloved. He planned to bathe, change and make himself more presentable but, in truth, Filliol was Death riding a horse: his arrogance, his determination to have his own way, were the real causes for what happened next. Yes?'

Prior Felix simply shook his head.

'Filliol was truly infected with whatever contagion ravaged *The Ragusa*,' Corbett pressed on. 'By the time he reached The Wodewose he must have been sick, debilitated. He'd be hot, fevered, though not yet delirious. On his arrival, mine host Crispin, totally ignorant of physic, showed Filliol up to a chamber. Only then, Prior Felix, do you enter this tragic tale.'

'I didn't, I never—'

'You did, Prior Felix. You became involved. God knows, I feel dreadfully sorry for you. Crispin the taverner did what he always did when he needed help. He despatched a messenger, the scullion or a stable boy, to St Michael's to ask for your assistance. Brother Norbert welcomed the messenger and, thankfully, kept him outside on the trackway whilst he sent for you. You came down to greet him. I can only conjecture what happened next, but you were informed about Filliol and others falling ill. Anyone else might not have been concerned, but you, learned and skilled in physic, realised you were listening to a nightmare last glimpsed when you studied in Salerno or elsewhere. You would escort the messenger away from Brother Norbert, or anyone else close to the postern gate. You listened very carefully then sent the messenger back to the tavern. You also gave him strict instructions, which probably included a lie. But it was the best you could do. You told the messenger you would come and cure all at The Wodewose but they had to follow your very precise instructions. They were to lock and shutter the tavern, every door and window in case the air outside deepened their ill humours. Of course, that was nonsense, but they wouldn't know that. They were receiving the advice of an established and trusted physician. You would order them to assemble in the taproom and wait for your arrival. They were to open the tavern to no one but you. I concede, Prior Felix, what confronted you was truly dangerous.'

Prior Felix however had turned away again, breathing noisily though his nose. 'How do you know all this?' he murmured.

'First, what you did that day, any other physician worthy of the name would have done. Secondly, Lord Janus, captain of the mummers, sent a boy to the tavern on some petty errand. Apparently, he knocked on the door and shutters without any response. So,' Corbett continued, 'you isolated The Wodewose, very similar to how the city states of Italy combat infections or in this country, the lepers, confining them to lazar houses isolated from the healthy and well. Later on, you tried to cover up what you'd done. You scratched the name of the messenger from The Wodewose out of Brother Norbert's visitors' ledger. This was to protect yourself against anyone who, as I did, might wonder if this abbey had any visitors from the tavern early on the day before the great fire. True, physician?'

'And then what?' Prior Felix abruptly asserted himself, turning round to confront Corbett as if he had made a decision and would adhere to it. 'What then?' he repeated.

'What then, Prior Felix? I say this in sorrow rather than in anger. You reflected carefully on what you had learnt from that messenger. It's not complex, but simple enough. Those who lodged and worked at The Wodewose were suffering from a deadly contagion. You could do little to help them but you could stop the infection spreading. You were like a captain of war on the battle-field. You decided to sacrifice ten for the sake of the thousand and that is precisely what I would have done. You then made the necessary preparations. You collected your chancery satchel and put in certain philtres and powders which only you had access to. You are cloaked and cowled against the cold. You are booted but, more especially, you have protected your mouth and nose. You donned a physician's mask against infection; you know the type, Prior Felix, the front is shaped like a horn to cover both nose and mouth. The horn is crammed with certain spices and herbs; more protection against infection. Indeed, you have covered yourself well, even wearing heavy gauntlets: these protect the hands but they are also fashioned so the fingers can easily move. As soon as darkness descended, you slipped out of the abbey and crossed God's Acre. You made one error. Our anchorite was also out, wandering and mumbling as he is wont. By chance you passed a fire left by the gardeners. The anchorite glimpsed you in your grotesque attire and now believes the devil has visited St Michael's. He probably has, but he's not that macabre figure striding through the darkness. So I ask you, Prior Felix, who else has the authority to pass so confidently through the abbey grounds? Despite your cowl and mask, you apparently knew your way, so who else could it be? A mummer? One of those camped out in Bloody Meadow? But why would they be dressed like that? Where were they going at such a late hour and for what?' Corbett held Prior Felix's gaze.

'*Jesu miserere*,' the accused moaned, beating his breast three times.

'I agree,' Corbett retorted. 'Jesus have mercy on you. Prior Felix, I repeat, I truly feel sorry for you. But to continue. When you reached that tavern, you beat on the door, shouting who you were.' Corbett paused. Prior Felix was now sobbing, face in hands, rocking backwards and forwards on his chair.

'I cannot . . .' he gasped, letting his hands fall from his face. 'I cannot continue to listen in silence. What you say, Sir Hugh, is true enough. Oh yes, I could go back and correct you on this or that, but what does it really matter now? Suffice to say, what the messenger from The Wodewose told me was dire, as if Satan himself had hired bed and board in that tavern. Oh, you are correct, Sir Hugh, I know all about that malignancy. I have seen it in Sicily and the kingdoms of the east. A blackening of the blood, swift and cruel, so your finger-tips and the end of your toes turn black. Boils and swellings erupt in your tender parts, between your legs or in your armpit. Physicians believe the worst of its kind is not spread by human touch but the fetid breath of victims. It is so easy to diagnose, absolutely impossible to treat.'

'And the taproom of The Wodewose?'

'Like Death's own kitchen. Mine host Crispin was in the most pitiful state, his family and household no better. Filliol, the royal courier, was dying, face all ravaged, coughing up black blood.'

'And then?'

'I moved very swiftly. I opened all the windows and doors and prepared a philtre for everyone. A potion, a deadly powder of crushed almond and henbane. I poured in a little water, stirred the powder until it mingled and made each and every one of them drink. God have mercy on them. They thought it was a cure, except mine host; I think he knew.' The prior's voice quavered. 'He smiled at me with his eyes. The effect was expected, the potion swift acting. They slipped from life into death as easily and as quietly as a shadow passes under a door. It was for the best,' Prior Felix's voice faltered, 'no pain or discomfort. Certainly nothing compared to the fever which ravaged them all. Afterwards, I sat outside on a fallen log. I remember picking at the bark, crumbling it between my fingers. I prayed, I wept, then I went back into the taproom: death's own chamber. All of them were gone, dead.

Some lay sprawled on the floor. Others crouched in corners or lolled from some stool or bench. I am a priest as well as a physician. I administered general absolution then I tried to conceal what I had done.' The prior straightened in his chair. 'Mine host certainly had enough oil both above stairs as well as in his cellars. I doused that tavern easy enough. I slit oilskins, broached barrels. All was ready.'

'And the outhouses?'

'Yes, I cleared the stables. The horses, pent up for so long, were only too willing to canter away.' Prior Felix rubbed his face in his hands. 'God knows what you must think,' he continued, 'but I had no choice. I fired that tavern and its outhouses. I stood and watched them burn. The Wodewose was ancient, its timbers and woodwork provided the best kindling, dry as dust. Once the flames roared up, I returned to the abbey. In a desolate part of God's Acre, I stripped off everything and rubbed my body and face with a rich pine juice. I also donned the shirt, loincloth, robe and sandals I had hidden away before I left. Ah well, Sir Hugh, so now you have it.'

'You also placed yourself in great danger.'

'No more than what I dealt with in the hospitals and leper houses of Salerno. I was very careful, prudent. I simply faced what confronts any physician who treats his patients. I put my trust in God . . .' Prior Felix folded his arms and let the tears stream down his face. 'It was so pathetic,' he murmured, 'so tragic, I felt a deep sorrow for the victims.'

'And a deep sorrow for yourself, surely?'

'Sorrow, guilt, a darkness of the soul! Yet, as I have said . . .' the prior gestured at the three men sitting before him, 'what else could I do?'

'Nothing,' Ranulf retorted. 'What would have happened if you had done nothing?'

'Can you imagine it?' Prior Felix replied. 'Filliol carrying letters to my brothers, all those who live here. Then there's the mummers in Bloody Meadow and the queen and her unborn child out at Windsor. Believe me, Ranulf, this infection is as swift and as deadly as a well-loosed arrow shaft. I did in conscience what I thought was the best. You are correct, Sir Hugh, I was like a captain of war prepared to sacrifice a few to save the many.' He smiled wryly at Corbett. 'I wondered when you would close with me. Yes, I made reference to Filliol leaving Queenhithe, but that's what he told me. I did meet the messenger. I opened his scroll container and emptied its contents. I did remove the entry from Norbert's visitors' ledger. I also tried to calm my conscience.'

'I understand,' Corbett replied. 'I could see you were profoundly troubled and I wondered why? You practise mortification in reparation for what you have done. Fasting and flagellation?'

'Oh yes, Sir Hugh. To quote the psalmist, "My sin is always before me; a sinner was I born, in guilt was I conceived."'

'There's nothing wrong, Father Prior, with conscience. I have met men and women with none and they are demons from hell. You're a man who cares, which is why you blessed the dead and the place where they perished. I returned to The Wodewose as you did. I noticed the fresh oil stains on some of the burnt timber and stones. You took a stoup of holy oil and an asperges rod. You blessed the site of The Wodewose, as you did the grave where the remains of all those who died at that tavern lie buried in God's Acre.'

'Ah well, "*Alea iacta*" – the dice is thrown. I cannot refashion the past.'

'Tell me,' Ranulf asked, 'Filliol journeyed from Queenhithe to The Wodewose, what about those he encountered on the road?'

'None, thank God. Filliol rode hard and fast.'

'And, of course, no one would dare to impede a royal courier.'

'Precisely, Sir Hugh. Filliol, as he lay dying, informed me of that, as he did . . .' The prior's voice trembled.

'What?'

'As he did, Sir Hugh, of his love for the Lady Beatrice. He begged me to take his last loving message to her, but . . .' The prior rubbed his red-rimmed eyes. 'How could I?'

'And *The Ragusa*?' Ranulf seemed determined on questioning the prior about every part of his confession. 'Filliol must have talked about it, yes?'

'Of course. He blamed himself and I agreed. He should never have boarded that galley. As for *The Ragusa*, God help its crew. They would have been devastated by the pestilence; it would have snatched all their souls, leaving their vessel to be battered by a cruel sea. The galley was doom-struck. Somewhere out on the great, mist-shrouded northern waters, *The Ragusa* undoubtedly came to grief, battered and shattered by wind and wave. The crew would try, but it would be fruitless.' The prior crossed himself. 'They joined the legions of the drowned awaiting the great call at the end of time when the sea shall give up its dead.' He patted the front of his robe. 'And so it was, and so it is. What now, Sir Hugh?'

'Nothing, nothing at all. What you did, I would have done with clear conscience.' Corbett smiled at the prior, who relaxed with a deep sigh which seemed to come from the heart. 'As we have said, you sacrificed a few, Prior Felix, to save the many, including everyone in this abbey and beyond. What I would like you to do for pity's sake is visit the Lady Beatrice. No, no, she is not to be told the full truth, but you could create some story, some kind fable.'

'Such as?'

'How you met Squire Filliol by chance on the road to The Wodewose. How he hoped to hasten to meet his beloved at Windsor. How he was filled with the joys of spring at the prospect of seeing her. How he loved her and wanted her to be handfast with him at the church door. Prior Felix, you are, despite your cowl, a man of the world. You know what to say. Leave the truth buried where it is, but give Lady Beatrice some comfort, some lasting, loving memory of her beloved.'

'And your verdict on the fire?'

'Oh, quite simple. The Wodewose was burnt to the ground by some mysterious fire which erupted in flames and sparks that spread to the outhouses. A devastating conflagration, the source of which will always remain a mystery.' Corbett spread his hands. 'We are finished, yes?' Prior Felix, openly relieved, quickly agreed and got to his feet. 'One further thing,' Corbett declared. 'Tomorrow morning, Father Prior, please celebrate the dawn mass in one of the chantry chapels. I shall attend. Afterwards I want you to return here with the Book of the Gospels and the reliquary stone from the altar you celebrated mass on.'

'The reliquary stone?'

'Yes. The stone contains fragments, relics of saints and martyrs. I want it brought here.'

'Of course, Sir Hugh. But why?'

'I need to conduct a swearing-in ceremony which will include all we have discussed here.' Corbett also rose, and he clasped hands with Prior Felix. They exchanged the kiss of peace and the Blackrobe left.

'Strange happenings!' Ap Ythel whispered. 'I sat and listened, Sir Hugh – your conclusions, your verdict are correct. And tomorrow?'

'Tomorrow,' Corbett replied, 'let us wait and see. We shall attend the dawn mass. Afterwards I will have urgent words with Prior Felix about his abbot, who will be leaving St Michael's. Her Grace the queen will also depart, de Craon soon afterwards in a desperate attempt to catch up with her. Before he leaves, de Craon will make one last desperate plea that Malpas be released. Of course, I will robustly refuse to hand the man over. If I know my enemy well, and I think I do, de Craon will be beside himself. He will fear for his beloved clerk and take his begging to our king, the Archbishop of Canterbury and the great earls,' Corbett waved a hand, 'and so on and so on. However, let us wait and see. We shall gather here tomorrow as soon as we can.'

Corbett's predictions proved correct. He attended the dawn mass in the chantry chapel of St Benedict of Nursia. Afterwards he met Prior Felix in his chamber, accepting the Book of the Gospels and the reliquary stone. Corbett informed the prior that he was now in charge of St Michael's Abbey, Abbot Maurice being taken to Wallingford. The prior tried to question Corbett on what had happened, but the Keeper of the Secret Seal refused to answer.

'I cannot,' he declared. 'What I found here is for your superiors. Suffice to say that I have recovered the diamond, which is now safe in my possession. I have also resolved who murdered Brother Mark. Prior Felix, you know your abbot's past, his deep absorption with finding his brother Didymus. My friend, you can read between the lines and that is your right. However, it is up to your superiors what conclusions they wish to publish. Now,' Corbett walked over to the hour candle, 'Monseigneur de Craon will soon be here to be the nuisance he always is. Then I must take my leave of the queen. Prior Felix, *Pax et Bonum*. Please let me know when Her Grace, not to mention de Craon, has left this abbey. I and my entourage will then meet and, God willing, leave soon afterwards.'

PART SIX

'He perishes on the rocks who
loves another more than himself.'

C orbett and his secret council gathered later that
same day. Ranulf assured Sir Hugh that the
abbey now seemed deserted. A comitatus of
mounted men-at-arms had taken Abbot Maurice to
Wallingford. The queen had left, hastily pursued by de
Craon, whose pleas on behalf of Malpas, Corbett had
vigorously rebuffed.

'Ah well.' The Keeper of the Secret Seal waved his
visitors to the stools and chairs he had arranged around
the room.

'Ranulf, Megotta and Ap Ythel, bosom friends and
the best of comrades. I need you to take an oath.'
Corbett pointed to the desk in front of him. 'One hand
on the Book of the Gospels, the other on the reliquary
stone. You will take the most solemn oath, on the pain
of your mortal souls as well as the forfeiture of both
body and goods, that you will never reveal to anyone,
whoever that might be, whatever you see or have seen

or heard in this chamber. Easter has come and gone at St Michael's with very little ceremony and certainly no liturgical festivities. You know the reason for this. Abbot Maurice has been dethroned and despatched. However, we were not only intent on recovering the diamond and resolving Brother Mark's murder, but also determining what truly happened at The Wodewose. There were other matters here at St Michael's, truly murderous. The Game of Kings has been ferociously fought out deep in the shadows of this abbey. De Craon lost and has retreated, but we are not yet finished.'

'Meaning?'

'Meaning, Ranulf, that I want you and Ap Ythel to bring Philip Malpas down here immediately.'

The French clerk looked surprisingly relaxed and happy when he arrived and sat on the cushioned chair Corbett pushed out for him. The surprise of the secret council deepened even further as Malpas warmly embraced Sir Hugh, who held him close for a while, exchanging the kiss of peace on each cheek. Corbett then urged Philip to sit, insisting he accept a goblet of the abbey's finest Bordeaux.

'Sir Hugh, what is this?' Ranulf exclaimed. 'He is our enemy.'

'A true enemy,' Ap Ythel echoed.

'A better mummer than I,' Megotta offered.

'My friends,' Corbett clapped his hands, 'the abbey now lies quiet, the bane of our life has gone. De Craon thinks young Philip here is my prisoner, my enemy, when, in truth, he is my dear comrade. Philip Malpas,'

Corbett continued, 'son of a notary and his wife Matilde. Philip was born under the shadow of the great fortress of Chinon and baptised in the castle chapel. A true scholar of the monastery school, Philip soon won the attention of the Masters of the Sorbonne and the other great halls and schools of learning in Paris. He studied the *trivium*, the *quadrivium*, scripture, Canon law and Roman law. He became an articled clerk recruited by the French Royal Chancery. He was eventually promoted to the Chambre Noire at the Louvre. Philip,' Corbett leant across the table, 'you can tell your story better than I. However, before you begin, I invite my friends here, who may have an inkling of what you are going to confess, to take the oath I described earlier.' There was no dissent: all three took the oath, one hand on the Book of the Gospels and the other on the reliquary stone. Once they had completed the ritual, Corbett gestured at Malpas. 'Tell them,' he urged, 'tell them who we are and what we do.'

'It is as Sir Hugh described,' Malpas began. 'I was a high-ranking clerk in the Chambre Noire, close to de Craon though not one of the Sacred Six. My own situation was that, although to the world I was a successful clerk, patronised and promoted by the Crown, in secret I was two persons. I felt as if I was a woman trapped in a man's body. I felt no attraction whatsoever for the ladies but I did fall deeply in love with another clerk, Simon Vancineat. I truly loved him, though of course we kept our passion and our relationship secret. I also discovered that de Craon was of the same persuasion as myself. On a number of occasions, he did approach me, and I courteously but firmly declined his invitation. Ah well, de Craon eventually fell in love with a young clerk of the royal household, but that is de Craon, he passes from one infatuation to another. Now, I and others of my kind used to gather in an *auberge*, Le Paradis, sited near the Tour de Nesle. We met, ate, drank and relaxed there.'

'Did de Craon join you?'

'Oh no, Master Ranulf, as far as de Craon was concerned, when it came to that love between David and Jonathan it was a matter of much suspected but nothing proved. De Craon kept to himself. Nevertheless, his involvement with that young clerk was like the Sword of Damocles which eventually fell. The clerk, Marcel or something like that, bitterly repulsed de Craon. We never realised the danger. De Craon kept his thoughts secret and we had no inkling of the storm fast approaching. In a word, de Craon used his authority to invade Le Paradis.'

'Sweet heaven,' Ranulf interjected. 'Any man found in such a place faces very serious accusations which could result in the most horrific death.'

'Too true, Ranulf. De Craon struck, surrounding the auberge. I was there at the time. Simon, God rest him, saved me. He would take no objection or delay, but thrust me through a hidden doorway and told me to run. God save me, I did. I fled like a bat into the night.'

'And the rest?'

'Taken up, Megotta, flung into dungeons beneath the

Chambre Noire. They were tortured, abused and eventually hanged most cruelly on the great gallows at Montfaucon. No pardon shown in life, no mercy in death. De Craon ordered the corpses to hang there until they rotted, slabs of putrid flesh dropping into the great pit below.'

'And this included Simon?'

'Yes, it did, Ranulf.' Malpas fought back the tears. 'We also learnt that the so-called Sacred Six, devils incarnate, visited Simon in his death cell. They abused, raped and sodomised him. They tortured a man condemned to a most horrific death and, on execution day, they watched him die, sipping wine as Simon strangled on the gallows.'

'And you were never suspected, taken up?'

'No, Megotta, I was most fortunate. I realised how Simon had kept our relationship very secret. He never mentioned it to anyone. No one could lay an indictment against me. Oh no, indeed, I was promoted, my career enhanced. But my life had changed. I vowed vengeance. I became eaten up with a desire for revenge on de Craon and his ilk. I let de Craon seduce me. He entered my life and my bed and I waited.'

'De Craon trusted Philip so much,' Corbett intervened, 'that he despatched him on important errands to Westminster and elsewhere, and to our queen in particular. On one of these occasions, he sent a secret despatch to me. We met and I listened to Philip's story. I carried out my own investigation and I concluded he was speaking the truth. He and I became handfast comrades. My enemy was his enemy. If the king of France works for the total destruction of the English Crown then, believe me, Philip Malpas does everything to impede his masters at the Louvre. We plotted and we planned. I gave Philip juicy morsels to take back to the Louvre. We set up an arrangement whereby my couriers would meet Philip in secret, they would never know who he really was. I continued to supply him with tasty scraps from our king's table; bits of information the Chambre Noire would find useful. At the same time, we began to drop the poison that perhaps there was an English spy deep in the heart of the French Court.'

'And de Craon?' Ranulf asked.

'De Craon was delighted,' Malpas replied. 'He became deeply infatuated with me. Once the time was right, I turned on the Sacred Six. I began to hint that the English spy in the Louvre was one of them, deep in the pockets of Sir Hugh Corbett. At first this was difficult, but the seed was sown.'

'I in turn,' Corbett spoke up, 'began to receive valuable information, especially on troop movements close to the bastide of St Sardos on the borders of Gascony. The French would love to seize that wine-rich province back from England. More importantly, late last year I began to learn of a plot by King Philip and his coven to seize the Glory of Heaven and cause utter disruption and chaos in this kingdom.'

'Of course,' Ranulf breathed, 'by then Gaveston was proving a real threat to the peace and harmony of the

Crown. The great earls were calling themselves the Lords Ordainer, demanding Gaveston's exile, even death. They were intent on seizing the reins of government.'

'Ranulf, it was very serious, it still is, and I became more and more dependent on our friend here.'

'Matters progressed,' Malpas spoke up, 'I made myself indispensable even as I moved against the Sacred Six. I did all in my power to prove that Corbett's spy was a real danger. De Craon and I eventually entered into a pact. We knew we could not dispense with the Sacred Six; they knew too much. They could not be hired by some other family and there was a grave danger that all six of them could do real harm to the interests of King Philip. We concluded that they had to be killed and that should be carried out here in England. De Craon would be able to purge his household then recruit clerks totally faithful to him.'

'Moreover,' Corbett added, 'de Craon would use their murders here in England to depict this kingdom as riven by unrest and lawlessness, where even sacred envoys are not safe.'

'So, you killed those clerks?'

'Yes, Ranulf, I did, with the full connivance and support of de Craon. Sir Hugh neither advised nor supported me on this matter. I had no scruples. My conscience was clear. I saw, and I still do, their deaths as legitimate executions; fit punishment for men who had abused and murdered someone deeply precious to me. They all had to die.'

'I did not intervene,' Corbett agreed, 'even though I

knew that the Sacred Six – and what a lie of a name for a coven of thirsty blood-drinkers – had killed Malpas' friend. Just as importantly, I knew that they had inflicted the same agonies on those captured working for me. So, in truth I had no pity for them. They lived by the sword, they certainly died by it.'

'De Craon gave me free mandate,' Malpas continued. 'We arrived in England and I played the diligent clerk. However, I am also a skilled bowman. I have trained at the butts, not as sharp as you, Ap Ythel, but good enough.' Malpas pulled back the cuff of his jerkin to show the wristguard all archers wore. 'Now, like any embassy,' Malpas declared, 'we carry a weapons chest. De Craon and I made sure it contained longbows and quivers of arrows. I decided to strike on our way back from Windsor. On our journey out there, we stopped in a small glade in the forest edge. We visited the same place on our return.'

'And you had the longbow and arrows hidden close by?'

'Yes, Ap Ythel. Before we ever left for Windsor, I stole out of the abbey and hid the bow and arrows deep amongst the trees and vegetation. I also secreted a bow in a narrow enclave overlooking the abbey stable yard and so the stage was set. We left for Windsor, only a short journey but we paused in that glade where I ensured all was well. It was. On de Craon's return from Windsor, I left him and the others. I quietly hastened to where I had concealed both bow and arrows. I let loose the shafts and killed two of the Sacred Six. I did this like death's own bowman. I then hid my weapons and returned to the glade. Of course, all was confusion, but nobody, apart from de Craon, knew that I had left and returned. He actually confessed that he'd been taken by surprise himself. There was no need for pretence. Those arrows sped out through the green darkness and two of his henchmen were dead.' Malpas clenched his fist. 'I had begun to carry out my blood oath. Once we had returned to the abbey I crept away again and seized the second bow I had hidden.'

'Did you intend to kill?'

'No, Ap Ythel. If I had sighted one of the Sacred Six, yes, I would have loosed at him, but of course the confusion and chaos protected them.'

'So why did you do it?'

'Ranulf, I wanted to show that death stalks St Michael's and was no respecter of persons. More importantly, just by loosing on everyone, it dispelled the suspicion that those two deaths in the forest were not just an assault on de Craon and his entourage, but on everyone else. Another group was also involved.'

'The Templars?'

'Of course, Ranulf. I left those Templar seals on the arrow shafts as I did after the attacks on the other members of the Sacred Six, including the next victim.'

'Ambrose of Amboise?'

'Oh yes, dear Ambrose! A true wolf in human clothing. Living proof of the adage, "man is a wolf to man". Sir Hugh will certainly verify that. Ambrose was a blood-gulper responsible for a great deal of cruelty.

I whispered my poison in de Craon's ear. I warned him that two of his clerks were truly dangerous, Ambrose and Gaston Foix. They could well be the traitors but they were also men of violence. We had to move quickly.' Malpas waved a hand. 'And so on, and so on. De Craon was soft dough in my hand. He cooperated in Ambrose's death. I went into that blood-drinker's chamber. Believe me, his death was much swifter than the one he inflicted on many of his victims. I got close, drew my dagger and stabbed him; a blow direct to the heart. As I pressed on the handle, I watched the life light fade in his eyes and I whispered Simon's name time and time again.' Malpas sat head down. Corbett watched. He truly believed he was a merry soul, his life blighted by the brutal death of his beloved Simon. Malpas was now a man consumed by that love but also the deep pain of loss and an insatiable thirst for vengeance. Corbett and Malpas had often talked in secret, though rarely at St Michael's. The Keeper of the Secret Seal always felt a profound sorrow for this young clerk. Yes, he had killed and killed again, but Corbett's conscience was not troubled. They were caught up in the deadly Game of Kings, fighting those shadow-battles which were never far from Crown and throne. Corbett believed he was a soldier, a captain of war. Some royal retainers commanded fighting cogs out on the Narrow Seas or soldiers along the Scottish March. This was no different. This silent war waged far from the light.

'How did you communicate with Sir Hugh?' asked Megotta.

'Easy enough,' Malpas replied, breaking free of his reverie. 'A scrap of parchment left here and there with symbols and ciphers which meant nothing to anyone else. They would look like fragments of a tavern bill or the jottings of some household clerk.'

'And Ambrose?' Ranulf asked. 'What happened after you killed him?'

'Ah yes, Ambrose. De Craon was party to all that. Usually, he left matters to me.'

'You killed Ambrose, opened the shutters and fled through the window,' Corbett declared. 'But not before pulling those same shutters as close as you could?'

'Yes,' Malpas agreed. 'And during the confusion of breaking into that room, de Craon insisted on his rights. He decided who could enter and who could not. He moved swiftly to lock that chamber. He made sure the shutters were sealed with the bar brought down, so a real mystery was posed. How could anyone enter a locked, barred chamber and kill a mailed clerk like Ambrose? How did they get in? How did they get out? Why hadn't Ambrose resisted? Why weren't there signs of a struggle? No, Ambrose's death was meant to puzzle and to confuse. As I have said, de Craon was party to this. He truly believed, thanks to me, that one or more of the Sacred Six were traitors. Only I could be trusted.'

'But surely the suspicions of the other clerks must have been roused, their fears deepened even further?'

'Of course, Megotta. After the murder of Ambrose, de Craon held a council meeting. The three clerks were angry at the slaughter of their comrades. They hinted that de Craon was not protecting them. More chillingly, for the first time Gaston Foix not only suggested that Corbett had a spy in de Craon's household, but amongst the Sacred Six. Of course, this was met by cries of denial. I firmly rejected such an allegation. However, Foix remained insistent. He and Jean-Claude certainly believed that the death of their comrades was the work of Corbett and his minions and that we should retaliate. Now de Craon was desperate to strike at you, Sir Hugh, or even Ranulf, but he was very wary. If they murdered king's men, such high-ranking members of the English Chancery, and were caught, not even King Philip could save them. Nevertheless, the debate raged on. Someone in Corbett's party should be killed.'

'And they chose me.'

'Yes, they did, Megotta. Gaston, however, said it was too dangerous for them to be directly involved. De Craon agreed, so Gaston went out and hired those ruffians who, like many of their kind, had drifted into Bloody Meadow. What happened then was simple enough. I kept Gaston under constant scrutiny then I watched the hirelings. You made ready to leave, so did they. I left the abbey and made my way into the forest. De Craon wouldn't have missed me, he spent most of his time in his chamber seething about this or that. Anyway, I watched your would-be assassins prepare the ambuscade. They captured you.'

'And they abused me.'

'Yes, and they paid for that with their lives.'

'You were my saviour,' Megotta gasped.

'I was certainly their death. I loosed the shafts. Stupid wolfheads, they milled around, perfect targets. Once they were down, I heard you call out. Of course, I did not answer. I was wearing a Lincoln-green jerkin with a hood, I blended with the trees. I simply watched and waited for you to leave. Once you had, I dragged the corpses to a woodland marsh, deep and cloying. Your would-be abusers can rest there until the Final Resurrection.'

'And Jean-Claude?' Ranulf demanded brusquely, ignoring Megotta's glare. 'You were saved out in the forest,' Ranulf soothed her, 'and thank God for that, but the clerk Jean-Claude . . .?'

'At de Craon's council meeting, Jean-Claude loudly voiced that he felt as if he was not trusted; that he and the Sacred Six had been viciously attacked. Unlike Gaston and de Craon, Jean-Claude believed that Sir Hugh should be killed immediately.'

'Hence all the mummery,' Ranulf declared.

'Oh yes, the claim that evidence was found on Jean-Claude, depicting him as the traitor. This, of course, culminated in the swordfight outside the abbey church; Jean-Claude's flight into sanctuary; his confession and desperate plea for help. Absolute nonsense! A complete farrago of lies, a scheme concocted between Jean-Claude and de Craon to trap you, Sir Hugh.'

'So, our noble French envoy decided on my death.' Corbett scowled.

'Why didn't he just wait for your murder during the mandatum?'

'No, Ranulf.' Corbett shook his head. 'De Craon was being fenced in: he had to retaliate and be seen doing it. Moreover, he had nothing to lose. If Jean-Claude was successful, the game was over. If he failed, well, Jean-Claude would pay the price, whatever that was. Nothing could be placed at de Craon's door, not even the murder during the mandatum on which he had pinned so much. Nevertheless, our French envoy must have been desperate.'

'Sir Hugh, he was,' Malpas confirmed. 'He was consenting to the deaths of his own clerks but he had to hide that. He had to retaliate otherwise suspicions would be roused.'

'And you?' Megotta asked.

'Of course I knew what was coming,' Malpas replied. 'My first duty was to warn Sir Hugh, but I protected myself. I begged both de Craon and Jean-Claude not to do it. I told them it was highly dangerous. Even if they killed Sir Hugh, there would be an investigation. Jean-Claude countered time and again, repeating that Corbett should pay. I was overruled, though of course I would use that later to protect myself. But yes, it was all mummery. Jean-Claude wanted to get very close to you, Sir Hugh, to carry out his murderous mischief. He argued that he could kill you in such a manner so that people might suspect, but no one could hold him to account.' Malpas spread his hands. 'I assure you, my friends, everything that Jean-Claude said was mummery, a blatant lie. Now I know that Jean-Claude was a poisoner, a constant visitor to the shabby shops near

Pont Neuf. He knows all about henbane, and hemlock, foxglove and all the deadly plants you can find growing in any garden. De Craon had often exploited Jean-Claude's skill to slip poison into some goblet or tankard on behalf of the Chambre Noire.'

'So . . . the business of the Vexin – the custom he spoke of, of reaching an agreement sealed by both parties drinking a goblet of wine in a church?'

'Oh yes, that's a custom I know and recognise, Ranulf,' Corbett replied. 'Indeed, they do the same in the south-west shires of this kingdom.' He grinned. 'But not with one of the goblets heavily poisoned. Malpas warned me that Jean-Claude was a sham, and to be wary of him, particularly with Jean-Claude's favourite weapon – poison.'

'And so?'

'And so, Megotta, I was determined not to drink. I used the confusion caused by the altercation with de Craon at the front door of the church to secretly exchange goblets.'

'And Jean-Claude was so easily deceived?'

'Megotta, Jean-Claude was arrogant. He insisted on pouring the wine and sharing out the cups and that was it. I knew what he would do. I happily obliged. Jean-Claude believed his victim was trotting like a lamb to the slaughterhouse. He was caught up with all the glory of what he was doing. He would win the accolade of being the French clerk who'd removed me permanently from the Game of Kings. He made an error, a terrible mistake: he was too confident so he paid the price. Of course, I kept my face impassive. I acted the startled spectator who could not understand or accept what had happened. I had to assume such a role.' Corbett spread his hands. 'Even to you, my friends, that was vitally important,' he grinned, 'and that's why afterwards I went through the events of Jean-Claude's poisoning. I had to ensure that I had not made a mistake in what really was Death's own drama. I did not want to provoke the suspicion, even amongst you, that I had been warned. Jean-Claude planned on me collapsing; you can imagine the chaos and confusion that would have caused. People would start asking who was in the church. Who had touched the goblets? Perhaps the Templars would be blamed? And so on, and so on. Believe me, de Craon wouldn't have waited. Jubilant, he would have collected his entourage, Jean-Claude included, and left St Michael's for a swift visit to Windsor and then on to the coast.'

'But that didn't happen,' Ranulf declared. 'Surely de Craon's suspicions must have been roused? The first question would be, who had informed Sir Hugh? How was it arranged that Jean-Claude, the author of Sir Hugh's planned murder, was killed himself?'

'Of course, Ranulf,' Malpas replied, 'but I could point the finger. Remember, I had warned them not to proceed with Jean-Claude's plan. In fact, I described it as a madcap scheme. I said there were all sorts of possibilities to explain the terrible mishap. Was it by accident or design or simply ill fortune? Jean-Claude would not be the first poisoner to die by his own hand. Accidents do happen.'

'And as I have said,' Corbett intervened, 'I was determined not to drink from either goblet just in case.'

'Of course, I did more,' Malpas continued. 'I continued my whispering against the rest. I said the poisoning might well be the work of Gaston, who had also supported Jean-Claude. Nor did I forget the other clerk, the tall, ever-silent, cadaverous-faced Augustin, who'd watched like some spectator, the murderous mystery unfolding around us.'

'So, Gaston supported Jean-Claude?'

'Oh yes, Gaston would have supported anything against Sir Hugh. And you did well to watch him, Megotta. After Jean-Claude's death, de Craon seemed to lose confidence. If I made a mistake, and I did,' Malpas cleared his throat and gratefully sipped at the cup Megotta handed to him, 'I underestimated Gaston: he did not trust me. I know he was jealous of my status, my relationship with de Craon. He certainly entertained deep suspicions about me.'

'Why didn't he voice those to de Craon?'

'He probably did, Ranulf, but de Craon would not believe him.'

'So why did he want you dead, murdered?'

'First, he hated me, deeply jealous of my relationship with de Craon, Secondly, I suspect he really did think I was the spy. Thirdly, Ranulf, once I had been removed, Gaston would have ransacked everything I owned looking for evidence and he might have found something. Fourthly, the chaos and confusion which had disturbed de Craon's household would disappear.

Gaston would argue that was so because the cause of the chaos and confusion, namely myself, had been removed.'

'Oh yes,' Corbett interjected. 'Gaston and the other clerk would fasten on that.'

'And time was passing,' Malpas continued. 'De Craon seemed at a loss, so Gaston took matters into his own hands. He hired a wandering wolfshead, an assassin amongst the crowds thronging into Bloody Meadow. Gaston hoped, did he not, to bring the assassin into the abbey, a shrewd throw of the dice, a murderous gamble. Sir Hugh told me what you did, Megotta, and I thank you for that. Gaston left to meet the assassin who, of course, had been warned off by you. Gaston never suspected. He came striding through the dark, and I was there near the ruined abbey wall waiting for him. It did not take long. Gaston drew his dagger and knocked mine from my hand so I clubbed him with a ferocious blow to the side of the head. He sank to the ground. I wasted no time, I was aware of the mummers, some of whom might come wandering; lovers looking for a lonely place for their tryst. I loaded pieces of stone beneath Gaston's clothing to weigh him down and tossed the corpse into a nearby marsh.'

'And his corpse has never been found?' Megotta asked. She smiled wanly. 'I watched your struggle with Gaston Foix, a true blood-gulper, a killer to the marrow, resourceful and cunning. Sir Hugh, we should ensure his corpse is where it should be.'

'Perhaps, perhaps, but soon we will have to leave.

For the moment I believe we are finished. Ranulf, you have searched the abbot's chamber?'

'As you instructed, Sir Hugh, but I found nothing remarkable. You said I would know what I was searching for when I found it.' Ranulf scratched his head and grinned sheepishly. 'Very mysterious.'

'Aye, it is, my friend. It's connected with the diamond. Rest assured, I will be glad to transfer the Glory of Heaven to the arca in the Secret Chancery.' Corbett got to his feet. 'That diamond may well be the Glory of Heaven, it is undoubtedly sacred, which means it must be managed very carefully.'

'What do you mean?' Malpas demanded.

'Perhaps, my friend, it should only be held by the pure of heart as in the stories of the Knights of the Round Table. Only Galahad was able to hold the Holy Grail.'

'Tell me,' Ranulf remarked. 'What I find mysterious is your hunt for the diamond, Sir Hugh. You found it. You resolved Brother Mark's murder, as you did the plot by the so-called Apostles who conspired to kill the king and, when he escaped their trap, they turned on you. Surely,' Ranulf gestured at Malpas, 'de Craon must have discussed this with you. Couldn't you have informed Sir Hugh about what you learnt?'

'Tell him, Philip,' Corbett urged.

Malpas rubbed his eyes. 'Oh no, Ranulf,' he replied slowly, 'look at the crimes we are discussing. Whoever stole that diamond, if he was caught, would be accused of the most heinous crimes and sins: the murder of the guardian, Brother Mark, a killing committed at the very heart of this abbey, whilst the subsequent theft of the Glory of Heaven would be deemed a truly sacrilegious act. Oh no, what happened here in St Michael's recalls what happened to Beckett in his own cathedral church, a truly sacrilegious act. The person responsible could expect no mercy whatsoever. He'd be torn apart but not before being excommunicated by bell, book and candle.' He paused. 'And the same is true of what the so-called Apostles plotted. Hideous murder in this abbey church during one of the most sacred ceremonies of Holy Week. Again, you can only imagine the outrage. Now I know, and you know, what King Philip and de Craon plotted. However, I would wager my life there is not a scrap of parchment either here or in the Chambre Noire which provides any hint of what they intended. So, to answer your question bluntly, Ranulf-atte-Newgate, de Craon may have known, may have suspected, but he was not directly responsible for the murder of Brother Mark, the theft of the diamond or the plotted attack during the mandatum. He left these matters to his mysterious secret henchman, Reboham, who, of course, Sir Hugh unmasked and so Abbot Maurice was caught.'

'So, is de Craon guilty?'

'In a word – yes, Ranulf,' Malpas replied. 'He wanted the diamond and he wanted that murder during the mandatum. Both acts were meant to cause chaos and confusion throughout this kingdom. However, I never overheard any conversation or read any document which could throw any blame for all of this on de

Craon or his royal master. Oh, I am sure both crimes were plotted by King Philip and his creature de Craon, but their execution was left to Reboham to organise and carry out.

'Reboham was their catspaw,' Malpas declared. 'So that precious pair, like Pilate, could wash their hands and shriek their innocence.'

'Very clever,' Corbett declared, getting to his feet again. 'So, my beloveds, let us adjourn. We must prepare to leave.' He stretched out his hand for Malpas to clasp. 'You, my friend, must revert to being our prisoner, bound for comfortable quarters in the Tower. Ranulf and Ap Ythel will see to that. Oh, by the way, captain, I want three of your best archers outside. They are to follow me wherever I go. Megotta,' Corbett took the moon girl's hands in his, 'my most grateful thanks. Tell your captain Janus that he is finished here. I am more than aware of how his planned masques and miracle plays were never staged. My deepest apologies for that. However, tell him to move to my manor at Leighton where the great meadow can house you all. The Lady Maeve will warmly welcome him and you, but I shall see you before we part.'

Corbett then asked them all to repeat the oath that they had taken at the beginning. All of them did.

'Sir Hugh.' Ranulf tapped the Book of the Gospels. 'Sir Hugh,' he repeated, 'why have you made us take this oath: a truly binding vow to what we witnessed here?'

'Life is strange, Ranulf, and events can take a sharp

and vicious turn. One of these days I might not duck fast enough. No, no,' he held a hand up to still their protests, 'we are soldiers. We fight battles deep in the shadows thrown by Crown and Throne. We wage war against those who would see good government crumble and the king's peace shattered. Two hundred years ago, civil war raged in this country. Foreign princes and prelates interfered and made matters worse; they called it a time "When God and his saints slept". We are part of that struggle; you've seen it played out here. Jean-Claude poisoned in a church; others brought down by well-aimed arrow shafts; Megotta nearly murdered, and so on, and so on. You can only successfully confront the tempest for a while and, one of these days, I too might go down. However, I am not thinking about myself,' he pointed at Malpas, 'but you, Philip. A time might well come when all the masks slip and the truth emerges. If that happens, and I have spoken to you before about this, you must flee as swift as a bird on the wing. You will have to reach either Ponthieu or Gascony, any place where the English king's writ runs. If that happens you will eventually have to make your way to Westminster to make a plea to the judges of King's Bench that you be given good shelter in England. You will have to tell the justiciars precisely what you have done on behalf of the English Secret Chancery. They will ask for proof but, of course, as you know, we keep no letters or memoranda. In fact, the opposite. I have told you time and again: nothing in writing, unless it's a brief message in a cipher only the two of us understand. However, even if you could produce those it would mean nothing.' Corbett paused and took a sip of wine from his goblet. 'When you appear before King's Bench you will be asked for evidence and you will reply that you have none. Then they will demand witnesses—'

'And we are that,' Ranulf interjected.

'Yes, my good friend – you, Ranulf-atte-Newgate, Captain Ap Ythel and Megotta the moon girl. All three of you must go before the royal justiciars and take a solemn oath that Philip Malpas is indeed a true friend of the English Crown and its Secret Chancery. If and when I return to Leighton Manor, I shall tell the Lady Maeve precisely what has happened and ask her to take a similar oath. She will also come forward to stand guarantee for Philip Malpas.'

'God forbid all this should happen,' Ap Ythel murmured.

'God keep us all safe,' Corbett replied. 'But now, my friends, I bid you adieu.'

Once they had gone, Corbett sat listening to the faint sounds of the abbey as he quietly marvelled at the sheer, sharp turn of events since he had arrived at St Michael's. 'And yet,' he murmured to himself, 'all is not finished.' He rose, seized a quill pen and scribbled a name on a scrap of parchment. He then strapped on his war belt, collected his cloak and left the chamber. Ap Ythel's three archers were waiting for him and they followed Corbett down the stairs and the long narrow galleries to Abbot Maurice's chamber.

'Why are you here, Corbett? You will keep your word?' The abbot spread his bony fingers out as if to embrace the warmth from the pine-log fire blazing in the hearth.

'I will keep my word and you will answer a question.'

'Which is?'

'The name of your accomplice in the robbery.'

The abbot just gaped.

'I, I . . .' he stammered, 'I did that alone. It's all my responsibility, my fault . . .'

Corbett leant over the abbot, his face only a few inches away from that of his opponent.

'Listen, Blackrobe,' he hissed, 'I am not in the mood for any further games. I know what happened, what actually happened. I don't care about your oaths or vows to this person or that! Promises to keep silent! I will show you a name on a scrap of parchment. I will ask if that person was your accomplice, you will answer, yea or nay. Nothing more, nothing less.' Corbett undid the scrap of parchment he held in the palm of his hand. He held it so that the abbot could read what Corbett had scrawled there.

'Yea or nay,' Corbett insisted. Abbot Maurice rubbed his face in his hands.

'Yea or nay?' Corbett repeated.

'Yes, yes, it is.'

'Thank you.' Corbett threw the scrap of parchment into the fire and re-joined his escort outside.

They went down into the ice-cold nave of the abbey church, which was both deserted and desolate except for Simon the Sacristan busy in his chamber. Corbett greeted him then walked on down to the ankerhold. He ordered the archers to wait close by and then knocked on the door, which swung open. The anchorite, almost hidden in a swathe of blankets, let him in. Corbett sat down on a stool close to the anchorite, who perched on the side of his cot bed.

'Sir Hugh, to what do I owe the honour?'

'My friend, you must have expected me.'

'Why?'

'Because of the diamond, the Glory of Heaven, you were there when it was stolen.'

'I was asleep,' the anchorite screeched. 'I drank,' he pointed to the pewter goblet on the table, 'I drank wine and fell asleep. Looking back, on reflection, the wine must have contained some sleeping potion.'

'I am sure it did. But, I suggest, you drank the wine *after* the murderous masque played out here. You know full well what actually happened. You could have saved me a great deal of time and energy as well as considerable heartache.'

'I, I . . .' the anchorite stammered.

'Oh, you can mumble and mutter your innocence for all you like, but you were, and you are, committed to that diamond. You venerate it as a truly powerful relic; it's also a strong link to the past, your years as a Templar, the tragedy of Acre and so on. Ah well, my friend, tell me what you saw that day.' The anchorite looked as if he was going to refuse, a stubborn set to his grizzled face. 'My friend,' Corbett warned, 'I can tear this ankerhold apart. I could indict you as an accomplice to the litany of heinous crimes committed here in this abbey church. Or, there again, you could cooperate with me, the king's justiciar.'

'And?' the anchorite interjected quickly. 'What then?'

Corbett smiled to himself; the anchorite was rising to the bait.

'I have the diamond, the Glory of Heaven. It will be locked away in the most secure arca to be found in the Secret Chancery at Westminster. I shall then recommend to the king, Her Grace the queen and the Archbishops of Canterbury and York that the Glory of Heaven be transferred to the Marian Shrine at Walsingham where it can be safely displayed for the devotion of pilgrims. However,' Corbett held up a hand, 'to display it properly and worthily, the diamond will need its monstrance or pyx. The sacred host is held in such a receptacle and I know, from the descriptions I have read of the Glory of Heaven, that the stone was set in a gold, jewel-studded pyx. A true work of art; a roundel with a most rare glass covering. The pyx rests on four gold, jewel-studded legs. Now,' Corbett leant forward, 'I seized the Glory of Heaven from our abbot's unholy grasp, but not the pyx, the container, specially fashioned for it.'

'And what makes you think I have it?'

'The abbot's possessions were searched. No pyx was found. Those who first discovered the robbery and murder make no reference to it. Now listen carefully for I have not yet finished. If and when the Glory of Heaven is displayed at the shrine of Our Lady of

Walsingham, I could arrange for you to be appointed to the ankerhold at the shrine.' Corbett caught the shift in this cunning man's deep-set eyes. 'So,' Corbett pointed a finger, 'you were there when the diamond was stolen and Brother Mark murdered. I know that because Abbot Maurice has confessed as much.'

'He wouldn't—'

'He did. I suspect you are going to say how Abbot Maurice would never break his solemn oath to an old comrade. Well, he didn't. As I said, I had his chamber searched and found nothing. I genuinely believe that the abbot does not have the golden pyx. You do. You were the only one in this church besides the abbot when the theft took place. You were here and somehow you seized it. Oh, and don't reply that Abbot Maurice would not reveal the truth. To be honest, he didn't break his oath. I simply wrote your name on a scrap of parchment and he nodded his agreement. He did not reveal the truth, I did. Do you want me to drag the abbot down here and ask him the same question again? Ask him to write down the name? So, if not, where is the pyx, monstrance, or whatever you want to call it? Come, come, the candle burns. I have other business.' Corbett paused as the anchorite raised his hand.

'You will keep your word, Sir Hugh?'

'You have my word.'

The anchorite crossed himself and murmured something under his breath.

'Abbot Maurice,' he declared slowly, 'has, however way you wish to portray it, Sir Hugh, dissolved our bond. So yes, I was present at the robbery and murder. I was sitting here staring at the wine jug wondering whether I should drink it immediately or leave it for later. I sensed someone was in the church, but the noises I heard were, I thought, caused by Brother Mark. He could be extremely clumsy, even more so after a goblet of Bordeaux. Nothing out of the ordinary until I heard raised voices. They came from Brother Mark and the abbot. I got to my feet, but of course the squint hole does not provide me with a good view of the Silver Shrine. I then heard a cry, a deep wounding cry. I left my ankerhold. God save me, it was the most chilling sight. Brother Mark was staggering away from the bars, blood pumping out from the deep wound to his chest. Abbot Maurice stood there as if paralysed, one hand grasping the dagger, the other his walking cane. I called out. Abbot Maurice turned, a stricken look on his face. I knew I should keep away from him but then glimpsed the monstrance or pyx lying on the ground next to the bars. I swiftly seized it and backed away. By then the abbot had regained his wits. "I have the pyx," I declared.

'"And I have the diamond," the abbot replied, patting the pocket of his robe. He then turned and fled, one shadow amongst many. I hastened back here.' The anchorite shrugged. 'As expected, there was chaos and confusion. Then you arrived, Sir Hugh. Abbot Maurice, however, had anticipated your investigation and he did what he could. He held on to the Glory of Heaven; he also realised I would not surrender the pyx, so we took an oath of mutual support. He would keep the diamond and maintain his silence. I would hold the pyx and do likewise. We remembered our time in Acre and called upon our glorious dead to witness our oath.' The anchorite rubbed his face.

'What did you intend to do with your treasure?'

'Before God, Sir Hugh, I don't really know. I cannot, I would not, sell such a precious and sacred item. I just felt that I had some part of the diamond with me – I mean, its purpose, perhaps a memorial of things that were. As you say, a link to the past. But now—'

'Hand it over!' Corbett retorted brusquely. 'And I mean now!'

The anchorite sighed, rose and went into a far corner. He picked up a coarse-haired horse blanket. He brought this back, undid the rope and carefully unrolled the blanket to reveal the pyx, an exquisitely beautiful roundel with a cross on top just above the circular glass door. Corbett held it up like a priest would the host, admiring both the pyx and its four legs, all fashioned out of the purest gold. He weighed it in his hand and it felt heavy. He opened the delicately hinged, round glass door and put his finger in the small hollow sculpted out of the gold where The Glory of Heaven was supposed to reside. He closed the small door and put the pyx on the ground beside him.

'Sir Hugh, you have the diamond on you?'

Corbett smiled bleakly at the anchorite.

'Of course.'

'And you will keep your word?'

'I have already assured you of that.'

'Can I look at the diamond, hold it once more? Will you repeat your promise? If you do, I will tell you something else. Information which might be of great interest to you.'

Corbett pulled the diamond out of the special wallet he had fastened to his war belt.

'Good, good,' the anchorite whispered. 'That's how I used to carry it.'

Corbett handed the diamond over and repeated his promise, staring at the sheer translucent beauty of the stone. The anchorite held it up. Eyes closed, he murmured a prayer then handed it back.

'It should,' he murmured, 'be kept in a most sacred place.'

'And it will be, it will be.' Corbett slipped the diamond securely back in his wallet. 'And now you have something of interest to tell me?'

'Oh yes. I go out into God's Acre, you know that. Sometimes for a walk, but I also have a secret cache, a wine skin and other comforts hidden away. I like the cemetery; I like to wander it, that's where I saw the demon striding amongst the dead.' The anchorite looked at Corbett quizzically. 'You have resolved that as well?'

'You said you had something to tell me.'

'Last night I was out in my hiding place behind a plinth, an ancient funeral slab. I heard a sound and stood at a half-crouch. I glimpsed the glow of a fire where the ground fell away into a hollow. Curious, I crept towards it. A man sat hunched over a meagre fire. I think he was wounded here,' the anchorite tapped the side of his head, 'he was pressing a rag against the wound. He looked wet as if he had fallen into water. He was shivering, talking to himself. I listened carefully; he spoke in French.'

'What?'

'Not English, Sir Hugh, but Norman French. I was curious but I dare not approach. There was something about him, sinister, threatening. At first he was nothing more than a bedraggled shadow, yet as I watched he seemed to become more assured and confident. Eventually he rose, stamped on the fire and disappeared into the darkness. That's all I can tell you.' The anchorite wiped his mouth on the back of his hand. 'I do talk to the brothers. I have heard about your clashes with de Craon and his clerks. I was here, remember, when one of them fled for sanctuary and was poisoned?'

'And you think the man you glimpsed was one of those French clerks?'

'He may well have been. He spoke their tongue; he had a war belt and I saw rings glittering on his fingers. When he walked away, I also noticed the boots. They looked high-heeled, of good Cordovan leather . . .' The anchorite's voice trailed away. Corbett ensured that both the diamond and the pyx were safely secreted. He then bade the anchorite adieu and left for his chamber.

Once there, Corbett took off his war belt and boots and sat staring into the fire, watching the flames rise and fall like dancers. He reflected on events. He had the diamond and the pyx. De Craon had been sent packing. Nevertheless, Corbett felt a deep sense of menace. 'I will be glad, my soul will rejoice,' Corbett whispered to himself, 'to be free of here. Ah yes, Gaston Foix!' He recalled that professional assassin's sombre face, a true street-fighter, a skilled dagger man. Was he still alive, Corbett wondered? Had he escaped from that marsh? Malpas had confronted him in the dark. A blow to the head might be serious but not necessarily lethal. Corbett had walked battlefields and seen men similarly struck rise to fight afresh. He recalled precisely what the anchorite had told him. There was no other logical explanation for it. The man in God's Acre must have been Gaston Foix. Corbett rose and opened the door, beckoning at one of the archers.

'Sir Hugh?'

'Fast as you can,' Corbett declared, 'to your captain and Master Ranulf. At first light they must drag and search the marsh close to the broken wall. They should ask Megotta for help, she knows what they are looking for.' The archer faithfully repeated the message and hurried off. Corbett returned to his chamber and knelt at the prie-dieu before the crucifix. 'Lord help me,' he prayed, 'but this truly is a fight to the death. But whose death, Lord, whose death?'

Monseigneur Amaury de Craon was also reflecting as he slouched before the fire in his chamber deep in the soaring donjon of Windsor Castle. He studied the rough carving above the hearth depicting St George thrusting his lance into the mouth of a dragon. De Craon blinked and glanced away. The insignia of the English Royal

Court did not concern him. What he had achieved in England did.

He had now left St Michael's, hurrying after the young queen, who loudly declared that she was making her last journey. She would stay in her chambers at Windsor until her Golden Boy, as she constantly proclaimed him, was born and her confinement brought to an end. The queen was certainly testy, giving de Craon the briefest of audiences when he reached Windsor. The French envoy didn't really care, he was exhausted, deeply agitated by the seizure of his beloved Malpas, desperate to return to the Louvre. He was certain he could convince Philip of the urgent need to exchange Thomas Didymus for this most cherished clerk of the Chambre Noire. Corbett had obliquely referred to such an exchange when de Craon met him just before leaving for Windsor.

De Craon plucked at the fur on his robe as he wondered how he could present his report to that most inscrutable of princes. He must try to depict himself in the best light. He must emphasise his achievements and dismiss any failings as the fault of circumstance or someone else.

First, the Glory of Heaven had eluded his grasp: that could be rectified in years to come. England was fast becoming fertile ground for France to till.

Secondly, Corbett had also eluded his grasp but, on reflection, that too was an apple waiting to be plucked. There would be other occasions when the tide could change.

Thirdly, he had culled the Sacred Six. Five of them now lay dead. One or more of them had been a traitor, so de Craon didn't give a fig. Punishment had been carried out: de Craon could not tolerate any traitor being close to him. If he'd left such matters alone it would be only a matter of time before Philip turned on him.

Fourthly, de Craon was pleased with the reports he had received on his return to Windsor. The queen's uncles, Louis and Charles, were insistent that the expected heir to the English Crown be baptised Louis after the saintly king of the Capetian royal line. De Craon smirked to himself – that would certainly set the cat amongst the pigeons!

In addition, he could relay favourable news. Edward the king may well be lusty and healthy but he would not give up Gaveston and the great earls were preparing for war. It was only a matter of time before the English king unfurled his banner and marched to meet them. Once he did, all sorts of possibilities emerged. *The Temeraire* could soon be re-equipped for sea, and French troops were within a day's march of their coastal ports. Oh yes, de Craon was determined to emphasise the widening rift between Edward and his leading earls.

His mind drifted back to St Michael's and the tangle of tortuous events at that abbey. Where was Gaston Foix, he wondered, what had happened to him? And poor Philip. Would he be treated well? Once his beloved was back in the Louvre, de Craon was determined to recruit fresh blood. He would re-establish a new Sacred

Six under the leadership of his beloved Philip. He would—

De Craon started at a swift knock on the door. The French envoy's hand went out to touch the small hand-held arbalest, fully primed, on the table to his right. He then felt beneath his robe and tapped the handle of his dagger. Again, the knock. De Craon rose and opened the door. Augustin stood there, face all startled, behind him a shadowy cowled figure.

'What is it?' de Craon demanded, tightening his grip on the hilt of his dagger.

'Monseigneur, see for yourself!' Augustin stepped back, ushering the figure forward. 'It is Gaston Foix!'

The new arrival now pulled back his hood. De Craon glimpsed the gruesome bruise to the right side of the man's head as well as the deep scratches along his face.

'By Saint Denis,' de Craon exclaimed. 'What is this? Augustin, thank you. Gaston, you are most welcome. Come in, come in.' De Craon pulled his visitor into his chamber, thanked Augustin once again, then closed and bolted the door. 'My friend, my comrade, do sit.' De Craon, mind all awhirl, beckoned Gaston Foix to a chair in front of the hearth. He then poured a goblet of wine and thrust it into his guest's hand. 'Drink, drink,' he urged as he returned to his own chair. De Craon let Gaston take a few sips as he tried to control his own whirling thoughts.

'Well.' Gaston took one last gulp then turned to face his master. 'Monseigneur, I have urgent news for you. When we last met, you know that I was intent on

PAUL DOHERTY

hiring an assassin to kill Corbett or at least one of his entourage.'

De Craon nodded, desperate to keep his face impassive.

'I arranged to meet the wolfshead,' Gaston continued, 'at a place in the abbey wall. I went there and waited. A man came slinking out of the dark, all masked and hooded. I thought it was the outlaw I had hired. I was sorely mistaken. The man immediately closed with me, lunging with a dagger. I knocked it aside. He stepped back, his hood and mask slipped and I glimpsed the top part of his face, certainly enough to identify him. It was Malpas! Monseigneur, I swear by all that is holy, it was Malpas! He is – he was – the traitor, the spy, the viper you nursed in your bosom.' Gaston paused to catch his breath. 'Monseigneur, I did warn you. I had the deepest suspicion about Malpas. Something about the way he acted. I know you cared for him but, from the start, he has been a deep-dyed Judas.'

'You are sure?' De Craon strove to conceal the panic within him.

'I am, monseigneur, and I would go on oath to declare that.'

'And then what happened?' de Craon croaked, picking up his own goblet, his lips and throat were so dry.

'I managed to knock his dagger away, but then he struck me here on the side of the head. I crumpled into darkness. When I regained my mind, I found myself half floating in a marsh, a place where the mud was

342

not so thick, constantly moved by some underwater spring. You see, the quagmire fell away in a row of muddy ledges. If I had been pushed out to float further, I would have been unable to escape. My attacker had placed rocks and stones in my clothing to weigh my body down. Some of these had fallen out and I quickly got rid of the rest. I turned and looked about me. I glimpsed lights from the abbey and this gave me some direction. I dragged myself back on a ledge and then up onto others. Eventually I reached firm ground and pulled myself out. No one was there. My attacker had pushed me into the quagmire confident that I would float away and drown. I did not. I staggered into the abbey cemetery; I knew I would be safe there. Who visits God's Acre after dark? I still had my war belt and one stiletto. More importantly I had silver in my purse as well as a dry tinder. I crept down into a hollow and lit a fire. Monseigneur, I have served our king in war, I have been in worse situations on the battlefield at Courtrai. I managed to get some warmth as I tried to make sense of what had happened. I was utterly shocked; Malpas was your henchman. He was our leader and you trusted him completely. He had access to all our secrets, plans and designs. He is young and capable, a mailed clerk who enjoyed your favour and that of the king. So why should he turn, monseigneur? We will ask that same question in Paris. Malpas must be brought to judgement; he must answer for his crimes, his treachery. Either being burned alive on a bank by the Seine or be torn apart at Montfaucon. Monseigneur, he knows everything. He was party to all your secret designs. Heaven knows what he is telling Corbett now.' Gaston cradled the goblet. 'I was, I am, deeply confused.'

'Continue. Tell me what happened next.' De Craon tried to remain calm. He wanted to do nothing to provoke Gaston's suspicions.

'I was determined to reach you, monseigneur, as well as to get safely out of St Michael's. The fire cheered me but I realised I must leave the abbey; it was too dangerous.'

'So how did you escape?'

'I was seething with rage, not just at Malpas but the wolfshead who had betrayed me. I hired him for a task which he didn't carry out and almost led to my death. I crept into Bloody Meadow. I reached the wolfshead's cart; thank God the villain was alone. He had packed everything ready to leave the following morning. He never even saw me coming. I killed him, put his body into his covered cart and left. I reached the trackway to Windsor. By then I had changed my wet clothes with whatever I could find in the cart. I stopped to get rid of the man's corpse. I thrust it deep into the vegetation, let it rot there. I reached Windsor and lodged at a tavern just within the main gate. I sold the cart and horse very swiftly, bought new clothes and armaments.' He toasted de Craon with his cup. 'And so, here I am.'

'So you are, Gaston.' De Craon stretched out and patted the man's arm. 'You did very well. You showed great courage. The king will be most pleased with you.' De Craon stared into the flames and tried to hide the agitation which gripped his belly and turned his flesh ice-cold. He must seek a way forward, but his mind tumbled like dice in a cup. De Craon sensed real danger. Time would pass and Gaston might prove to be a most deadly threat. 'Monseigneur, we have to report all this to the king. I still cannot believe it.'

'Neither can I, my friend, neither can I.' De Craon closed his eyes at the surge of hate which swept through him. Malpas! A man he had favoured and cherished above all others.

'He's been seized,' de Craon declared. 'Malpas has been taken up by Corbett on what I now regard as a spurious charge.'

'I agree,' Gaston interjected. 'You know what's happened, monseigneur. He has been taken into custody to deepen the illusion that he is Corbett's enemy. All a pretence.'

'Ah.' De Craon raised his hand. 'But we will, after the shock is over, smile and smile again. Once back in Paris, I will seek Malpas's return to face the consequences of his treachery.' To curb his own inner turbulence, he rose and walked to the door. He unlocked it and peered out. Augustin had moved away, probably downstairs into the tavern buttery. De Craon, taking deep breaths, realised he had to act. He was committed. He walked back to his chair and sat down, staring at the floor.

'Monseigneur?'

'Gaston, my friend, have you informed anyone, including Augustin, of what you have told me?'

345

'No, monseigneur.'

'Think, man. Anyone at all? Does anyone here or at St Michael's know what happened to you?'

Gaston raised a hand. 'Monseigneur, I have told no one because I trust no one except you.'

'Then, Gaston, I will take the same blood oath of comradeship you and all the Sacred Six swore when you were inducted to my service, but this time, I shall take it with you.' De Craon rolled back the sleeve of his jerkin. 'Draw your dagger, Gaston.' He did so. 'Now,' de Craon turned his bare arm, 'a slight cut here just below the elbow.' Gaston leant forward and made the cut. De Craon winced. 'A second one, again just a simple slit.' Gaston, fully immersed in the ritual, agreed to do so. He then, head down, wiped the blood off the blade of his dagger, polishing the steel with a rag.

'Gaston!' The man looked up. Before Gaston could even react, de Craon released the catch of the arbalest, sending the bolt to smash into the left side of his henchman's chest, a mortal blow direct to the heart. Gaston, eyes popping, dropped his knife. He tried to stretch out his arms but then coughed on the blood spurting through his nose and between his lips. One final cough and he fell back, eyes half closed in death. De Craon watched for a while then he sat down. He placed the arbalest on the floor, picked up his goblet, toasted his victim and gulped a mouthful of wine.

'My apologies, Gaston,' he whispered, 'but it was necessary. I cannot, I will not have you return to the

Chambre Noire to tell your tale. How Amaury de Craon allowed himself to be fooled and tricked, not only by Corbett of England, but Malpas of France. How I, under his direction, permitted, nay, even encouraged, the needless slaughter of four French clerks of the Chambre Noire, loyal to the Crown. Oh yes, Philip of France would soon realise that.' De Craon took another gulp of wine. 'And there's worse, that same Malpas betrayed the secrets of his king and brought many of Philip's hidden designs to nothing.' De Craon wiped the sweat off his face. 'I nourished a spy as close as possible to the French Crown. A traitor who supplied Corbett with vital information whilst causing utter confusion within the Chambre Noire. And I was responsible for that. Questions would be asked. Oh yes, wolves turn on each other and you, Gaston, along with the likes of Augustin, would smell blood and close in for the kill. But not before I became a laughing stock.' De Craon took a deep breath. 'And then, of course, there's my love for Malpas. King Philip would soon conclude that I was guilty, that it was all my fault and that I should pay the price. He would bring in his inquisitors. They would question others, torture me. So, my friend, you had to die.' De Craon rose and stood over the corpse of his victim.

'But not now, eh?' He kicked the dead man's booted feet. 'I will peddle the tale that you were the traitor. How my suspicions were first aroused in the abbey. I'll garnish it with scraps of information. How I found a war bow hidden away close to your chamber. Of how you came here and I caught you out when questioning you. Your first mistake was over the poisoning of Jean-Claude. You made a slip, Gaston. You talked of Corbett exchanging the cups in the church. How did you know that, eh, Gaston? Of course you cannot reply, what a pity.' De Craon, warming to his theme, walked up and down the chamber. 'And then of course there's the murder of poor Ambrose. You talked of his corpse, or I will say you did, being slumped in the corner of his chamber where he'd fallen after being stabbed to the heart. But how could you possibly know that? You never entered that room. You never examined the corpse. Remember, I had the remains moved to the death house? I will even embellish it a little further. How Abbot Maurice, at the time Ambrose was murdered, glimpsed Ranulf-atte-Newgate outside the guest house, close to the window of poor Ambrose's chamber. You see,' de Craon crouched down and stared at the dead man's stricken face, 'you needed help to create that perfect mystery and Ranulf-atte-Newgate supplied it and, again, what answer can you make? You are now busy defending yourself at Heaven's Gate. So, by the time I am finished, the indictment against you will be most telling. I shall then describe how you came here. I caught you out in the questioning, you drew your dagger but I was prepared. You made a cut to my arm, nothing serious, and I defended myself. I carried out legitimate execution. I unmasked the real spy and killed him. I will see to your corpse. Augustin can hand it over to the constable for swift burial in the poor man's lot and I,' de Craon patted the front of his jerkin, 'will prepare for a hasty departure to Dover. I will cross the Narrow Seas and inform the king of my momentous discovery and how I dealt with it. Of course, there's Augustin. I don't really trust him either. He may have seen things he shouldn't have; heard whispers of things best left unsaid. However, accidents can be arranged, be it on a cog bound for France or some narrow street in Paris. I will go back. I'll heal my wounds. I'll bring this murderous mayhem to an end then I'll return. I will meet Corbett again deep in the darkness and, believe me, Gaston, I will settle accounts.'

Breathing heavily, de Craon walked up and down. 'I have little time.' He wagged a warning finger at the corpse. 'I must marshal my thoughts correctly. I would love to get my hands on Malpas; I would love to see him torn apart at Montfaucon, but of course I must be prudent. Oh yes, Gaston! Malpas must never ever come back to France. If he returned, under question he might confess to those things best kept hidden. So, Corbett will offer Malpas in return for Thomas Didymus.' De Craon laughed loudly. 'But that exchange will never ever happen. Malpas can stay and rot in England. If I am given the opportunity, if that possibility occurs, then I'll strike him down. But, time will tell, time will tell . . .'

AUTHOR'S NOTE

*R*ealm of Darkness is a work of fiction, but the novel contains a number of themes deeply characteristic of life in fourteenth-century England. Relics were big business and gave rise to some jaw-dropping sums of money, a better source of profit than many a harvest! Professional relic sellers, festooned with strings and cords loaded with relics, preyed upon the faithful devout. Shrines such as Walsingham, Glastonbury and Canterbury drew in tens of thousands, with great profit to those who guarded and managed such holy places. Of course, there was also a great deal of fraud. The poet Chaucer savagely ridicules such charlatans with his portrayal of the Pardoner in the prologue of *The Canterbury Tales*. Nevertheless, the confidence tricksters had a heyday. One wit even declared that if all the pieces of the so-called True Cross were put together it would provide enough wood to build a fleet of ships!

The bubonic/pneumonic plague was the most hideous pestilence. It actually blossomed to full rottenness in England and elsewhere during the years 1348–1350. Some commentators believe it wiped out more than two thirds of this country's population. The kingdom was certainly devastated, and even today you can still visit the lost villages of England. However, it is a mistake to believe that the plague first emerged in the fourteenth century: this is not true. We know that the plague, or something very similar to it, surfaced in the late Roman Empire as well as in kingdoms beyond the Silk Road. Of course, medieval medicine could not cope with such an onslaught. Instead, our ancestors seized on two defences. First, isolation and quarantine: many cities developed a strict quarantine procedure. A fine example of this is the fortunes of St Ignatius Loyola, founder of the Jesuits. He tried to get into Venice but failed because he could not produce a health certificate or medical passport!

Medieval society also carefully developed quarantine to deal with lepers. These unfortunates were confined to a certain area and looked after in its special hospitals and hospices known as lazar houses.

The second defence, which I refer to in my novel, was fire! Fire consumes everything, the good and the bad, the healthy and the sick. Some historians wonder if the Great Fire of London may have been deliberately started so as to eradicate the plague, which had been raging for the previous year. It's sobering to remember during these Covid years that viruses have been plaguing human society for many a year. Indeed, some predict that man's last final battle will be against the virus.

Philip of France was also a reality and the way I depict him is fairly accurate. Philip truly believed the Capetian blood was sacred and that he had been raised to kingship by God himself. Philip nursed and cherished dreams of Empire. A direct descendant of St Louis, he viewed himself as Pope and Emperor. He was the new Charlemagne and strove to give France the very borders it now enjoys.

Philip was surrounded by men like Amaury de Craon; individuals such as Nogaret, De Marigny and Dubois were real enough and very sinister with it. Philip's daggermen, under the direction of these clerks, seized the hapless Pope Boniface VIII and forced him to become a mouthpiece for the French Crown. These same lawyers and clerks organised the vicious assault on the Templars. The number of theories and legends about the Templars only emerged after their fall: most of them actually originate from Philip's attack on the great military order. He and his council accused the Templars of every sin under the sun and a few more: witchcraft, sorcery, sodomy, treason, blasphemy. Philip's lawyers created one hideous fiction after another. Nothing was sacred. The Templars themselves were rounded up and tortured in a most barbaric way. They were beaten and broken and would confess to anything that might bring them relief.

One example of this will suffice as it also touches on a theme in my novel. Philip's lawyers accused the

353

Templars of worshipping a severed head. The accusation was a twisted version of the truth. The Templars probably did possess a number of very precious relics. One of these was the mandylion: a cloth which either Veronica used to wipe Christ's face as he was hustled to crucifixion or, possibly, the funeral cloth which covered Christ's face when he was later laid to rest in what is now known as The Holy Sepulchre. Either way, the story demonstrates the underlying truth of what I have written about Philip perverting the facts for his own sinister purposes.

Edward II of England was another casualty of Philip's bounding ambition. Edward succeeded to the throne in July 1307. Philip immediately concentrated on him, sending secret messages of support to Bruce and other rebellious Scots whilst reminding the young Edward of the Treaty of Paris of 1303, which declared Edward would marry Philip's beloved daughter Isabella. Edward was desperate to break free of this commitment. He tried to make life difficult for Philip by openly proclaiming that he believed the Templars were innocent. Consequently, he could see no reason why he should seize them or their property in England. Philip immediately retaliated, cultivating friendly relations with Edward's barons who, from the very start of the reign, were protesting at the rapid promotion and advancement of Edward's beloved favourite, the Gascon, Peter Gaveston. At the same time Philip became even more amicable to Bruce. Edward tried to break free, openly questioning the Treaty of Paris and his obligation to marry Isabella. Philip immediately began to mass troops close to the border of English-held Gascony and Edward fully capitulated. Despite his earlier proclamations, Edward turned on the Templars. He also agreed to marry Isabella, which he did at Boulogne in January 1308.

For the next four years, Edward fought to save his favourite, Gaveston. By 1312 matters were approaching a crisis. Philip intervened and French envoys were sent to meddle in English court politics. They did try to have Isabella's male child christened Louis; however, on this issue Edward would not budge and his son (the future Edward III, the great warrior king) was given the same name as his father.

Isabella's pregnancy and the events leading to the birth of her firstborn, the future Edward III on 13 November 1312 were certainly shrouded in both intrigue and mystery. There is no doubt that the prince's actual birth was long overdue so, when it actually occured, there was a veritable eruption of joy across the kingdom, especially in London. I touched on this in my doctorate on Isabella – that there is considerable evidence to suggest that the Queen, only 15 to 16 summers old at the time, exploited the news of her pregnancy and all the drama surrounding it, to elicit sympathy and support for both herself and her misguided husband. In 1312 antenatal care was nonexistent. Consequently, Isabella was left 'fully in charge' of her own pregnancies as well as how to present them to the outside world. In this she succeeded brilliantly.

Isabella was an extremely beautiful, gifted and talented

young woman. She proved herself to be a good and faithful wife until thirteen years after the events in this novel. In 1325 Isabella, provoked beyond measure, sided with the rebels against her husband. She brought Edward down and, some argue, was instrumental in his death at Berkeley Castle in 1327. One of the great ironies of history is that Isabella also brought her father's dreams of Empire to a fairly horrific conclusion for the kingdom of France. Isabella had three brothers but their wives were caught up in the great Tour de Nesle scandal. Fresh marriages were arranged but not one of the three brothers had a male child. Isabella's son therefore, the warlike Edward III, then laid claim to the throne of France as the only male heir to the Capetian crown. The Hundred Years' War broke out and the darkness deepened . . .

Of course, I have written enough. What I describe is fertile ground for fresh investigations by Sir Hugh Corbett.

Pax et Bonum, Paul Doherty

~

For further information about Paul Doherty's books, visit: www.paulcdoherty.com